SHADOWS
in TIME

SHADOWS
in TIME

A Kendra Donovan Mystery

JULIE McELWAIN

PEGASUS CRIME

NEW YORK LONDON

SHADOWS IN TIME

Pegasus Crime is an imprint of
Pegasus Books Ltd.
148 W 37th Street, 13th Floor
New York, NY 10018

First Pegasus Books edition August 2020

Interior design by Maria Fernandez

Library of Congress Cataloging-in-Publication Data is available.

ISBN: 978-1-64313-474-1

10 9 8 7 6 5 4 3 2 1

Printed in the United States of America
Distributed by Simon & Schuster
www.pegasusbooks.us

To Justin and Kaitlin,
wishing you much love on your new life together

SHADOWS
in TIME

1

The lion looked pissed.

Kendra Donovan couldn't blame it. She'd be pissed too if she'd once been free to roam the wilds of Africa and was now confined to a fifteen-foot cage in the rather gloomy Tower of London. The majestic beast padded back and forth, its tail furiously swishing. Its black lips were peeled back in a contemptuous snarl, and feral yellow eyes glared at the visitors who'd paid one shilling each to wander the Royal Menagerie and gawk at the exotic animals.

"My most vivid recollection of visiting as a child is of the monkeys," Lady Rebecca Blackburn, standing beside Kendra, said. "Fascinating creatures."

Kendra glanced at Rebecca. After ten months of friendship, she barely noticed the pockmarks that marred Rebecca's face, the result of a nearly fatal bout of childhood smallpox. Instead, Kendra saw a pleasant countenance and fiercely intelligent cornflower blue eyes beneath arching eyebrows. Rebecca's most striking feature was her glorious auburn hair, which, except for a few loose tendrils brushing her cheeks, was mostly hidden beneath a silk, primrose-hued bonnet, decorated with flowers and three jaunty ostrich plumes. The bonnet matched the color of her fur-lined wool pelisse. At twenty-three, Rebecca was just three years younger than Kendra.

Or two hundred years older, depending on your point of view.

For just a moment, Kendra's ears buzzed, and her stomach roiled. Time traveler. *Freak.*

Being a time traveler was new, but she'd always been an oddity. Her parents—Carl Donovan, a biogenetic engineer focusing on genome research, and Eleanor Jahnke, a quantum physicist—were brilliant scientists who advocated positive eugenics, believing society would be improved if genetically gifted individuals married with the intention of producing equally superior offspring. She'd been the result of their union, her childhood a bleak routine of academia, her destiny preordained by her parents. Then she'd expressed a desire to forge her own path—to explore possibilities that went beyond their focus on science—after entering Princeton at the tender age of fourteen. As teenage rebellions went, it was hardly a revolt. But it had been enough for Carl and Eleanor to walk away, washing their hands of her.

Kendra knew her father had kept a file on her, charting her growth, checking off her academic achievements—or, by his ruthlessly high standards, the lack thereof. She was certain the final note that he'd tacked into the manila folder had been: *Failed experiment.*

She *knew* that was bullshit. Her chosen career path had been successful. She was the youngest person ever recruited to the FBI, working first in their cyber division and then in the Behavioral Analysis Unit. She *knew* that she had a lot to be proud of. She'd been a damned good FBI agent—until she'd thrown it all away.

She couldn't even blame her parents for how her life had imploded. She was the one who had made the decision to go rogue, seeking justice against the man responsible for the disastrous last mission that had killed most of her team. It was ironic that she hadn't been the one to kill Sir Jeremy Greene. Instead, he'd been taken out by a hit man hired by one of his former criminal associates.

And yet her life had changed irrevocably, though in a way she could never have predicted when she'd made all her plans. Her skin prickled as she recalled her escape from that same hit man using a hidden passageway in Aldridge Castle.

She'd never made it out the other side.

Something had happened, a wormhole or vortex. She didn't know. It had been like plunging into an icy electrical current and being spun around, then shredded and knit back together. When she'd emerged from the horror, everything had changed. Goodbye, 21st century; hello, 19th.

"Of course, His Majesty ordered the monkeys removed from the Royal Menagerie after one of the creatures tore off a young boy's leg," Rebecca continued.

That pulled Kendra's thoughts away from the past—*future*.

Rebecca gave a delicate shudder. "It was truly horrible. After I read about the incident, I had night terrors for weeks."

"How did the animal get out of its cage?" Kendra asked.

"Oh, well, at the time they were never kept in cages. They're so humanlike, after all. They were kept in a room decorated like a drawing room."

Kendra stared at Rebecca, wondering if she'd heard correctly. "You were allowed to . . . to *interact* with the animals?"

It wasn't like people in her own era didn't sometimes treat dangerous wild animals as children. Sometimes a person even jumped into a zoo habitat, maybe because they felt they needed to or on a dare. But Kendra couldn't imagine being allowed to roam freely inside a primates' habitat. Or having said habitat fashioned into a drawing room.

"No one realized how dangerous the creatures were, despite being so humanlike," Rebecca said. "Then again, one could argue that they *are* like us, given our own propensity for violence." She tilted her head to the side thoughtfully. "One has to wonder if there is any animal that is not vicious in some manner. I dare say it's part of nature."

"Bats are pretty peaceable. And porcupines," Kendra said without thinking, then shrugged when Rebecca regarded her with surprise.

Rebecca asked, "How do you know?"

"I read it somewhere." In a science journal while she was at Princeton, she remembered. Another one of her peculiarities was her nearly eidetic memory.

Rebecca shook her head and laughed as they strolled to the next cage, where a beautiful Bengal tiger was stretched out with lazy grace, its expression bored. "I was so pleased when I heard that His Grace decided to venture to London for the same lectures that Papa is attending at the Royal Society, and you were able to join me this morning."

"Are you kidding? You saved me. Lady Atwood was talking about bringing out the embroidery. She hates me."

Rebecca laughed again. "Embroidery is considered an acceptable pastime for young ladies, you know. Mama and I have spent many an afternoon doing fancywork. I don't think the countess hates you so much as she is attempting to guide you in what she considers more suitable entertainments. Duke's sister tends to be a stickler for propriety."

Kendra said nothing. On a good day, the countess viewed her with thinly veiled tolerance. Unfortunately, there weren't many good days with Lady Atwood.

Rebecca smiled, correctly reading the put-upon expression on Kendra's face. "How long will you be staying in London?"

"It depends on His Grace. Or Lady Atwood."

But not on me, Kendra thought with a flash of irritation. There were a lot of things that grated on her nerves about living in the early 19th century. Chamber pots. The lack of central heat. No Internet. How damn *slow* everything was. No chocolate candy bars.

But nothing, *nothing*, chafed as much as losing her independence.

She was twenty-six years old, an Ivy League graduate. An *FBI agent*, for Christ's sake. And yet in this world, she needed a guardian. It made her want to scream. The only saving grace was that her guardian was Albert Rutherford, the seventh Duke of Aldridge. Despite his lofty title and enormous wealth, the Duke was a man of science, with a mind flexible enough to eventually believe her bizarre time-travel story. In fact, he'd been delighted by it. While Kendra continued to be cautious about saying too much—the worry that she could inadvertently change history, and therefore the future, was always at the back of her mind—the Duke never stopped quizzing her about life in the 21st century.

It had been the Duke's idea to claim her as his ward, giving her a place in his grand household, but it wasn't always a comfortable fit for either of them. She had to acquiesce to having a chaperone whenever she wanted to step outside when they were in London—today it was Rebecca's maid, Mary, who drifted behind them like the tail of a kite—and the Duke was forced to look the other way about her relationship with his nephew, Alec Morgan, the Marquis of Sutcliffe.

That was another thing that had changed. Kendra's palms grew clammy just thinking about it. For the first time in her life, she'd fallen in love—sheer insanity. Even more insane, Alec appeared to love her as well. Hell, he wanted to marry her. No one had loved her before, and she wasn't sure how to handle it, so she'd so far resisted his pleas to marry. Initially, she'd thought her stay in the past was temporary, that whatever phenomenon had brought her here would eventually whisk her back to her own era. It would have been too weird to leave behind a husband in the 19th century.

But as that hope faded, her resistance to his proposal had become more complicated. Like her, Alec had been born to fulfill a destiny. He was heir to one of England's great estates, and thus his duty was twofold: to keep his estate financially solvent and to produce heirs—*male* heirs—to continue his family's legacy.

It was that latter duty that made Kendra balk at their marriage. Not for her sake, but for *his*. She'd been seriously injured during her last mission in the 21st century, an injury that had reduced her chances of becoming pregnant. At the time, she hadn't thought too much of it. Marriage and motherhood were still far enough into the future to be nebulous concepts at best, and, at the time, she'd been focused entirely on her career. If and when she wanted to have children, she had believed that there were enough medical advancements to help her overcome any difficulties.

Here, there were no fertility specialists. She'd seen the advertisements from quack doctors touting cures for everything, and supposedly taking two teaspoons of a certain elixir and then burying a lock of your hair at midnight would combat infertility. She didn't know who was gullible enough to believe that kind of nonsense, but she was a realist. No matter what Alec said now, if she married him and couldn't give him the children that were practically a requirement, he would begin to resent her. How long before he abandoned her?

"Is something amiss?"

Rebecca's question again jerked Kendra back to the present. She turned and saw that Rebecca was eyeing her with concern.

"Sorry. What?" Kendra said.

"You look . . . unhappy. What's wrong?"

"Oh. Nothing." She forced a smile. "I guess I'm still thinking about Lady Atwood forcing me to do embroidery."

Only two people in this world knew about her origins—the Duke and Alec. She'd often considered sharing her secret with Rebecca, but it wasn't easy to tell someone that you were a time traveler. Like Alec and the Duke, she thought Rebecca would eventually believe her. But what then? Would Rebecca start looking at her like she was a freak too?

Kendra lifted a gloved hand to press against her chest, an automatic gesture. Through several layers of material, she could feel the outline of the arrowhead pendant that lay heavy against her breastbone. A couple of months ago, the Duke had had the ancient artifact from America fashioned into a necklace. He'd given it to her to remind her that anything could adapt and have a new purpose, even if it was out of its original time and place.

It had been a thoughtful gesture. Still, she knew that she was as out of place in 19th-century England as the exotic animals were in the Tower of London.

She stifled a sigh, aware that Rebecca's sharp gaze was still fixed on her. She could tell that her friend didn't believe her, but how could Kendra explain how bizarre it was for her to be standing in this ancient fortress with the scent of wild beast and hay in the air around her? The first and last time she'd been in the Tower had been four years ago when she'd attended a joint training exercise between the FBI and Scotland Yard. Like any other tourist, she'd come to view the crown jewels and marvel at its long and often violent history. *Now I'm living in that history.*

She supposed it could be worse. She could have traveled back to the medieval era, when the Tower was a prison and plenty of famous folks were losing their heads. At least May 7, 1816, was considered part of the modern age, with the Industrial Revolution in its infancy.

"Perhaps you ought to take up painting," Rebecca finally said with a quick smile. "'Tis a suitable pastime as well, and infinitely more enjoyable than embroidery."

"Maybe for you. You're actually an accomplished artist," Kendra said, but her attention was drawn to a couple standing in one of the chamber's shadowy alcoves. A man and a woman.

She probably wouldn't have noticed them if not for the disparity in their dress. The woman was wearing a navy-blue bonnet trimmed with ribbons, flowers, and feathers. Her pelisse was a lighter blue than the bonnet, but just as high quality. In contrast, the man was disheveled, with a grubby brown wool coat thrown over a black jacket and pantaloons. His boots were scuffed and his shirt and cravat crumpled and stained. He wore a battered tricorn hat. Kendra might have thought they were mistress and servant, except for the belligerent expression on the man's face and intimidating aura he projected as he invaded her personal space. The woman was holding herself stiffly, her face averted. When she moved back one step, the man's hand snaked out to grasp her arm to prevent her from fleeing.

Kendra glanced around. A few other people had noticed the couple, tossing them curious looks. But no one made a move to intervene. For a brief moment, Kendra imagined the same scenario taking place in the 21st century. The majority of onlookers probably wouldn't intervene there either. Instead, they'd be whipping out their cell phones, ready to record the fight that might happen so they could be the first to post it on YouTube.

Technology advanced with time; human behavior, not so much.

Kendra let out a sigh and strode purposefully toward the couple.

"Excuse me, is everything all right?" she asked, looking at the woman. She was older than Kendra had initially thought. Mid-forties, she estimated. Hazel eyes—wide now with surprise at the interruption—and strong, elegant features. Not beautiful or pretty, but what one would describe as handsome.

"This ain't none of your business, missy," the man answered, swinging toward her without letting go of the woman's arm. He thrust out his chin aggressively. "Take your long nose off and poke it elsewhere!"

Kendra took a moment to size him up. Average height, maybe five-ten. Beneath the coat and jacket, he had bull-like muscles that banded across his shoulders, giving him the look of a pro wrestler. *An aging, out-of-shape pro wrestler,* Kendra amended silently, eyeing the belly that protruded over his cracked leather belt. She brought her eyes back to his face. Beneath his hat, his hair was light brown, liberally threaded with gray, framing a ruddy face, heavy in the jowls. His brown eyes were small and sparking with hostility as he glared at Kendra.

Kendra shifted into a defensive stance. She didn't think the man would be so bold as to attack her in the middle of the Tower, but her training as an FBI agent meant she never took anything for granted. Rebecca was right; human beings weren't that much different than any other species of animal.

"I think the lady has a say in whether she wants to continue this conversation," Kendra said coldly. "I suggest you let her go."

His lips curled back, revealing tobacco-stained teeth. "And what are you gonna do about it if I don't, eh?"

"I shall fetch one of the Yeoman Warders to deal with the likes of you!" Rebecca said as she joined them. "We shall not stand aside while you manhandle this lady, sir. Release her this instant and be on your way!"

Whether it was the threat of involving the Tower guards or Rebecca's unmistakably upper-class accent, the man let the woman's arm go, and retreated back two steps. He threw up his hands in surrender.

"Oy, there's no need to make such a blasted fuss! We were having a private conversation."

"Well, it's finished," Rebecca snapped. "Be gone, sir!"

The man's face tightened, flushing with anger. He threw a narrowed-eyed glance at the woman. "We'll speak another time, Horatia," he warned, and glowered at Kendra and Rebecca before he hurried away.

"What an insufferable creature," Rebecca sniffed.

"Are you all right?" Kendra asked the woman.

It wasn't lost on her that the man had used her first name. Kendra had been in this world long enough to know that such informality meant either the two had an intimate acquaintance, or he'd just insulted the woman.

The woman cleared her throat and finally spoke. "Yes, thank you. I didn't mean to cause such a scene." She shot a quick glance around and seemed relieved that everyone's attention had returned to the animals.

"*You* didn't cause a scene," Rebecca said, and smiled. "Please forgive the unorthodox introduction, but I am Lady Rebecca, and this is Miss Donovan."

"How do you do? I am Mrs. Gavenston." The woman smiled back at Rebecca and dropped into a curtsey. "Thank you for your assistance. I . . ."

She swung around to gape at Kendra, surprise and recognition registering on her face. "Miss Donovan? Pray, are you by any chance connected to the Duke of Aldridge?"

Kendra lifted her eyebrows. "Do I know you?" She was usually good at remembering faces but couldn't remember meeting Mrs. Gavenston. Still, the last time she'd been in London, she had been forced to attend several balls. She could have met her at one of them. Or the woman could have seen her, without a formal introduction.

Mrs. Gavenston clasped her hands tightly together as she regarded Kendra with a strange intensity. "You were involved in solving the murder of Sir Giles. It was in some of the papers and people were talking about it."

Kendra frowned. She was aware that she'd achieved a certain notoriety in London because of her involvement in Sir Giles's murder. A few of the more titillating broadsheets had reported on the crime and even identified her by name, until the Duke or Alec had managed to suppress them. Of course, it was impossible to stop the gossip, and the Beau Monde had become fascinated by her, like the monkeys that had once been housed in the Tower. Kendra didn't want that kind of fame.

Mrs. Gavenston surprised her by reaching out to grasp her hand. "Please," she whispered, her eyes glittering with some emotion that Kendra couldn't identify. "Please, Miss Donovan, I beg of you. I am in desperate need of assistance. Will you help me?"

2

Rebecca's maid, Mary, stayed in the carriage while they found a table at a nearby coffee shop that catered to a wealthier clientele. Mostly matrons, but a few gentlemen—a blend of nobility, Kendra surmised, and London's increasingly affluent merchant class.

Kendra tugged off her gloves, tossing them on top of her reticule, and regarded Mrs. Gavenston with keen interest. Her earlier wariness had been replaced by curiosity and anticipation.

"How can I help you, Mrs. Gavenston?" she asked.

"Forgive my boldness, Miss Donovan. If I wasn't so anxious, I would never have approached you in such a brazen way." She paused when a young serving maid approached to take their order—chocolate for Rebecca, coffee for Kendra, and tea for Mrs. Galveston.

"My business manager has disappeared," the woman said once the maid left. "I'm quite concerned. I thought perhaps you . . ." She drew in a breath, let it out. "Well, if you could discover the fiend who killed Sir Giles, you might also be able to find Jeremy—Mr. Pascoe."

Mrs. Gavenston leaned forward, her hazel eyes filled with entreaty. "I shan't insult you by offering you money for your services, but I have need of your help."

Only in this era was it considered an insult to offer those in the upper class money for work, Kendra thought wryly. Then again, the very notion of *work* was something the Beau Monde seemed to abhor. It was a strange system, one that she was still learning to navigate.

The maid returned with a tray filled with silver pots, floral-patterned bone china cups and saucers, and creamer and sugar bowls. They remained silent as she served them and left.

Kendra picked up her coffee cup, studying the other woman over the rim. She saw intelligence and strength in the attractive face. And desperation.

"When was the last time you saw your business manager?" Kendra asked, taking a sip of her coffee.

"Saturday, at the brewery. I didn't expect to see him on Sunday, as it's his day off. But Monday . . ." She frowned. "He should have returned yesterday."

"The brewery?"

"Barrett Brewery." She said it matter-of-factly, but there was a glow of pride in her eyes.

"And what is your connection to Barrett Brewery?"

"'Tis my company."

"I see. And Mr. Pascoe runs the brewery for you as your business manager."

Mrs. Gavenston's face changed subtly. "No, *I* run Barrett Brewery, Miss Donovan."

In Kendra's ten months in this timeline, she'd encountered female costermongers peddling flowers and fruit on the street and dressmakers who owned their own shops. But she'd never met a woman in a position of power in the business world, holding real responsibility in running a company.

Mrs. Gavenston misinterpreted her silence, continuing in a chilly tone, "Barrett Brewery has been in my family for generations, with its recipes passed down from mother to daughter. Given the rumors that I have heard about you, Miss Donovan, I would think you would not be a person who was critical of a woman in my position."

Kendra wasn't sure she liked the bit about rumors circulating about her, but she raised a placating hand. For all her pride at being in charge of Barrett Brewery, the older woman was clearly defensive. Kendra understood. Mrs. Gavenston was probably as much an oddity in this era as Kendra was.

"I didn't mean to offend you, Mrs. Gavenston," Kendra said. "I'm not being critical—just surprised." She found herself studying the older woman again. "I was under the impression that once you married, a woman's property became her husband's."

Rebecca spoke up for the first time since they sat down at the table. "Unfortunately, that is true. One wonders why a woman of any means would marry at all," she said as she set her cup down on the saucer and leaned forward. "I applaud your resourcefulness, Mrs. Gavenston, on avoiding this sad state of affairs that bedevils our sex. Your father was wise in your marriage settlement to ensure your independence."

Kendra smiled slightly. Rebecca was a follower of the early feminist Mary Wollstonecraft, and rarely ignored an opportunity to espouse her own views on the subject.

Mrs. Gavenston appeared mollified by Rebecca's words, some of the stiffness going out of her shoulders. "Thank you, my lady. Of course, my family is not part of the aristocracy, so nothing was entailed. And as I said, the women in my family have always been brewsters—my mother and her mother before her. I intend to pass the brewery to my eldest daughter, Hester. It's not only tradition, it's our legacy."

"Impressive," said Kendra.

Mrs. Gavenston glanced at her, unsmiling. "It shouldn't be. Englishwomen have been brewsters in this country for centuries. My husband passed away seven years ago, but even without my father's provision, he had little interest in running the brewery. He understood that Barrett was my company when we married. But that is neither here nor there."

Mrs. Gavenston sighed, lifting her hand and waving it as though to dismiss the subject. "I did not force an introduction with you, Miss

Donovan, to discuss Barrett Brewery or the beer industry. Will you help find Jeremy?"

The pleading look was back, so at odds with the proud tilt of her head. Kendra suspected that the other woman didn't often ask for help.

"I'll do whatever I can, Mrs. Gavenston," Kendra said. She'd been involved in a few missing persons cases, though usually involving children or teenage girls.

Still, she frowned as she considered the length of time Mr. Pascoe had been missing. It had been less than forty-eight hours—not long when dealing with an adult.

"It's only Tuesday morning," Kendra said. "He hasn't been gone that long."

"He did not come into work on Monday, and he was not at home."

"Did you just knock on his door, or did you go inside?"

"I went inside. I have a key. The cottage is owned by Barrett Brewery. I offered it to Jeremy when he came to work for me."

"How long has he worked for you?"

"A little over a year."

"And he's never disappeared for a couple of days before?"

"No. Never." Mrs. Gavenston was adamant.

"Do you have any reason to think he met with foul play? When you went into the cottage, were there indications of a fight?"

"No."

"Okay." Kendra took a long sip of coffee. "Tell me what his mood was like when you saw him on Saturday. Did he seem upset? Can you think of any reason why he might leave voluntarily?"

Mrs. Gavenston bit her lip, and her gaze slid to the side. It took her a moment to answer. "He . . . he was distressed, but I cannot believe that he would simply leave."

Kendra eyed her closely. "What was he distressed about?"

She waved her hand. "It's not relevant."

"Mrs. Gavenston—"

The woman shook her head. "He would never have left without speaking to me. And even if he had been so ill-mannered—which he is *not*—he would have returned to his home. To his . . . his family. After

I realized he wasn't at the cottage, I went to speak to Mr. and Mrs. Pascoe. They live in Maidenhead, a short distance from Cookham, where I live. They haven't seen him. I told them to send me a message if he returned. I have received nothing."

Kendra kept her gaze on the older woman. "What was Mr. Pascoe upset about on Saturday?" she asked again.

"I'm telling you that he would never have left without resigning, regardless of the argument."

"So, you argued?"

"It was a disagreement."

Kendra frowned. "Mrs. Gavenston, if you want me to find your business manager, you can't hold anything back."

"I am telling you everything."

But again, she avoided looking at Kendra, dropping her gaze to her teacup.

Kendra waited a moment. Silence and eye contact were useful tools during interrogations. And while Mrs. Gavenston was a client—an *unpaying* client—rather than a suspect, Kendra's inner antennae was quivering at her evasiveness.

"Whether you think something is irrelevant or not, I need to know," she pressed. "I won't be able to help you otherwise. So, what did you have a disagreement about?"

Mrs. Gavenston continued to study the pretty pattern on her china teacup as though trying to memorize it. Then she released a sigh that sounded either frustrated or exasperated (or both), and raised her eyes to meet Kendra's.

"I've decided to expand the brewery," she said. "There is new machinery in which I am considering investing to increase production. Jeremy does not agree. We had words about it."

"But he is your business manager!" Rebecca stared at the other woman, shocked. "He works for you. Surely, he would not dare to contradict you?"

Mrs. Gavenston shrugged. "The machines will replace a few workers. Jeremy is tenderhearted and frets over the loss of jobs. He was vexed with me, but he would never have left without handing in a letter of resignation. Or speaking with his parents."

"That's unusual," Kendra said. "Most business managers are about the bottom line."

Mrs. Gavenston looked like she was going to say something, but then pressed her lips together.

Kendra asked, "How old is Mr. Pascoe?"

"He turned nine and twenty last Friday."

Kendra was surprised. She wasn't sure why, but she'd gotten the impression that Pascoe was much younger, more boy than man. This information changed the picture. A younger man might be more impulsive, storming off after an argument. Then again, if Pascoe was as compassionate as Mrs. Gavenston seemed to think, maybe he was holed up somewhere reevaluating his career choice and figuring out his options.

All of that was assuming he'd left voluntarily, despite Mrs. Gavenston's refusal to believe he'd do such a thing. It was too early to rule anything out.

Kendra took another swallow of coffee, then asked, "Did Mr. Pascoe have any enemies? Anyone make any threats against him recently?"

Mrs. Gavenston knitted her brow. "I never heard of such a thing."

"If you were considering bringing in machinery to replace workers, someone in the brewery might have blamed Mr. Pascoe," Kendra noted. Several months earlier, she had seen firsthand the tensions in factories in the wake of the Luddite movement. Whether it was machines in this century or AI in the 21st century, no one liked being replaced. Especially when their replacement lacked a heartbeat.

"It was a private discussion," Mrs. Gavenston replied.

"Sometimes private discussions, especially when they affect business, have a way of leaking out."

Mrs. Gavenston shook her head. "I think I would have heard complaints, if that were the case."

"What about something more personal? Maybe he rubbed someone the wrong way. Not everyone likes being managed."

Mrs. Gavenston frowned as she sipped her tea. "Jeremy was well-liked inside Barrett Brewery," she said. "But the brewery industry is competitive. Disagreements among brewers are common. 'Tis the nature of the business. Still, I cannot imagine anyone wishing him harm."

"What about before he was in your employ?" asked Kendra. "Did he mention anyone from his past that he may have been having problems with?"

Mrs. Gavenston's frown deepened, but she shook her head. "He never mentioned anything."

Which only means he didn't tell his employer, Kendra thought. Not surprising. "Where did he work before you hired him?"

"He was a clerk in the Maidenhead Banking Company. I cannot conceive that Jeremy would have made any enemies there."

Kendra shrugged. "He worked in a place that loaned money—or refused to. Money has a way of bringing out the worst in people."

Worry darkened Mrs. Gavenston eyes.

"I'll need to speak with the Pascoes about their son," Kendra continued briskly.

"Of course. I shall provide you with their address."

"I'll need your address as well. And Mr. Pascoe's."

"Certainly." Mrs. Gavenston reached for her reticule and withdrew a flat silver case of her calling cards. She flicked it open with her thumb and slid out a thick ivory card, which she handed to Kendra. It read, in lovely embossed letters: MRS. WILLIAM GAVENSTON. WHITE POND MANOR. COOKHAM, BERKSHIRE.

"The cottage's address is 1 Milton Road." Mrs. Gavenston looked around. "Mayhap someone has paper to write it down on."

Kendra waved that off. "I'll remember."

"If I may ask, what are you doing in London, Mrs. Gavenston?" Rebecca asked, gazing at the older woman. "Shouldn't you have asked your local magistrate and constable to search for Mr. Pascoe?"

It was a good question. Kendra looked at Mrs. Gavenston, interested in her answer.

"Of course, I considered that, but Cookham is a small village," she said slowly. "I confess that I did not wish to feed the rumor mill. I thought it would be more discreet if I hired a Runner."

Kendra searched the other woman's face. It made sense and yet . . . *Something's not right.*

"You'd probably have better luck finding a Runner on Bow Street than inside the Tower of London," she said.

Mrs. Gavenston's jaw tightened at Kendra's dry tone. "I am quite aware of that, Miss Donovan," she said coolly. "I wanted a moment of privacy to gather my thoughts before I requested the services of a Runner. I have always enjoyed the Royal Menagerie."

"Who was that man with you at the Tower?" Kendra asked.

Mrs. Gavenston's eyes widened, clearly unprepared for the question. She shook her head. "He has nothing to do with Mr. Pascoe."

"Mrs. Gavenston," Kendra said with a sigh. "I told you. I need to know everything."

"He has no connection to Mr. Pascoe," she insisted.

Kendra was beginning to recognize that mulish look on Mrs. Gavenston's face. She supposed any woman who ran a business in this male-dominated era had to have more than their fair share of stubbornness. At any other time, Kendra would have admired her for it. But not when it interfered with an investigation.

"Actually, they do have a connection—you," she pointed out. She fixed her gaze on the other woman as she raised her cup and took a sip. "I'm going to be frank with you, Mrs. Gavenston," she said as she lowered the cup. "If you want me to find your business manager, I'll be asking a lot of questions. They may seem intrusive. You may think that they're none of my business. You may even think they have nothing to do with locating Mr. Pascoe. But I can tell you that I'm not asking idle questions. They are all necessary—even if just to weed out false trails. Do you understand?"

Mrs. Gavenston glanced away, then huffed out a sigh, looking resigned. "His name is Albion Miller. His father worked as a cooper at the brewery before he died. I have known Albion since we were children."

"Cooper?" It rang a distant bell.

Mrs. Gavenston gave Kendra a strange look. "Surely you must have coopers in America, Miss Donovan? Craftsmen who make casks and barrels."

"What did he want from you?" Kendra asked.

"What he often wants." She said it in a weary sort of way. "To persuade me to put money into one of his investment schemes."

"He seemed pretty aggressive for a guy trying to persuade you to part with your money," said Kendra. "How did he know you were going to be at the Tower?"

"As far as my household knew, the Tower *was* my destination—not Bow Street. I had planned to tell my driver to continue on after my visit to the Royal Menagerie. Then I met you."

"You're saying that someone in your household told Mr. Miller?" Kendra said.

"Perhaps. Or he followed my carriage. It wouldn't be the first time." Mrs. Gavenston's mouth tightened, but she gave an impatient flick of her wrist. "He's harmless. And has nothing to do with Mr. Pascoe."

"As your business manager, I would think he would have been involved if Mr. Miller wanted you to invest in something."

"No. Mr. Pascoe is the manager at the brewery—not my personal business manager. There is no connection."

The lady doth protest too much. But who is she trying to convince? Kendra wondered. She decided to let it go—for now.

"Does Mr. Pascoe have any close friends? Or a . . ." She bit her tongue on the word *girlfriend*. ". . . a lady that he may have formed an attachment to?" she asked instead.

"I haven't noticed him showing partiality to any particular young lady at the village assemblies or at our ball—my family throws one at White Pond Manor every Michaelmas. I think I would have heard something if he had developed a tendre." Her lips curved in a wry smile. "Cookham is a small enough village for gossip to circulate quickly."

Maybe, maybe not, thought Kendra. "What about friends?"

Mrs. Gavenston pursed her lips, considering the question. "I don't know about his acquaintances in Maidenhead, but I believe he and Mr. Elwes are friends. They've been known to dine together at the local taverns and hostelries. I confess I never considered approaching him to ask about Jeremy's whereabouts."

"Who is Mr. Elwes?"

"He's a schoolmaster at the Cookham Grammar School. Jeremy's father, Mr. Pascoe, is also a schoolmaster in Maidenhead, at one of the

Bluecoat schools. No doubt that provided common ground for Mr. Elwes and Jeremy. I should speak with Mr. Elwes."

"I'd rather you leave that to me. You did ask for my help," Kendra reminded her.

Mrs. Gavenston hesitated, but then inclined her head in acknowledgement. "Very well, but I insist that you keep me apprised of your investigation, Miss Donovan. I would like daily reports."

Kendra leaned back in her chair to study the strong face beneath the fashionable bonnet. Mrs. Gavenston was every inch the businesswoman she purported to be, used to issuing orders. She might not have blue blood running through her veins, but she had the same kind of arrogance that Kendra often observed in the upper classes. Besides, Kendra wondered how she could manage daily updates. It wasn't like she could pick up the phone and call the woman. And writing—with quill and paper—tended to be a painstaking process for someone used to keyboards. She'd rather stick a fork in her eye.

"You know, for someone who is not even paying me, you're a little demanding," Kendra said lightly.

Mrs. Gavenston looked startled. "You aren't suggesting you *wish* to be paid?"

"Heavens no. Why would I want that?" Kendra said, knowing her sarcastic tone bewildered the other woman even more. "I'm joking."

Mrs. Gavenston eyed her dubiously.

"Miss Donovan is an American," Rebecca remarked, hiding her smile behind her cup of hot chocolate. But Kendra caught the glint of laughter in Rebecca's eyes.

Kendra said, "I'll keep you updated about what I find out, Mrs. Gavenston."

The woman nodded, satisfied. "Thank you, Miss Donovan. You shall be able to find me at White Pond Manor or Barrett Brewery." She reached for the dainty teapot and poured. "What will you do first? Speak to Mr. and Mrs. Pascoe?"

"It's a good starting point." Kendra glanced at the grandfather clock at the other end of the room. Rebecca had wanted to go to the Royal Menagerie in the morning because her mother had insisted that she accompany her on morning calls—which were done mostly in the afternoon. *Go figure*. It was now twenty minutes past ten o'clock.

"Where exactly is Maidenhead?" she asked.

"No more than an hour from London. Half of that, if you take a wherry."

Getting from Point A to Point B was a pain in the ass in the 19th century, especially for a woman—and *especially* woman who hadn't learned to ride a damn horse. But the boat option was appealing.

"I can go this afternoon," she said. "Do you have any objection if I call in a Bow Street Runner to assist me?" Her mind flashed to Sam Kelly, the Bow Street Runner who she'd come to trust. "We'd cover more ground together."

Mrs. Gavenston looked surprised but shook her head. "Of course not. As I told you, I had intended to hire a thief-taker. I shall pay him whatever he requires."

Kendra stifled the urge to roll her eyes. *Sure, I'm supposed to work for free while Sam gets paid.*

Putting her exasperation aside, she asked, "Did you check the public coaches to see if Mr. Pascoe left on his own accord?"

Another glint of surprise. "It never occurred to me," Mrs. Gavenston admitted.

"Did Mr. Pascoe have a horse or carriage?"

"No. He doesn't need one. The cottage is near enough to the brewery to walk. Of course, he is allowed to use the stables at White Pond Manor, but he prefers walking."

Rebecca spoke up. "You ought to quiz the wherrymen as well, if Mr. Pascoe chose to leave by boat."

"Good idea." Kendra slipped Mrs. Gavenston's calling card into her reticule, which was heavy with the muff pistol inside. She looked at the older woman. "I'll see what I can do to find Mr. Pascoe, but I'm going to warn you. You might not like what I uncover."

Mrs. Gavenston looked genuinely puzzled. "Why ever not?"

Kendra could think of various scenarios. Mrs. Gavenston obviously had a high regard for her business manager, but if Pascoe had gone off in a temper, maybe he was on a bender, drunk or on drugs, or shacked up with a woman. In her experience, those who put people on pedestals were often disappointed.

She shrugged, deciding to forego that conversation for the moment. "If you need to contact me, I'm at Number 29, Grosvenor Square."

For the first time, a small smile flitted around Mrs. Gavenston's mouth. "Everyone knows the Duke of Aldridge's London residence, Miss Donovan." She fished out several coins from her reticule and left them on the table as she pushed herself to her feet. She paused, allowing her gaze to move from Rebecca to Kendra. "Thank you, Miss Donovan. Our meeting was fortuitous."

"Don't thank me yet," Kendra cautioned. "I'll be in touch."

Mrs. Gavenston nodded, then glanced at Rebecca. "My lady."

"Good day, Mrs. Gavenston," Rebecca said.

Kendra was silent as she watched Mrs. Gavenston thread her way through the tables. She glanced over and met Rebecca's amused eyes.

"What?" Kendra asked.

"I must say, Miss Donovan, the unexpected always seems to happen around you," she replied with a grin. "Do you think you shall find the elusive Mr. Pascoe?"

"Unless he's deliberately hiding, I don't think it will be that difficult." Except she wouldn't be able to track the missing man through his credit cards, cell phone, or social media posts. This search would have to be done the old-fashioned way, questioning his friends, family, and acquaintances.

Excitement thrummed through her veins as she stood up. It was grunt work, really. But it beat the hell out of spending the afternoon embroidering.

3

⠄

Normally, Grosvenor Square, the wealthy enclave where the Duke's sprawling mansion was located, was a haven of tranquility in the clatter of London. But upon arriving in London the afternoon before, the Duke's household had been vaguely appalled to realize that they would be living next to a construction zone. Lord and Lady Yarborough had decided to renovate their residence, disrupting the peace of the square with hammering, sawing, and the shouts of the mason workers who had invaded the space next to Number 29.

After waving goodbye to Rebecca, Kendra paused to study the construction. The mansion was early Georgian, with traditional exposed red brick, white sash windows, and ornate pilasters on either side of the door. But the Yarboroughs had been swept up in the Greco-Roman craze that had come to dominate the architecture of the time, a trend pushed by celebrated designers like John Nash. In addition to expanding the mansion by bumping out walls, the workmen were changing the exterior by slathering on stucco, which would eventually be painted a creamy white.

It would be, Kendra knew, the style most familiar to anyone who lived in or visited London in the 21st century.

Her skin prickled. A disorienting sensation swept through her. *The city is changing before my eyes.* It was strange to know already what London would look like after the transformation was complete.

She took a step back and nearly collided with one of the masons maneuvering a wheelbarrow filled with bricks. The wheelbarrow wobbled.

"Whoa! Careful there, lass!" warned the workman. He had a soft Scottish burr that went with his red hair. His bright blue eyes twinkled as he grinned with cheeky familiarity. "You are too bonnie a lass ter take a tumble. Although I suppose that would allow me ter play the knight and sweep you up in me arms."

A true gentlewoman of the time would have been offended by the man's overfamiliarity. They'd probably have delivered a stinging set-down. Kendra, who'd endured some colorful catcalls walking past a few construction sites in her own era, ignored him. Instead, she nodded at the work being done on the Yarboroughs' residence.

"When do you think the construction will be finished?" she asked.

The man looked surprised that she'd spoken to him. "Can't rightly say. Couple of months, maybe."

"Wonderful," Kendra muttered as another round of hammering pierced the air. "Well, I suppose I'll be seeing you around."

She walked up the path toward the Duke's residence, but a tingle between her shoulder blades made her look back. The Scotsman was staring after her with a strange expression on his face. Kendra's lips quirked. Undoubtedly he had expected to shock her with his forwardness, but she'd been the one to surprise him.

Feeling oddly satisfied by the encounter, she hurried the rest of the way up the path, then climbed the steps and slipped through the door. Inside the entrance hall, the noise from next door was reduced to a muffled pounding.

"Has His Grace returned from the Royal Society?" she asked Harding, the Duke's solemn-faced butler, when he materialized out of one of the doorways.

"His Grace and Lady Atwood are having tea in the morning room."

A very good reason to avoid the morning room, she decided. "I need to send a message to Mr. Kelly."

Harding's expression remained perfectly blank. "Is there something amiss?"

"Not really. I just need his assistance on a matter that has come up. I'll write a note. Can you have someone deliver it to Bow Street?"

"Certainly. I shall inform His Grace."

She scowled at the butler. "I wasn't planning on hiding it from the Duke, you know."

"Of course not, miss."

She started for the grand staircase, aware that Harding was watching her. "I'll be in the study."

"Ring the bell when you need your message delivered."

She jogged up the sweeping staircase and down the hall to the Duke's study. Daylight poured through the three glazed windows. Though the clanging and banging from the construction zone penetrated the walls, as an urbanite, she was used to city noises. At least she didn't have to listen to the abrasive thud of jackhammers or high-pitched whine of a power saw.

She dropped her reticule on one of the damask chairs with legs carved into a griffin's talons, dispensed with her gloves, bonnet, and pelisse, and sat down at the Duke's desk. She found foolscap in the center drawer and went through the lengthy process of scribbling a note to Sam with quill pen and ink, sanding the paper to dry the ink faster, then folding the sheet into a small square. The Duke walked in while she was pressing a wax wafer to seal the missive.

The Duke was a man of average height with blond hair fading to gray and thinning on top. His face was longish, with a bold nose and pale grayish blue eyes that often sparkled with intelligence and curiosity—both of which she recognized in their depths now.

"Is that the note for Mr. Kelly?" he asked, glancing at the now neatly folded piece of foolscap in her hand. He pivoted over to the bellpull, yanking the braided cord.

The butler must have gone straight to the morning room. "Harding told you," she said.

"He said that you required assistance from Mr. Kelly, but not why."

She grinned. "I've got a case. Missing person."

"Who is missing? How did this come about? I thought you and Rebecca went to the Royal Menagerie this morning."

"We did." She stood up and told him about Mrs. Gavenston and the disappearance of her business manager. "He hasn't been gone for very long. He's an adult—twenty-nine. I think Mrs. Gavenston is feeling guilty and that, in turn, is making her anxious."

"Why would she feel guilty?"

Kendra leaned a hip against the desk. "I'm not really sure. She admitted that they had argued on Saturday. She said it was about business."

He eyed her with interest. "But you don't believe her?"

"I believe her when she said that they argued. But whether it's about business . . .." She shrugged. "I feel like she's hiding something."

She straightened when there was a soft knock at the door. The footman entered and she crossed the room to hand him the note. "Make sure this gets to Mr. Sam Kelly," she directed.

The Duke settled into the chair behind his desk. "Still, I can understand Mrs. Gavenston's concern," he said. "If he was supposed to be at work on Monday but failed to show up . . . well, that is not the usual, especially in this time when too many Englishmen are finding work scarce and fighting for survival. Who would be so blasé about their position of employment?"

"I hadn't thought of it like that. But Mr. Pascoe is an educated man. He worked at a bank before Mrs. Gavenston hired him to be the brewery's business manager. I would think he would find other employment if he left."

"How will you go about trying to locate him?" the Duke asked.

"The usual way. Talk to his family and friends. Neighbors. Co-workers."

"I thought you said that Mrs. Gavenston had already spoken to Mr. Pascoe's family."

"She did, and they told her that they didn't know where he was. But that's only one question, and the least significant one. Most parents probably don't know where their grown children are after they've moved away from home." She paused. "Assuming they even told Mrs. Gavenston the truth."

The Duke opened a drawer, retrieving his clay pipe and tobacco bag. "Why would they lie?" he asked.

She watched him open the hemp bag and carefully tip the dried tobacco leaves into the bowl. "To cover for their son, who doesn't want to speak to his employer after an argument, maybe," she said. "I'll know more after I talk to them."

"And if they genuinely do not know where their son is?"

"Then I need them to tell me *who* their son is." She sat on the arm of one of the chairs facing the desk. "What he might be capable of."

The Duke glanced up from the process of tamping down the dried leaves into the pipe's bowl. "What do you mean?"

"When an adult goes missing, their state of mind is important. Were they upset? Depressed? Anxious? Afraid? There are a lot of reasons why an adult male—or female, for that matter—might want to disappear from their everyday life. It doesn't have to mean something sinister happened."

"He could have had an accident."

Kendra nodded. "That's definitely a possibility." She glanced at the clock, feeling the press of time. "Mrs. Gavenston said Cookham and Maidenhead aren't far, faster by water."

"By wherry, yes. I shall accompany you."

"That's not necessary. I don't want to interfere with your schedule at the Royal Society. I know that's why we came to London."

The Duke smiled. "The Royal Society will be there tomorrow. Once Mr. Kelly arrives—" He broke off when Harding came into the room.

"Forgive the interruption, Your Grace, but a young lady is at the door, demanding to speak to you." The butler frowned in disapproval. "She has no calling card. However, she is quite insistent that she see you, sir. She says that it is a matter of great importance. Shall I tell her that you are not at home?"

The Duke raised an eyebrow in Kendra's direction, his eyes brightening with amusement. "Well, my dear, it would seem to be a day of unexpected encounters." He turned back to the butler. "What is the young lady's name?"

"She would not say," Harding sniffed, then hesitated. "She does not appear low-born, but she is alone, sir. Quite unusual, if I do say so."

"Hmm. How odd." The Duke rubbed his chin thoughtfully. "Well, send her up, Harding. I shall deal with her."

"But, Your Grace . . ." The butler looked horrified at the suggestion. "I can put her in one of the lesser drawing rooms, sir."

"That will not be necessary." He glanced at Kendra and smiled. "Miss Donovan shall act as my chaperone."

Kendra laughed and wandered to the window. The sky remained a clear azure, which boded well for travel, although the lack of breeze might not be a good thing if they planned to sail down the Thames. She was pondering that when Harding returned with their unexpected guest.

Kendra had wondered why Harding hadn't chased the woman off without bringing her to the Duke's attention, but now she thought she understood. The woman had the kind of fragile beauty that would always have men running to help her if she showed the tiniest bit of distress. Beneath the plain, rose-colored bonnet, her hair was raven black, and pulled back in a severe bun that did nothing to detract from the creamy cameo of her face. Her dark brown eyes were wide and thickly lashed under winged brows, her nose delicate above a mouth that could be described as lush, her cheekbones high, colored with the faintest blush—natural, not from a jar. Her gaze swept the room, touching briefly on Kendra before fixing on the Duke. Some emotion—Apprehension? Excitement?—flared in the dark depths of the stranger's eyes as the Duke pushed himself to his feet, his expression politely quizzical.

Kendra took stock of the rest of the woman. Gray wool cloak trimmed with fur at the collar. Well-made, Kendra thought, but showing signs of age. Underneath, her gown was a lavender muslin, pale from being laundered countless times. The woman's hands were small, encased in kid gloves, and clenched tightly on the gray velvet reticule that she held.

The Duke said politely, "How do you do?"

"Your Grace," the woman began, then bit her lip, looking uncertain. "Forgive me, but I do not know where to begin."

She had a lovely voice, low and husky. Unconsciously seductive, with a faint accent. Spanish, Kendra thought.

The Duke offered her an encouraging smile. "Why don't you begin by telling us your name?" he suggested gently.

The woman stared at him, transfixed for a long moment. Then she drew in a trembling breath, deep enough to raise her small breasts. Slowly, she exhaled.

"My name . . ." She hesitated, then tried again. "The name that I was raised with was Carlotta. Carlotta Garcia Desoto. Yet that is not the name I was given at birth."

She looked at the Duke expectantly. For some reason, Kendra felt a chill. She found herself holding her breath, a strange trepidation washing through her as she waited to hear what the woman would say.

"My name . . . I am . . ." Carlotta let out a hiss. One hand let go of the reticule to press against her abdomen as though she were trying to push the words out. Her large, dark eyes remained locked on the Duke.

"I am . . . I am Charlotte, Your Grace. Your daughter."

4

Aldridge stared at the woman, shock rippling across his skin like the electrical currents in a Leyden jar. Maybe he hadn't heard her correctly. Maybe . . .

His gaze flicked to the bookshelf that held two miniature portraits. The beloved faces of his wife and daughter stared back at him, immortalized in oil. His chest tightened with white-hot pain that slowly ebbed, and then was replaced by rage. He had to clench his jaw to control his fury. He trembled with the urge to leap across the room to where the brazen creature stood and shake her senseless for her cruelty.

"Do you jest?" he finally demanded. His throat was so tight, he could barely utter the words.

"No." The woman shook her head, her dark brown eyes locked on his.

Charlotte's eyes. The very thought jolted him. *No!* He refused to even consider such a thing. Down that road lay madness.

"I do not find this amusing, young lady," he said harshly. "My daughter is dead."

He nearly jumped when a hand brushed his arm. He glanced down, and realized that Kendra had moved to his side.

She asked, "Do you want me to escort her out?"

He lifted his gaze to meet the American's worried eyes.

"*Por favor* . . . please." The other woman lurched forward, raising the hand that had been pressed to her stomach. Palm up, fingers splayed. An entreating gesture. He noticed that her hand was trembling. "Please, I would like to tell you my story. I beg of you . . . I only ask for a very small amount of your time, and then if you order me to go, I will go."

"Don't come any closer," Kendra warned with a hard look pinning the stranger. She glanced at Aldridge. "Your Grace?"

His gaze moved between Kendra and the creature calling herself his daughter. They both had Charlotte's coloring, he realized. Black hair, brown eyes so dark they looked like onyx. They were both the age his daughter would have been. If she had lived. If her body hadn't been swept out to sea, never to be found.

Dear God in Heaven. His stomach churned and the world seemed to tilt around him. He remembered when Kendra had suddenly appeared in his study at Aldridge Castle. Alec had feared that the Duke's affinity for the American had been due to her resemblance to Charlotte. But in that moment when she'd first appeared, he'd only been concerned, reacting to the panic he'd seen on her face. She'd been lost and frightened, and desperately trying to conceal both. He'd wanted to help her. Never once, not even for a moment, had he been so foolish as to think that she was his daughter.

He wouldn't play the fool now.

Carlotta's mouth quivered. "I-I am aware this is a shock—"

He gave a sharp bark of laughter, the bitterness surprising even him. "Madame, this is a *farce*. I suggest you take yourself off before I call the watch."

Tears filled her eyes and her hand fell away. If she hadn't evoked his daughter's name, he would have felt sorry for her, much as he had for Kendra. Now, though, he had to keep his hands clenched, or else he may still give in to the desire to throttle her.

"I had hoped you would spare me a few minutes," she whispered tragically. Again, she pressed her hand to her stomach, but her fingers weren't still. They began to tap nervously.

"I will not spare one more second for you," the Duke said. But his gaze was transfixed by her tapping fingers. Not a random pattern, he realized. *One, two, three* . . . Pause. *One, two, three* . . .

Kendra advanced toward the other woman. "Come on. You've had your say."

"Please." Carlotta threw a desperate look at him as Kendra's hand closed over her arm.

"Wait!"

Aldridge barely recognized his own voice, it was so harsh. He was aware of Kendra's eyes searching his face, but he ignored her, staring at Carlotta.

"Why are you doing that? *That!* With your hand!" He forced himself to take a breath. "Why are you tapping your fingers in such a way?"

"Oh." She glanced down at her hand, as though surprised to find her fingers moving at all. She flushed, embarrassed. "It's nothing. A nervous habit, I suppose. Superstition."

"Superstition in what way?" he demanded.

She gave a self-conscious laugh, flexing her hand. "If you tap three times, it's magic. 'Tis silly, I know. I don't believe it's truly magic, but . . ." She shrugged. "As I said, 'tis a habit that I've had since I was a small child. I don't even remember how I came to do it."

Aldridge stared at her.

Charlotte's body was never found . . .

"Your Grace?"

Kendra was looking at him. He shook his head, his mind racing with possibilities. *Charlotte's eyes . . . Charlotte's body was never found . . .*

"My daughter had a doll that she prized," he finally managed to say. His eyes never left the woman's delicate face. "If you are truly Charlotte as you claim, you ought to remember the doll's name."

He heard Kendra's swift intake of breath.

Carlotta searched his face for a long moment, then she nodded. "*Si.* It was a long time ago, but I remember that doll. I loved her. Annie. My doll's name was Annie."

The room spun. He felt like he'd drunk a full bottle of whiskey. He lifted a hand; it was shaking.

"Your Grace?"

Kendra's voice seemed to come from far away. He stumbled forward, made it to his chair before his legs gave out and he abruptly sat down. He struggled to control his erratic breathing, to keep hold of his composure even though it felt like it was shattering into a million pieces. He thought he heard Kendra say something, but her voice was drowned out by the roar of blood in his ears.

"I think," he said carefully, his gaze on the stranger, "I would very much like to hear your story now."

Something had changed, Kendra realized. Something that had to do with the woman's habit of tapping her fingers. And the doll. She'd obviously guessed the correct name for Charlotte's doll. What were the chances?

What were the chances that this woman was actually Charlotte?

She glanced at the Duke. A minute ago, his face had been flushed with anger. Now he'd lost every drop of color, his complexion gray. Concern propelled her across the room to where the decanters were scattered across the side table. She pulled out a stopper to one of the bottles and splashed a generous amount of brandy into a glass. She hesitated, then added brandy to another glass. Carrying both tumblers, she hurried across the room.

"Here. Take it," she said, handing him the glass. "Drink it."

His hand trembled violently as he grasped the crystal. She pivoted, walking to the woman who claimed to be Charlotte, and thrust the other glass at her. Surprise registered on the pretty face.

"Oh. *Gra*—thank you."

Kendra noticed that the other woman's hand was steady now. Apparently, she'd managed to calm her nerves. Or her earlier apprehension had been an act. Kendra's jaw tightened.

"Please sit down." She gestured to a wingback chair. "We might as well get comfortable. I assume this is going to be a long story?"

If Carlotta heard the sarcastic edge in Kendra's voice, she gave no indication. She sank down into the chair, looking small and fragile. Deliberately, Kendra eased a hip on the corner of the Duke's desk. It was a strategic position meant to align herself with the Duke, to show the other woman that he wasn't alone.

She said, "Miss Garcia Desoto—"

"Missus," Carlotta corrected, long dark lashes fluttering. "I was married. M-my husband died."

Kendra raised her eyebrows. She was surprised, still sometimes caught by surprise by the era's societal standards. She and Carlotta looked to be the same age, and Kendra was well aware that she was dangerously close to sliding into spinster territory. Most twenty-six-year-old women were not only married but also mothers. And in this grim, pre-vaccination world, many had already buried children.

"Tell us why you believe you are my daughter, if you please," the Duke said abruptly.

Kendra glanced down at him, pleased to see that his color had returned to normal.

"I'll take notes," she said, straightening. She shot Carlotta a warning look. "I want names, dates, details."

Carlotta drew in a long breath. "I was a child, you understand. There is much I do not remember."

Convenient, Kendra thought, but remained quiet.

The Duke handed Kendra sheets of foolscap and a graphite stick.

"Thank you," she said, and moved to a chair. She motioned to Carlotta. "We'll take it one step at a time. Tell us what you do remember."

"Mamá . . ." Carlotta frowned, then glanced at the Duke. "Forgive me, but I shall always think of the woman who raised me as my mother."

The Duke took a sip of brandy, nodding. "I understand."

"Mamá said I was found floating unconscious on a piece of wreckage by the crew of *La Rosa Negra*. Diego Garcia was the ship's captain. He brought me to San Sebastian. I was quite ill with brain fever. Mamá nursed me back to health."

"What's your mother's name?" Kendra asked.

"Camila."

"And her connection to Captain Garcia?"

"She was married to Captain Garcia's brother."

"Your father?" Kendra clarified.

"I never thought of him as my father. I scarcely remember him. He died two years after I was found."

"What was his name?"

"Raul."

Kendra scribbled the name down. "How did he die?"

Carlotta frowned. "Why does this matter? It was so long ago."

The devil was always in the details. The best way to trip up a con artist was to collect as many details as possible.

She bared her teeth in a smile. "Everything matters."

Carlotta regarded her for a moment, then shrugged. "He was a brick-layer. I think it was an accident at work, but . . . I was so young. I only know what Mamá told me."

"Okay. After you recovered from your illness, why didn't you tell them who you were? You spoke English, so they must have known you were English. Even with the language barrier, surely, they would have understood your name, that you had family in England."

The small chin lifted; the gesture haughty. "Mamá spoke English. I told them my name when I recovered my wits. However, they could not bring me home."

"Why not?"

"There was terrible upheaval," she said simply.

"War," the Duke clarified, meeting Kendra's eyes. "Spain and France had joined forces against Britain in 1796—the year Charlotte . . . when she was lost."

The Anglo-Spanish war. It rang a distant bell. Kendra remembered the conflict from European history classes she'd taken at Princeton.

"Captain Garcia would not have been welcomed in England," Carlotta said softly. "Mamá never spoke of this directly, but I think he was a privateer. Or perhaps a smuggler. I believe that was why he was sailing near England at the time."

Kendra glanced at the Duke, curious to see how he was taking her story. His expression was impossible to decipher, but it was as though he didn't dare look away, for fear that she'd vanish like a puff of smoke. Kendra's stomach knotted.

"I think he brought me to Spain for another reason, too," Carlotta said.

With an effort, Kendra pulled her gaze away from the Duke to refocus on the other woman.

"What's that?" she asked.

"Mamá was childless. She wanted children. Wanted me." With a burst of defiance, as though daring them to contradict her, Carlotta insisted, "She loved me."

Kendra looked down at her notes. She said, "We'll need Captain Garcia's address."

Carlotta shook her head. "He was killed when Napoleon captured San Sebastian."

"What about the crew of the *La Rosa Negra*?"

"I . . . I don't know. Mamá and I left San Sebastian before the city fell." Carlotta lifted the brandy glass, took a cautious sip. "I remember very little of our time in San Sebastian. Only fragments. In many ways, it feels like a dream."

Kendra asked, "Where did you go?"

"Eventually Madrid."

The Duke leaned forward. "How did you survive? Did you have family to take you in?"

"No. No family. Mamá worked."

Kendra searched the other woman's face for subterfuge. "Where did she work?"

"A *panadería*—a bakery. A sweet shop. A laundry." She shrugged. "Many places."

"Can you be more specific? The name of the bakery or laundry would be helpful." Kendra raised a brow. "You must remember a name."

"I'm sorry, no. I was a child. I remember the smell of the bread, and Mamá sneaking me *pan basico*." A smile flickered on her face, and then was gone. She lowered her gaze back to the brandy she held. "Mamá found a . . . a protector."

Carlotta peered at the Duke through veiled lashes. He said nothing; his face remained expressionless.

"Who?" Kendra asked. "What was his name?"

But Carlotta shook her head. "I only know he was a wealthy merchant. For a time, we lived in a lovely house with servants. I had a governess."

"You lived with this wealthy merchant, but you *don't* know his name?" Kendra didn't bother to conceal her skepticism.

Carlotta's jaw tightened; her dark eyes flashed at Kendra. "We did not live with him. He had his own family. He gave us a house—for a time. Mario. Mamá called him Mario."

The Duke took another swallow of his brandy, his gaze shadowed. "How old were you at this time?"

"I was thirteen when Mamá . . . when the affair was over, and we moved to Seville."

"Why did you move?" he asked.

"I don't know. Mamá found work as a *modista*."

The Duke brought up a good point, Kendra thought. "Why did you move around so much?"

"Spain was at war . . ." She shrugged. "But I do not know. I was a child."

"At thirteen, no longer a child. Weren't you curious?"

"She was my mother. I didn't question her decisions."

Kendra tapped the graphite stick against the paper. But it reminded her of Carlotta's strange tapping habit and she stopped. "Neighbors? Friends? You must have had some."

"Of course. But, as you said, we moved often. It is difficult to maintain connections."

Kendra didn't like it. But perhaps it wasn't unreasonable. People here wrote *letters*, for Christ's sake. As far as Kendra was concerned, that was hard enough during peacetime. She couldn't imagine people maintaining long-distance relationships in a time of war.

"We lived in Seville for two years. Then Mamá married Jorge, and we moved with him to Barcelona. He was a soldier." She shot a combative look in Kendra's direction. "He was also killed in one of the battles."

"What was Jorge's last name?"

"Cortez."

"Any relatives? Friends? Fellow soldiers?"

Carlotta sipped her brandy. "I'm certain he had all of those, but he and Mamá were married only two years. And it was war."

"You've had a tragic life," Kendra murmured neutrally.

Carlotta said nothing, merely looked at her with an unreadable expression.

Kendra went on, "Tell me about your late husband."

"What do you wish to know?"

"Everything."

Carlotta nodded. "I met Fernando when I was seventeen. He was a good husband. He provided for me and Mamá until she died."

"When did she die?"

"The year I turned twenty." Carlotta's face changed, softening with memories and sorrow. "It was on her deathbed that she begged Fernando to bring me to England . . ." She looked at the Duke. "To find you."

"What did your husband do?" Kendra pressed.

"He was a carpenter."

"Your husband was aware of your claim to be Charlotte?" Kendra asked. She didn't want to give the impression that she was buying her story.

"My husband knew who I was," Carlotta replied evenly. "He wanted to bring me home."

"Six years ago."

"We had no money for smugglers to bring us to England. My husband had people in Toledo, but he . . . he died on the journey there. It took me another three years, but I finally managed to buy passage to England."

"Where did you work?"

She shrugged. "At a bakery for a time, a dressmaker's shop as a seamstress."

"Quite a story," Kendra said, offering her a tight smile.

Carlotta eyed her. "You don't believe me," she said flatly.

The Duke, who'd been silent throughout the exchange, finally spoke up. "What do you remember about your life *here*?"

She shifted her gaze to look at the Duke. "Only bits and pieces. Annie, of course. And a woman with dark hair. Laughter like church bells. It's hazy, but . . . lavender. I smell lavender." She tilted her face up, and closed her eyes, smiling slightly. She opened her eyes. "It's a happy memory.

"And I remember . . . you," Carlotta continued quietly. "But only like a dream. The scent of tobacco. The laboratory. You let me help you there. You carried me to the roof of the castle and allowed me to look through a telescope at the stars. Orion, Scorpius, Pegasus. I remember that."

"My God," the Duke breathed, his gaze fixed on Carlotta. His hand shook as he set down his glass. He stood abruptly. "Can this be true?"

Kendra saw the wild glimmer in his eyes, and felt the air evaporate from her lungs. She scrambled to her feet, tossing aside the paper and graphite stick.

"Can we take a minute? We need to take a minute here, Your Grace."

She stepped toward him, reaching out to grasp his arm. She tried to capture his gaze, but his eyes remained locked on Carlotta.

"Charlotte?" he said. "Good God, *is it really you?*"

5

Y our Grace—" Kendra tried.

The Duke kept his blue gaze fixed on Carlotta. "Where are you staying?"

"The Royal Oak Inn in Ealing."

"Sir." Kendra had a horrible suspicion where this was going. She tried to catch the Duke's eye again. "Can I speak to you? Privately."

The Duke ignored her. "Do you have a maid or chaperone with you?"

"I hired a *criada*—a maid—for the journey, but I could not continue to engage her services." Carlotta lifted a hand, palm up in a helpless gesture. "She has returned to Spain. I know it is not proper, but I *am* a married woman—a widow."

Aldridge frowned. "You are still young and beautiful, regardless of your marital status. And London is a dangerous city for a lone woman."

Carlotta smiled slightly. "I have faced greater danger before."

"Still—"

"*Your Grace*," Kendra raised her voice.

The Duke finally glanced at her, but shook his head. His gaze returned to the other woman.

He said, "Mrs. Garcia Desoto, I am not certain I accept this fantastical story of yours, but I cannot disregard it either. I think it would be best if you stayed here whilst I investigate your claim."

Carlotta hesitated. "I am aware how this must seem to you, that I am some sort of fortune hunter." She put her glass of brandy to the side and slowly rose, her gaze never leaving the Duke's. "If I accept your generous invitation, it is only to further our acquaintance, sir. I do not want anything from you."

"Really?" Kendra could feel her lip curl.

Carlotta glanced at her. "I cannot prove my intentions."

The Duke said, "I shall have my coachman drive you back to the inn so you can pack your belongings. A room shall be readied for you when you return."

Carlotta bit her lip, searching his face. "Are you certain?"

"I would not have issued the invitation if I were not."

She nodded, offering him a slow, shy smile. "Thank you, sir. I shall accept your invitation. But I want to say again that I wish nothing from you but your company."

For a long moment, the Duke said nothing, simply allowing his gaze to rove over the woman's lovely face. Then he seemed to give himself a mental shake and came around the desk to cross the room to the bellpull, yanking the cord to summon a servant.

Kendra's unease only grew when she caught the expression that flared for only a second in the Duke's eyes before he managed to bank it. *Hope*, she thought. It could be dangerous.

"You don't believe her, do you?" Even to Kendra's own ears, the question sounded like an accusation.

The Duke had returned to the study after seeing Carlotta off. Slowly, he walked back to his desk and lowered himself into his chair. He picked up his clay pipe, weighing it in his hand, a familiar gesture that indicated he was lost in thought.

Like Carlotta's tapping three times? Kendra wondered.

He sighed. "I do not know what to believe," he admitted quietly.

His gaze traveled to the windows, but Kendra suspected he wasn't seeing the blue sky beyond the glazed windowpanes. For a long moment, the only sound was the crackle of burning logs in the fireplace and the construction and voices drifting in from next door.

Kendra swallowed against the golf ball–sized lump in her throat and tried again. "Your Grace—"

"She knew things," he cut her off. "She knew that Arabella's scent was lavender. And the name of Charlotte's doll."

"A good imposter would do their research. It's part of the con. Finding out what scent your wife once wore and the name of your daughter's favorite doll would be easy. Anyone who lived in Aldridge Village or worked in or around the castle would know that information." Kendra sat down in the chair that Carlotta had vacated and leaned forward. "We need to find out if anyone has been asking questions around the castle in the last couple of months."

The Duke turned back to Kendra. "She remembered me taking her—Charlotte—into my laboratory, up to the roof to show her the stars. The names of the constellations."

"Also information easily obtained. Or an educated guess. Your interest in astronomy and science is well known. Hell, we're in London because you're attending lectures at the Royal Society. Everyone is aware that you installed a telescope on the castle's roof. It would be odd if you never tried to include your daughter in some of your interests."

"You forget, my dear, that astronomy and science are not interests encouraged in young ladies. This is not your America."

Kendra shook her head. "I'm not forgetting. Anyone who knows you would realize that you are not the kind of person to exclude your daughter from less conventional interests."

His mouth twisted. "Charlotte was always an inquisitive child." He hesitated. "She has the look of my daughter."

"It's been two decades," Kendra argued. "You don't know what Charlotte should look like as an adult." She paused, then asked, "What was that about tapping three times?"

The Duke abandoned the pipe, picking up his brandy glass. He took a slow sip.

"Charlotte had the same habit," he finally said. "When my daughter was four, she was besieged with night terrors. Nanny MacTavish didn't know what to do. For a time, Arabella arranged for a cot to be brought into her bedchamber so she could comfort Charlotte during the night. This went on for weeks. Naturally, we were distraught." His studied his brandy as if fascinated by the amber liquid. "You are aware that my wife was a brilliant mathematician."

Kendra nodded. "You told me, yes."

"Well, one evening, Arabella came up with a scheme. She told Charlotte that three was a magical number. Stuff and nonsense, I know." He raised his gaze to meet her eyes, smiling wryly. "However, it *is* the first odd prime number, which gives it the power of indivisibility. Pythagoreans actually believed it was the perfect number. It is the first number to form a geometrical figure, that of a triangle. And, of course, three has a special meaning in the Bible."

"The Holy Trinity," Kendra acknowledged with a nod. "The number three is considered a sacred number in many religions and philosophies. There are three primary colors from which all other colors are derived. In fairytales, one gets three wishes . . . I understand the superstition behind the number three."

The Duke smiled. "As you know, normally I am not an advocate of spreading superstitious gibberish, but I recognize that it can be a powerful tool. 'Tis why so many cultures have superstitions, as a method of easing a population's fears.

"My wife told Charlotte to tap three times if she ever felt anxious or afraid, because she would be protected. It appeared to comfort her, and eventually the night terrors went away. But Charlotte continued to tap three times, because she thought it was magical."

He took another swallow of brandy. "It seems reasonable that she would continue a habit into adulthood even if she may have forgotten its origins."

"You think Carlotta tapping three times and saying that it was magic proves that she's your daughter?"

"Not proves . . . but how do you explain it? Mrs. Garcia Desoto did not even realize why she was doing it."

"So she says."

The Duke shook his head. "Charlotte's night terrors were not common knowledge. Arabella and I did not discuss it, nor did we speak of Arabella's method of comforting our daughter."

"Maybe you didn't talk about it, but Charlotte's nanny probably discussed it with the cook, and the cook shared it with Mr. Harding, who spoke to Mrs. Danbury about it."

"Mrs. Danbury was not the housekeeper at the time."

"My point is that whoever the household staff was, it would be natural for them to discuss what was going on. They weren't gossiping. They were *concerned*. But that's how information flows."

"I cannot dispute that. You believe a charlatan came across this information twenty years later, and is using it as a way to convince me that she is my daughter?"

"It sounds like it's working."

He said nothing, his expression pensive.

Kendra's stomach churned. Her gaze drifted to the glass that Carlotta had discarded. She'd been wearing gloves, so she wouldn't have left behind fingerprints. Though even if she had, there was no way to collect them and no database to check them against.

She said, "We have to investigate her claim."

"I am not arguing the point, Miss Donovan. But what if she *is* my daughter?" The hand that held the brandy suddenly trembled, and he put the glass down. He scrubbed his face with his palms, looking dazed. "My God . . . what if? It would be a miracle."

"Did you *listen* to her story?"

Kendra sprang up and reached for the pages of foolscap she'd tossed down. She shook the papers at him.

"Look at these. There's hardly anything written here! Everyone who could corroborate her account is dead or will be almost impossible to trace because she and her mother kept moving around, conveniently losing touch with neighbors and friends throughout the years."

"Spain was ravaged by war," he countered. "It is not as incredible as you think for the population of a war-torn country to move about, to escape the brutality."

"And her lack of relatives, extended family, friends?"

The Duke regarded her. "Misfortune happens. And miracles. In fact, I remember listening to another young woman tell me a fantastical story of how she came from the 21st century."

Kendra jerked back. "It's not the same."

"Pray tell, what is the difference?"

"None of this has been in my control!"

The paper she held fluttered as she waved her hand, gesturing to the room, him, the entirety of the 19th century.

"If Carlotta is my daughter, much of her life has not been in her control either."

He looked as though he were going to say something else, but he paused at a knock and Harding's entrance.

"Mr. Kelly has arrived," said the butler. "Shall I bring him up?"

The Duke agreed, then waited until Harding had left to push himself to his feet, looking at Kendra.

"I shall leave you to speak to Mr. Kelly about your investigation into the missing Mr. Pascoe," he said. "I must inform Caro of our guest."

Kendra drew in a breath. "Will you tell her about her claim that she's your daughter?"

"Of course. Although I think we ought to be prudent about sharing that information with too many people. I would like to develop my acquaintance with Mrs. Garcia Desoto without the scrutiny of the Beau Monde."

"I'd like to talk to Mr. Kelly about sending a couple of his men to Spain, follow the trail," Kendra said. *What little trail there is.*

"Are you asking my permission?"

"Would you give it?"

The Duke was quiet for a long moment, his gaze brooding. "Yes," he finally said. "I am not such a fool as to accept her story without trying to verify it." His expression lightened. "It took me a few weeks to accept your story, you know."

That surprised Kendra. "You seemed to accept it immediately. At least you didn't throw me out on my ass. What made you believe me?"

"I was there when you arrived, remember? You came out of the passageway like you were being chased by a madman. I thought you were going to burn yourself on my candles. You seemed mesmerized by them." He smiled at the memory. "Little did I know that in your time, you've harnessed the forces of electricity to push buttons and have lights come on. What a wondrous time you come from, my dear."

Kendra had to smile at the marvel she saw in the Duke's face. "It beats using a tinderbox."

"Still, your claim of being from the future was fanciful, to put it mildly," the Duke reminded her. "So, I continued to observe you. You were not like any other lady—or man, for that matter—of my acquaintance."

"Which is another way of saying I'm weird."

He laughed. "You were different. But your story somehow . . . fit." He tilted his head as he regarded her. "You and I both approach life with deductive reasoning. I am a man of science. But I am also a man of faith. How can you look at the heavens and not see the hand of God? I don't believe your arrival here was random, especially given what happened during that time."

He was talking about the serial killer that had been stalking young prostitutes at the time. Kendra had been instrumental in capturing the killer. She'd been raised by scientists, so her natural inclination was to be leery of attributing anything to the divine. At the same time, even she'd been struck by the coincidence of being the only person who was capable of recognizing the kind of killer they had in their midst. But if that had been the purpose of her arrival, why was she still here?

"You must have a little faith, my dear," the Duke said, a small smile on his lips. "I shall pay Mr. Kelly whatever is needed to send men to Spain. And now I shall leave you."

He walked to the door, but paused to look back at her. "You ought to leave immediately for Maidenhead. I would like you home before evening."

Kendra hesitated, worry gnawing at her. "Maybe I should postpone my trip until tomorrow."

"Do not be concerned about me, my dear." He offered her a lopsided smile that faded. The gray in his eyes seemed to overtake the blue as his expression grew somber. "You *must* find this missing man. He has loved ones waiting anxiously for his return."

6

Sam let out a low whistle that was quickly carried off by the wind. Kendra was sitting with the Bow Street Runner and her maid, Molly, on narrow wooden seats, their backs against the rails of the wherry. It was a sleek, low-slung boat manned by three muscular watermen, all vigorously rowing. Their efforts were aided by the breeze that was stronger here on the Thames, pushing the boat forward through the choppy waters. Kendra suspected they'd make good time to Maidenhead.

The vessel itself was small, with the capacity to seat six passengers comfortably, and maybe ten not so comfortably. Thankfully, there was only one other man besides their party, who looked to be a merchant in a greatcoat of brown wool, clutching a worn satchel to his chest. He was hunched on the seat across from them, his attention fixed on the water. He wore the same nervous expression as Molly, which Kendra attributed to her maid's earlier revelation that capsized wherries and drownings were not an uncommon occurrence on the Thames.

"Do you reckon there's a chance that the lass really is His Grace's daughter?" Sam asked, rubbing his nose.

Kendra looked to the Bow Street Runner. He was a short, muscular man with an elfin face, reddish-brown hair, and the graying sideburns of someone who'd recently entered their fourth decade of life. His eyes were so light brown that they appeared gold, and currently held the hard, flat expression that she'd always associated with those in law enforcement.

She'd waited until they were away from the Duke's residence and settled on the wherry before sharing Carlotta's story.

"It's pretty convenient," she replied. "Everyone who could verify her story is either dead or she lost touch with them a long time ago. But the Duke isn't willing to dismiss the possibility."

Sam frowned. "The child's body was never recovered." The Bow Street Runner had been acquainted with the Duke long enough to know the circumstances surrounding his wife and daughter's death.

"No," Kendra conceded, though it wasn't a question.

Sam huffed, then said, "She wouldn't be the first charlatan ter try ter pass themselves off as one of their betters."

"She knew enough information to get His Grace to think that she could be his daughter and invite her to stay with him," Kendra said. "Carlotta may think she's clever by pretending to 'remember' these things, but it's also her weakness. You have to send someone to Aldridge Village, find out if anyone has been around asking questions in the last year. Even if they don't remember questions, they still might remember a stranger in the area."

Sam's eyebrows shot up. "A full year?"

"Or more. Carlotta is playing the long game. The Duke of Aldridge is a powerful man. This scheme wasn't hatched overnight. It takes planning. She had her story down."

Sam's gaze drifted to the brackish water of the Thames as he considered that. "It'll be a hard trail ter follow in Spain," he said slowly. "And it'll probably take considerable time."

"I realize that."

And she didn't like it. Frustration burned like an ulcer in her belly. She thought of how easily a DNA paternity test could be conducted in the 21st century. Blood tests were not as reliable to determine a biological connection, but she didn't even have access to that technology. Hell, it would be another 85 years before Austrian scientist Karl Landsteiner would even begin identifying different blood types in human beings.

She sighed and said, "We still have to try."

Sam nodded. He looked as though he wanted to say something, but hesitated.

"What?" Kendra prodded, gazing at him.

"You've given a lot of thought ter the woman being a fraud. But have you considered the other possibility, lass? That she really is the Duke's missing daughter?"

The chill that raced down Kendra's arms had nothing to do with the cool breeze coming off the Thames.

"I'm considering everything."

But she had to put it aside to focus on the task at hand.

The market town of Maidenhead was about seven miles from its more famous neighbor, Windsor. As Sam explained, it had begun as a small hamlet along the River Thames, but its geographic position between London and England's West Country along the Great West Road made it a desirable location for public coaches and private carriages to stop and water, rest, or change horses, and for passengers to have a meal and a drink, and refresh and relieve themselves before continuing their journey. It was here where King Charles I met with his children to say their final farewells before he traveled to London to be executed.

The Maidenhead of today wasn't much changed. The city jostled with activity and boasted a heavy concentration of ancient inns, hostelries, stables, and blacksmith shops. Because of it, the air was heavy with the scent of horse, hay, and manure.

Sam secured a gig from one of the public stables nearby, a two-wheeled vehicle pulled by a horse. The contraption seated two comfortably, but three in a pinch. Molly managed to squeeze herself between Sam and Kendra without compromising the Bow Street Runner.

The gig was high enough off the ground to make Kendra's palms itch. She'd first traveled in a gig a couple of months ago in Yorkshire. At the time, she'd been terrified about being catapulted out and breaking her neck. Now, as Sam jiggled the lines and the horse jolted forward, she realized her fear hadn't subsided. She grasped the seat's edge in a white-knuckled grip, tightening her jaw to stop herself from crying out or cursing.

The vehicle shook as the wheels traveled over the macadam, dirt, and cobblestone roads that wove through Maidenhead. Kendra focused her attention on the buildings rather than the street below. The town was a mixture of architecture cobbled together from different centuries. She recognized Jacobean, Tudor, and the more modern Georgian styles. Kendra had never been to Maidenhead in her own timeline, but she imagined glass and steel would eventually replace some of the stone and stucco that she saw now.

Sam expertly steered the gig through streets congested with wagons, horseback riders, and carriages. Pedestrians—working-class folks, mostly—were going about their daily chores. Maybe because Maidenhead was both a travel center and a market town, where food and goods were brought in several times a week to be bartered, Kendra didn't see the grinding poverty that was so prevalent in London.

The Pascoe residence was a picturesque, whitewashed, two-story cottage with its door and shutters painted a shiny lapis. The roof was steeply angled and thatched, the straw old enough to have gone gray. Kendra hopped off the vehicle before Sam could come around and assist her, but waited for him to help Molly down, then hobble the horse.

The gravel crunched beneath their shoes as they walked up the path. A chilly breeze swept down on them, stirring the honeysuckle and rose bushes.

"Gor, we've 'ad an uncommon cold spell," Molly complained, pulling the collar of her coat closer. "Oi 'ope it gets warm soon. Everybody is comin' down with the snuffles. Cook and Beth were laid up just last week."

"Aye," Sam agreed as he lifted his hand to grasp the plain brass knocker. "'Tis goin' around London Town too."

"It ain't natural, ter be freezing in the month of May," muttered Molly.

It was actually completely natural, Kendra knew. The colder than normal temperatures would one day be traced to the previous year's volcanic eruption of Mount Tambora, half a world away in Indonesia. In history books, this period would one day be called the Year Without a Summer.

She kept that all to herself.

The cottage door opened to reveal a young girl about Molly's age wearing a beige linen mobcap and servant's garb. She gazed at them curiously. "May I help you?"

"Is this the Pascoe residence?" asked Sam.

"Aye."

"I'm Mr. Kelly and this is Miss Donovan." He didn't bother introducing Molly, who's status as a servant was obvious. From his coat's deep pocket he pulled the gold-tipped baton that identified him as a Bow Street Runner. "We need ter speak ter your master."

The girl's eyes widened at the sight of the baton. "The master ain't home yet. He's still at school. But my mistress is in the kitchen. Come inside, and I'll fetch her."

They followed the girl into a well-appointed parlor off the foyer, where she bobbed a quick curtsey and scurried out of the room. Light streamed through the bow window, touching on the slew of books that filled the shelves and sturdy mahogany furnishings in deep browns threaded with ambers and oranges. The room was as cold as outside, but the fireplace remained unlit. Unlike the Duke's wealthy household, most people didn't waste precious coal or wood to heat rooms that were unoccupied.

Kendra moved over to one of the bookshelves, scanning the titles. The Pascoes' reading material was diverse, ranging from several Henry Fielding novels to works by Thomas Paine and Jonathan Swift. Kendra was reminded that Mr. Pascoe taught at a boy's school here in Maidenhead. Her gaze fell on a small miniature of an attractive young man with a mop of curly, dark blond hair.

"Good afternoon."

Kendra turned to survey the woman who'd appeared in the doorway. She was a tiny, round woman, wearing a serviceable, high-necked, long-sleeved brown wool dress. Tendrils of medium brown hair escaped the undyed linen mobcap she wore and drifted around an unassuming face dominated by large, light brown eyes magnified slightly by gold-wired spectacles. Like most women in this era, who had spent a lifetime protecting their complexions from the sun, Mrs. Pascoe looked younger than her age, with only a few lines around her eyes and bracketing her mouth. Kendra suspected she was in her late forties, maybe early fifties, but she based that deduction more on the age of her son.

"Good afternoon, ma'am." Sam bowed. "My name is Mr. Kelly, and this is Miss Donovan."

Mrs. Pascoe *tsk*ed as she looked at them. "Martha should have taken your coats and things and asked you to be seated."

"Apologies, ma'am," the maid said, coming up behind her mistress. "I'll take them now."

Mrs. Pascoe waited for the servant to collect their outer garments, though Kendra kept her reticule (and the muff pistol concealed within).

"Please sit down," Mrs. Pascoe said, indicating the chairs. "Do you want tea? Ale?"

Kendra said, "No, thank you."

Mrs. Pascoe looked at Sam, her expression anxious. "Martha said that you were a Bow Street Runner. Does this have anything to do with Jeremy? Do you know something?"

"Nay. He ain't here, then?"

"No." Worry dug a notch between her eyebrows. "Mrs. Gavenston came here yesterday to inquire about his whereabouts. Did she . . . did she speak to you?"

Kendra leaned forward. "She asked us to look for your son," she said carefully. "We have a couple of questions, if you don't mind."

Mrs. Pascoe's frown turned to puzzlement as she regarded Kendra. "Forgive me. Who are you?"

"Kendra Donovan. I'm an acquaintance of Mrs. Gavenston's." As of that morning, but she didn't feel the need to point that out. "She's concerned about Jeremy."

The other woman nodded. "She told Mr. Pascoe and me that he didn't come in to work yesterday. Mr. Pascoe said we ought not be concerned, but it is not like Jeremy. He has always taken his responsibilities very seriously."

"When was the last time you saw your son, Mrs. Pascoe?" asked Kendra.

"I suppose it's been nearly a month. He came for Sunday dinner." She clasped her hands together, shooting Sam an apprehensive look. "Do you think something has happened to him?"

"We've got no reason ter think that," Sam said, adopting a reassuring tone. "There's plenty of reasons why a man might take off for a day or two."

Surprisingly, Mrs. Pascoe nodded. "Writing."

Sam and Kendra exchanged surprised looks.

"Writing?" asked Sam.

"Jeremy is a writer." She beamed at them, all motherly pride. "Poetry. He is a great admirer of Mr. Wordsworth and Mr. Shelley. Oh, I know Lord Byron is all the rage these days, what with the females swooning over the rogue. But Jeremy said that is more about his wicked conduct than his prose."

Sam frowned. "I don't understand. I thought he was a clerk at a bank before he became Mrs. Gavenston's business manager at the brewery."

"Well, one must make a living, you know. Mr. Shaw—he's the bank manager—approached my husband to inquire whether Jeremy would clerk for him after Jeremy finished with his schooling. Jeremy is quite good at mathematics. Mr. Pascoe . . . my husband is a schoolmaster here in Maidenhead. Even though it's a Bluecoat school, as one of the schoolmasters, my husband was allowed to teach Jeremy. He was adamant that Jeremy excel in all subjects. Jeremy was an excellent student."

Kendra remembered Mrs. Gavenston mentioning the school. "What exactly is a Bluecoat school?" she asked.

"'Tis a charity school," Mrs. Pascoe replied with a smile. "The boys wear blue coats."

Kendra had forgotten that a school system during this time was pretty much nonexistent for the poor and lower middle classes. The upper classes or wealthy merchants sent their boys to boarding schools like Eton or tutored them at home.

Mrs. Pascoe went on, "Anyway, how could Jeremy turn down Mr. Shaw's offer? Still, writing has always been his true passion. He told me that he found himself inspired in Cookham. 'When I look out my window and see the rolling green hills and woolbirds lolling about, my mind takes flight,' that's what he told me. Isn't that lovely? My Jeremy has always been clever with his words."

"Woolbirds?" wondered Kendra aloud.

"Sheep," Mrs. Pascoe and Sam said in unison. The older woman grinned at him, but her smile faded as her worry returned.

"I know Jeremy tends to have his head in the clouds when he's scribbling, but he wouldn't miss a day of work," Mrs. Pascoe said. "That's not like Jeremy at all. He is quite conscientious. I know Mr. Shaw was distressed to lose him from the bank when Mrs. Gavenston offered him employment as her business manager."

Kendra asked, "When you last saw your son, how was his mood? Upset? Depressed?"

"No. In fact, he was in excellent spirits. I had hoped he'd developed a tendre with one of the young ladies in Cookham. I have begun to despair that he will ever marry. I had thought a few years ago he and Miss Rogers—the vicar's daughter—might make a match of it, but she ended up running off with the blacksmith. Silly creature. Caused quite a scandal. Poor Jeremy was downcast for months." She let out a sigh. "I do so long for grandchildren."

Sam offered an encouraging smile. "I imagine you ain't alone in your wishes, Mrs. Pascoe. Is Jeremy your only son?"

"He is our only child." She unclasped her hands, allowing her fingers to pluck nervously at her skirt. "God will uplift."

Kendra eyed her. "Excuse me?"

"Oh—that's what Jeremy means. *God will uplift*. I have a fondness for researching the etymology of names. 'Tis my hobby. When Jeremy was a boy, we would do it together."

Kendra thought about what Mrs. Gavenston had said regarding Pascoe's love life, that he hadn't appeared to be interested in anyone, but she still asked, "Did Jeremy say he'd developed a tendre for someone? Is there a young lady we should speak to?"

"Jeremy said no when I quizzed him, but I suspect there is someone fluttering their lashes at him enough to turn his head." She smiled. "He is someone any young lady would set their cap at—Miss Rogers notwithstanding."

"Any idea who?"

"I'm afraid not. I'm not familiar with the young ladies in Cookham."

"What about his job at the brewery? Was he upset for any reason? Mrs. Gavenston said that they argued the other day over her decision to bring in machinery."

"He made no mention of it when he was home last month. But I can imagine how that would upset him. These are difficult times. I've read about the hostilities in the north, with lost wages because of the new machines. I would hate for that to happen here." She pursed her lips. "He did speak of tension in that household. I think it upset him."

"What household?" Kendra asked, "Mrs. Gavenston's?"

Mrs. Pascoe nodded.

Sam looked at her. "What was that about? Did he say?"

"Something to do with Mrs. Gavenston's family wanting more involvement in the brewery. Still, whatever the problem, what could it possibly have to do with Jeremy?"

Kendra was more interested in why Mrs. Gavenston hadn't mentioned those tensions. She'd felt the other woman hadn't been completely upfront with her. However, Mrs. Pascoe was right; what would that have to do with her son?

"If he was upset, do you have any idea where he might have gone?" Kendra asked.

Mrs. Pascoe lifted her hands. "I would think he would come home. He knows he is always welcome."

Kendra nodded, and pushed herself to her feet. "Thank you for your time, Mrs. Pascoe. If Jeremy contacts you, I'd appreciate it if you could send word to the Duke of Aldridge's address, Number 29, Grosvenor Square."

Mrs. Pascoe's eyebrows shot up as she hastily got to her feet. "You are connected to the Duke of Aldridge?"

"He's my . . . guardian." Would that word always stick in her throat?

"Oh, I see," Mrs. Pascoe said, and surveyed Kendra with something approaching awe. "I didn't realize. What will you do now, Miss Donovan?"

"Go to Cookham. Maybe your son has returned home." Kendra walked to the bookshelf that held the miniature portrait. She picked it up. "Is this your son, Mrs. Pascoe?"

She smiled automatically. "Yes."

"Would you mind if I borrowed it? If your son isn't at home, this will help in trying to find him. I promise to return it."

"Of course. I shall have Martha bring your things."

Mrs. Pascoe hurried out of the room.

Sam studied the portrait. "Good thinking, lass. I'll take it around ter the hostelries and public houses ter see if he got on a stagecoach."

"If we don't get a lead today, I will have Rebecca make a copy of it, so I can return the original to Mrs. Pascoe."

Mrs. Pascoe and Martha returned with their outerwear.

"Thank you for your time," Kendra said as she put on her pelisse and tugged on her gloves. "We'll be in touch."

She didn't offer anything more. No assurance that everything would be all right. She'd been an FBI agent too long to make that kind of promise.

7

Cookham wasn't bustling with commerce like Maidenhead, but it was busy enough. Half-timbered and redbrick buildings, many of which probably dated back to the Elizabethan era, rose up in heavy concentration along its high street. A handful of men were unloading barrels from a wagon, while young boys pelted down the street, laughing, with two dogs yapping excitedly at their heels. Sam drew the gig to a halt next to the wagon and asked the men for directions to 1 Milton Lane. Kendra knew that in London such an inquiry would have been met with hooded, suspicious eyes, but here she only saw bright curiosity. They didn't hesitate to supply the information.

Kendra thought about the villagers near Aldridge Castle. If a stranger had come around asking questions about the Duke's family, would anyone have thought twice about answering? It wouldn't have been a direct question, but a conversation. Casual. Probably at the village tavern. People talked more when they were drinking, not even realizing how much information they were divulging.

The gig jiggled to a stop outside a charming, buff-colored stone cottage nearly identical to the other stone cottages along the tree-lined street. Thin strips of greenery and gardens—pops of purple from buddleia, lilac, and hydrangea bushes, pale yellow primrose and daffodils, brilliant red roses—separated the houses from the pavement. The air was heavy with the syrupy scent of flowers.

They walked up to the door. Sam used the brass knocker crafted into a lion's head.

"Looks like Mr. Pascoe still isn't home," Kendra said after several attempts of knocking. She reached down to twist the knob. When it didn't open, she frowned. "I didn't think to ask Mrs. Gavenston for a key."

Sam said, "She probably thought you'd come and get it from her. She lives around here, you said."

"White Pond Manor."

"Do you have the address?"

"Yes, but I don't think that will be necessary."

Kendra was already drawing two long pins from her hair, which earned a squeak of dismay from Molly.

"Oh, miss . . ." the maid muttered woefully, clearly more upset about having her creation destroyed than what Kendra was about to do.

Kendra bent to insert the pins into the keyhole and worked the tumblers. She released a sigh of satisfaction when she felt the lock give way. Straightening, she turned the knob again, and smiled when the door swung inward.

"You have a right interestin' skill, lass," Sam murmured as he watched her remove the hairpins from the lock, and randomly shove them back into her chignon.

Kendra grinned at him. "It serves a purpose."

Inside, the cottage was small, the layout simple. The entrance hall was narrow, with a staircase at the other end, bisecting the drawing room on the right and the dining room on the left. By unspoken agreement, Kendra and Sam separated, with the Bow Street Runner angling toward the left, and Kendra walking through the door on the right. Molly drifted behind her.

Kendra scanned the drawing room. A brown brocade sofa and two leather chairs were arranged in front of an unadorned fireplace. A desk was shoved against the wall opposite the fireplace, flanked by heavy walnut bookshelves. A single mullioned window allowed the sunshine to stream in, dust motes dancing in the beams. The dark wood floor was covered by a brown woven area rug. Except for a thin layer of dust that Kendra could see on the furniture, the space appeared tidy.

She walked to what she considered the most interesting thing in the room—the desk. On its polished surface was a tray filled with foolscap; a brass inkwell stand that held two crystal inkpots, half-full; a quill pen; a container of sand; a candelabra, its four tapers burnt down to stubs; and three books stacked neatly on top of one another. Kendra picked up the first book. *Songs of Experience*, a collection of poems by William Blake. Her gaze dropped to the next book. John Milton's *Paradise Lost*. Below that, Alexander Pope's *Dunciad*.

Kendra imagined the aspiring poet spent many evenings at this desk.

Kendra began searching through the drawers, and found the usual assortment of stuff—for the 19th century. Nibs separated from their quills. A couple of graphite sticks. A penknife to sharpen the nibs or the graphite. A box of wax wafers for correspondence. More paper—but not the blank pages that were in the desk tray. Almost every square inch of these was covered in writing. Some of the words were crossed out, with arrows pointing to the notes in the margins or at a diagonal.

This was what writing looked like before the age of computers, before you could delete, add, rewrite with a stroke of a key. Chaotic and messy.

"Nothing in the dining room or kitchen," Sam said, coming into the room. "What've you got there, lass?"

"Mr. Pascoe's attempt to become a poet, I believe," she replied, and shrugged. "Nothing that would help us find him."

And because it felt a little invasive, Kendra slid the sheets back and closed the drawer.

"The lad cleans up after himself, right enough," Sam said, looking around the drawing room. "Everything was tucked away in the kitchen as well."

"Could 'ave a maid-of-all-work ter come in and tidy up for 'im," Molly put in, running a finger along the sideboard. She wrinkled her freckled nose critically as she inspected her smudged finger. "Needs more polishin'. Mrs. Danbury would 'ave 'er 'ead ter leave it like this."

"If he has a maid, maybe she only comes once a week," Kendra speculated, and looked at the Bow Street Runner. "What about food? Any perishables?"

"Nay. Tea kettle full of water on the stove, but that's all."

"That only means he doesn't cook much. Mrs. Gavenston said that he often ate in the taverns with his friend, Mr. Elwes." Kendra crossed the room to the door. "All right. Let's check the bedrooms upstairs."

There were only two bedchambers. The first door Kendra opened revealed a room that was furnished but clearly unoccupied, the bed stripped of its linens. More light dust covered the furniture.

"Pascoe definitely has a maid," Kendra said before closing the door. The wooden floor creaked beneath their feet as they walked across the hallway to the chamber that had been claimed by Pascoe.

"How'd you reckon?" asked Sam.

"Mrs. Gavenston said that she's employed Pascoe for over a year. There would be a lot more dust in the spare bedroom if someone didn't occasionally come in and wipe down the furniture. And I don't see a man dusting an unoccupied room, do you?"

Sam cocked his head, gold eyes gleaming. "Nay, but I can't say that I see a man dusting an *occupied* chamber either."

Kendra's lips quirked. "In all fairness, I don't see a woman doing it either. Not unless you were paid to do it. What's the point?"

Unless you were anal about cleanliness, which would mean no dust at all. She made a mental note to find and interview the maid.

Kendra opened the other door and surveyed Pascoe's bedchamber. The bed had been made, but not particularly well. The probability was high that Pascoe had done it himself; a maid would have done a better job. The ceiling was slanted, dormer windows letting in the light. In the corner was a wooden washstand with a mirror, a towel, toiletries for shaving, toothbrush and powder, and a comb.

She joined Sam, who was opening the doors of a large wardrobe. Inside were several jackets, shirts, and pantaloons on hooks. Two pairs of shoes were tucked at the wardrobe's bottom. Kendra opened the drawer to reveal a neatly folded nightshirt and cravats.

"Well, it looks like Pascoe is planning on coming back." Kendra closed the drawer and looked around the bedchamber again. "You don't leave without taking your things."

Molly looked at her wide-eyed. "Do ye think something 'appened ter the gent, then?"

"Not necessarily. Maybe he's stranded somewhere. Or needed a couple of days away." Although he would have taken his toiletries if he planned an overnighter, she thought. "There is the possibility that he had an accident."

Kendra moved to the windows, which overlooked a tiny patch of land separated from the neighbor's backyard by a low gray stone wall. A gnarled oak tree provided shade. Birds hopped on the branches, trilling to each other.

She turned abruptly and hurried out of the bedchamber. She retraced her footsteps to the ground level. Frowning, she went to each window.

"What are you doin', lass?" Sam asked, puzzled, as he watched her push aside the gauzy curtains in the kitchen to stare out at the gnarled oak tree.

She let the curtains drop, turning to look at the Bow Street Runner. "We need to find Pascoe's other place."

Molly stared at her. "W'ot other place, miss?"

"The one where he's been writing. The one where he told his mother that he can look out the window and see rolling green hills and sheep."

The maid frowned. "But there ain't any 'ills and sheep 'ere."

"Exactly."

8

Kendra walked outside, and stopped abruptly, her gaze immediately going to the handsome man sitting astride a beautiful Arabian stallion.

"Miss Donovan."

Alec Morgan, the Marquis of Sutcliffe, swept the hat off his head in greeting. The breeze ruffled the dark hair framing a face that could easily have graced one of the sexy designer ads that dominated Times Square in the 21st century. Straight nose, chiseled cheekbones, square jaw with the shallow dent in the chin. The sensual mouth was now curved in a rakish smile. His eyes—at a distance, the same shade as his forest green riding habit, although close up she knew there were gold flecks radiating around the pupil—met hers. That smile and the accompanying gleam in his eyes still had the power to steal her breath and start a delicious flutter in her stomach.

"Milord," Sam hailed when he stepped outside. "I reckon your appearance here ain't a coincidence."

"His Grace informed me of your quest to find a young man who has disappeared." He raised an eyebrow at Kendra. "Always a surprise, Miss Donovan."

"How did you find us?" she asked.

"Duke gave me Mr. and Mrs. Pascoe's address in Maidenhead. I spoke with Mrs. Pascoe, who sent me here." He looked beyond them at the cottage. "I assume you did not find Mr. Pascoe?"

"Not yet."

"How do you plan on finding him?"

Kendra smiled. "Right now, we need to start knocking on doors. You can help."

Alec swung down from his horse, tying up the reins to a nearby hitching post. He gave her a slight bow. "I am your servant, Miss Donovan."

They divided up the neighboring houses, with Sam and Alec taking the side of the street that Pascoe's house was on, and Kendra, followed by Molly, taking the other. No one answered the door to the pretty stone cottage directly across from Pascoe's residence. She moved on to the next house on the right, and a middle-aged woman wearing a black lace cap and black bombazine gown came to the door. Obviously still in the deep stages of mourning, but probably at the end of that period, since no black wreath or ribbons decorated the door.

"Hi . . . ah, good day." Kendra offered a friendly smile. "My name is Kendra Donovan. I'm sorry to interrupt, but we're looking for Mr. Pascoe. He lives across the street. Do you know him, Mrs.—?"

The widow's eyebrows rose. It probably wasn't every day an American knocked on her door looking for her neighbor. The rules governing introductions in this era were complicated; Kendra knew she was breaking them. As she watched, the other woman's gaze slid past her to rest briefly on Molly. She seemed reassured by the maid's presence, but kept her hand on the door, ready to slam it shut if Kendra made the wrong move.

"Mrs. Bunting," the older woman finally answered, her expression still suspicious. "I am only slightly acquainted with Mr. Pascoe. He works for Barrett Brewery. I expect you'll be able to find him there."

"He hasn't been to work in a few days. When was the last time you saw him?"

"Oh, dear." Concern—or maybe it was just the desire to gossip—made Mrs. Bunting open the door wider, revealing a small foyer that was painted mint-green and smelled of lemons. "Has something happened to him?"

"We're just trying to locate him. It would help if you could tell us the last time you saw him."

Mrs. Bunting frowned. "Walking home from the brewery, I should imagine. Last week . . . Wednesday? Or possibly Thursday. I'm not certain. The days speed by so quickly. 'Tis difficult to remember specifics."

"You didn't see him on Saturday?"

"I wasn't at home. My first grandchild was born, and I was there helping with her birth until Monday afternoon."

"Did you hear if Mr. Pascoe mentioned leaving town for a few days? Maybe he said something to you in passing, or one of your neighbors."

"No. And I'd think he would have told Mrs. Gavenston if he planned to do such a thing."

"What about mentioning another place where he liked to write?"

"I assume you are referring to his poetry?"

If this had been the 21st century, Mrs. Bunting would have made quotation marks with her fingers, Kendra thought. Clearly the widow didn't think much about his extracurricular activity.

"He told you that he wanted to be a poet? I thought you were barely acquainted."

"That's true, but I encountered him at the circulating library. He had a volume of poems by Robert Burns. When I mentioned his interest in poetry, he confessed that it had always been a passion of his. You can imagine my surprise when he admitted to dabbling in verse himself." She wrinkled her nose. "One would think Mr. Pascoe would be too old to dream of such things."

Kendra wasn't sure at what age a person was supposed to give up on their dreams but shifted to a more relevant question. "Can you tell me where I might find sheep around here within walking distance?"

Mrs. Bunting stared at her like she'd lost her mind. "Sheep?"

"Sheep and rolling green hills."

"Well, if you're interested in sheep, Miss Donovan, you ought to find them on the commons or Squire Prebble's lands, as he's got a fair amount of the beasts. However, have care. You don't want to be downwind from them."

"And those would be where?"

"The squire's land is to the west. The commons is northwest."

"Rolling green hills?"

She gave Kendra a quizzical look. "Both have hills."

"Thank you, Mrs. Bunting."

They left the widow and retraced their footsteps to the street, where Sam and Alec were waiting. Sam looked at Kendra and said, "I spoke ter a lady who says she saw Mr. Pascoe take off down the street Saturday afternoon. She said he was carrying a satchel."

Kendra frowned. "A satchel? Then he did leave town."

"Nay, I don't think so. Mrs. Booth said that was his habit ter go off early in the mornin' with a satchel slung over his shoulder, though normally on Sunday mornings."

"What time exactly? Did she say?" asked Kendra.

"Mrs. Booth thought it was near three, but couldn't be certain of the exact time, as she wasn't near a clock."

"That is the same information I was given," Alec said with a nod. "Except Mr. Gayle said that Mr. Pascoe appeared blue-deviled about something. He was working on his rosebushes when he saw Mr. Pascoe leaving. Called out a greeting, but Mr. Pascoe either ignored him or didn't hear."

"Aye. Mrs. Booth thought he looked upset as well."

Kendra pursed her lips. "Mrs. Gavenston said they had a disagreement about her decision to bring in machines."

Alec studied Kendra's face. "You don't believe her?"

"I don't know. Something seems off." She shifted her gaze to the west, imagining rolling green hills dotted with sheep. "Mrs. Bunting said that we can find sheep on the commons or Squire Prebble's land. I think we can eliminate the commons. It sounds like Pascoe was looking for the privacy and inspiration of a bucolic setting. He wouldn't get the former on the commons."

Sam nodded. "Aye. You'd have every farmer bringing their cattle in ter feed."

"We're also looking for an abandoned structure of some kind—maybe it's just a shack. Something that Pascoe felt comfortable taking over as a writer's retreat. I don't know how much Mrs. Gavenston was paying him, but I doubt it was so much that he could afford two residences."

"I thought Barrett Brewery owned this one," Sam said.

"Good point. I don't know if he pays rent to Mrs. Gavenston or not. But I still don't see him renting another residence."

The Bow Street Runner regarded Kendra with a puzzled frown. "Doesn't make sense. He's got a perfectly fine cottage here. Why'd he need another one?"

"Maybe he just wanted space, a different environment to get the creative juices flowing," Kendra said with a shrug. "Let's see how much ground we can cover in the next couple of hours."

Squire Prebble's estate was nearly nine hundred acres, a fact that Sam learned when he stopped by the local stables to get directions. That translated into roughly 1.4 square miles. The size, Kendra knew, of New York's Central Park. She also knew that it was going to be a long walk, especially for someone wearing thin-soled shoes and a dress.

They started at the point nearest to Pascoe's cottage in the village and farthest from where the squire's manor was located. Within walking distance from his house, and yet still isolated. They hobbled the horses near the low stone wall that marked the boundary to the squire's land, then Sam peeled off to the left while Alec, Kendra, and Molly headed in the opposite direction.

Kendra would have pointed out to Alec that his decision to walk beside her was not the most efficient use of their time, but this was her first opportunity to talk to him privately. Molly was far enough behind to give them privacy and yet still perform her chaperone duties by keeping them in her line of sight. People in the 21st century chafed about losing their privacy by having cameras everywhere. They should try being a single, upper-class woman in the 19th century with a permanent shadow.

They were both quiet as they set off across Squire Prebble's land. Kendra's gaze roved over the hills and hallows stretched before them. Above, the sky reminded her of skim milk, white with a bluish tinge. Wildflowers dotted the lush greenery. Woods nestled in valleys. No sheep that she could see, but the grass was short enough to make her think the animals had been around within the last couple of weeks.

She broke the silence, glancing at Alec out of the corner of her eye. "Have you talked to the Duke about his new guest?"

"Yes." His mouth tightened. "He was waiting for the woman to return."

Kendra watched a series of emotions flit across his handsome face. Anger, she recognized. And worry.

He looked at her. "You met with the woman. What do you think?"

"I think she's a clever con artist," she said bluntly. "But I have nothing to base that on."

She paused as she maneuvered over a rocky patch, accepting Alec's hand when he reached out to steady her.

It was becoming natural to accept his assistance. She wondered if that should concern her. She'd fought so hard to become self-reliant in her own era. When her parents had discarded her, she'd felt helpless. She never wanted to feel that helpless again. So it was ironic that she'd been forced to accept help in one form or another since she'd arrived in this timeline. She'd borrowed a little money from the Duke to invest in the Exchange and made enough to pay him back and create a small savings account for herself. But the clothes on her back were still purchased at the Duke's largesse. She lived in luxury because of the Duke, not her own efforts. And she knew that she was allowed to question members of the Ton because of her connection to the Duke of Aldridge. Even Sam, who was a servant of the Crown, didn't have that kind of access.

Aware that Alec was looking at her, Kendra forced her thoughts back to Carlotta.

"Physically, she *could* be his daughter," she said. "Black hair, dark brown eyes. She's very pretty. Charlotte was only six when she was lost at sea."

Kendra had worked a few times with artists specializing in age-progression and remembered what they had told her.

"Children change the most at seven and eight years old. They lose their baby teeth, which changes the shape of the mouth and jaw. Facial bones also grow and change the most during those ages."

"Duke says the resemblance is uncanny."

"The Duke may be seeing what he wants to see. But based on the paintings of Charlotte and Arabella, there *is* a resemblance," Kendra admitted reluctantly. "The resemblance is probably more striking with Arabella, but that makes sense. Charlotte took after her mother. I've hired Mr. Kelly to send men to Spain to check out Carlotta's story."

Alec nodded. "I shall take care of the expenses."

Kendra smiled slightly. "The Duke also offered. I'm less worried about the expense than I am about the investigation. The history she gave is conveniently scarce in specifics. Everyone who could corroborate her account is either dead or lost. I think she's relying on the war as cover."

Alec frowned. "No matter what is discovered, it could take a long time."

Kendra sighed in frustration. "I know. And it pisses me off, because in that time, she's going to be working on the Duke."

"Working on?"

"Trying to convince him that she's his daughter. She didn't even have to try to get him to invite her to stay with him. He offered immediately. I think that surprised her."

"You can't expect him to leave her at an inn?"

"No, probably not. But now she's under his roof. I don't like it."

For several minutes, they trudged along in silence except for the breeze whispering through the blades of grass, the occasional trill and tweet of birds in the trees. Behind them, Molly paused every now and then to pick a wildflower.

"Mr. Kelly is also going to send someone to Aldridge Village," Kendra told Alec. "Carlotta knew things that would require research. And that kind of research would mean talking to villagers and the staff at the castle. That could be her downfall."

At least she hoped so.

Alec looked over at Kendra as they began to climb a hill. "What if her claim is true?"

Kendra stumbled. Alec's hand flashed out, caught her elbow.

"You can't believe that!"

"I don't know what to believe," he admitted and shook his head. "It is incredible to think Charlotte may have survived her ordeal, that she may be alive. And yet people do survive shipwrecks, you know."

"Twenty years later?"

He gave a shrug. "She was a child and Spain was at war."

"Why are you taking her side?"

"I'm not taking her side. But we need to at least consider the possibility. My uncle is."

Kendra's stomach pitched and rolled. She remembered the bright flare of hope that she'd seen in the Duke's eyes. *He wants it to be true.*

"What do you remember about Charlotte?" she asked. She sounded a little breathy, but she could attribute that to the hike up the hill.

Alec was silent for a long moment. "Adorable," he finally said, and he smiled at the memory. "Intelligent, of course. Always running about like a hoyden. She'd follow me around like a puppy during my stays. She'd quiz me about everything, chatter nonstop."

His smile faded. "It broke my heart when I heard that Charlotte and Arabella died. Duke was beside himself in his grief. I shall never forget it."

Hearing the pain in his voice, Kendra reached out to clasp his hand, offer a comforting squeeze. Assistance took many forms, she realized. And it wasn't one-sided. Give and take; take and give. They balanced each other out.

He gave her a sideways look, smiling slightly, and squeezed back. They walked a bit more in silence.

"If this woman is a charlatan playing on Duke's affections and memories, she shall regret it," Alec finally said. The dark promise in his voice nearly made Kendra shiver.

"Think about the Charlotte you remember. It's those memories that can be used to trip her up. And hopefully Mr. Kelly's men will find something, either in Spain or Aldridge Village. I don't think she's working alone."

He looked at her sharply. "Why do you say that?"

"Educated guess. She would have stood out if she went to Aldridge Village, asking questions. A beautiful young woman without a chaperone?" She glanced automatically over her shoulder at Molly. "Someone would remember her. That's also vital to a good con. When you're doing research, you want to be low-key."

"She may have disguised herself as a servant or someone from the lower classes, where she wouldn't need a chaperone. Like someone else I know," he said dryly, a not-so-oblique reference to times when Kendra had made use of a maid's uniform to go about London incognito.

Kendra dismissed that with a wave. "London is different than Aldridge Village. And she still would have been noticed, unless she disguised her looks. Possible, I suppose, but—" She stopped when Alec put a hand on her arm and looked at him. "What?"

But now she saw what had caught his attention. They'd reached the crest of the hill. Below them was a charming glen, thick with woods, and a stream cutting through the fields. The land rose again in the distance, rolled green against the milky sky and dotted with bits of white.

"Sheep," Kendra said.

"Not that." Alec turned her slightly and pointed.

It wasn't easy to see through the copse's foliage. But there was enough space between the branches and leaves to identify something else: gray stone jutting upward.

A chimney stack.

9

The cottage wasn't much in size—less than four hundred square feet, if Kendra had to guess—but looked like something straight out of a fairytale. It had gray stone and lichen-covered walls and a steeply slanted slate roof. Time had worn the paint off on the door, making it impossible to discern its original color. Two small windows were cut into the stone, on either side of the door. The forest, cool and green and slightly mysterious, surrounded the tiny building.

"It looks abandoned, but it's not," Kendra murmured.

"W'ot makes you say that, miss?" Molly eyed the structure dubiously.

"The windows have been cleaned," Kendra pointed out, and strode forward.

They'd skirted the forest and were now approaching the cottage from the other direction. It was too quiet, Kendra thought. She'd been sure, so sure, that they'd find the missing man here.

She knocked on the door, and called out, "Mr. Pascoe?"

Silence.

She knocked again, then tried the doorknob. It turned easily beneath her hand. She pushed inward. The foul smell hit her then, as vicious as a punch in the gut. Unmistakable. Instinct made her retrieve the muff pistol.

"Wait here," she ordered.

Alec glanced at her sharply. He didn't bother arguing, merely joined her, and they cleared the threshold together.

Kendra's gaze swept the room—one room only. Four hundred square feet; she'd been right about that, she decided. The size of a studio apartment in New York City. A narrow cot covered with a sage-green wool blanket and two plush turquoise pillows was shoved against one wall. A stone fireplace filled the other wall, a half-consumed log and cold ashes in the blackened hearth. A skinny pinewood cupboard was wedged between a cast iron stove and a washbasin. There was a small rustic pine table and two equally rustic chairs, all of which would have cost a small fortune in the 21st century, but had probably been made by whoever had once lived in the cottage. A wool coat was draped over the back of one of the chairs.

Kendra processed the room with a quick glance before her gaze dropped to the man lying face-up on the floor, the smooth hilt of a knife protruding from his stomach.

"Shit," she muttered, and slipped the pistol back into her reticule. Even though the stench made her eyes water, she started forward. She didn't need to fish out the small miniature portrait from her pouch, but she did so anyway. Taking shallow breaths, she angled the tiny painting toward Alec, who'd joined her.

"Mr. Pascoe isn't in his best looks," Alec murmured, stripping off one of his gloves to hold against his nose.

Since that wasn't a bad idea, Kendra followed suit with her own glove. "Being dead for several days has a way of doing that to a person."

Molly came up behind them and let out a shriek. She whirled around and stumbled back out the door, gagging.

Kendra ignored the commotion, her gaze traveling over Pascoe's swollen features, noting the marbling and greenish tinge to his skin. Flies buzzed in the air and crawled across the corpse, feasting on putrid flesh.

"I'd say that he's been dead since Saturday, but the colder temperatures have slowed decomposition," she said. "You know, really, he could look a lot worse."

"Except for the knife sticking out of his gut."

"Yeah, except for that." She straightened and looked at Alec. "You need to get Mr. Kelly."

"I'm not leaving you alone."

She lifted an ironic eyebrow. "Pascoe is hardly in the position to compromise me if I'm left alone with him."

"And what if the fiend who murdered this poor wretch returns?"

"I'm not defenseless, Alec," she said, exasperation making her terse. "Besides, the killer is long gone."

She recognized the expression on his handsome face.

"Fine," she hissed, moving to the door.

Outside, Molly was looking almost as green as the corpse.

"Molly, you need to find Mr. Kelly and bring him here," Kendra said.

The maid hesitated. "Oi shouldn't leave ye and 'is lordship alone."

Kendra was done with the archaic rules that governed this society. "Oh, for God's sake! Who will know? We're in the middle of nowhere."

She didn't wait to see if Molly obeyed; she swung around and surveyed the room more thoroughly. Alec was in the process of opening the two windows, letting in fresh air to chase away the overwhelming stink of death. *Impossible*. The odor of decay had seeped into the wood and walls, and long after this day, the whiff of it would remain.

She ignored the smell; focused on the visuals.

The room had been kept tidy, except for the table, which was cluttered with items. Several stout candles of varying sizes, the tallow wax having pooled and hardened into stiff bubbles at each base, were scattered across the surface, along with an inkwell, its cap off, several quill pens, pages of foolscap, and a small teak chest. Next to that was a tin plate that held a half loaf of stale bread and a wedge of yellowish cheese, waxy and hard. Kendra let her gaze travel to two earthenware bowls—one filled with crystallized lumps of sugar and one with clumps of loose-leafed tea—and a dented silver spoon next to an earthenware mug. Bits of tea leaves floated in a thimbleful of brown water. A copper tea kettle, dented and tarnished, was on the stove.

It only took three steps to reach the table. Holding the glove pinched to her nose, Kendra lifted the lid to the chest. Inside was a removable top tray, which held wax sticks, a penknife, and more inkwells.

"'Tis a traveling writer's chest," Alec identified.

Kendra left the lid open and circled the table to the skinny pine cupboard. Opening the door, she surveyed the empty shelves. She closed the cupboard door, turning to look at Alec.

"What is this place?"

"I'd say it was probably once a cottage for one of the squire's tenants who farmed the land," he replied. "Most likely abandoned after the property was enclosed. There are similar cottages on many estates throughout England."

"And Pascoe found it and cleaned it up so he could use it as a writer's retreat." She glanced at the window and saw the rolling hills that Pascoe had mentioned to his mother, although from this angle, she couldn't see the sheep. "It's cozy. Plenty of solitude. He didn't have to worry about the neighbors bothering him."

"I'm not certain that he had that worry regardless," Alec commented.

Grimacing, he crouched down next to the dead man. Keeping the glove pressed against his lower face, he used his other gloved hand to carefully lift up Pascoe's jacket.

"I don't see a purse. I can't imagine a brewery manager being too plump in the pockets, but it must have been a robbery."

"It wasn't a robbery," Kendra said, and shook her head.

Still, she reached down to check the pockets of the coat hanging on the chair. Nothing except for a handkerchief. The worn, brown-leather satchel that the neighbor had mentioned was resting on the same chair. She lifted the flap, poked through. More papers, many crumpled and some torn, filled with scribbling, and a small dog-eared book. She lifted the book, saw that it was a collection of poems by Walter Scott. (It would be a couple more years before the Prince Regent granted him a baronetcy.) She slipped the book back into the satchel.

"This was a crime of impulse," Kendra narrated. "The killer didn't bring the knife. Pascoe brought it with him to cut his bread and cheese. One plate, one cup. He didn't invite the killer to lunch."

She knelt down beside Alec to inspect the knife in question. The hilt was plain brown, stained in places. Splattered with Pascoe's blood. Maybe some of the killer's, but she doubted it. Still, this was the type of disorganized crime that had tons of trace evidence scattered throughout the scene. If she were in her timeline, they'd have the killer by nightfall.

Damn, damn, damn.

She huffed out a frustrated breath and turned to examining the body.

"He was stabbed repeatedly," she murmured. Pascoe's wool waistcoat had once been canary yellow, but was now nearly black. Pascoe's blood had seeped into the wool that was stretched taut across his bloated abdomen. More blood spatter was visible on the trousers and jacket, a dried lake on the floor beneath the body.

Kendra pointed to the tears in the material. "At least five times. But I'd like Dr. Munroe to verify that." She lifted her gaze to Alec's. "Will that be a problem? I know Cookham is probably outside his jurisdiction."

"The local doctor or sawbones will have authority, but mayhap we can convince him to relinquish it to Dr. Munroe. But what do you expect to learn from an autopsy that we don't already know? Clearly he died from the knife wounds."

"It's part of the process. You never know what else you might find," she said with a shrug. Maybe it was foolish, but she wanted to stick with the procedures she'd been trained in as much as possible.

She leaned forward, put on her glove, and picked up the dead man's hands, first one, then the other, to scrutinize the fingers and palms.

"Defensive wounds," she said, noting several cuts that gouged the flesh. "He tried to take hold of the weapon at one point." She lowered his arm to the floor. "He's no longer in rigor mortis."

"Which means?"

"He's been dead longer than thirty-six hours."

"God's teeth!"

They glanced around to see Sam reel back slightly in the doorway. He lifted his arm, burying his nose in the crook of his elbow, then determinedly advanced into the room. Amber eyes hard, he studied the dead man for long minute before looking at Kendra.

"Well, lass . . . I guess Mr. Pascoe ain't missing any longer."

10

"T his ain't good," Constable Leech said, casting a leery eye toward the open door of the cottage. He was a short, chubby, middle-aged man with a shock of bright blond hair and a florid face that could probably be traced back to the ale he'd been drinking in the tavern where Sam had finally located him.

"Mrs. Gavenston ain't gonna like it one bit that her man has cocked up his toes." Leech shook his head, his brow creasing. "Mr. Pascoe seemed a decent enough fellow."

"How well did you know him?" Kendra asked curiously.

"Ack, not well, I suppose. We weren't friends, if that's what you're askin'. But he was friendly enough when he came into my shop."

"Your shop?"

"Aye. I've got a tea shop on High Street."

The job of a parish constable was unpaid and part-time, which meant whoever held it also had another job. Last fall, Kendra had dealt with

75

a thoroughly unpleasant constable-cum-blacksmith. So far, Constable Leech appeared to have a more congenial disposition.

"He was an Assam man," confided the constable.

"Excuse me?"

"Mr. Pascoe. Always came in for my Assam black tea blend."

"Oh."

Constable Leech went on, "A very robust tea. I was a bit surprised he favored it, to be quite honest. Mr. Pascoe never struck me as a particularly robust man. More . . . studious, I suppose." He rocked back and forth on his heels, with his hands clasped behind his back as he pondered the dead man's choice in tea. "Thought he'd be a Darjeeling man."

Kendra caught the amused glint in Alec's eyes and had to suppress an answering smile. She focused her attention on the constable.

"What can you tell me about Mr. Pascoe? Was he involved in any altercations recently?" *Besides the disagreement he'd had with Mrs. Gavenston,* Kendra amended silently.

"Nay. Least-wise, not that I heard." Leech glanced at the door to the cottage again, frowning. "What's he here for anyways? Mrs. Gavenston gave him a fine cottage in the village."

"Apparently Mr. Pascoe was trying his hand at poetry, and found inspiration in this area," Alec answered. "He made the cottage comfortable enough."

Constable Leech scratched his chin. "I wonder if Squire Prebble knew?"

"Would that be a problem? If he discovered Mr. Pascoe on his property?" asked Kendra.

"Hard to say. If he knew, he wouldn't have made a fuss, since Mr. Pascoe worked for Mrs. Gavenston. Barrett Brewery holds powerful sway here in the village."

"Even with the squire?"

That was a surprise. A squire was landed gentry, while Mrs. Gavenston was only a merchant.

"Squire Prebble likes his ale as much as the next man," the constable said.

"What kind of temperament does the squire have?" Kendra persisted. "If he came across a stranger squatting in his cottage . . . some people like to shoot first and ask questions later."

"Well, Squire Prebble would definitely be shooting, not stabbing someone in the breadbasket, if it came to that." He pursed his lips, shaking his head. "Nay, miss. Mr. Pascoe is a recognizable enough figure. He attended the assemblies in the village; danced with the squire's daughters, if I recollect properly. In fact, the squire's been in London for the last month because he's got to marry them off. All three of them, God help him. They're all a bit whey-faced, if you must know, so it ain't gonna be easy. The villagers are placing wagers on whether the squire and his wife will be able to unload them in the marriage mart before the season is over."

Sam asked, "Does the squire have any sons to run the estate while the family is gone ter town?"

"No sons, more's the pity. Mr. Cox is his land steward."

"We'll need his address," Kendra said. "Would you object if we have the body transported back to London for the autopsy?"

"Why would you want to do that?"

"Dr. Munroe is an anatomist that we've worked with before." *And he's one of the few men in this era who treated me with respect,* she thought, but didn't say it.

Leech stared at her, clearly baffled by the request. "We've got a village surgeon, you know. Although it seems clear as day how the poor wretch died. What could a London sawbones tell you that Hobbs couldn't?"

"I don't know," Kendra had to admit.

Constable Leech shook his head. "We've got to keep Mr. Pascoe in Cookham until the inquest. The autopsy needs to be done here. Since you and Lord Sutcliffe discovered the body, you may be called upon to testify too."

"What if Dr. Munroe comes here?" asked Kendra, reluctant to let the matter go.

"It's up to Hobbs, I reckon," he said and peered at her closely. "Your man is a real doctor?"

She understood the question. The medical field in this era had a strange social hierarchy, with doctors at the top, surgeons on the middle tier, and apothecaries at the bottom. Most doctors shied away from getting their hands dirty—literally—which meant they were socially acceptable and invited into the homes of the Beau Monde.

Dr. Ethan Munroe was something of an anomaly. He had trained to be a medical doctor in Edinburgh before switching careers to work as a surgeon. And if that wasn't shocking enough, he had then turned his attention to the world of the dead. An anatomist didn't even rank on the medical hierarchy. It probably fell somewhere in the category of an occultist.

It occurred to her that she wasn't the only freak in this timeline.

"Yes, Dr. Munroe is a real doctor," she finally answered. "Yours isn't?"

"Nay. Like most sawbones, Hobbs got his training on the battlefields during war. I'll make arrangements to transport the body to his farm." He glanced at the cottage. "Best get him out of there. The air ain't gonna get any fresher."

"I'll go with you, and speak ter Hobbs," Sam said. "If he's agreeable, I'll fetch Dr. Munroe from London Town." He met Kendra's eyes. "Does that meet with your approval, Miss Donovan?"

She smiled. "Yes, thank you, Mr. Kelly."

"And while I'm there, I'll make arrangements for that other matter we discussed."

She nodded, silently thanking him for setting up the investigation into Carlotta's background in the midst of this case.

Constable Leech sighed, looking troubled. "This is a nasty bit of business. Cookham is a peaceable village. Someone passing through must have come upon Mr. Pascoe and thought to steal from him. We've had peddlers come from Maidenhead during market days. And Gypsies. Course I've chased them off whenever I can, but they still come."

"I don't think that's it; Mr. Pascoe knew his killer," Kendra said slowly.

Constable Leech gaped at her. "How'd you know that?"

Kendra walked back to the cottage door. No, the air wasn't going to get any fresher. From the threshold, she studied the room with a critical eye.

"The crime scene tells us what we need to know. Nothing indicates a struggle of any kind. Nothing has been knocked over or is on the floor—aside from Mr. Pascoe," she said drily. "Mr. Pascoe even allowed his killer to get close to him.

"He stood up or was already standing when his killer came into the cottage. The knife was on the table, next to the bread and cheese." She made a mental note to ask Munroe to check the blade under his microscope for traces of food, although knowing the doctor, he would do it without needing to be asked. "If Pascoe had felt threatened in any way, why wouldn't he have picked up the knife, used it as a weapon? And if the killer had surprised him, the scene would be a lot more disorganized; chairs and the table tipped over, the bread and cheese and mug on the floor."

Leech came over to peer into the cottage. "Huh." He turned to look at her. "What if he didn't feel threatened? Maybe it was one of those Gypsy women."

It was possible. A man might not feel threatened by a stranger, if the stranger was a woman.

"Why would a Gypsy woman kill him?" asked Sam.

Leech glanced at the Bow Street Runner. "They're all thieves. Mayhap Mr. Pascoe objected to being robbed."

Sam shook his head. "That may be, but the Romany I've dealt with wouldn't have stopped at taking just his purse. They would've taken his coat and boots, the dishes, those nice pillows on the bed, *and* the feather tick mattress. They'd have stripped the place bare."

Kendra glanced at the Bow Street Runner with surprise. "You make an excellent point, Mr. Kelly," she said. She wasn't willing to categorize all the Romany people as thieves, but a thief who was willing to kill would probably take more than the victim's wallet. *If* that was even missing. They needed to search Pascoe's cottage in the village more thoroughly.

"There was a handkerchief in Mr. Pascoe's pocket as well," she added, and saw the constable's eyebrows shoot up in understanding. Oddly enough, she'd learned months ago that handkerchiefs were prized in this era, often targeted for theft.

"Well, that's a different kettle of fish," conceded Constable Leech. "A Gypsy wouldn't have left that behind."

"How long will it take to bring Dr. Munroe here?" Kendra asked Sam.

"I'll rent a horse; faster ter get ter town. No more than a couple of hours, I'd say."

"It would make more sense if you took Chance," Alec said, offering his stallion. "I will take over the gig. And, I suggest after you make your arrangements with Dr. Munroe, borrow a carriage from His Grace's stables. At this rate, we won't be returning to London until nightfall. I'd rather be in a carriage than on a wherry up the Thames in the dark."

Sam nodded. "If I have time when I return with Dr. Munroe, I'll try to find Mr. Cox."

"While you do that, I need to have a talk with Mrs. Gavenston."

Kendra's stomach twisted into knots. It didn't matter the century; some things never got easier.

First things first, though. Kendra sucked in a deep breath of fresh air, and then went back inside the stone shack. She gathered up the loose papers from the table. Like the foolscap she'd found in his cottage in Cookham, Pascoe had filled up the pages. But he'd apparently found his writing wanting, because angry slashes crossed out words, sentences, sometimes the nib digging so deeply that he'd torn tiny holes in the page.

She stuffed the papers into the writing chest and satchel. Later, she'd read through them. Studying the victim was a vital part of any murder investigation.

For a long moment, she stood with her hand resting on the wooden writing chest as her eyes roamed across the room to imprint the scene in her mind. Narrow cot, pillows, candles, tea kettle, mug . . . What was she missing? What was she not seeing?

Her gaze fell on the dead man lying at her feet. Leech said that he'd soon be hauled away to Hobbs's farm. A *farm*, for God's sake. She wondered if the autopsy would be conducted in the barn. It made her uneasy to leave without cordoning off the crime scene, but what would be the point? Crime scenes were preserved to allow the CSI unit time to collect trace evidence. The cottage was remote enough; maybe it would remain undisturbed.

Biting back a sigh, she started to hoist up the travel chest, but Alec came around to take it from her. She hadn't realized he'd been standing behind her. He raised an eyebrow.

"Do you really think Mr. Pascoe's poetry will help you find his killer?"

"You never know." She gave a noncommittal shrug and moved to the windows, shutting them. She didn't know how long it would take to remove the corpse, but it was best not to give larger predators an opening to get inside to feed.

She grabbed the satchel and followed Alec outside.

"God, Ramsey may quit on the spot when he gets a whiff of these clothes," Alec muttered, waiting while she closed the door. "It might be better to toss them in the dustbin where they cannot offend my valet's sensibilities."

"Aye, the dead have a way of staying with a person," Sam spoke up. He was already sitting astride Chance, controlling the skittish stallion by sawing at the reins. He looked at Kendra. "I'll see you at Hobbs's farm, then?"

Kendra nodded.

"Mrs. Gavenston is most likely at the brewery at this time of day," said Constable Leech after Sam galloped off. He looked at Kendra. "Should I come with you to inform Mrs. Gavenston about Mr. Pascoe?"

"Thank you, but no. I'd like to talk with Mrs. Gavenston privately, if you don't mind."

The constable couldn't hide his relief as he followed Kendra to the gig, where Alec helped her up onto the seat. "We ain't never had anything like this happen in Cookham," he confided. "The worst I've had to deal with in the six years I've been constable was Mrs. Mason's housemaid selling used tea leaves to an unscrupulous peddler. Didn't know I was the constable when he came to my store, or that I'd insist on boiling a pot 'cause the leaves didn't look fresh. Plenty of nasty business in the tea trade, you know."

"I guess you can't trust anybody."

"Ain't that the truth." He shook his head.

At that moment, a two-horse wagon came barreling down the hill. The 19th-century version of a coroner's van.

Constable Leech waved at the three men on the seat. He looked back to Kendra. "I'll ask around the village to see if anyone's heard any gossip about Mr. Pascoe."

"That would be helpful." Kendra hesitated. "What about Mrs. Gavenston's family? Have you heard any gossip about them?"

Leech frowned. "Like what?"

"I don't know. I heard there might be tensions in the family."

"I know Mrs. Gavenston's uncle is back from India, living at White Pond Manor. There's some gossip about him wanting a hand in Barrett Brewery." The constable shrugged. "The family ain't gentry, but the brewery is a sizeable operation. And it's prosperous. Money always has a way of bringing out the worst side of a person. I've seen it often enough in the tea business. But what does that have to do with Mr. Pascoe? It's not like he was family."

Kendra remembered the worry in Mrs. Gavenston's eyes when she begged Kendra for her help that morning. *Had it only been that morning?*

"Mrs. Gavenston seemed to care a lot for Mr. Pascoe," she said. "Maybe that rubbed someone in the family the wrong way."

For no reason at all, a vision of Carlotta sprang up in Kendra's mind. *Not the same at all.* Irritated, she pushed the thought away and looked at Alec. "After we talk to Mrs. Gavenston, we need to go to Maidenhead." Her stomach squeezed. No, it never got easier. "Mr. and Mrs. Pascoe need to be informed of their son's death as well."

11

Barrett Brewery was a massive compound located next to the Thames. It had an oddly cobbled-together look: four-stories of orange-red brick, narrow mullion-paned windows, steeply pitched slate roofs, and soot-darkened chimney stacks thrusting upward into the sky. A small gravel courtyard hummed with activity. A narrow one-story building, which looked like it had been attached to the main building at one point, had its bay doors open, showing a handful of men busy sawing and hammering wood, pounding metal into hoops. The finished product—casks—were stacked row upon row against the furthest wall. More men were gathered around a wagon still hitched to a draft horse, unloading large hemp bags. The air smelled of dust, grain, something citrusy, smoke, and the ever-present dung.

Even with the dung, it smelled better here than inside the cottage, Kendra decided.

A stable boy came running up to them, catching the reins that Alec tossed down. Kendra had a vision of tossing her car keys to a valet in the 21st century.

"A shilling to secure the horses," Alec offered, and leapt down to the ground with athletic grace, before coming around to assist Kendra and Molly.

"Aye, gov'ner," the boy said with a grin, and began to lead the horses and vehicle away.

"Wait," Kendra called out. "Where can we find Mrs. Gavenston?"

"Over there," he said, pointing a grimy finger toward a two-story attachment to the main building, opposite where the casks were being made.

"Thanks."

Kendra caught the curious glances of the workers as they crunched their way across the gravel to a low stoop and a black painted door. A crest featuring the image of a woman holding a flask in one hand and what looked like shafts of barley in the other was attached to the door. The Barrett Brewery name was emblazoned across it.

The door opened to a small foyer with a wooden staircase and a set of double doors that stood ajar, revealing an office with shelves, cabinets, and three wooden chairs. An archway led to a hallway on the left. A man who looked to be in his mid-twenties was hunched over the desk, busy scribbling in a ledger with one hand and wiping his nose with a linen handkerchief with the other. He glanced up as they entered the room. His eyes were watering and as red as his nose.

"May I help you?" he asked in a nasal voice.

"We're here to see Mrs. Gavenston—Kendra Donovan, Lord Sutcliffe," she identified.

"Do you have . . . have a . . ." He managed to capture the sneeze with his handkerchief. "Oh, pardon me," he said, blowing his nose. "Do you have an appointment?"

"She'll want to see us."

He hesitated, shifting his gaze to Alec. "Lord Sutcliffe, did you say?"

Alec inclined his head. "Yes."

"I shall inform Mrs. Gavenston of your presence." He rose, bowing briefly. He swept through the archway and down the hallway. He was gone for only a moment before he returned, beckoning them. "Mrs. Gavenston will see you."

Kendra and Alec started forward, but Molly plopped down in one of the chairs. "Oi'll wait 'ere for ye, miss."

Kendra couldn't blame the maid; the next few minutes wouldn't be pleasant.

They followed the clerk down the hallway, which smelled like the outside of the brewery, minus the dung. The clerk opened the door at the end of the hall and stepped aside, allowing them to enter.

Kendra glanced around, curious to see what the office of a business-woman in this era would look like. The space was large, less showy and more utilitarian. Shelves held both books and glass jars filled with pellet hops, which, to Kendra's eye, looked a lot like the dried marijuana she'd seen in dispensaries. Other jars were filled with rich amber grains and what appeared to be potpourri, but was probably something relevant to the beer trade. A large map of the world and a smaller map of the East Indies were on the wall, speckled with tiny yellow flags anchored by needle-like pins. There was an elegantly carved mahogany mantel surrounding a hearth that had a coal fire blazing, and a long, gleaming credenza. Dark amber bottles, decanters, and crystal glasses were arranged on its surface. Two low-backed leather chairs faced an enormous desk.

Mrs. Gavenston stood behind the desk, in front of a large window that overlooked the Thames. Kendra could see boats bobbing and skimming across the choppy waves.

Quite a view, Kendra thought. Strategic too. Framed by the window, Mrs. Gavenston exuded strength.

"Miss Donovan, my lord." Mrs. Gavenston's eyes flicked between them. "Would you like something to drink? Tea? Of course, we have ale." She smiled slightly. "Or something stronger?"

"No, thank you," said Kendra.

Mrs. Gavenston looked at the clerk. "Thank you, Mr. West. You may leave us now."

She waited until the clerk closed the door, then her gaze returned to Kendra. "I confess that I didn't expect to see you so soon, Miss Donovan. Do you have news?"

Kendra hated seeing that hopeful look on the other woman's face, hated knowing that she would be the one shattering it. "Perhaps you should sit down?"

"Of course. Please forgive me. My manners have fled . . . . Please sit."

Mrs. Gavenston sat, as well, but her expression altered subtly. "You have news. I can see it in your faces. What . . . what have you found out?"

"We found Mr. Pascoe in an abandoned cottage on Squire Prebble's land," Kendra explained. "He was using it as a writer's retreat. I'm sorry, but he's dead."

"Dead?" Mrs. Gavenston gasped, her face draining of color. "But . . . that can't be. That simply can't be." She shook her head. "I don't believe it."

"I'm sorry," Kendra said again. She kept her gaze on Mrs. Gavenston's pale face. There was no way to soften the next blow. "He was murdered."

Murdered?" The other woman lifted a hand to her mouth. "No. I don't believe you. Why would anyone murder Jeremy?" But tears were beginning to shimmer in the horrified eyes. "This can't be happening."

Alec stood and crossed the room to the credenza. Without invitation, he pulled the stopper from one of the decanters and poured what looked like brandy into a glass.

"This might steady your nerves," he said, bringing the glass over to Mrs. Gavenston and pressing it in her palm.

Mrs. Gavenston's hand shook as she took a swallow. "I cannot believe it," she whispered, staring at nothing. "I was worried, but . . . but *this*. Jeremy is dead."

She set the glass down abruptly and pulled out a dainty handkerchief from her sleeve, dabbing at the tears that trickled down her cheeks. "Forgive me," she muttered. "I'm overwrought. What happened? Who would hurt Jeremy?"

"That's what I intend to find out," Kendra said. "I'm going to ask you again, Mrs. Gavenston: was there anyone that Jeremy was having a problem with? Someone he might have fought with recently?"

"I already told you, no. Everyone likes—liked Jeremy."

"You need to think about that very carefully. I believe that Mr. Pascoe was killed by someone he knew."

Mrs. Gavenston stared at her, shocked. "How could you know such a thing? How—" she broke off when the door opened, and a young woman came in, holding a sheaf of papers.

"Mama, I have the numbers on—Oh, pardon me. I didn't realize you had visitors. What's wrong?" she demanded suddenly, her tone sharpening as she noticed her mother's tears. She hurried forward, dropping the papers on the desk and whirling to confront Kendra and Alec. "What's going on here?"

Mrs. Gavenston drew in a shuddering breath, using the handkerchief to mop up the tears. "Don't fuss, Hester." She made an effort to pull herself together, straightening her shoulders. "Miss Donovan, Lord Sutcliffe, this is my daughter, Hester. Hester, this is Miss Donovan, Lord Sutcliffe."

"Miss Gavenston," Alec murmured.

The daughter resembled her mother in the strong, elegant planes of her face and stubborn chin. Hester's hair was lighter and brighter, more of a strawberry blond than her mother's chestnut brown, her eyes turquoise blue rather than hazel. Unfortunately, the woman appeared to be suffering from the same cold as the clerk; her eyes were red-rimmed, her nose rubbed raw from blowing. Kendra's throat itched just from looking at her and she made a mental note to drink some echinacea tea later. Maybe she could ask Constable Leech if he had any in his store.

Hester was frowning. "Miss Donovan . . . Mama told me that she asked you to find Jeremy—Mr. Pascoe." Her face changed then, her eyes rounding in horror. "Oh, dear heavens. This is about Mr. Pascoe, isn't it?" She looked at her mother. "Mama?"

"Jeremy . . . he's dead . . ." Mrs. Gavenston said, her breath hitching. "Jeremy is dead."

Hester's hand went to her throat. "No."

"I'm sorry," Kendra said, and wondered how many times she would say those useless words that day.

"I can't believe it." Hester made it to a chair before collapsing.

"He was murdered," Mrs. Gavenston told her daughter.

Hester shook her head. Her gaze wandered to the window, becoming unfocused. Tears welled swiftly. "This doesn't seem real."

"We're going to find out who killed him," Kendra promised. "But I need to ask you a few questions. They could help find who killed him. Can you tell me your connection to Mr. Pascoe?"

Hester brought her eyes back around to stare at Kendra blankly. "What?"

"I know he was your mother's business manager here at the brewery. Did you work with him?"

"Oh. I . . . Yes," Hester mumbled, dazed and distracted.

"What is your role at Barrett Brewery?"

"My daughter is my successor," Mrs. Gavenston spoke up. "I told you that Barrett Brewery is passed from mother to daughter—the eldest daughter. One day Hester will take over."

Hester produced a hankie much in the same way her mother had, out of the cuff of her sleeve, like a magician. She wiped her nose. "Mr. Pascoe was responsible for controlling Barrett Brewery's cash flow, tax liabilities, bookkeeping . . ." Her voice trailed away.

"CFO," Kendra said.

Hester frowned. "Pardon?"

"Chief financial officer," Kendra supplied. "Where I come from—in America—Mr. Pascoe's duties would make him chief financial officer. Did you know that he was interested in poetry?"

"Of course. We . . . we would talk about it often. Poetry happens to be an interest of mine as well. Not writing it, but reading—"

She broke off with a ragged sob and pressed a hand against her mouth, much like her mother had. "Forgive me but I . . ." Tears glittered in her eyes as she looked at Kendra. "How can something change so quickly?"

Kendra felt a pang at the desolation she saw swimming in the other woman's eyes. She had no answer for that. Unless you were dealing with a lingering illness, death tended to strike without warning. Too often Kendra had seen the same shattered expression on the faces of those who'd lost loved ones to senseless crime. *Why? Why them? Why me? How could this happen?*

Alec splashed brandy into another glass and brought it to Hester.

Kendra asked the young woman, "Did he mention to you if he'd argued with anyone recently? Had any trouble with anyone? Anyone giving him trouble?"

Hester struggled to compose herself. "No. Well, yes. There was Mr. Logan. They had words the other week."

"Jeremy quarreled with Mr. Logan?" Mrs. Gavenston's tone was sharp. "This is the first I am hearing about this."

Kendra looked at the older woman for an explanation.

"He's a local farmer. We buy hops and apples from him," said Mrs. Gavenston. Her gaze returned to her daughter. "What did they argue about?"

Hester wiped her eyes and her nose, sniffling. "Mr. Logan was being difficult about selling us what he'd promised."

"Why didn't I hear of this?" Mrs. Gavenston demanded, then shook her head. "Never mind. 'Tis not the time to speak of this." She brought her hands up to rub her temples. Grief cut lines into her face, making her appear suddenly older. "I can't think."

"We'll need to talk to Mr. Logan," Kendra said. Even though she didn't believe Pascoe had been murdered because of an argument over crops, he still needed to be questioned and ruled out as a suspect. "And anyone else who worked with Mr. Pascoe."

Mrs. Gavenston dropped her hands. "Will you really find out who did this, Miss Donovan? The . . . the monster who murdered Jeremy?"

Hester drew in a harsh breath, shaking her head as though to ward off the truth. "I cannot believe he's gone," she murmured, wiping away more tears.

"I will do everything I can," Kendra promised. She shifted her gaze to Hester. "When was the last time you saw Mr. Pascoe?"

Hester's brow creased. "Friday? I did not go into the brewery on Saturday."

"My daughter has been in her sickbed. She probably should be there still."

"When you saw Mr. Pascoe on Friday, how did he seem to you?" Kendra asked. "Was he upset in anyway?"

Hester shook her head. "No. Everything was normal." She suddenly thrust herself to her feet. "I'm sorry, but I can't . . ." Her lips trembled. She pressed them together. She looked at her mother, eyes glazed with tears. "Forgive me, Mama, but . . . I cannot speak of this anymore."

"Miss Gavenston—" Kendra began, rising.

"Leave her be," Mrs. Gavenston said as her daughter raced across the room in a flurry of skirts. She was weeping openly by the time she opened the door and disappeared. "This has been such a shock. For both of us. I was afraid . . . but I never expected this. Who would ever expect *this*?"

Kendra bit back the desire to express her sympathy again. "Do you mind if we speak to your employees? They may have heard something."

Mrs. Gavenston's eyebrows pulled together. "I would have heard."

"You didn't hear about Mr. Logan," Kendra reminded her mildly.

Mrs. Gavenston drew in a swift breath, anger flaring in her eyes. But as quickly as it came, the anger vanished. "You are correct. I shall get my coat—"

"I think it will be better if we introduce ourselves." Employees were always more talkative without their boss hovering around.

Mrs. Gavenston looked like she was about to protest, then reconsidered. The fight went out of her shoulders abruptly and she sighed.

"Very well. I ought to look in on Hester, convince her to go home. She shouldn't have even come in today." She hesitated, her gaze leveling on Kendra. "And . . . thank you, Miss Donovan. I am aware this is not what you first agreed to do when we met this morning."

Kendra thought of how often missing persons case turned into murder investigations in the 21st century. Too damned often, the lost beauty queen ended up in a garbage heap, the five-year-old in a drainage ditch.

She exchanged a look with Alec. There was nothing more to be said, no comfort to be offered. He gave an imperceptible nod, and they crossed the room together.

Kendra glanced back briefly. Horatia Gavenston had moved to the window, rubbing her arms as though chilled, fresh tears trickling down her cheeks.

12

They started in Jeremy's office, which was next to Mrs. Gavenston's. Similar look—cabinets, shelves, maps on the walls, desk and chairs—but smaller, and no fireplace or window. The map on the wall was of Great Britain rather than the West Indies but also thick with the yellow flag pins. The desk reminded Kendra of the one in the Cookham cottage, except most of the papers were filled with the calculations of a bookkeeper, not the lyrical brainstorming of poet. She opened drawers, sifted through more papers. There were no poetry books or novels here, only ledgers containing what looked like contracts.

"Pascoe clearly made a delineation between his work and his private life," she murmured, putting away a ledger.

"I wonder which one got him killed?"

"I can't imagine he got in an argument over poetry."

"I shall have to introduce you to Bryon." Alec smiled. "Suffice to say, poetry has a way of inflaming passions. And poets have been known to be . . . eccentric. And temperamental."

"And we're back to Lord Byron."

Alec laughed. "Not just him. William Blake is considered mad, but it probably didn't help that he denounced the Royal Academy as idiots. Of course, the man was also charged with assaulting a soldier. And there was that incident with Lady Caroline Lamb at Lady Heathcote's ball, when she broke a wine bottle and attempted to slash her wrists because Bryon insulted her."

"Jesus. Never mind. You've made your point. We won't ignore it if we run into a rabid poet who took exception to Pascoe's unpublished work. For now, though, I suggest that we concentrate on his day job."

For the next forty minutes, they roamed the brewery, pulling aside workers to break the news that Jeremy Pascoe wouldn't be coming in the next morning—or ever again. Most of the men seemed genuinely shocked. A few didn't seem to care. Everyone expressed the same sentiment: Jeremy Pascoe had been a pleasant enough fellow, although a bit bookish. But no one held that against him. Certainly, they couldn't imagine anyone disliking him enough to do him in.

"Never heard a bad word spoken against him," insisted Wilbur. The old man was one of the brewery's coopers. He was sitting on a stool, using a drawknife to expertly shave bits of oak wood, shaping the staves that would form the body of the keg. He paused, cocked an eyebrow at Kendra. "Are ye sure it weren't Gypsies who did this vile thing?"

"Aye." Another man nearby looked up from measuring the top of a barrel with a compass. "They're heathens. They'd cut yer heart out just as soon as look at ye."

Molly, who was waiting near the bay doors, overheard and shuddered.

Kendra tried not to roll her eyes. Every society had their bogeyman. "It was someone Mr. Pascoe knew."

Wilbur scratched behind his ear. "Makes no sense."

"What about Mr. Logan?" Alec asked. "We heard that he and Mr. Pascoe argued recently."

"Ack, that weren't nothin'," said the second cooper. "Andy Logan was just tryin' ter renegotiate the price of his crop. Mr. Pascoe didn't take kindly ter it, but Andy ain't gonna kill him over blunt words."

"How long have you both worked at Barrett Brewery?" Kendra asked the men.

"I've been a cooper 'ere for nearly forty years," said Wilbur. "Bevin there"—he jerked a thumb at his coworker—"almost as long."

"Thirty-seven years come September," said Bevin.

"So, you know Albion Miller?" Kendra asked, referencing the man Mrs. Gavenston had argued with at the Tower the day before. "I was told that his father was a cooper here before he died."

"Aye," the old man nodded. "George Miller, God rest 'is soul. Been gone for about . . . what do ye think, Bevin? Eight years?"

"Thereabouts."

"We worked together. He was a good God-fearing man. Wish Oi could say the same of his son."

Kendra raised an eyebrow. "He's not God-fearing?"

"He's a wastrel, that's what he is. Nothing like 'is da. Hard ter believe there was a time when Miss Horatia—Mrs. Gavenston, before she married, o' course—was sweet on him."

Before Kendra could comment on that, the other cooper waved his compass in the air. "Nay, it weren't Albion that Miss Horatia was sweet on. It was his brother, Robby. They were as thick as thieves until Robby went up ter London Town and cocked up 'is toes."

The older man nodded and grinned. "Aye, that's right. Thought for sure George would be visitin' his son in the big house one day."

Bevin snorted. "Not bleeding likely. Mrs. Dyer wouldn't let Miss Horatia get leg-shackled ter a cooper's son, even though Robby went ter London ter apprentice as a silversmith. That's why she sent Miss Horatia off ter that fancy finishing school, ter get her away from Robby. But then he goes and dies anyway . . ." He shook his head, clucking his tongue. "Terrible thing ter happen. Would have been better if Albion had been the one ter take ill. But it's always the good ones, ain't it? Robby, George, now Mr. Pascoe."

Kendra felt like she was losing the thread of the conversation. "Mrs. Dyer is Mrs. Gavenston's mother?"

"Aye," said the first cooper, nodding. He leaned forward, gliding the wickedly sharp blade over the slates. Wood shavings curled and dropped to the floor. He peered up at her. "What do ye wanna know about Albion for, anyways?"

"I'm curious," Kendra replied. "Do you know if he ever met with Mr. Pascoe? I was told that he sometimes comes around here looking for investors. Maybe he spoke to Mr. Pascoe about it, and it didn't go over so well. Maybe they argued too."

The first cooper snorted. "Investors, is that what ye call it? More like gulls." He paused in his wood shaving, considered it, then shook his head. "Albion is around, doing this and that. The devil takes care of his own. But I don't recall him fighting with Mr. Pascoe. You should speak ter Mrs. Doyle."

"Who's Mrs. Doyle?"

"She owns the Green Knight. It's a tavern on High Street. No one knows the rumor mill better than Mrs. Doyle."

"That's because she's churning out most of it," laughed the other cooper.

Kendra thought that both men were doing a pretty good job at churning out gossip themselves, but put Mrs. Doyle on her list of people to interview.

"Were you working on Saturday? Did you see Mr. Pascoe?" she asked.

"Aye, I was here Saturday morning," the first cooper said. "I saw him come in. But I didn't see him leave."

"I saw him leave," Bevin said, then frowned. "It was early yet. We keep the doors open." He used his compass to point at the bay doors, which had a view of the larger building beyond. "I saw when he left. Now that I think on it, he seemed ter be pettish. Tore up the gravel leavin'. Miss Horatia came after him, called his name, but he paid her no mind. Just kept walkin'. Thought it was peculiar, but . . ." He shrugged.

"What time was this?"

"Two. Around that time, anyway."

"I heard they argued that day. Any idea what that was about?"

He frowned and shook his head. "Nay."

The first cooper rolled his shoulders. "Miss Horatia is . . . was fond of Mr. Pascoe. Took him under her wing ter show him the business after she pensioned off Mr. Carter."

"Her previous manager?"

"Aye."

"Was Mr. Carter upset about being let go?" Kendra asked.

"Nay," Bevin said. "Mr. Carter worked here even longer than us, eh, Wilbur? Worked for Mrs. Dyer, maybe even *her* ma. He's at least five-and-eighty, if he's a day."

The old man—Wilbur—laughed. "Spry, though. Said Barrett ale kept him youthful. Probably misses the free sampling, but he was pleased ter move up north where his two sons live. His wife passed on more than twelve years back, if I recollect rightly. Don't think he had any other family around here. Leastwise not living."

"Thank you," Kendra said. "If you think of anything else, send word to Number 29 Grosvenor Square in London." She started to turn, but hesitated, then glanced back at the two old men. "How are people reacting to the news of new machinery coming in, replacing a few workers?"

Both men stared at her. Bevin was the first to break the silence. "What are ye talkin' about? I haven't heard about any new machinery. Have ye, Wilbur?"

"Nay." He shook his head. "Not a word. And I don't believe it."

"Maybe I was mistaken. Thank you for your time."

She summoned a smile and walked toward the bay doors with Alec.

"Mrs. Gavenston might not have told the brewery workers yet," Alec said in a low voice as they walked outside, Molly trailing behind them.

"Maybe. Or maybe she lied to me." Kendra frowned.

"Why would she do that?"

"I don't know."

The boy who'd taken charge of their horse and gig spotted their approach and went to fetch them.

Alec asked, "Do you wish to go to the Green Knight and speak to Mrs. Doyle or to Mr. Hobbs's farm to see if Mr. Kelly has arrived with Dr. Munroe?"

Kendra huffed. "Neither. We have to go to Maidenhead. The Pascoes have to be told."

Mrs. Pascoe knew the moment she opened the door and met Kendra's eyes. She took a step back and pressed a hand against her trembling mouth. "No. Oh, no."

"I'm very sorry, Mrs. Pascoe," Kendra said sincerely. "May we come in?"

"Who is it, Hazel?"

A man materialized behind Mrs. Pascoe—her husband, Kendra guessed. He was tall and thin, with a long face and studious air that suited his role as a schoolmaster at a boys' school. His hair was salt-and-pepper—more salt than pepper—and receding, giving him a high forehead that somehow served to make him look even more intellectual. Like his wife, he wore glasses, and behind the lenses, brown eyes flashed with concern when his wife turned and clutched at him.

"What is it?" His voice sharpened and his arm came around his wife protectively as he glared at Alec and Kendra.

"We are here about your son, Mr. Pascoe. May we come in?"

"He's dead, isn't he?" Mrs. Pascoe's glanced over her shoulder at Kendra, tears welling up and flowing down her face. "You've come to tell us that Jeremy is dead."

Kendra had to brace herself for the awful pain in Mrs. Pascoe's eyes. "I'm afraid so. I'm sorry."

Mrs. Pascoe gave a raw sob and buried her face in her husband's chest. Kendra met Mr. Pascoe's stunned eyes over her head.

"How?" he asked hoarsely.

"May we come in?"

For a moment, he stared at her in blank shock. Then he drew in a harsh breath, his face tightening as he made the effort to compose himself.

"Of course. Pardon me . . ." He shifted his wife to the side so Kendra and Alec could enter the narrow foyer. Molly had again chosen to wait outside. *Lucky her*, Kendra thought.

Mr. Pascoe gestured to the door that led to the drawing room. "Please go into the parlor while I . . . I must take care of my wife." The maid came trotting down the hall and Mr. Pascoe looked at her. "Oh, Martha. Good. Take Mrs. Pascoe to her bedchamber. And find the laudanum, give her a spoonful—"

"No." Mrs. Pascoe straightened. She removed her spectacles and wiped away tears. "I must hear what happened. I'm his mother." Her breath hitched, but she steadied it. "Let's go into the parlor. Martha will take your coats. Would you like tea? Martha . . ."

"No, thank you. We won't be staying long," Kendra said. In times of great stress and grief, she had noticed that people often fell back on banalities. There was comfort in the mundane when nothing in the world would be normal again.

"Please, be seated." Mr. Pascoe indicated the chairs.

After Kendra and Alec sat, he and his wife settled on the sofa. Mr. Pascoe reached for his wife's hand. In a matter of minutes, anguish had etched itself in his face, deepening every line.

Mr. Pascoe cleared his throat. "My wife told me of your earlier inquiry, that Mrs. Gavenston asked you to find Jeremy. You are Miss Donovan and Mr. Kelly, correct?"

Mr. Pascoe's somber gaze traveled between Kendra and Alec, and he frowned slightly as his eyes rested on Alec, whose exquisite tailoring didn't match with the idea of a Bow Street Runner.

"I'm Kendra Donovan, but this is Lord Sutcliffe," Kendra introduced. "Mr. Kelly . . ." She thought of how the Bow Street Runner was bringing Dr. Munroe back to Cookham to attend the autopsy of their son. "Mr. Kelly is performing another task at the moment."

"I was so certain there was nothing to worry about." Guilt seeped into Mr. Pascoe's grief. "Was it some sort of accident?"

There was no way to soften what was coming next. Kendra said, "Your son was murdered."

Mrs. Pascoe let out a gasp, her knuckles whitening as she squeezed her husband's hand. "*Murdered*. But . . . *why*? Who would wish to hurt Jeremy?"

"That's what we're going to find out—I promise you," Kendra said gently. "But I need you to help us. Mrs. Pascoe, you said that the last time she saw Jeremy was a month ago."

She nodded, dabbing at her eyes.

Kendra looked at her husband. "And what about you, Mr. Pascoe?"

"Yes. He came to Sunday dinner."

"How did he seem to you? Did he seem worried about anything? Anyone?"

"I told you earlier that he was . . . he was in excellent spirits," Mrs. Pascoe said. Her breath hitched. Abruptly, she pushed herself to her feet. Her husband and Alec quickly stood as well. "Forgive me, but I . . . If you'll excuse me . . ." Tears falling, she ran from the room.

Mr. Pascoe stood for a moment at loss, then crossed the room with a jerky stride to a small table. "Would you care for a brandy?" he asked, reaching for a decanter.

Alec said, "No, thank you."

He nodded vaguely, splashing brandy into a glass.

"Mr. Pascoe, I realize this is a difficult time for you and your wife, and I am sorry," Kendra said. "But it's important for me to ask these questions now. They could lead me to your son's killer."

Pain bracketed Mr. Pascoe's mouth as he stared down into his brandy. "Jeremy did not want to worry Hazel," he said. "But once we were alone, he confided to me that he was considering leaving Barrett Brewery."

This was news. "Why?" Kendra asked, searching Mr. Pascoe's face as he sat down again.

"Because he was becoming uncomfortable with some things that were happening." Frowning, Mr. Pascoe took a long sip of his brandy. "What do you know of Barrett Brewery?"

"Not a lot, except Mrs. Gavenston owns and runs the company. That is both unusual and impressive, I think, for a woman during this time." Kendra caught Alec's eye briefly before focusing her attention again on the older man.

Mr. Pascoe nodded. "Mrs. Gavenston is a formidable woman."

"Why was your son thinking of leaving Barrett Brewery?"

"There have been family challenges. Mrs. Gavenston's uncle, Captain Sinclair, returned from living in India about nine months ago, a few months after Jeremy began his position. Initially, Jeremy had little to do with him. Or Captain Sinclair had little to do with Jeremy. But in the last few months, the captain has been pressuring Mrs. Gavenston to create a position for him in the company. He is of the opinion that Barrett Brewery is too large a company for a woman to run."

Kendra could just imagine how Mrs. Gavenston reacted to that but kept her focus on the murder. She asked, "How was your son involved?"

"Captain Sinclair approached Jeremy, hoping to receive his support."

Kendra raised her eyebrows. "Mrs. Gavenston's uncle is attempting a coup?"

"I don't know if it would be considered that, but he is trying to form alliances. My son is a good man. He would never behave in such a shabby manner toward Mrs. Gavenston, and told the captain so. Unfortunately, Captain Sinclair was put out by Jeremy's rejection. I believe he became quite intimidating to Jeremy whenever he was around the man."

"He threatened your son?"

"Not physically. At least I don't believe so." Mr. Pascoe frowned as he considered the possibility. "No, I think Jeremy would have said something to me. But even so, I cannot imagine him hurting Jeremy. Why would he? What would he accomplish with Jeremy's death?" He took another swallow of brandy.

"It's too early to say," Kendra said. "Did Jeremy talk to Mrs. Gavenston about her uncle's intimidation?"

"He warned her. He told me that she wasn't concerned." Mr. Pascoe shook his head, his face crumbling a little. "Again, I have to say, what does Jeremy have to do with this?"

Mrs. Pascoe came into the room again. Her face was blotchy from crying, but she'd managed to compose herself. Mr. Pascoe and Alec rose.

"What was Jeremy involved in?" she asked her husband, searching his face. "Was it something dangerous?"

"No. No, of course not." He crossed the room, laid a hand on his wife's shoulder. "That is what I was explaining to Miss Donovan. Though he was upset by it, the politics and family drama at Barrett Brewery had nothing to do with Jeremy."

"Did he mention to you that he was upset about Mrs. Gavenston's decision to bring machinery into the brewery?" Kendra asked.

Mr. Pascoe frowned. "No. He never said anything."

Mrs. Pascoe twisted her hands together, looking at Kendra. "How was he killed? Where did you find him?"

"He was using a vacant cottage on the local squire's land to write."

"And someone hurt him there? How?"

Kendra had considered sparing the Pascoes the details, but they would find out the truth soon enough. "His assailant stabbed him."

Mrs. Pascoe gasped, tears spilling over again. "Why? Who? Who would do such a thing?"

Because everyone else was standing, Kendra rose too. "I intend to find that out."

"You think someone from Barrett Brewery killed Jeremy?" Mr. Pascoe said slowly. "How do you know that it wasn't done by a vagrant, just a horrible, random act? We rarely deal with murder in these parts, and when it happens, it's usually a robbery."

"It wasn't robbery," said Kendra.

"How do you know?" Mr. Pascoe pressed.

Kendra hesitated, then said, "Your son never attempted to protect himself. He let the killer enter the cottage and get close enough to pick up a knife from the table. I think—based on the crime scene—your son didn't feel threatened by his killer until it was too late."

At length, Mr. Pascoe shook his head. "Then it would not have been Captain Sinclair. While I don't believe he threatened Jeremy physically, Jeremy would have been uncomfortable if the captain had interrupted his solitude."

"Not necessarily. Most people don't think someone they know will become violent. I think the person came in and talked to your son. They were standing next to the table." In truth, given how small the cottage was, there weren't many places to stand. But the proximity went to her theory, regardless. "They argued, perhaps, and, in an impulsive act, the assailant grabbed the knife and struck out."

Kendra opened her reticule and retrieved the tiny portrait of Jeremy. For a moment, she studied the painted features. Jeremy Pascoe would never get older than this. And that was heartbreaking. "I'm sorry for your loss," she said again, feeling inadequate, as always. She offered the painting to Mrs. Pascoe, who reached out and clasped it tightly to her breast.

Kendra and Alec stood to go.

"Champion." Mrs. Pascoe said the word softly.

Kendra glanced back at the grieving woman. "Excuse me?"

"After you left, I researched your Christian name." Mrs. Pascoe's red-rimmed eyes met Kendra's. "I told you researching names is a hobby of mine. Jeremy and I used to . . ." She bit her trembling lip. She had to clear her throat before she continued. "Kendra is an old Welsh name. It means *greatest champion*." She searched Kendra's face, a bit desperately. "I pray that is true, Miss Donovan. I pray that it is true, because my Jeremy needs a champion now."

13

The day was fading into the soft purplish hues of twilight by the time they reached Hobbs's farm, which was located right on the border of Cookham, within easy walking distance of the village. A handful of plump chickens pecked and scratched the ground inside a fenced-in area that contained a rickety-looking coop. There was a pen of about half a dozen snuffling pigs on the other side of the stone barn. Kendra was relieved to discover that the country doctor had set up his practice in the large, two-story stucco house with black shutters rather than the barn.

The Duke's gleaming black carriage, his crest on the door, was parked on the pebbled drive. Coachman Benjamin and another man, both with blunderbusses tucked in their wide leather belts—highwaymen were a concern for nighttime travelers—watched the younger groom brush down the four horses.

"Molly, why don't you wait in the carriage for us?" Kendra suggested, eyeing her maid.

"Aye." Relief flooded the girl's face. "Thank ye, miss."

They walked up the path. There was no knocker to use, so Alec banged his fist against the sturdy black door. A pretty, dark-haired woman opened it a moment later. She wore an unadorned dress that countless laundering had faded to a peach hue. She curtsied after Alec introduced himself and Kendra.

"I'm Mrs. Hobbs. Come in. We've been expecting you. Mr. Kelly and Dr. Munroe are with my husband. May I take your coats, hats?" She smiled at them as they divested themselves of their outerwear. "Would you like tea? Or something stronger? Dr. Munroe certainly appears to enjoy his spirits."

Kendra looked at her in surprise. She hadn't known the London anatomist to indulge any more than anyone else in this era. "Why do you say that?"

"Because he brought his own bottle of whiskey." Mrs. Hobbs's brown eyes twinkled with amusement as she folded their coats over her arm.

Kendra had to suppress a smile. The last time she had dealt with Dr. Munroe, she'd introduced washing their hands with whiskey as a quasi-antiseptic after autopsy. Despite her worry that the littlest things might change history—and therefore the future—in ways she couldn't imagine, she was also gratified to know that the doctor had listened to her and modified his behavior.

They followed Mrs. Hobbs down the hallway to the back of the house, which had been converted into an office and examining room. Oil lamps cast a golden light across dark bookshelves filled with heavy medical tomes, glass cabinets, and an old-fashioned desk cluttered with papers and medical instruments. A narrow table near the windows held the naked corpse of Jeremy Pascoe.

The room's floor was stone tile instead of the wood throughout the rest of the house. Better for mopping up blood, Kendra supposed.

Sam, Dr. Munroe, and Constable Leech were standing next to a slim blond man, who looked to be the same age as his wife. They broke off their conversation as Mrs. Hobbs, Alec, and Kendra swept into the room.

"His lordship and Miss Donovan," Mrs. Hobbs said unnecessarily.

Hobbs leapt forward to grab a linen cloth from a nearby cabinet and drape it over Pascoe's nether regions. "Apologies, Miss Donovan," he said and blushed a bright red. "We didn't expect you so soon."

"Forgive me, but the door was open," his wife said. "I shall leave you to it, then. If you need me, I'll be in the kitchen." Her gaze traveled over the occupants in the room briefly before she departed, pulling the door shut behind her.

Dr. Ethan Munroe came forward with a smile. He reached out to take Kendra's gloved hands in his. "'Tis good to see you again, although the circumstances leave much to be desired."

Kendra smiled at the doctor. He was in his early fifties, and his most distinctive feature was a thick silvery mane that he wore longer than was fashionable and tied into a queue. His light hair contrasted with his heavy black brows. His eyes were dark gray and shrewd behind round gold spectacles he'd pinched onto the bridge of his hawklike nose.

"We always seem to meet because of murder," Kendra replied, and tilted her head toward the corpse. "You haven't started the autopsy, but is there anything you can tell me? I estimate that Pascoe was killed on Saturday based on the state of decomposition. I'm factoring in the colder temperature, which would have preserved the body somewhat."

Munroe's eyes gleamed with amusement, as though he still found it funny to have a female speak so freely and matter-of-factly about such topics. "We have just arrived, but I can tell you that Mr. Pascoe was stabbed exactly five times in the lower abdomen. The tears in his clothing are consistent with the puncture wounds, so he was dressed when the assault took place."

Kendra nodded. She'd figured as much, but that was why she wanted to work with the doctor; he took nothing for granted, which made him extremely thorough in his approach.

"Hobbs had already removed the knife . . ." Munroe pivoted, picking up the item in question. Pascoe's blood, dried to a blackish rust, was on the blade. Kendra tried not to wince to see a murder weapon handled without gloves.

The doctor went on, "'Tis a French knife—the blade is eight inches in length, one-and-a-half inches in width at its base, tapering to the tip. If you notice, the tip is broken. I have already measured Mr. Pascoe's injuries. Three are fully eight inches deep, the remaining five inches and seven inches. Given the width of the two other injuries, I would say the same knife—this knife—was used to make the other injuries as well, indicating only one assailant. Although I shall caution you that the very act of stabbing, possibly twisting, the knife can change the size of the wound, so I cannot confirm that is one hundred percent positive. I can say that the assailant did not twist the knife upon withdrawal, as that would have resulted in more of an *X*-shaped injury to the flesh."

Thorough, Kendra thought again. "That's consistent with the crime scene. The killer didn't bring the knife with him. Pascoe had it on the table, had been using it to cut his bread and cheese. You could check the blade under a microscope for that. I don't see this as a premeditated murder, but more a crime of opportunity."

"But why?" Hobbs spoke up. "Mr. Kelly said this wasn't a robbery. I've met Mr. Pascoe." His troubled gaze traveled to the man lying on the autopsy table. "I was not an intimate acquaintance of his, but he seemed harmless enough. Certainly not a man to whom someone would wish ill-will."

Kendra regarded the surgeon curiously. She hadn't realized that he knew the victim, but Cookham was a relatively small village. "Did you ever treat Mr. Pascoe?"

"I only met the man a few times at the village assemblies." Hobbs lifted his gaze to look at her. "He's had no need of my services while he's been in Cookham. Most folks go to the apothecary for their maladies, unless they're dealing with broken bones or a serious accident. Such things mostly result from farming accidents. I've never had a corpse on this table who was murdered. I'm grateful for Dr. Munroe's assistance." Hobbs cast an admiring look at the doctor. "I had the pleasure of attending one of Dr. Munroe's lectures when I was in London last year."

Dr. Munroe graciously waved off the compliment, although Kendra could tell that he was pleased. "Obviously I cannot tell you why the fiend decided to attack our victim, only how Mr. Pascoe died. Once I open him up, I'll be able to give you more information."

"It doesn't take a huge amount of force to stab someone," Kendra mused. "Our killer could be a man or a woman."

Constable Leech's eyes widened. "You can't think a female would do such a terrible thing, do you?"

"You thought a Gypsy woman could have done it," she reminded him.

"Well . . . aye. But that's a *Gypsy* woman, not a proper English female." He flushed then, as though just realizing that Kendra was an American.

"We can't rule anyone out," Kendra said.

"I would have liked to have seen the body at the crime scene, but Kelly here tells me that he was inside the cottage, near the table," Munroe interjected. "Being stabbed in the abdomen results in exsanguination, but the time that it actually takes for a person to bleed out varies widely. The fact that the victim didn't attempt to crawl away suggests that he died quickly. Again, I will not be able to determine this until I perform the postmortem, but I suspect the killer managed to puncture the aorta, which would collapse the circulatory system as he bled internally and externally."

Hobbs *tsk*ed. "If that happened, he would die within minutes."

"And fall unconscious immediately," Kendra added. "He tried to grab the knife—he's got defensive wounds on his hands," she pointed out when Hobbs looked at her. "He reacted, but not quickly enough to stop the assailant from striking again. If the aorta was penetrated, it was probably the last blow. He would have crumpled to the floor right after. The killer let go of the knife as Pascoe fell, so it was still in him when we found him. He was already unconscious, so he never attempted to remove it."

Stabbing victims often instinctively tried to yank out the knife. Ironically, in some cases, removing the knife—or other object—was what actually caused the victim to bleed out.

"At least that fits with the crime scene," she murmured with a shrug. "Can I have some paper and a pencil?"

Mr. Hobbs was staring at her like she was a new species. *Which I probably am to him*, Kendra thought wryly. Still, he went to the desk to retrieve foolscap and a graphite stick for her.

Aware of his puzzled gaze on her, Kendra quickly made a crude outline of a man, front and back. Carefully, she marked the position of the knife injuries, noted the defensive wounds, then handed the graphite pencil back to Hobbs.

"What's that for?" he asked, as she folded the sheets and tucked them into her reticule.

"A visual reminder of what we're dealing with," she said.

Constable Leech edged toward the door. "Ah, well, I don't think I need to be here for the postmortem."

"If you wait, I'll walk out with you," Kendra said.

Munroe raised his dark brows in surprise. "You're leaving, Miss Donovan?"

Normally, she would have stayed. But she thought about Carlotta having already moved into the Duke's mansion. She wanted to be on hand for dinner. Besides, an idea had come to her that might aid Sam's men with their investigation in Spain.

But she only said, "I've got a few things to do; I'll touch base with you tomorrow."

"I shall be testifying at the inquest along with Mr. Hobbs," he told her.

"When is the inquest?" Kendra asked.

Constable Leech said, "I've sent word to the parish coroner to find out. Considering Mr. Pascoe ain't exactly smellin' like a posy, it'll probably be tomorrow afternoon. I'll send word when I hear."

As soon as Kendra, Alec, Sam, and Constable Leech stepped into the hall, Mrs. Hobbs materialized with their outwear. "Such a dreadful thing to happen to Mr. Pascoe," she murmured, watching them as they put on their coats and hats.

"How well did you know him?" Kendra asked, tying the ribbons of her bonnet under her chin.

Mrs. Hobbs shook her head. "Not well at all. We danced at a few assemblies and at White Pond Manor's annual ball. I never heard that he was involved in anything scandalous. I cannot believe that someone from Cookham did this vile thing."

No one wanted to believe that, but everyone had the capacity to kill. In self-defense. To protect someone else. To protect one's country. In cold blood. In a hot flash of temper.

Kendra didn't try to reassure the woman. Instead, she said, "If you hear of anything, let me know."

Outside, the shadows had grown longer, and the temperature chilly enough to prompt Kendra to draw her fur-lined collar closer. She looked at Constable Leech. "Did you find out anything in the village?"

"Nay. Been querying the tradesmen along High Street, but everyone who met the man said the same thing I told you. He was a pleasant fellow.

The worst I heard about him was he could be frugal with his coin. But I'll keep askin'."

Sam spoke up. "I'll pay a visit ter a couple of the taverns in the area before I return ter London Town. I've found that folks talk more freely in pubs, with a few pints in them."

Kendra grinned. "Excellent idea, Mr. Kelly. I've been told that Mrs. Doyle at the Green Knight would be a good person to talk to."

"Aye, she would be," the constable said, and touched his hat before hurrying off to his horse tied near the stables.

"I'll take the gig and return it ter the stables in Maidenhead," offered Sam.

Kendra looked at him. "When are your men leaving for Spain?"

"They've booked passage on a galleon ship tomorrow at noon."

"Good. I'm hoping Rebecca will be available for dinner tonight so she can meet Carlotta. I want her to do a couple of sketches for your men to take with them and show around."

Sam smiled. "Lady Rebecca is a clever artist. Her sketches will help considerably."

"You can pick them up tomorrow morning and tell me what you learned from Mrs. Doyle."

"Aye, lass. Milord. Good evening." Sam gave them a little salute and climbed up onto the gig.

Benjamin was already folding down the steps to the carriage, and he opened the door when they approached. Molly looked at them when they ducked inside.

"Are we off ter London, then?" she asked hopefully.

"Yes. You'll be coming to dinner, my lord?" Kendra asked, her gaze meeting Alec's as he settled into the seat across from her. His handsome face hardened, at odds with the smile that curved his mouth. Unless you noticed how predatory that smile actually was, Kendra thought.

"Oh, I shall come," he said softly. "I am eager to meet my little cousin again."

14

While Kendra dashed off a note to Rebecca explaining why she was inviting her to dinner and letting her know that Alec would pick her up if she was so inclined, Molly went about the task of having servants haul up buckets of steaming water for the copper bathtub in the dressing room. Once they were alone, Kendra stripped as Molly sprinkled bath salts into the water. The scent of honeysuckle floated up in the steam.

"We'll need ter wash yer 'air as well, miss," the maid said, picking up a bowl and vigorously whisking.

Kendra let out a hiss as she eased herself into the hot water. After the initial shock, the hot water felt wonderful against her skin. She sank down, leaning her head against the lip of the tub, eyeing the bowl. She knew what was in it—egg whites. Unless she wanted to wash her hair with the lump of rose-scented soap made out of lye, egg whites were the preferred method of washing one's hair in this era. The first time she'd asked for shampoo, Molly had tried to massage her head with scented oil. It was only then that she'd learned that shampoo or, rather, *champo*, was the practice of oil massages that British traders had brought back with them from India and had nothing to do with washing one's hair. She was learning something new every day.

"Oi 'eard that Lady Atwood put the foreign lady in the Chinese bedchamber," Molly said, kneeling down to rub the frothy mixture into Kendra scalp.

Kendra closed her eyes. "Anything else you heard?"

"The 'ouse'old is in a right dither about whether she's 'Is Grace's daughter come back from the dead."

"I can imagine. How many of the household were here when Charlotte was alive?"

"Oh, Mr. 'Arding, for certain. But 'e was a first footmen back then. Or maybe 'e was the under butler. And Cook. But Oi don't think she was the cook then either. Gor, it's been some twenty years, ain't it?" Molly pushed herself to her feet. "Oi'll go on down ter the kitchens ter make the rinse."

The rinse was equal parts rum and rose water. Kendra really only needed two cucumber slices for her eyes and a pumpkin mask slathered on her face to feel like she was in a high-priced spa in the 21st century.

"Oi'll take yer clothes for the laundry."

"I would suggest burning them. I can smell them from here. What on earth were you doing? Rolling about in a pigsty?"

Kendra gave a startled jolt, opening her eyes. The Duke's formidable sister, Lady Atwood, was standing in the doorway of the dressing room. *Oh, shit.* Kendra briefly entertained the idea of submerging herself underwater, but the countess would just wait her out.

Or take the opportunity to hold her head under the water.

Lady Atwood was not one of her admirers, though she'd begun to thaw a bit after their last visit to London, when Kendra—despite being involved in investigating the murder of a prominent citizen—had become a moderate success with Polite Society. Or, rather, *because* she was investigating the murder, she'd become a success. Human nature was surprisingly—sometimes depressingly—consistent. People loved rubbing shoulders with individuals who thumbed their noses at conventions. Still, people had their limits. Lord Byron had been a darling of society, but only last month word had reached Aldridge Castle that the poet had left the country because the Beau Monde had begun to shun him over his possible bisexuality and rumors of incest with his half-sister.

It was that fear that Kendra would cross the line—and, by association, bring the Duke down as well—that made Lady Atwood's face rigid with disapproval. Molly eyed the countess nervously as she scooped up the offending clothes and fled.

"So, you've been at it again, Miss Donovan," Lady Atwood sniffed, moving into the room. She was already in her evening dress, a Prussian blue silk brocade trimmed with black lace around the neckline and cuffs of her long sleeves. The material shimmered richly in the soft light cast by the many candles and oil lamps. She'd hidden her graying blond hair beneath one of the many turbans that she favored. A three-tiered pearl necklace centered with a sapphire the size of a robin's egg encircled her throat.

The countess was not the kind of person who believed in dressing down, even for family dinners.

Kendra hunched her shoulders, trying not to feel stupid sitting there naked, with her hair slicked back with egg whites. "I don't suppose you could be a little more specific?"

"Don't be glib with me, young lady." Her grayish blue eyes—the exact same shade as her brother's—sparkled with annoyance. "I have been told that you are involving yourself in yet another murder. A manager of a brewery, of all things."

Kendra wondered what offended Lady Atwood's sensibility more, the fact that she was investigating a murder or that the victim was not a member of society. There was no cachet in being involved with the merchant class.

The countess gave an imperial wave of her hand as though to dismiss the subject, and her diamond and sapphire rings glittered. "But that is not why I have sought you out." She looked away for a moment, frowning. "I am here about this other thing."

"Carlotta," Kendra guessed. "Have you met her yet?"

"Of course. Bertie told me about her claim and introduced me to her when she arrived. She resembles Arabella."

"It would be hard for her to pass herself off as His Grace's daughter if she were blond-haired and blue-eyed." Kendra felt ridiculous sitting in the rapidly cooling water without doing anything, so she reached for the square linen rag and lump of soap that Molly had placed on the three-legged stool near the tub and began to wash. She still felt self-conscious. "What do you think of her story?"

Lady Atwood toyed with the large sapphire at her throat. "'Tis far-fetched, to say the least. And yet she seems to know information." She frowned. "I remember Charlotte's nonsense for tapping three times and believing it was magic. How could she know that?"

"The same way you know. It was discussed, witnessed by family, friends . . . servants. I'm having Mr. Kelly send a couple of men to Spain to see if they can verify her story. Oh, and I've invited Rebecca to dinner tonight."

The countess regarded her coolly. "You take a great deal upon yourself, Miss Donovan."

Kendra shrugged, sending ripples through the bathwater. "I'd like Rebecca to meet her."

"Rebecca was three years younger than Charlotte. I'm not certain she remembers anything about her."

"Still, it might be interesting to see what Carlotta remembers about Rebecca. I was thinking more about Rebecca's artistic skill, anyway. It would be helpful for Mr. Kelly's men to have a drawing of Carlotta."

Lady Atwood's eyes brightened, and she nodded. "Clever." She bit her lip, then said, "I'm worried that Bertie is too eager to believe that this woman is his daughter. My brother can be too easily swayed by a pretty face and a story of misfortune."

Kendra saw the pointed look that Lady Atwood leveled at her and stiffened. "I've never asked His Grace for anything."

The older woman raised her pencil-thin eyebrows. "And yet here you are, in a bedchamber far away from the servant's quarters. Last August, you arrived at Aldridge Castle claiming to be a lady's maid. Now you are the Duke of Aldridge's ward."

"Also something I never asked for," Kendra muttered, but she knew where this was heading. "What do you want me to do about Carlotta?

I'm already sending Runners to Spain to see what they can find out about her and to Atwood Village to find out if anyone has been around, asking questions."

"You appear to enjoy solving puzzles. Instead of finding out who killed this strange man you know nothing about, mayhap you ought to focus your attention on this brazen creature who is claiming to be my niece."

"I can do both," Kendra retorted, then drew in a steadying breath. Arguing with the countess—especially when she was sitting naked in a bathtub—would get her nowhere. "What do you remember about Charlotte?"

Lady Atwood was silent for a long moment as she considered the question. "She was a delightful child," she finally said, "although at the time I was raising my own family at Atwood's estate in Somerset, so I wasn't as well acquainted with her as I would have wished. It was something I regretted after . . ." Pain darkened her eyes. "Charlotte was very much like her mother—quick of wit, beautiful, generous, and endlessly curious. Arabella and my brother suited each other perfectly. The deaths of his wife and child very nearly destroyed Bertie. I will *not* have this woman hurt him."

Kendra said slowly, "Are you so sure that Carlotta is an imposter?"

Emotions, too quick to identify, flitted across the countess's face. She let out a troubled sigh. "No," she finally admitted. "As I said, she has the look of Charlotte. And those mannerisms. What do you think, Miss Donovan?"

Kendra was a little surprised that Lady Atwood would ask her for her opinion, but shook her head. "My gut says no. The story she gave about her childhood will be hard to verify—so hard that it makes me think it's deliberate. Or at least designed to slow down the investigation."

"For what purpose? Never mind." Lady Atwood shook her head. "I know the purpose. To work her way into this household and my brother's good graces. If Bertie begins to believe the creature, there will be nothing that he won't do for her."

For reasons that Kendra didn't quite understand, the idea of the Duke becoming entranced by the woman claiming to be his daughter formed a hot, hard lump in her throat.

Lady Atwood surveyed her. "This puts us in a very odd position, does it not, Miss Donovan?"

Kendra eyed her uneasily. "What is that?"

There was nothing friendly in Lady Atwood's smile. "Why, on the same side, of course. We want the truth, Miss Donovan, no matter what that truth may be. No matter if the person who we're trying to protect will not thank us for that truth. On some level, my brother wants this woman to be Charlotte."

Kendra said nothing; Lady Atwood was right.

The countess pivoted toward the door, silken skirts flaring. "Stop dawdling, girl, and help your mistress finish her bath," she snapped at Molly, who had been hovering at the dressing room door, holding an earthenware jug filled with the rum and rosewater rinse. "Dinner will be served at half past eight."

Lady Atwood glanced back at Kendra. "And, Miss Donovan, do try to refrain from speaking of your *gut*. Whatever you were in America, you are now the ward of the Duke of Aldridge—not a fishwife."

15

I t took a full two hours to get Kendra's hair washed, dried, and styled into an elegant bouffant, silk violets complimenting the sumptuous velvet evening gown Molly had chosen. Kendra had been in this era for almost a year, but she still found it surreal to look in the mirror and see a version of herself that resembled a fairytale princess with flowers in her hair.

She thought of the classic black dress she had tucked away in the bedroom closet at her spacious Arlington apartment. She'd bought it for the occasional formal affair that the Bureau had, and the even less frequent date. That, too, was velvet, but the design was short, sleeveless, and sexy. What a difference a couple of centuries made when it came to fashion.

What happened to it? she wondered now. And the rest of her things? The FBI would have gone through her apartment with the proverbial fine-tooth comb, then her landlord had likely contacted her next of kin. Neither one of her parents would have wanted anything. The little black dress, along with everything else, had probably been donated to Goodwill. Or her landlord had given the cocktail dress to his wife or kid.

A chill danced across her flesh. It was a little like being dead, knowing your stuff had been sifted through, sorted, and dispersed to strangers or thrown in the trash. If she returned to her own timeline right now, would she feel like a ghost, drifting through a life that once had been hers?

Then again, she hadn't planned on returning home after going rogue. Maybe she would have been too busy being on the run, hiding in the shadows, too busy being someone else to think about her former life. Here, she didn't have to change her name, but she was still living a life of subterfuge, pretending to be someone she was not.

Her mind flashed to Carlotta. Someone else who was pretending to be someone she was not. *Or is she?* Miracles happened. Or, at least, events that were so bizarre and improbable that they looked like miracles. As the Duke had pointed out, her own circumstance could be classified as both miraculous and improbable. What were the odds that the Duke would be connected to two improbable occurrences? Kendra didn't need to do the calculations in her head to know that they were astronomical.

Of course, so was the possibility of being sucked into a vortex and transported to another time. But it had happened. If that could happen, who was she to say that a child presumably lost at sea had not been rescued and lived most of her life in another country? Really, which was the most fantastical? If Kendra was being honest with herself, Carlotta's story made a hell of a lot more sense than her own.

Kendra stifled a sigh and left the bedchamber. A liveried footman was standing outside the drawing room and opened the door for her. The Duke, Carlotta, and Lady Atwood were sitting in front of a crackling fire, drinking sherry. At her entrance, the Duke rose to his feet, smiling at her.

"Ah, my dear. You are looking well after your ordeal this afternoon. I heard that your missing young man is no longer missing." He searched her face. "Do you want a sherry? Or Madeira?"

"Sherry is fine." Kendra shifted her gaze to Carlotta. The other woman had swept up her gleaming raven hair into the familiar topknot, leaving thick sausage curls to frame her pale, beautiful face. Kendra wondered who'd styled it. For that matter, she wondered who'd helped her into the heavy cream silk gown she was wearing. Getting dressed was always a chore for women in this timeline. "Have you settled in, Mrs. Garcia Desoto?"

"Yes, gracias. His Grace has been most kind. And her ladyship," she said, smiling as she looked from one to the other. "I am grateful for Miss Beckett's services."

Ah. Miss Beckett was Lady Atwood's personal maid. Now Kendra knew who'd helped Carlotta get ready for the evening.

"Until other arrangements are made, I shall be delighted to share my lady's maid with you, Mrs. Garcia Desoto," the countess said, a small smile playing about her lips as she raised the sherry glass and took a sip.

Delighted, my ass, Kendra thought. A lady's maid had many duties to perform, but one of the major ones was to tell their mistress what was happening belowstairs, or any other gossip that they had picked up. By sharing her lady's maid, the countess was guaranteeing that whatever Carlotta happened to say would be funneled back to her.

The Duke looked at his sister as he set down the decanter. "I would like you to make an appointment with your modiste, Caro," he said as he brought a small glass of sherry to Kendra. "Carlotta ought to have a new wardrobe."

Kendra's fingers convulsed around the delicate stem of the wineglass. *Carlotta.* Fast work. She'd been here more than nine months, and the Duke rarely called her by her first name. At least he wasn't calling her Charlotte.

"I do not need a new wardrobe, Your Grace," Carlotta demurred, running a slender hand down the bodice in a gesture that brought attention to the gown that even Kendra could see was at least five years out-of-date, the skirt narrower than was the current fashion. "I did not come here for gowns."

"Nonsense, my dear—" The Duke broke off when the door opened.

"Lord Sutcliffe, Lady Rebecca," Harding announced, and then withdrew quietly as Alec and Rebecca swept into the drawing room, bringing with them the faint scent of cold and smoke from outdoors.

Kendra took a step back to watch the Duke introduce Alec and Rebecca. If Carlotta was nervous at all about meeting two people that

Charlotte had known in her childhood, she didn't show it. Her lovely face remained carefully composed, even when there was an awkward beat of silence after the Duke identified her as Mrs. Carlotta Garcia Desoto.

"Mrs. Garcia Desoto . . . I confess, if you are really who you say you are, I find such formality odd," Alec said, his mouth curving to take the sting out of his words, although his green eyes remained sharp. Kendra suspected the smile was more for his uncle's benefit than Carlotta's.

The Duke said, "I admit that I was in the same predicament. Carlotta gave me permission to not stand on ceremony and allowed me to call her by the Christian name with which she is most familiar."

"I would be pleased if you would call me Carlotta," she said to Alec and Rebecca, and smiled.

"Sherry?" the Duke asked Alec and Rebecca.

"Thank you," Rebecca said, and glanced briefly at her godfather before returning her gaze to Carlotta. "Do you remember me at all?"

Carlotta's dark eyes were unreadable as she scanned Rebecca's scarred face. "I'm not certain," she said slowly.

Rebecca waited, but when the other woman didn't expand upon that, she shrugged. "I was only three when Charlotte was lost to us." Rebecca accepted the sherry the Duke had poured for her. She lifted the glass, eyeing Carlotta over the delicate rim. "Are you certain you don't remember anything? We were playmates."

Amused by Rebecca's fishing, Kendra sipped her sherry and watched Carlotta study Rebecca's face for another long moment.

"I think I do remember you," Carlotta said slowly. "It's only fragments, mind you. A little girl with red hair. I let you play with Annie—my doll. I believe you were crying at the time."

"I sound very ill-mannered," Rebecca said with a faint smile.

Carlotta glanced at Alec. "I have some memories of you, as well, my lord. I remember you staying with us at the castle during the holidays." A frown puckered her smooth brow. "I have a feeling of sadness with the memory. Your father had died . . . You had a mother and brother, but you never saw them."

"Stepmother," Alec corrected coolly.

Carlotta's eyes darkened. "I never understood why you were so alone." She hesitated, then gave a quick laugh. "I always looked forward to your visits, though. I am certain I made a pest out of myself, following you about."

Alec lifted a silky eyebrow. "I would never be so ungentlemanly as to say so."

Carlotta laughed. "Which tells me everything."

Kendra regarded Carlotta. "*¿Qué más recuerdas de las visitas de Sutcliffe?*" she asked in Spanish, to see how the other woman would react. "*¿Algo más específico? Quizás sea algo que solo lo sabe Charlotte y Sutcliffe?*"

There was a moment of silence. As far as Kendra knew, only Alec was fluent in the language and understood that she'd asked the other woman if she could remember something specific about his visits to Aldridge Castle.

"*Lo siento,*" Carlotta finally said, smiling slightly. "*Como le dije, mi memoria . . . me falla. No sabía que hablabas español, Sra. Donovan. Su acento es excelente pero es de mala educación hablar un idioma que los demás no entienden y yo he pasado muchos años sin hablar mi lengua materna.*"

She glanced at their audience. "I have told Miss Donovan that her Spanish is commendable, but I would prefer to speak in English. I have spent too long not speaking my native tongue."

"Yes," the Duke immediately agreed. "My French is much better than my Spanish, I'm afraid."

"Dinner is ready," Lady Atwood said abruptly, rising. She held out her hand for her brother, who dutifully offered his arm. Alec politely escorted Carlotta out of the room, leaving Kendra and Lady Rebecca to follow behind. Rebecca deliberately slowed her step.

"Why did you speak to her in Spanish? You know that she was raised with the language," Rebecca said.

"Do I? I only know what she has told us. She has a slight accent, and she sprinkled a few Spanish words around . . ." Kendra shrugged. "I wanted to confirm that she really speaks the language."

"I never considered that she may be pretending in that as well."

"Well, she's not. She speaks fluent Spanish. Her accent is Castilian Spanish, consistent with someone who was raised in Madrid."

Rebecca was silent for a long moment. "She's very good, isn't she?" she finally murmured, looking troubled. "Ingenious of her to remember my hair, but not my face."

Kendra smiled. "You contracted smallpox three years after Charlotte went missing."

"Yes, and we could have dispensed with this entire charade if she would have remembered my disfigurement."

"Maybe. Maybe not. Memory is a funny thing." Kendra hesitated. "She used the past tense."

"Pardon?"

"When she mentioned Alec's mother and brother, she used the past tense. She didn't say, 'You *have* a mother and brother.' She said, 'You had.'"

"Charlotte shouldn't know that." Rebecca's eyes gleamed with triumph. But the light vanished as quickly as it had come, and she let out a heavy sigh. "Of course, she could have picked up the gossip since arriving in London."

"And she was talking about the past. Maybe that's all it was. Not so much a slip of the tongue but that she misspoke."

Rebecca gave her a long look. "This isn't going to be easy, is it?"

"Proving her to be an imposter? No, but your artistic skills may help. You'll be able to give me what I need tonight?"

"Yes. Harding put my box of pastels in the study. Whether it will help you . . ."

Rebecca's troubled gaze drifted down the hall toward the dining room. Another liveried footman stood waiting for them outside the double doors.

Kendra drew in a breath, let it out. She needed to be objective. "There's also the other possibility we need to think about."

"What is that?"

"That she really is Charlotte."

Once all were seated and beneath Harding's stern regard, the footmen served the first course of artichokes slathered with hollandaise sauce. Kendra kept her attention on Carlotta, watching every expression that flickered across her beautiful face as she fielded questions about her childhood from Rebecca, Alec, and Lady Atwood. Maybe because the Duke had already heard the story, he sat quietly, staring at Carlotta with a fixed fascination.

The story was exactly the same. Kendra thought Carlotta even smiled at the same moments that she'd smiled before, her eyes taking on the same sad glow as she recited events from her past. But that could be Kendra's imagination. As she had just told Rebecca, memory was a funny thing. She could be reconstructing it to suit her own predisposition. She believed Carlotta to be a con artist, so was she unconsciously building memories to support that belief?

The china plates from the first course were cleared for the main course: pheasant under glass, accompanied by various jellies, and silver serving platters filled with boiled, buttered potatoes sprinkled with bits of parsley, and tender asparagus shoots. The delicate white wine was replaced with a more robust red, poured by Mr. Harding.

"Sutcliffe told me that you found Mr. Pascoe murdered," Rebecca said, turning her attention to Kendra when there was a natural lull in the conversation with Carlotta. She picked up her knife and fork, smoothly slicing into the pheasant breast. "Poor Mrs. Gavenston. I imagine she was devastated. What happened?"

"He was killed in the cottage that he was using as a writer's retreat," Kendra said. "Crime of opportunity, since the murder weapon was the knife that Pascoe had brought with him. There was bread and cheese on the table."

For the first time that evening, the Duke seemed to really focus on Kendra, his gaze sharpening with interest. "Do you know why someone would murder this young man?"

"No. But I intend to find out."

Carlotta looked confused. "I do not understand. Why would you take it upon yourself to find who killed this man, Miss Donovan? Was he known to you? You . . . you are a woman."

"I believe the truth is important," Kendra said, making a point of staring across the table into the other woman's dark eyes. "And I don't see why I would be less interested in the truth because I'm a woman."

"In Spain, women are not so . . . bold as to be involved in such things."

"Nor are they in England," Lady Atwood said stiffly. "Miss Donovan is somewhat unorthodox. But she is an American. And I will confess, she has a remarkable ability to ferret out the truth."

Carlotta smiled faintly, picking up her glass to sip her wine. "How will you go about seeking the truth, Miss Donovan?"

"Simple. Human error. People tend to get overconfident. They don't realize that they've left a trail. It's only a matter of finding that trail and following it to the truth."

She leaned forward to spear a potato, smiling across the table at Carlotta. Not exactly subtle. But she wanted to send a message.

Carlotta said nothing, but judging by the glint that appeared in her dark eyes Kendra thought that the message had been received.

Two hours later, Kendra scanned the two pastel sketches that Rebecca had made of Carlotta. She'd captured not only the physical beauty of the woman, but her artistic eye had managed to capture her spirit as well. Kendra frowned, because what she saw wasn't a hardened grifter. Instead, Carlotta seemed softer, not necessarily innocent—there was a shrewdness there—but younger, her lips curved in humor.

Kendra glanced up at Rebecca and Alec. They'd escaped to the study shortly after dinner, leaving the Duke and his sister with Carlotta in the drawing room.

"Thank you. This will help," she said, rolling up the foolscap and tying it with a ribbon. "I'll give it to Mr. Kelly when he comes tomorrow morning."

"Tomorrow morning?" Rebecca shot her a speculative look. "Breakfast?"

Kendra grinned. "I think that can be arranged."

"She was not what I expected," Alec admitted softly from where he was standing, staring broodingly into the fire simmering in the hearth. Earlier, he'd poured himself a short whiskey, and he now took a drink.

Kendra glanced at him. "What did you expect?"

He shrugged his broad shoulders. "I'm not certain. Less personable, I suppose."

"Less attractive, you mean," Kendra said drily.

Alec's white teeth flashed in a rakish smile as he turned toward her. "Was she attractive?"

Kendra laughed.

"When will you be returning to Cookham?" Rebecca asked Kendra as she gathered her pastels back into her art box.

"I'm not sure. Constable Leech thinks the inquest will be tomorrow. I've only begun interviewing people." She glanced at the slate board that had very little writing on it. "I need to make notes, get a timeline going." She needed to get organized, follow procedure.

Alec set down his empty glass and picked up Rebecca's box of pastels. "We shall leave you to that then. Becca, I'll escort you home."

Rebecca glanced between them. "I shall bid the Duke good evening, and meet you downstairs, Sutcliffe," she said breezily, leaving the room.

Alec smiled as he tucked the art box under one arm and walked over to Kendra. "Try not to stay up all evening," he murmured, and lifted his hand, trailing a finger along Kendra's jaw before leaning down to brush his lips against hers, lightly at first, then deep enough to make her toes curl. "You need your rest," he whispered, straightening.

Kendra said nothing as she watched him leave the room. It took a full minute after he was gone for her toes to uncurl.

16

Kendra needed to jot down notes, maybe scan Pascoe's papers from the cottage, but she was having a difficult time concentrating. Twice she caught herself standing in front of the slate board, staring at nothing, her mind straying to what might be happening in the drawing room with the Duke, Lady Atwood, and Carlotta.

She wondered if Carlotta knew how to play the pianoforte. Maybe at this very moment, she was entertaining the Duke and his sister with a rendition of Beethoven's *Moonlight Sonata*. Or maybe they were playing cards, or dice games. Both were popular activities when a family chose to stay home for the evening instead of venturing out to the steady swirl of balls, fetes, and salons offered by London's elites.

Family. Kendra's stomach curdled like she'd eaten a bad piece of meat. If Carlotta really was Charlotte, then they really were family. And she was the outsider.

Damn it. She couldn't think about it. And she certainly wouldn't think about how, at any other time, the Duke would have been in the study with her, holding his pipe or sipping a brandy as she talked to him about the investigation. She hadn't realized until now how much that mattered, how she enjoyed discussing possibilities and theories with him. How much she relied on his perspective.

Annoyed with herself, she paced the room. Of course, he would be spending the evening with Carlotta. It didn't mean he was buying into her claim that she was his daughter.

Stop thinking about it.

Jiggling the piece of slate in her hand, she wandered over to one of the windows. The day's thin layer of clouds had broken apart, leaving patches of night sky exposed. Stars pulsed. The moon wasn't full, but it was bright enough to limn the trees in the park across the street and the piles of brick and wood from the construction zone next door. She remembered her errant thought from earlier that morning, that London was changing before her eyes.

In three months, she would be here a year. She tilted her head back to gaze at the moon. It had been a full moon on the night she'd ended up in the 19th century. She'd thought that maybe it had something to do with the vortex opening, similar to its gravitational pull on the tide. The theory was asinine, of course, but at the time, she'd been desperate. She'd tested it out a month later, climbing the stone steps to the hidden stairwell and waiting for the wormhole to open and whisk her back to her own timeline.

Even then she'd realized the chance she was taking. She could have been transported to anywhere in time. There were no guarantees. She knew that now, more than ever.

Suddenly impatient—she'd never been so damned maudlin in the 21st century—Kendra spun away from the window. *Focus.* Whatever was happening in the drawing room between the Duke and Carlotta, it was Jeremy Pascoe who was dead. He was the one who deserved her attention. He deserved justice.

She stalked to the slate board. Timeline. That was the first order of business. It would be impossible to know with one hundred percent certainty, but Kendra believed that Pascoe had been murdered on Saturday afternoon, not Sunday. He'd left the brewery at two or two-thirty that day. She would have to walk the distance between the brewery and his house, but she doubted that would have taken more than fifteen minutes. At home, he'd filled his satchel with bread, cheese, and a knife. The neighbor had seen him leave around three.

How long would it take to walk from his house to the cottage on Squire Prebble's land? They'd driven the distance and it had taken them about twenty minutes, plus the time for them to walk, but they hadn't known where they were going. And you could take shortcuts when walking that weren't possible when driving a gig. He could have been in the cottage by four, easily.

Then what? Mrs. Gavenston had admitted that he'd been distressed when he'd left the brewery, and his neighbor had remarked that he'd seemed in a foul mood.

Kendra closed her eyes and visualized the crime scene. Pascoe had made himself tea, put out the bread and cheese. She thought about how Mrs. Pascoe had fallen back on the mundane, offering them tea after she'd been informed of her son's murder. That's what people did when they were upset. Common, everyday rituals.

So, Pascoe had lit a fire in the stove for the tea, probably also in the fireplace because of the chilly temperatures, even during the day. Then he sat down to lose himself in his poetry.

She glanced over at the traveling writer's chest that Alec had placed on the side table. She opened it and retrieved several pages, which she spread across the Duke's desk. She examined not the words, but the angry, savage slashes that marked the foolscap. Was Pascoe already in a temper and took his anger out on these pages? Or was this the result of the natural frustration of a poet unable to express himself in the way that he wanted?

If it was the former, then Mrs. Gavenston had lied to her. She'd downplayed the argument, all but dismissed it. But if Pascoe was still so enraged that he'd taken his quill-pen to the pages, then there was clearly more to it than she was willing to let on.

Kendra jiggled the slate in her hand again as she pondered that. From what they'd pieced together so far about Pascoe, he had been a nice, even-tempered kind of guy. Even if Mrs. Gavenston was telling the truth, that they'd argued over displacing workers with machines, would that really have pushed Pascoe into such a fury that he would walk off his job and more than an hour later begin violently marking up his work?

Times were tough. The loss of a job could mean the workhouse, debtor's prison, starvation. There was no social safety net to capture those who fell. Maybe Pascoe had caught the spark of revolution, like the Luddites in the North.

It was a stretch, she decided. Which left her with the alternative: Mrs. Gavenston wasn't being truthful.

People lied. They lied to law enforcement; they lied to themselves. Everyone had secrets that they didn't want exposed. Hell, she was a freaking poster child for that.

She thought of Carlotta. Another person who had secrets, she was sure.

Focus.

She returned to the board and wrote, *Suspects.* She hesitated for just a second, then put Mrs. Gavenston's name in that category. Beneath the brewery owner, she wrote, *Albion Miller.* Now that was a man everyone seemed to dislike. From what little she'd seen of him at the Tower, he had struck her as a blowhard and a bully. Yet his connection seemed more to Mrs. Gavenston than Pascoe. At least on the surface.

But it was the stuff beneath the surface that made all the difference.

She needed to speak to Captain Sinclair and Mr. Logan—maybe split them up with Sam. She'd take Sinclair and the Bow Street Runner could take the farmer. Those were the only two men with whom Pascoe had argued. So far.

She sighed. Hopefully, Sam would get more information from the town gossip, Mrs. Doyle. Something to point them in a direction. Tomorrow she'd try to talk to Pascoe's friend, Mr. Elwes. Maybe Pascoe had confided to him what was going on in his life.

Kendra started pacing again, thinking about the crime itself. This was not a random attack. The killer had to know that Pascoe was at the abandoned cottage—or would be at some point on Saturday. Of course, Cookham was a small village. How hard would it be to figure out where Pascoe spent his time?

The door opened. Smiling, Kendra turned, expecting to see the Duke walk through the door. Her face fell when a footman entered instead. She hastily composed her expression as she met the servant's eyes.

"Pardon, miss," he apologized. "I was ter see ter the candles and fire. Thought everyone had went ter bed."

Kendra glanced at the clock, startled to see that it was nearly midnight.

"I'll come back later," he said and began to withdraw.

"No, that's all right. I'm leaving." She moved to the desk, concentrating on the task of gathering up Jeremy Pascoe's writings rather than the disappointment that had rushed through her. It was not like she had expected the Duke to check in on her.

Her head was beginning to pound as she left the study and exhaustion made her steps heavy by the time she opened the door to her bedchamber. She had a momentary twinge of guilt when her gaze fell on Molly, sleeping on the striped satin divan near the fireplace, knowing that the maid had fallen asleep waiting to help her undress.

Molly's eyes popped open the minute Kendra shut the door with a soft click. "Ack, sorry, miss. Oi must've dozed off." She yawned hugely and stretched before standing.

"I'm the one who should be sorry." Kendra dumped the foolscap on the bed. "I didn't realize how late it was."

Molly gave her a strange look. "Ye're my mistress. 'Tis me duty ter take care of ye."

"Well, I apologize nevertheless," Kendra said, presenting her back to the maid, feeling the tug and release of the material as Molly began unbuttoning the gown. "Any more gossip about Carlotta?"

"She's good at playin' the pianoforte and singin'."

"I *knew* it." Kendra huffed, aggravated. She caught Molly's eyes on her as she stepped out of the evening gown. "Is that what they did tonight?"

"Aye. Mr. 'Arding said she entertained 'Is Grace and 'er ladyship with some foreign songs. 'E said 'e didn't know w'ot she was singing, but she sang it very well." Molly went to the wardrobe and hung up the gown, returning with a filmy ivory nightdress. "'Er ladyship is gonna bring 'er ter 'er dressmaker for a new wardrobe tomorrow," she added, waiting as Kendra stripped off her stockings, shift, stays, and petticoat. "Miss Beckett says 'er clothes are fine quality, but outdated."

"Hmm. How does the wife of a carpenter afford such nice clothes?" Kendra wondered, slipping on the nightdress. She carefully took off her arrowhead pendant and placed it on top of the vanity dresser before sitting down in front of the mirror.

Molly shrugged, coming up behind her to take the flowers and pins out of her hair, putting them in a small jeweled box. "Second'and shops."

"You still have to have money to buy the clothes," Kendra murmured. "She said that she worked as a seamstress for a time. I suppose she could have made them herself."

"Aye, that's possible. Even could 'ave gotten better quality material in 'er shop. Spain 'as nobility like us. Least-wise, Oi think they do. They weren't loppin' off their betters 'eads like the Froggies were." She picked up a silver-backed hairbrush and began brushing Kendra's hair. "Polite Society is gonna want fine fabrics."

"Here, let me do that." Kendra held up a hand for the brush. "It's late. Go to bed."

"It ain't no trouble."

Kendra smiled. "It's no trouble for me to brush my own hair either. Goodnight, Molly," she said firmly and waited for the maid to hand over the brush. Before leaving, Molly added another log to the fire.

Kendra was on the fourth brushstroke when the door opened again. Her heart accelerated when Alec slipped into the shadowy bedchamber and a strange sort of giddiness assailed her as their eyes met in the mirror.

"You took long enough," he murmured huskily, shedding his greatcoat, hat, and gloves.

"I didn't realize you were waiting for me." She turned, gazing at him as he sat on the bed and tugged off his boots. "What if someone caught you skulking in the halls?"

His white teeth glimmered in a half smile. "First of all, I am a lord, and lords don't skulk. Second, I spent many months on the continent during the war operating as an intelligence officer. I was never caught."

She rose, going to him. "I'll bet you didn't have to hide from someone like Mrs. Danbury or Mr. Harding."

"I confess my uncle's servants offer more of a challenge than Napoleon's army. Still, I spent a great deal of my childhood in this house." He shrugged out of his jacket. "I know where the hiding places are. Besides . . ." He grasped her waist, smiling at her. "Some things are worth the risk." He shifted his position, turning his head when he heard the pages of foolscap crackle on the bed. He lifted a brow. "What's this?"

"A little late-night reading—until I found something better to do."

She grinned at him, allowing herself the indulgence of threading her fingers through his silky dark hair. Alec swept his hand across the bedspread, sending the papers flying and fluttering to the floor. Kendra laughed as he took hold of her, rolling her beneath him in a fluid movement and nuzzling a particularly sensitive spot on her neck.

"I thought you said that I needed rest," she murmured breathlessly.

Alec lifted his head to gaze down at her. "Shall I go?"

She grabbed his arms when he began pushing himself off her. "Hell, no. Sleep is overrated."

17

Of course, he was gone in the morning. Kendra pushed aside the twinge of regret and slipped out of bed to retrieve her shift and stays. She donned the undergarments and picked up the pages of foolscap that were scattered on the floor. Putting them on the small, elegant writing desk in the corner of the room, she began stretching. She was halfway through her yoga routine when Molly came into the bedchamber, carrying a folded note.

"This came for ye," the maid said.

Surprised, Kendra straightened out of warrior pose and snatched the note. She scanned the contents. "I need to get dressed."

"'Oo's it from?"

"Phineas Muldoon."

"Ain't 'e the scribbler from the *Mornin' Chronicle?*"

"Yes." And because it was impossible to get dressed in less than five minutes, Kendra crossed the room to the desk. She wrote a quick reply and gave the note to Molly. "Have a footman take this to Mr. Muldoon across the street in the park."

"'E's in the park?"

"Yes, but probably not for long. So, hurry." Kendra watched Molly dash out of the room, and nearly shook her head. *This is how people sent messages before texting*, she thought wryly. Would she ever get used to it?

She tugged on her stockings, anchoring them with garters, and was pulling a green-sprigged walking dress over her head when Molly jogged back into the room. Efficient as always, Molly had dashed up to her room in the servant's quarters to retrieve her wool coat.

"'Ere, let me button ye up." Molly dropped the coat on the bed before she scooted behind Kendra, tugging the gown into place so she could button it. "W'ot does Mr. Muldoon want with ye, miss?"

"I'm not sure. He said that he knows about the investigation and wants to meet. Where are my shoes?"

Molly pulled open a drawer at the bottom of the wardrobe to reveal a neat row of them. She retrieved a pair of low-heeled leather shoes. "Oi 'ave ter still do up yer 'air, miss."

There was no point in arguing. Her maid could be surprisingly obstinate about such things. With a sigh, Kendra plopped down to let Molly brush and twist her hair into a low chignon. As soon as she stepped back to survey her handiwork, Kendra thrust herself to her feet, moving to the wardrobe to grab a dark gray pelisse trimmed with mink and a simple bonnet—really, what was the point of styling your hair if you were just going to cover it up again?—before heading downstairs. Molly followed. It was still early enough—not quite eight—for there to be only two maids sweeping and polishing in the entrance hall.

Outside, Kendra paused on the front steps, blinking in the strong morning sunshine. The sky was an Easter egg blue, but Kendra could see gray-tinged clouds boiling on the horizon, along with the strange yellowish smog that was part of daily life in London. The clatter of construction from the Yarborough residence had already begun, disturbing the normally peaceful square.

Kendra spotted the Scotsman from yesterday. When he caught her gaze on him, he doffed his knit cap and called out, "A fine day to you, lass!"

Kendra grinned. "Good morning."

Molly scowled at the man as they walked past him. "Forward cove, 'e is, talkin' ter 'is betters. Ye really shouldn't encourage 'im, miss. 'E's beneath yer touch."

Kendra raised an eyebrow. "We barely exchanged pleasantries."

Molly had begun to adopt the snobbery that many upstairs servants had for what they considered the lower classes. The maid colored but lifted her chin. "'E's got a shifty look about 'im."

Ignoring the maid, Kendra looked across the street to the park. Muldoon lounged with one shoulder propped carelessly against an ancient oak, near the entrance. His face was shadowed both by the outstretched leafy branches and the battered tricorn cap that he'd squashed on his bright red-gold curls. Even at that distance, Kendra thought she could see the gleam of crafty intelligence in his cerulean blue eyes.

She'd first met Phineas—Finn—Muldoon a couple of months earlier, in the course of another murder investigation. She'd found him to be both irreverent and resourceful.

"Miss Donovan." He swept off his hat as they approached and gave a bow that was mocking in its flamboyance. "Your humble servant."

Kendra snorted. "Humble is not a description I'd use for you, Mr. Muldoon. You said in your note that you knew I was investigating a murder. How'd you find that out? Listening at doors again?"

He grinned at her. "I have ears. I use them. Which is how I heard that you requested Dr. Munroe's assistance for an autopsy in Cookham. You could say my curiosity was piqued."

"Ah. You talked to Barts," she guessed, naming Munroe's pale, weak-chinned apprentice.

Muldoon tapped his finger against the side of his nose. "I shall never tell. I came here hoping you'd reply to my note, but I didn't expect an audience. Shall we walk?"

"I'm not the queen." Still, she put her hand on his arm when he offered her a courtly elbow.

"Praise the saints, as that poor woman is stuck with the mad king."

"Walk and talk," Kendra said.

He laughed, and they began strolling on the pale, pebbly path that cut through and curved around trees and shrubbery inside the park. Molly trailed after them, close enough to chaperone but far enough not to intrude. Kendra scanned the area. She could still see the blue sky above, but the trees transformed the space into a cool, green oasis. Birds trilled from outstretched tree branches. Insects buzzed. The construction noise and the clip-clop of horses' hooves, the rumble of wagon wheels on cobblestone, all faded into the background.

"We're walking, but you're not talking," Kendra pointed out after several beats of silence.

Muldoon laughed again. "I had forgotten how forthright you are, Miss Donovan. It's refreshing. No doubt it's because you're an American." He waited, but when Kendra said nothing, he went on, "I heard Mr. Jeremy Pascoe was murdered. Gutted like a fish, they say."

"Graphic. You're not telling me anything I don't already know."

His blue eyes lit up. "So, it's true then?"

Kendra realized her mistake. "Clever, Mr. Muldoon. I have just confirmed what had only been a rumor to you."

"I would have found out the information eventually," he said graciously.

Kendra considered the tall Irishman. The reporter had his uses, one of which was his knack for ferreting out information. And right now, she needed information.

"Why does this murder interest you, Mr. Muldoon? I thought you wrote about government intrigue and corruption. Mr. Pascoe wasn't part of government."

"My interests are wide and varied."

"Mr. Muldoon?"

"Yes?"

She met his eyes. "Stop the bullshit. How's that for being forthright?"

He looked startled, but chuckled. "Very forthright. Not very ladylike, but—" He held up a hand when she gave him a stony stare. "I confess I know very little at this point, except that Mr. Pascoe was an employee of Barrett Brewery. What do you know about the company or the brewery business?"

"The brewery industry, next to nothing," she admitted. "Barrett Brewery . . . I know it's a woman-owned business, run by Mrs. Gavenston."

"I can tell that appeals to you. You have radical leanings, Miss Donovan."

She rolled her eyes. "Having businesses run by women shouldn't be viewed as radical, Mr. Muldoon. Besides, I've been told that brewers in this country have always been women."

"Brewster—that's the correct terminology when you speak of a female brewer. That is true. Did you know that in the last century, nearly eighty percent of the brewery licenses in the kingdom were actually held by women?"

"No. And how do you know it?" She regarded him curiously.

"I'm a scribbler, Miss Donovan. I know a great many things." He gave her a quick smile. "Monks began brewing ale in their monasteries and selling it to passing travelers. However, alewives were the ones tasked with brewing beer locally."

"But? I sense a *but* coming."

"*But* a revolution is taking place in this country, Miss Donovan. Our world is changing before our very eyes. Cottage industries and craftsmen are being crushed by soulless factories powered by steam, companies whose thirst for profits are destroying the common folk. Ale is no longer a domestic art, brewed by women in their households to serve to their family and friends and sell to local taverns. It's become a *business*."

"It was always a business. It's just become a *big* business," Kendra corrected. Muldoon's argument was one she'd heard often enough in the 21st century. Corporate Goliaths crushing the little guy. *The more things change, the more they stay the same.* "As fascinating as the history of beer making is, what does it have to do with Mr. Pascoe's murder?"

"Maybe nothing. Or maybe something."

They'd walked full circle and were coming to the entrance of the park again. It allowed them a view of the street, and the sleek yellow carriage parked in front of the Duke's residence. The coachman had already released the steps, opened the door, and was assisting Lady Rebecca to the ground. She spotted them as she shook out her heavy wool carriage skirt, the color of apricots and trimmed with ivory ribbons. She waited until a wagon loaded with bricks, obviously meant for the Yarborough residence, lumbered past, then she briskly crossed the cobblestone street to meet them.

"Ah, good morning, Princess," Muldoon greeted, his lips twisting into a roguish grin.

Kendra expected Rebecca to fire back with a cutting retort over the Irishman's flippant and overly familiar manner, but was surprised to see her friend's cheeks color faintly.

"Mr. Muldoon." Rebecca inclined her head graciously. "I didn't expect to see you this morning."

"Apparently, Mr. Muldoon felt the urgent need to give me a lesson on the beer industry," Kendra remarked drily. "Although I'm still not sure why it's relevant to Mr. Pascoe's murder."

"I was getting to that," he grumbled.

Kendra made a quick decision. "We might as well go inside. You, too, Mr. Muldoon."

Muldoon's face brightened at the invitation.

"I dare say you've consumed enough ale to be an expert on the subject," Rebecca said, giving the reporter a pert look as they crossed the street.

He grinned at her. "I do what I can to support the business, Princess."

"I'm inviting you inside, Mr. Muldoon, but it's the same deal as before—whatever is said inside is off the record," Kendra warned as they went up the steps into the entrance hall.

Her chaperone duties over, Molly peeled off from the group while they climbed the grand staircase to the study.

"Agreed—unless I uncover the information from other sources," the reporter said.

"Okay," said Kendra. "But I hope you have more to offer than a history lesson. I visited Barrett Brewery yesterday and it's not a homespun operation. In fact, I'd say it's the very definition of a big business—"

She broke off as she opened the door to the study, and saw the Duke standing inside the room. The table had been laid out with silver pots and porcelain dishes. The smell of bacon, eggs, and—praise the Lord—the brown bread that Kendra had grown so fond of drifted toward them. The Duke had been pouring himself a cup of tea, but he smiled at her and set down the pot.

"Good morning, my dear. I had heard there would be a meeting this morning and took it upon myself to supply breakfast."

"Briefing," Kendra corrected automatically, then waved her hand. "Never mind." She looked at him, realizing she was smiling. "I didn't expect you."

He raised his eyebrows. "I have always been fascinated with these investigations."

"I know, but you've been preoccupied with other matters lately," she said carefully, aware that Muldoon was in the room. And as the reporter had said, he had ears.

The Duke seemed mindful of their audience, as well; he turned to acknowledge the Irishman. "Mr. Muldoon, I didn't realize you would be here."

"Your Grace." Muldoon bowed. "I've come to offer my services to Miss Donovan regarding the poor wretch who was murdered yesterday."

"Oh? And what services are those?"

"Mr. Muldoon *says* he can be useful. He has yet to prove it." Kendra dumped her coat and bonnet on a chair and joined the Duke at the table.

Muldoon put a hand to his heart and struck a dramatic pose. "Your lack of faith does me a most grievous injury, Miss Donovan."

"It won't be my lack of faith that will cause you injury if you're leading me on, Mr. Muldoon."

The Duke laughed. "I suggest we dine before anyone begins brawling." The door opened to admit two more guests, and the Duke greeted them, "Good morning, Mr. Kelly, Alec."

Sam stopped and frowned at Muldoon. "What's he doin' here?"

Muldoon paused in heaping eggs onto his plate. "Thank the stars that me sainted mother didn't raise me to be a sensitive lad, otherwise I would feel that I wasn't welcome."

"Mr. Muldoon feels he can help with the investigation," said Rebecca, pouring a drop of cream into her teacup, followed by tea. She used a tiny spoon to stir. "Whether that proves to be the case I am awaiting with breathless anticipation."

"I shall do my best not to disappoint, Princess," the reporter said, looking into Rebecca's eyes. Again, Kendra was surprised to see a blush rising on Rebecca's face.

"Keep a civil tongue in your head," Sam growled, giving him the gimlet eye.

"Did you talk to Mrs. Doyle?" Kendra asked the Runner after everyone had filled up their plates and sat down at the table.

Eyes narrowing, Sam jerked a thumb at Muldoon. "What about him?"

"Same deal as before—everything said here is off the record," Kendra assured him.

Sam glowered as the reporter grinned at him, but he said, "I went ter the Green Knight, but Mrs. Doyle wasn't there. Laid up with the grippe or something. The illness seems ter be going around the village."

Kendra thought of Mr. West and Hester's red eyes and noses.

"Who's Mrs. Doyle?" Muldoon asked, then picked up a slice of brown bread, stuffed it into his mouth, and chewed.

"Town gossip," Kendra said.

"By the by, the inquest is set for two o'clock today," Sam added, forking up his eggs. "You can testify, lass, unless His Grace deems it unseemly. Then his lordship's testimony will suffice, since you were together when you found Mr. Pascoe."

"I'll testify," Kendra said, irritated that would even be a question.

Sam picked up his glass of ale. "I did pick up a bit of gossip. Did Mrs. Gavenston speak of her uncle, Captain Lucian Sinclair, or her son-in-law, Mr. Mercer?"

"No, but Mr. Pascoe Senior mentioned Captain Sinclair. He's on my list. What about the son-in-law? Who's he married to?"

"Mrs. Gavenston's other daughter, Sabrina."

Kendra blinked. "How many children does Mrs. Gavenston have?" She was just beginning to realize how little she knew about her client.

"Just the two—Hester and Sabrina. As the eldest, Hester will inherit Barrett Brewery. Sabrina married Mr. Mercer, the youngest son of a viscount. Lord Redgrave."

Alec nodded. "I believe I've been introduced to Lord Redgrave. From what I remember, he seemed a proud sort. I can't imagine he would have been pleased to have a son marry into the merchant class."

"It must have been a love match," Rebecca said, and smiled.

"I don't know about that, but folks around Cookham aren't keen on him. Although no one could tell me precisely why." Sam shrugged. "Folks also don't like Captain Sinclair, either, even though he was born in the village."

"Maybe because the captain is trying to push his way into Barrett Brewery," Kendra said. "Mr. Pascoe Senior said that Captain Sinclair had approached his son, wanting to get his support in . . . I don't know if you'd call it a coup against Mrs. Gavenston, or if that's too strong a word."

Rebecca gasped. "What a despicable thing to do to your own niece."

"Very Richard III of him," Muldoon said, breaking off a piece of bacon. "The English are a treacherous lot."

They ignored him. Kendra said, "Pascoe didn't appreciate the duplicity either. It sounds like he told him so, and Captain Sinclair responded in a threatening manner."

Alec raised an eyebrow at her. "And Mr. Pascoe ends up dead. Convenient."

Kendra looked back to Sam. "What did you hear last night about the captain?"

"Captain Sinclair is Mrs. Gavenston's uncle on her mother's side. As the brewery is passed down ter the women of the family, he joined the army and headed off ter India, where he's been for a good forty years or better. He returned to White Pond Manor last year. The house has been in the family since his grandmother—Mrs. Gavenston's great grandmother—founded Barrett Brewery."

The Duke spoke up. "It cannot be a comfortable environment if the captain has been vocal on his displeasure over how the brewery has been passed down."

Kendra caught the Duke's eye and wondered if he could relate to that kind of familial tension. God knew his sister had been vocal about her displeasure regarding Kendra's position in his household.

"I, for one, find the brewery being passed to the firstborn female, rather than the more common male primogeniture, enormously refreshing," Rebecca said, her eyes glinting as she buttered her bun. "The laws in this country are really quite insufferable toward my sex."

"Aye, well . . ." Sam eyed Rebecca uneasily. "Captain Sinclair says that it's improper these days for his niece ter be in control of a company as large as Barrett Brewery. The on-dit is they've had rows about it."

"Ah-hah!" Muldoon shot Kendra a smug look. "This is what I was trying to tell you! Times are changing!"

"Times are always changing," Kendra said mildly. She tapped her coffee cup with her index finger. "How heated were their arguments, I wonder?"

"Obviously heated enough to set tongues wagging," said Alec.

"Like I said, the captain was born in Cookham, but folks don't like him," Sam said. "They're quiet about it, though. I get the impression that if they had ter wager on who is gonna win the battle and run the brewery, it might be the captain."

Rebecca frowned. "Does he have a family of his own?"

"He was married, but his wife and daughter were killed several years ago during an uprising by the natives," Sam explained. "He has a son who's living in those parts. Working for the English East India Company."

"So, the captain may wish to wrest control of Barrett Brewery for his son as much as for himself," the Duke speculated.

Kendra looked at Muldoon, who was finishing up the last bit of eggs on his plate. "Is that what you had information about, that Captain Sinclair is attempting to take over Barrett Brewery?"

The reporter chewed and swallowed. "Actually, no. He wasn't the one that I'd heard wants to take over the brewery. My information is Mr. Fletcher—Mr. Oscar Fletcher—has been moving in on Barrett Brewery. He owns Appleton Ale."

Kendra leaned back in her seat. "A competitor?"

"A competitor. And possibly a murderer."

Kendra stared at Muldoon, who looked smug after delivering that bombshell. "Excuse me?"

"Aye, lad, spit it out!" Sam growled, annoyed by what he considered the Irishman's theatrics.

The reporter raised his hand, as though to deflect Sam's ire. He even delayed his story by taking a long pull of his ale. Sam's eyes narrowed, and Kendra wondered if she might have to step between the two.

"In the last twenty years, Mr. Fletcher has grown his business from a local operation here in Southwark, supplying nearby taverns, to one of the largest breweries in the kingdom," Muldoon finally said, setting down his glass. "Like Barrett Brewery, Appleton Ale is now shipped throughout England and has begun expanding into foreign markets. Unlike Barrett Brewery, one of the ways that Mr. Fletcher has increased the size of his company is by taking over other smaller breweries."

"God's teeth, you take your time telling a tale," Sam grumbled, lifting his own glass of ale to take a swallow.

Muldoon grinned, wagging a finger at the Bow Street Runner. "I am simply giving you an understanding on how large Appleton Ale is, and how powerful Fletcher has become as a result."

Kendra nodded, leaning back in her chair as she thought it over. "So, Fletcher is eyeing Barrett Brewery for acquisition. But I was at Barrett Brewery yesterday. Like I said, it's not a small operation. And Mrs. Gavenston seems to be powerful in her own right."

"From what I've managed to learn in the little time I've had to investigate, Barrett Brewery is shipping to more foreign markets than Appleton Ale. Probably that's what got Fletcher interested in the brewery in the first place."

Kendra recalled the yellow pins and the map of the West Indies in Mrs. Gavenston's office.

Muldoon went on, "Barrett Brewery is a solid enough company. I suspect that's why Fletcher hasn't been able to force Mrs. Gavenston to sell. Unfortunately, there have been other breweries in a similar position that didn't want to sell either."

Alec cocked his head, surveying the reporter across the table. "Unfortunately?"

Muldoon lifted his shoulder in a half shrug. "Odd things seem to happen to those who refuse Mr. Fletcher. I was told he wanted to buy a brewery up north. When the brewer declined his offer, one night his brewery inexplicably caught on fire and burnt to the ground."

"Dear heavens," Rebecca breathed, pushing away her empty plate. "Pray tell, are you suggesting Mr. Fletcher had something to do with the fire?"

Muldoon glanced at her, his eyes darkening. "Nobody could prove anything. Radicals were blamed, and the brewer himself. It was said that he must have left a candle burning, or some other rot. Maybe if that had been the only incident . . . but he wasn't the only competitor of Fletcher's who suddenly found themselves born under a halfpenny planet."

Kendra had to ask. "A what?"

"Unlucky," the Duke supplied, rubbing his chin as he considered Muldoon's words. "It appears as though Mr. Fletcher's competitors suddenly found themselves very unlucky."

Muldoon nodded. "If it wasn't fire, then it was vandals who wrecked mashers, machinery, barrels of ale." Almost absently, he reached for another slice of bread and tore it in two. "These are the stories that I was told."

Mafia tactics, Kendra thought. She asked, "And what about the murder you mentioned?"

Muldoon's eyes went flat. "That happened in Fletcher's tavern, which is attached to his London brewery. Apparently, he took exception to something that was being said at the time by one of the tavern customers. The two men fought. Fletcher ended up breaking a bottle and stabbing the cove to death with it."

"Good God!" The Duke stared at the reporter in horror. "Why is this man not in Newgate? Or transported? He *must* have been charged!"

"The crime, which happened more than a decade ago, was investigated by the local magistrate. But no charges were brought. It was an argument that got out of control. The publican and several witnesses swore that the costermonger was a disagreeable fellow who had provoked Fletcher. There was a claim that the dead man was the one who broke the bottle, and Fletcher managed to disarm him. He was only protecting himself." Muldoon's lips twisted into a savage smile. "Or so it was said."

"You've done fast work, Mr. Muldoon, for a murder you learned of only yesterday," Kendra commented. "Impressive."

He grinned at her. "I could say the same of you, Miss Donovan. You learned that Mr. Pascoe was missing only yesterday morning and by nightfall you not only found him but are now investigating." He paused, then added with sheepish honesty, "I'm not as impressive as you may think."

"Do tell," Sam muttered sarcastically.

Muldoon ignored him. "I've been hearing about Fletcher for several years," he said. "When his name came up in connection to Barrett Brewery . . ."

"You became interested enough to come here," Kendra finished for him. She pushed away from the table and crossed the room. Picking up the jagged piece of slate, she added Oscar Fletcher's name to the suspect list.

"Why is Mrs. Gavenston's name up there?" Rebecca asked as she studied the board. "You cannot possibly imagine Mrs. Gavenston to be the killer?"

Kendra jiggled the slate as she looked back at Rebecca. "Why can't I imagine that?"

Rebecca appeared nonplussed. "Why, because . . . because she is the one who brought attention to her business manager's disappearance in the first place. Why would she want him found if she was the one who killed him?"

"The two aren't mutually exclusive, you know. Think about it. The cottage on Squire Prebble's land is fairly remote. Someone would have to stumble across Pascoe's body by chance. How long would that take? Days, weeks, months. In that time, Mr. and Mrs. Pascoe would be in agony, not knowing what happened to their son."

Kendra thought of the missing children cases that she'd worked. Never knowing what had become of their child was purgatory for parents. They were caught in a closed time-loop, bouncing endlessly between hope and despair.

"If Mrs. Gavenston killed her business manager, maybe she didn't want to put the Pascoes through that," she pointed out quietly.

Sam scratched the side of his nose. "Aye, I can see how that would explain her wantin' Pascoe found. Doesn't explain why she'd kill him, though. I thought she was fond of the lad."

Kendra had to smile at that, although there was no amusement in it. "Human beings kill people they're fond of all the time. They even kill people they profess to love." She allowed that to sink in before continuing, "Mrs. Gavenston was the last person to speak with Pascoe before he left the brewery. And they had argued."

"Exactly!" Rebecca pointed a finger at Kendra. "By her own account, she admitted to arguing with him. If she had killed Mr. Pascoe, wouldn't it be in her best interest to keep that sort of thing quiet?"

"She actually downplayed it. Said it was a disagreement."

"Still—"

"Mrs. Gavenston isn't a stupid woman. She had to think that others might have seen or heard them arguing. If she didn't address it and we found out about it, she knew we'd wonder. She would look guilty, like she had tried to hide it. But by bringing it up—even though she downplayed it—she neutralizes the damage."

Sam looked at her. "You think she followed him ter the cottage ter kill him?"

Kendra shook her head. "Remember the crime scene. We're not dealing with a premeditated murder. If it was Mrs. Gavenston—and let me remind everyone, we're theorizing here, nothing more—she followed him to continue the argument or maybe to reason with him. That seems more likely. The eyewitnesses said that he was the one who left the brewery and Mrs. Gavenston tried to call him back to talk to him. So, she could have gone to the cottage with the hope of diffusing whatever tensions were between them. But they started arguing again . . ."

"And she knifed him," Muldoon said.

"*If* Mrs. Gavenston was responsible—and that's a big *if*—I don't think she intended to stab him," Kendra concluded.

"She didn't intend to stab him *five* times?" Alec didn't bother to hide his skepticism.

Kendra shrugged. "It happens. A moment of rage, then when she came to her senses, Jeremy was on the floor, dying or already dead. Later, remorse sets in, and she realizes there is a good chance he'll never be found. Never have a decent burial. His parents would never know what happened to him."

"It would cast them into hell," the Duke said softly.

There was a short, charged silence. Muldoon frowned, perplexed, the only one in the room who didn't know about Charlotte.

Rebecca broke the silence. "I don't believe it," she said emphatically. "I do not believe that Mrs. Gavenston is capable of such . . . such perfidy. Or is the sort of woman who succumbs to that kind of rage. She is a businesswoman, for heaven's sakes!"

Kendra remembered the occasional flashes of temper that she'd seen in Mrs. Gavenston's eyes. "Sometimes it's the people who seem to be the most in control who end up snapping."

"She was distraught when she asked for your help," Rebecca argued, looking at Kendra. There was a combative light in her eyes. "I was there. She was genuinely distraught over the disappearance of Mr. Pascoe."

"Again, two different things. Maybe she was distraught *because* she'd killed him. Even if she murdered Pascoe, she still mourns him," Kendra said slowly. She remembered Mrs. Gavenston's tears when they'd told her that Pascoe was dead. They'd been genuine, Kendra was certain. Although they could have been genuine tears of remorse.

"But . . . I *like* her," Rebecca whispered, but her expression had lost some of its belligerence, becoming more uncertain.

"So do I. This isn't a popularity contest. And I'm not saying she did it. I don't know who is responsible for Pascoe's death. I'm saying that she can't be discounted as a possibility."

There was another short silence. "Who is Albion Miller?" Muldoon asked, eyes dropping to the next name on the list.

"A far more likely suspect than Mrs. Gavenston," Rebecca said tightly.

"He was harassing Mrs. Gavenston when we met," Kendra told the reporter. "Mrs. Gavenston says there's no connection between Pascoe and Miller."

The Duke regarded Kendra closely, reading something in her face. "You don't believe her?"

Kendra hesitated. "I don't know what I believe," she admitted. "She says he's harmless."

Rebecca said, "He didn't seem harmless when we met him yesterday."

"She's known him for a long time, since they were children together. His father used to work at the brewery as a cooper."

Alec leaned back in his chair, stretching out his long legs. "The coopers mentioned Mrs. Gavenston having a tendre for the brother, who later died. Bonds formed in childhood can be surprisingly strong throughout one's life. Perhaps it's her remembered affection for the brother that makes her tolerate Mr. Miller."

"Possible," Kendra agreed. She moved on to the last name on the list. "Mr. Kelly, I'd like you to interview Mr. Logan today. He's a local farmer who recently argued with Pascoe."

"What did they have a row about?"

"Some sort of supply issue. He's low on the list, but he still needs to be checked out, if only to be eliminated. Hopefully he'll have an alibi for Saturday afternoon. I think Pascoe was killed on Saturday between four and . . . when is sunset? Eight?"

"Aye, thereabouts," Sam nodded.

"If it had been night, he would have lit the candles," Kendra continued. "There was a burnt log in the fireplace, lots of ash. He could have lit that, and then it went out on its own accord without anyone to keep it going. But the candles . . . if he'd lit them, they would have burnt down to puddles of wax.

"After the unsub stabbed Pascoe, he would have been panicking, horrified at what had happened. I just don't see the killer taking the time to go through the cottage, blowing out candles before he left. Do you?"

"Brilliantly done, my dear," the Duke shot Kendra an approving look.

She smiled back at him, more gratified than she should have been at his admiration. "We can't eliminate the possibility that he may have been killed during the daylight hours of Sunday, though. Pascoe had a bed with blankets and pillows, so one has to assume there were a few times he stayed overnight. He could have kept the bread and cheese for the next morning when he made himself tea for breakfast."

Muldoon shook his head, his gaze on the timeline on the slate board. "No, I don't think so. If he left the brewery at two and his home at three, as you've written here, to make his way to the cottage, he wouldn't have eaten since breakfast. He's not gonna wait until the next day to have his meal. I know I would have been gutfoundered if I had to wait so long to eat."

"He could have eaten a little bit on Saturday and brought out the remainder for Sunday," Rebecca pointed out.

"If he was a mouse, maybe," Muldoon muttered, and grinned when Rebecca narrowed her eyes at him. "But as he was a man, I think he ate on Saturday."

Kendra looked at him. "You make a good point, Mr. Muldoon. But we can't ignore the slight possibility that it could have been Sunday, so we ask about both days." Time-wise, the window was big enough to fly a 747 through. She didn't like it, but there was nothing she could do to narrow it down further.

"I spoke ter Mr. Cox—Squire Prebble's land steward—last night," Sam spoke up. "He didn't know that Mr. Pascoe was making use of the cottage. He didn't think the squire knew either. But if he had known, he didn't think he would've cared. Not like he had tenants ter make use of it."

"Mrs. Gavenston must not have known about it either or else she would have pointed us in that direction," Rebecca said. "Surely, that absolves her as a possible suspect?"

Kendra thought Rebecca was trying too hard to prove Mrs. Gavenston's innocence, but didn't argue the point. She understood what was behind Rebecca's advocacy, but she wouldn't look the other way just because she admired the brewster.

"Not necessarily," she said. "If she was the killer, pretending that she didn't know about the cottage is in her best interest."

Rebecca's nostril's flared with annoyance, but she said nothing.

"The killer might not have known about the cottage, either, but followed Pascoe there," Alec pointed out.

"That's another possibility," Kendra nodded. "It works with the spontaneity of the murder. The unsub didn't follow him immediately. Pascoe had enough time to unpack his lunch, make tea, even look over his poetry."

Muldoon's eyebrows bobbed up. "How do you know he looked over his poetry?"

"There were pages on the table, and he had time to cross out a lot of words. I think he was still angry, considering how violently he marked up the pages."

The journalist grinned. "Well, I can sympathize with the poor wretch in that regard." Muldoon's smile faded as he looked at Kendra. "What you're really saying is that there is no motive behind Mr. Pascoe's demise. It was only a moment of uncontrolled temper."

"That's what I'm saying, yes."

Muldoon's jaw tightened as he nodded. "In other words, it's like Fletcher's uncontrolled temper when he broke that whiskey bottle and stabbed that poor bloke to death."

A chill raced down Kendra's arms as she met the Irishman's eyes. "Yeah. Exactly like that."

Fletcher's involvement in a death similar in style to Pascoe was an interesting coincidence, and Kendra had never been a fan of coincidences. But making connections because of coincidences could also ruin an investigation. She decided to push it to the back of her mind for now, let it percolate.

Rebecca stood up. "Well, I must go. I promised Mama to accompany her to the dressmaker to retrieve our new gowns for Lady Merriweather's ball tomorrow night."

"I shall escort you out, Lady Rebecca," Muldoon offered, scrambling to his feet.

Rebecca looked briefly surprised, then smiled. "Thank you, Mr. Muldoon."

Kendra frowned at them. Was Rebecca blushing again? Christ, was *Muldoon?*

Rebecca dragged her gaze away from the reporter to look at Kendra. "You will attending the ball, won't you?"

Kendra froze. "I'm a little busy—"

"Caro has already sent our acceptance," the Duke interrupted, also standing.

Damn, and double damn. The countess believed it was her sacred duty to make sure her brother—and by extension, his ward—attended all of the Ton's functions whenever they were in London.

"Don't look so Friday-faced, Miss Donovan," Rebecca said with a laugh. "It should be entertaining—but not as amusing as Sir Howe's fete at Vauxhall on Saturday. *That* is a masquerade ball. I'm quite looking forward to it."

Kendra cut her eyes to the Duke, who inclined his head and said, "Yes, we shall be attending that as well. I believe Caro was going to seek you out about shopping for costumes."

Alec lifted his coffee cup, green eyes gleaming. "I think you would make a lovely Cleopatra, Miss Donovan."

She glowered at him. Then an idea came to her. She managed to keep a straight face as she gave him a look. "Maybe I'll go as a woman from the future."

Alec choked on the swallow of coffee he'd just taken. "Good God. Pardon me," he muttered, reaching for a linen napkin.

Kendra smiled.

"That would be . . . unique," Rebecca said, her eyebrows drawn together in a perplexed frown. "Pray tell, what would a woman from the future look like?"

That was a question no one in the 21st century would ever ask. In her era, imagining the future was commonplace. Hell, you couldn't go to a Halloween party without bumping into a Princess Leia or a Trekkie. But here, literature swung toward the Romantic movement, not science fiction.

"I've read *Memoirs of the Twentieth Century*," said Muldoon. "But I don't recall it describing how those in the future dressed."

Startled, Kendra looked at him. "I've never heard of the book."

He grinned. "No doubt because it was little read. The author was a fellow countryman of mine—Samuel Madden. As an Anglican clergyman, he was more interested in vilifying the pope and decrying Catholicism than writing an interesting novel. Although the time-travel aspect was a fascinating premise, I thought. Probably why I read it." He peered at her closely. "Are you all right, Miss Donovan?"

"I'm fine." She was little faint—maybe she needed Lady Atwood's smelling salts. It was strange to talk about time travel with people who didn't know her secret.

"Well, no doubt I shall see you later at the inquest," Muldoon said, glancing at Rebecca, waiting for her signal to leave.

Rebecca said, "I want all the details later." She spoke to the room at large but looked at Kendra specifically. Then she lifted her hand, and Muldoon hastily offered his elbow. What was going on with them? If Kendra didn't know better . . .

"You must take the carriage to Cookham for the inquest," the Duke said, interrupting Kendra's thoughts.

She looked over at him. He was standing, preparing to leave as well. She followed him to the door. "You're not coming with us?"

"No. Last night, I promised Carlotta that I would take her and Caro in the barouche for a drive in Hyde Park, weather permitting." He glanced at the window, as though to assure himself that the sun still shone. "We should be able to do the Ring before they visit Caro's dressmaker."

"Whose idea was that?" Kendra winced a little. Even to her own ears, the question came off as strident. The Ring was the road in Hyde Park where the fashionable people would show off their expensive carriages, horses, and finery. Or their guests.

"I'm not certain. Still, Caro thought a drive in the park would be an excellent way to ease Carlotta into society. We shall introduce her as a family acquaintance from Spain."

Kendra felt a thrill of alarm at how quickly Carlotta was insinuating herself into the household. "Are you sure that's wise?"

"Well, tongues will most certainly wag if the Polite World knew we had a guest in our home but chose to hide her away," he pointed out mildly.

"Mr. Kelly's men will be leaving for Spain soon. Maybe you should wait to show off your guest—"

"You know as well as I do that it could be weeks, even months, before we hear word," he said gently.

"I'm going to find out the truth about Carlotta."

"I have no doubt you will, my dear. Your skill as an investigator is without parallel. However, we cannot ignore Carlotta's existence. *I* cannot."

"I understand that, but—"

"Enough has been said on the subject," the Duke interrupted, his voice suddenly needle-sharp and as cold as ice. He paused, perhaps recognizing his own harsh tone. "I understand your concern, my dear, but I'm hardly a lad wet behind the ears. I will proceed with this situation in the manner I think best. Now, I do have other matters to attend to. Good day."

Kendra bit her lip at the rebuke. He rarely used what she always considered his "duke voice"—coldly autocratic, brooking no opposition—and never with her. She swallowed against the hot lump that had suddenly lodged in her throat and automatically lifted a hand to press against her breastbone. She could feel the bulge of the arrowhead pendant beneath the fabric. She drew in an unsteady breath, feeling unexpected tears in her eyes.

Get a grip, Donovan. You're twenty-six, not six. And he's not your father.

Thank God, since her own father hadn't been so great.

She leaned against the doorframe, drawing in a steadying breath to regain her composure. Behind her, she heard the murmur of Alec and Sam's voices. And ahead of her, the creak of floorboards.

Kendra straightened, skin prickling. Then she heard the stealthy tread of footsteps moving away. Instinct more than anything propelled Kendra down the hall to where it branched off into another corridor. She caught the flutter of a skirt disappearing around the corner.

"Miss Donovan?"

Kendra glanced back. Sam had stepped outside the study, his coat on and his hat in his hands.

"I need ter meet me men at the docks before they sail. Did Lady Rebecca sketch the lass's face like you wanted?" He peered at her more closely. "Is somethin' wrong?"

"No. I thought . . ." She sighed, shaking her head. "It's nothing. I'll get you the sketches."

She retraced her footsteps to the study and retrieved the rolled foolscap from the desk. She handed the pages to the Bow Street Runner, watching as he untied the ribbon and unrolled the paper to study the pastel sketches that Rebecca had done the night before.

Sam nodded approvingly. "Good thinking, lass. You know, Bow Street ought ter come up with a system of using sketches like these. 'Tis a clever idea you have, much more useful than offering a description. This should help me men considerably—there aren't gonna be many who'd forget a face like this. She's a prime article, ter be sure." Quickly, he rolled up the foolscap and retied the ribbon, tucking the sketches under his arm. "I'll find my own way ter Cookham. See you at the inquest."

After the Bow Street Runner departed, Alec walked over to Kendra. He framed her face with his palms, his gaze searching hers. "What is wrong?"

"What makes you think anything's wrong?"

"Because I know you."

For some reason, the lump returned to her throat. She gave him a tremulous smile. "I think Carlotta was eavesdropping," she said, instead of the truth.

Alec gave her a long look, seeming to know that she was hiding something from him. But he didn't press it, for which she was grateful. Instead, he asked, "Are you certain it was Carlotta? Servants have been known to listen at keyholes." He snagged both of her wrists. His thumbs began making circles against the delicate skin. "Duke's household isn't usually so raggedy-mannered. Maybe it was a young maid still being trained."

"Hmm," was all Kendra managed. Her heart was accelerating, which, by his smile, he could probably feel against his thumbs.

He leaned down, his breath feathering against her lips. "It occurs to me that I have yet to wish you a good morning, Miss Donovan."

She pretended to frown. "Apparently the servants aren't the only ones who are raggedy mannered."

He laughed. "I'll do my best to make up for it."

She kissed him. *This* felt right, she thought, and gave herself up to the joy of the moment.

But in the back of her mind, she saw the flutter of skirt before it disappeared around the corner. She knew she hadn't seen the light blue fabric from a maid's uniform, but rather a deep, dusky rose.

18

Kendra had attended an inquest before, so she wasn't surprised that Pascoe's would be held in the Green Knight tavern. Nor was she surprised to find a rowdy, almost jovial crowd already inside the taproom when she, Alec, and Molly arrived fifteen minutes before the inquest was to begin at two. However, she was a bit disconcerted to see the dead man laid out on a table in the center of the room, naked except for a linen sheet draped over his loins. Someone had also placed posies on the table around the body, an attempt no doubt to counteract the stench of rotting flesh.

"Gor," Molly whispered, eyes rounding as she stared at the corpse. Without the embalming process, the gases from natural decomposition had rapidly turned Pascoe's skin a putrid green, the flesh blackened and shriveling where he'd been cut open with the standard Y incision during autopsy and stitched back together.

"We ought to be thankful they left Mr. Pascoe with a little dignity," Alec murmured.

Kendra lifted her eyebrows. "This is what you call dignity?"

"'Tis normal to leave them in the buff, you know."

"They knew Miss Donovan would be here to testify," Dr. Munroe said, overhearing Alec's comment as he shouldered his way through the churning knot of humanity to join them. "They thought it would be unsuitable for a duke's unmarried ward to see such a sight." His gray eyes gleamed at Kendra from behind his spectacles. "They don't realize you are not a faint-hearted miss. Good afternoon."

"Dr. Munroe." Kendra nodded in greeting.

"Come. Mr. Kelly and I have saved a table," he said. "These affairs tend to draw most of the village and beyond, so we thought to arrive early."

They followed Munroe's gaze to where the Bow Street Runner was guarding a table across the room. Even as they watched, several men tried to sit down, only backing away when Sam brought out his gold-tipped baton and thrusted it under their noses.

"What did you discover in autopsy?" Kendra asked Munroe as they pushed their way through the mob to the table.

"Nothing unexpected." The doctor paused when they reached the table. Sam stood up until Kendra and Molly were seated. Once everyone had settled into the chairs, he continued, "Mr. Pascoe's wounds were not caused by the assailant slashing at the victim. The fiend *thrust* the knife into Mr. Pascoe's abdomen. As I suspected, the aorta was punctured, which resulted in Mr. Pascoe's death. The assailant stabbed him once, twice, *thrice*, puncturing the stomach, spleen, and small intestine. I found the tip of the knife, which had broken off, embedded in the pelvic bone. This, I believe, was the last thrust the killer made, with the knife remaining in the body. Unfortunately, Mr. Hobbs could not remember the exact wound from which he'd removed the knife, but I suspect it was the injury that had the most downward trajectory."

"Because Pascoe was already falling," Kendra said.

"Yes. And that injury, I suspect, perforated the abdominal aorta. As you are aware, death would have been rapid."

Kendra could visualize it, the unsub withdrawing the knife only to plunge it back with enough force to nick the pelvic bone. Pascoe crumpling to the floor could have caused the assailant to release the weapon.

"With only five stab wounds—compared to fifteen, twenty-five, or even fifty—this was not a frenzied attack," Munroe went on. "Yet there was rage behind it."

Sam snorted. "Gotta have some rage ter stab someone in the belly, even if it was only five times."

"Yes, but there are different levels," Kendra said. "A frenzy implies uncontrollable fury and hatred. The difference between the two is the hatred. Pascoe's killer did not hate him, but he did lose control. If he'd hated him, he would have followed Pascoe to the ground and continued to stab him, even after he was dead."

"All the injuries that the victim sustained bled considerably, internally and externally," said Munroe.

"Which means the heart was still pumping for most of the attack," Kendra added, pausing when a buxom barmaid with riotous red curls poking out of her mobcap and a slightly harassed expression approached the table.

"What can I get for ye?" She looked at Sam. "Another whiskey?"

"Aye." Sam picked up his glass with its drop of whiskey and drained it.

"Do you have coffee?" Kendra asked after Alec, Munroe, and Molly ordered ale.

The barmaid gave her an incredulous look. "Do we look like a coffee shop to ye?"

Smart-asses didn't originate in the 21st century, Kendra thought wryly. "Okay. I'll have an ale."

"Another, if you please," Muldoon said, materializing next to her.

The woman snatched up Sam's empty glass and shoved her way through the crowd to the bar.

Muldoon scanned the taproom. "The proprietor of the Green Knight ought to be pleased. His purse will be plumper for certain after today."

"Her," Sam corrected with a scowl at the reporter. "Mrs. Doyle owns the place."

"Cookham appears to be a progressive town," Kendra said, and smiled.

"Well, *Mr.* Doyle actually owned the Green Knight, but he stuck a spoon in the wall more than fifteen years ago, I was told," said Sam. "Now his wife's the proprietress."

Kendra studied the occupants in the room. Mostly working-class men, based on their rougher clothing, and about a dozen fashionably dressed men with starched cravats and pressed superfine coats. She guessed those to be merchants and office clerks. Besides herself and Molly, there were only four women in the room. Two were barmaids. The other two women were sitting at a small table near the tap. One looked middle-aged, wearing sober colors on her petite frame and a lace cap that hung limply on her head. The other woman looked ancient, gray hair also covered by a frilly lace cap. She was twice as large as her companion, although that could have been an optical illusion, created by the many shawls that she'd wrapped around her. Kendra counted at least six. The woman was smoking a long, skinny pipe, her beady eyes in the fleshy, wrinkled face, darting around the room. Kendra wasn't surprised to hear Sam identify her as Mrs. Doyle.

"I guess she's out of the sickroom," commented Kendra.

Sam grunted. "Probably should still be there—she's up barkin' creek."

Which Kendra took to mean that she was having coughing fits. The old woman began hacking, each shawl shuddering with the force of her wheezing. In what looked to be a practiced move, the other woman bent over and produced a porcelain vase from below the table. She tilted it toward Mrs. Doyle, who spit into it. Then the vase—or, rather, spittoon, Kendra realized—vanished back to its spot on the floor. The old woman tossed back a shot of hot whiskey with the flick of her wrist and was already sucking her pipe by the time the dark-haired barmaid hurried over to replenish her drink.

Kendra didn't know whether to be impressed or appalled by how smoothly the entire process had been done.

Muldoon leaned over to whisper in Kendra's ear. "Mrs. Gavenston's uncle, Captain Sinclair, is the gentleman standing next to the portrait of the Prince of Wales. Brown as a Christmas pudding. Looks like he thinks all his geese are swans."

"What?"

Alec translated, "Mr. Muldoon apparently thinks Captain Sinclair is a boastful sort."

"Definitely has that look about him," the reporter insisted.

Kendra fixed her eyes on the gentleman in question. Forty years in the hot Indian sun had baked his complexion into a permanently swarthy state. His hair was silvery white, which probably made him look even more tanned. He wore a beaver top hat, which gave the illusion that he was taller than his average height of five-ten. He had a military bearing in the way he stood, in the way that he appeared to size up the crowd as though expecting trouble. Then she remembered that his wife and daughter had been killed in an uprising in India. After such a tragedy, maybe he always expected trouble in crowds.

Muldoon said, his voice hardening, "Fletcher is here too. Not surprising, really. Inquests have a tendency to bring out the curiosity seekers."

And murderers, Kendra thought.

The barmaid returned, carrying a full tray. Kendra waited until she'd deposited the glasses on the table, collected the coins that Alec tossed, and once again was twisting her way through the knots of humanity.

Kendra's gaze was already scanning the crowd again. "Where is he?"

Muldoon pointed. It took a moment of shifting bodies before she saw a tall, broad-shouldered man leaning against the bar, one hand wrapped around a tankard of ale, the other holding a silver-tipped cane. The crowd shifted again, obscuring Fletcher but revealing another familiar face.

Albion Miller.

"Oy! Quiet down, you lot!" Constable Leech yelled, coming into the room. He was followed by a man who was older, shorter, and rounder than Leech, and had a book tucked under his arm. "Make way for the Honorable Mr. Peyton! Make way for His Honor!"

Like the Red Sea parting on Moses's command, the crowd split to make a path for the Constable and Mr. Peyton to walk to where nineteen chairs had been arranged across the room. Mr. Peyton paused briefly to eye the corpse on the table, then moved ahead, plopping down on the chair nearest a small table. He set the book down. The redheaded barmaid hurried over with a tankard of ale, earning a smile (but, Kendra noticed, no coin) from the coroner. He lifted the tankard, gulping down the beer like he'd been wandering in a desert for the last week.

"Let's begin," he finally said, lowering his tankard and wiping his mouth with his sleeve. "Swear in the jurors, if you will, Constable Leech."

Seventeen men, a mixture of working class and merchants, separated themselves from the crowd. Constable Leech swore them in on a bible while Mr. Peyton finished his ale. The same barmaid hurried over to replenish the tankard, not looking impressed when she again received nothing but a smile and thank you from the coroner.

"Who gave the hue and cry?" Mr. Peyton asked, setting his half-finished tankard down on the table after taking another long swallow.

"That would be Lord Sutcliffe and Miss Donovan," Constable Leech supplied. "She's the ward of the Duke of Aldridge, like I told you."

Heads swiveled to gawk at Kendra.

"You and Lord Sutcliffe discovered the body?" Mr. Peyton addressed her directly, frowning. "I was given to understand the deceased was found in a remote cottage on Squire Prebble's land, which is why the jury couldn't view him in situ."

Although she didn't understand the disapproval she saw in the coroner's face, she nodded. "Yes, we found the body."

"Miss Donovan had her maid with her," Constable Leech hastened to add.

"Ah." Mr. Peyton's expression cleared. "Very good."

Kendra's lips parted in disbelief. Had the coroner really just concerned himself with her virtue? During a *court proceeding*? She glanced at Alec, and caught the gleam of laughter in his eyes.

"Mr. Hobbs, if you'll please come up and give the name of the deceased, and how he came to be in such a sorry state," the coroner ordered.

Hobbs pushed his way to where the jurors were sitting. "I can testify that the victim's name is Mr. Jeremy Pascoe. As to the rest, I'd rather have the esteemed Dr. Munroe explain. He was the one who conducted the autopsy."

"A doctor, you say?" Mr. Peyton raised his brows. "What's a doctor doin' poking about in someone's innards?"

"I was trained as a doctor, but I am now an anatomist," Munroe said, stepping forward. "I run an anatomy school in London."

His answer caused a startled murmur to ripple through the room.

"Huh." Mr. Peyton seemed genuinely baffled. "Why'd you lower yourself to such a degree, Dr. Munroe?"

Munroe smiled. "I confess that I am more fascinated by the secrets of the dead than I am in writing out prescriptions for laudanum to ladies of the Ton."

That drew a mixed reaction, with some chuckles, some nodding of heads, and a few looks at the doctor like he'd just admitted to necrophilia.

"Huh," Mr. Peyton said again. "Well, I suppose you have a right to choose your own living, no matter how peculiar it might be. Now, then . . ." He picked up the tankard, finished the ale, then waved the empty mug at the redheaded barmaid. With an increasingly disgruntled expression, she marched over to grab the stein. Mr. Peyton flicked a hand at Munroe. "Carry on, doctor, with your testimony regarding how the poor wretch came to cock up his toes."

Munroe faced the jurors as he explained Pascoe's injuries, as well as estimating the time of death as Saturday afternoon, though he couldn't rule out Sunday. As he spoke, the barmaid returned with a fresh tankard for the coroner. Mrs. Doyle began coughing with enough force to give Munroe pause. Everyone looked at the proprietress.

"Bloody hell," she gasped, hacking, and spat into the spittoon that her companion produced once more. "Carry on! *Carry on!*"

Looking amused, Munroe concluded his testimony. Mr. Peyton allowed him to return to his seat and ordered the jury to examine the body. The seventeen jurors pushed themselves to their feet and walked over to the table to inspect Pascoe for about five minutes, and then they were back in their seats.

Mr. Peyton cleared his throat. "Let's swear in the witnesses who found the body. Miss Donovan, if you would please come forward?"

Constable Leech held out a bible and swore her in, and then Mr. Peyton said, "Tell us how you found the body, Miss Donovan."

"Mr. Pascoe was lying on the floor next to the table. He was face-up. He'd been stabbed five times."

"Did ye see anything suspicious?" asked one of the jurors.

"Aye," another nodded. "Did you see anyone in the woods?"

It was a little odd having the jury question her directly, but she took it in stride. "No. We found the body late Tuesday afternoon. As Dr. Munroe said, the victim was most likely killed on Saturday."

"And he was killed there?" someone else asked. "Maybe somebody killed him someplace else and put him there?"

It was actually a reasonable question, but Kendra shook her head. "There was no indication that the body was moved. The unsub—ah, the killer used the knife on the table. Mr. Pascoe had been using the knife for bread and cheese, which were also on the table."

"Is it true that yer lookin' inter who murdered the poor sod?" demanded an elderly juror. "Oi heard that Mrs. Gavenston hired ye to find Mr. Pascoe, and now yer set on finding who murdered him."

That caused even more murmurs to break out in the room than Munroe's admission that he was a doctor for the dead. Mr. Peyton banged his empty tankard on the table and glared at the juror.

"That ain't a proper question for these proceedings, and you know it, Mr. Rooker! We ain't here to identify the fiend who has done this terrible deed. The Crown only wishes to know if Mr. Pascoe's death was the result of murder, manslaughter, self-murder, an accident, or a visitation by God. Now, does anyone else wish to question this witness? A *relevant* question, if you please!" When the jurors remained silent, the coroner nodded. "Very well. Miss Donovan, you may return to your seat. And you there"—he pointed at the redheaded barmaid—"bring me more ale!"

Kendra turned to go and found herself staring into Albion Miller's narrow, hostile eyes.

"Still poking your long nose where it don't belong, I see," he growled, his lips peeling back into a sneer.

"Let's have the next witness," the coroner announced. "Your lordship, if you could come up here and testify to what you saw when you found Mr. Pascoe, though I suspect it'll be the same as Miss Donovan."

Kendra moved back to the table while Alec took his place as a witness. She scanned the crowd. Albion Miller was gone.

After Alec added his testimony, the coroner declared that the inquest had concluded. The jury deliberated for several minutes before the foreman announced their verdict: death by stabbing. Whether that was caused by murderous intent or manslaughter, they couldn't say. Kendra wanted to roll her eyes. Mr. Peyton opened the book that he'd carried with him, and produced a coroner's inquisition document for each juror to sign. The room was oddly silent, like everyone was holding their collective breath. This was a solemn act—even if it took place in a tavern.

"Very good." Mr. Peyton huffed in satisfaction when the last man scratched his name on the paper. He picked up the quill pen, dipped it in the inkwell, and added his own name to the document. "I suggest Mr. Pascoe be removed from the premises forthwith. He's a bit moldy."

Chairs scraped back, some men shuffled toward the corpse to remove it, and most of the crowd headed toward the tap, talking and laughing. Kendra noticed coins exchange hands. It wasn't unheard of for those attending inquests to wager on the outcome.

Kendra pushed herself to her feet. Oscar Fletcher apparently had finished his ale and was setting the tankard on the bar. She started forward. "I need a word with Mr. Fletcher."

"Not alone, you don't," Alec muttered, coming after her.

Kendra ignored him as well as Molly, who had leapt up in pursuit. Maybe she was getting used to having an entourage; she was barely irritated. Fletcher was pulling open the tavern door.

"Mr. Fletcher!" she called, threading her way through the crowd. "Excuse me! Mr. Fletcher!"

He didn't seem to hear her, disappearing through the door.

She finally reached the door and yanked it open. Fletcher was walking on the pavement, about twenty feet away. "Mr. Fletcher?"

He halted and turned. His expression was only mildly curious as he studied her. His eyes were pale blue beneath heavy lids. But Kendra recognized the hard, calculating gleam in the icy depths. His face was long, with sharp features and thin lips. She estimated him to be in his late forties or early fifties.

"Miss Donovan," he acknowledged. In a gentlemanly gesture, he raised his black beaver hat to reveal grayish blond hair cropped close to his head. He shifted his gaze to Alec. "My lord. How can I help you?"

Kendra stepped forward to catch his attention again. "You can answer a few questions," she said. "I'm curious, what is a London brewer doing at an inquest in Cookham? Did you know Mr. Pascoe?"

Something flashed in his eyes. Maybe humor. Maybe irritation. "I was acquainted with the man, yes. Hardly unusual. The brewery business is relatively small, compared to other trades."

"I heard you're trying to make it even smaller. You've been expanding your operation by buying out your competitors, and you want Barrett Brewery. But Mrs. Gavenston doesn't want to sell."

He smiled without warmth. "For the moment."

"You think you can change her mind?"

"I think Mrs. Gavenston is a reasonable woman. She recognizes that the industry is becoming increasingly competitive, with costs rising, suppliers and clientele becoming more discriminating in who they do business with. Barrett Brewery does not have the wherewithal to survive with Mrs. Gavenston running it. Mrs. Gavenston's own family understands this."

His patronizing tone set Kendra's teeth on edge. "It seems to me that she's been running the business just fine for years."

"You speak of the past, Miss Donovan. I speak of the future. Many brewers do not wish to do business with a female." He glanced at Alec. "You must agree with me, my lord? A brewery is no place for a woman."

"I've sampled Barrett Brewery ale and found it exceptional," Alec said coolly. "If that is the kind of product Mrs. Gavenston offers, I have no complaints."

A gleam of amusement came into the cold eyes. "I agree that Barrett's recipes are excellent, which is one of the main reasons I am interested in acquiring the brewery. I am, of course, speaking of the realities of the beer trade." Fletcher paused to flick a piece of lint off his cuff. He smiled and continued, "It is those realities that will eventually force Mrs. Gavenston to sell."

Kendra drew in a breath, but she wasn't here to argue on Mrs. Gavenston's behalf. Pushing aside her desire to become the brewster's advocate—much like Rebecca had been that morning—she asked, "How well acquainted were you with Mr. Pascoe?"

"I would say not at all. I met the man less than a handful of times. Mrs. Gavenston invited him to sit down with us at our initial meeting, along with the chit . . . her daughter. Hester, I think is her name. There were other times. I scarcely remember," he said dismissively.

"We have witnesses who said that you argued with Mr. Pascoe," she lied, watching him closely. Fletcher's sleepy eyelids fell even more, but she saw how his eyes bounced from side to side as though reading an invisible newspaper. Trying to recall his meetings with Pascoe, she decided. Wondering who had seen them and whether to bluff or not.

"I don't recall arguing," he finally said. "He may have taken exception to my blunt talk on why Mrs. Gavenston ought to sell." Now his thin lips curled. "There is no place for chivalry in business, which is why there is no place for females. Men must feel free to speak with a frankness that would offend the delicate sensibilities of the fairer sex."

"Mrs. Gavenston doesn't strike me as delicate."

"Nevertheless, Mr. Pascoe felt the need to act as her personal knight." His hands tightened on his cane, his expression contemptuous. "I must bid you good day, Miss Donovan, my lord. As I am not Quality, I have to work for my bread and butter."

"One more question." Kendra said, and waited for him to look at her again. "Where were you Saturday, four to eight?"

He hesitated for only a moment. "I was where I spend most of my time—at Appleton Ale, working."

"And Sunday?"

"Also working."

Kendra raised an eyebrow. "On the Sabbath?"

His smile was cold again. "I am not a religious man, Miss Donovan. Nor do I have a wife and children. The business requires my full attention. If you don't believe me, I have plenty of witnesses. You have my permission to query them."

"Are they the same witnesses who backed up your claim of self-defense when you killed a man?"

He stared at her for a long moment. The look made her feel like something cold and scaly had slithered across her foot. Alec said nothing but shifted closer. She didn't look up at him; she kept her gaze on Fletcher and summoned a smile. "I thought you appreciated frankness, Mr. Fletcher."

"Touché." Instead of answering, he touched the brim of his hat. "Good day, Miss Donovan . . . my lord."

Fletcher turned, the skirt of his greatcoat flaring, and strode to a gleaming black carriage with the steps already down. His coachman hurried to open the door.

Kendra glanced up at Alec, who looked grim.

"Cor," Molly breathed next to her. "Oi 'ope ye don't 'ave nothin' more ter do with 'im, miss. 'E's a queer cove. Evil." She shivered. "Ye can tell in the eyes. 'E's got evil eyes."

Kendra said nothing, mainly because she thought Molly was right.

19

Inside the Green Knight, Sam pushed his way through the press of bodies across the room to where Mrs. Doyle and her companion were still sitting. By the way the old woman was continuing to hack, he suspected that she would soon be seeking her sickbed, so he wanted to talk to her before she left.

"Mrs. Doyle," he said, pulling out his baton from his deep pocket. "Sam Kelly. If I could have a word?"

Her dark brown eyes, set deep in a round face that had gone crepey with age, were as cunning as a street whore eyeing a gentry cove. "Ye're the thief-taker that was asking ter speak with me yesterday."

Sam disliked the term thief-taker, with its taint of past corruption, but he nodded. "Aye, I'm lookin' into Mr. Pascoe's murder."

"Ye, and that chit—the Duke of Aldridge's ward—by the look of it." She studied him for a moment, her expression sly. Her face crumbled into irritation, though, when she was overtaken by another fit of coughing.

Her companion thumped her on the back. She muttered hoarsely, "Blasted influenza!"

"I told you, you should've stayed in bed," chided her companion.

"Don't start, Myrtle," gasped Mrs. Doyle. She snatched the whiskey on the table and tossed back the remainder of the drink, then wheezed a couple more times. "I ain't staying," she warned Sam. "But I could hardly miss an inquest in me very own tavern, could I? Especially with that bloody Peyton presiding." She shot a look in the direction of the coroner, who remained though his duties were finished. He was currently at a table with a group of men, laughing and drinking. "If the River Thames were ale, I swear that blasted creature could drink it dry. And never leavin' a coin for all our troubles."

Sam grunted. He knew most tavern owners supplied free drink to the coroner. Given the business that the tavern received from the inquest, Sam considered it a fair trade. However, he'd seen the number of tankards the coroner had gulped down. Maybe Mrs. Doyle had a point.

"Gawd, me lungs are burning somethin' fierce," she muttered, her talon-like fingers tugging closer the many shawls she'd wrapped around her body. She picked up the pipe, which she'd left burning on the table, a delicate stream of white smoke curling around the tiny bowl. She put the stem between her lips and sucked. She caught Sam's eye. "Ye've got five minutes afore I take meself home."

Sam sat down. "Heard tell not much goes on in this village that you don't know about."

Mrs. Doyle grinned, revealing stained, crooked teeth. "I keep me ears and peepers open, I do."

"So, what have you heard about Mr. Pascoe? Who'd want ter kill him?"

She sucked the pipe's stem in contemplative silence. "I don't know anyone who was murderous against him. Oh, there were complaints, but nothing vicious-like. And from what I saw over there"—she nodded toward the spot where Pascoe had been laid out on the table—"that was vicious."

"What sort of complaints were lodged against him?"

"Maybe it weren't so much complaints as it was a few people grumblin'. Horatia's kin weren't happy at how she seemed ter indulge the boy."

"Horatia?" Sam lifted his eyebrows.

Mrs. Doyle's chuckle turned into another bout of coughing. "You're thinkin' I'm being too familiar with me betters, but I've known that girl since she was Horatia Dyer, runnin' around in braids. Elizabeth—her ma, God rest her soul—and I did business together. Mr. Doyle—me husband, God rest his soul—may have owned this tavern, but we ran it together. Elizabeth had inherited Barrett Brewery from her mother. Ye know about Barrett Brewery?"

"I know it's passed down the female line."

"And ye think that's queer, don't ye?"

Before he'd met Kendra Donovan, he'd have thought it was damned queer. But now . . . He shrugged. "As far as I can tell, the women have been doing a bang-up job of it."

"Aye, they all have, since Violet Taylor married Will Barrett back in 1722 or thereabouts. Like most wives at the time, she began brewin' ale in her kitchen. But she had the gift, no two ways about it. Those days, ye sold small lots ter the locals. Now the tale is that Will weren't no fool and saw his wife's talent in the area."

"And he started Barrett Brewery," Sam finished for her. He'd learned a long time ago to let people talk. Besides, by letting the old woman talk, he'd already gone over the five minutes she'd allowed him.

Mrs. Doyle nodded. "They had four children that lived. Daisy was the oldest and took a keen interest in ale making. Like her mama, she had the gift."

"The other children didn't have any interest?"

"I reckon not, since the other daughter married and emigrated ter Scotland or some other heathenish place. The two sons joined the army. Mind ye, at the time, Barrett Brewery was still a homespun trade. So maybe they didn't see any reason ter stay in the village. But Daisy took ter it like a duck ter water. When she married George Sinclair, a local boy, she was smart enough ter protect Barrett Brewery, wantin' it ter be passed ter the eldest female daughter, just like her ma had passed it ter her."

Mrs. Doyle waved at the redheaded barmaid, who came over with a tray of drinks. She set a glass down in front of Mrs. Doyle and eyed Sam. Her harassed expression eased a little when he tugged out a coin from his breast pocket to give to her.

"Still, that must've created grumblin' with the other children, ter be cut out like that," he said finally, raising his glass and eyeing the old woman over the rim. "I know Mrs. Sinclair had a son—Lucian Sinclair." He sipped the whiskey, enjoying the pleasant fire it lit in his belly.

"They actually had three children who lived—Elizabeth, Lucian, and Diana. As the eldest female, Elizabeth inherited Barrett Brewery." Mrs. Doyle sucked on her pipe, wheezed a bit. "Daisy took her under her wing when she was a babe ter teach her the business, just like Horatia is teachin' her eldest, Hester. But don't ye think that the other children were forgotten, because they weren't. They each got a sizeable inheritance and shares in the company. More than some second sons of the Patrician order get," she sniffed. "Gave Diana a plump dowry ter marry herself off ter one of those second sons, just like Sabrina. Heard tell she's living in Ireland."

Sam blinked. He was losing the thread of the conversation. "Who? Sabrina?"

"Don't be daft! *Diana* is in Ireland. Sabrina is Horatia's other daughter. Married herself a viscount's son who's got four older brothers, so no chance ter inherit that title. Which is the only thing left ter inherit. Poor as a church mouse, Mr. Mercer was, until he married the chit and moved inter the manor." Mrs. Doyle began to cough. "Damnation! This bloody grippe will be the death of me!"

Sam waited while Myrtle brought up the spittoon for Mrs. Doyle.

"They live at White Pond Manor as well?" he continued after she was finished.

"It's big enough," she said, wiping her mouth with the edges of the shawl. "Leastwise, Mr. Mercer don't have creditors knockin' on his door anymore since he and Sabrina got spliced."

"And when was that?"

She thought about it. "Two years ago. Caused a bit of a stir here in the village, 'cause they ran off ter Gretna Green ter do the deed."

The only reason couples eloped to Gretna Green in Scotland was if the family didn't approve of the marriage. "Why would they do that?" Sam asked. "I suppose his family was against the match, beings Mrs. Gavenston is in trade."

Mrs. Doyle snorted which turned into another hacking cough. Myrtle thumped her a couple of times on the back, and she took a swallow of whiskey. "Aye. They might be in dun territory, but that don't mean they want any connection ter folks in trade," she finally said. "Especially the ale business. Closed their doors ter him, the family did. They cut him off, but from what? Eh? They have nothin'."

Except entry to the Beau Monde, Sam thought. Now Polite Society's drawing room doors would be closed to Mercer and his wife. He would, in effect, be shunned from the social circle that he had once occupied. But Sam didn't say any of that. He had a feeling Mrs. Doyle wasn't impressed with the lineage of the Ton.

She proved it a moment later when she said, "They may be our betters, but if ye ain't got any money, I ask ye, how's that any better than Horatia or *her* family line? She's as much a lady as any gentry mort. Elizabeth even sent her off ter a fancy finishin' school to polish up her manners. She's as good as any of 'em."

Sam eyed her. Mrs. Doyle sounded aggrieved on Mrs. Gavenston's behalf. "How did Mr. Mercer get on with Mr. Pascoe?" Sam asked.

"Ack, Mr. Mercer's too busy getting his wardrobe tailored and acting like a lord ter bother with Mr. Pascoe. Mark me words, he'll have went through Sabrina's dowry and inheritance by the end of the year." She picked up her pipe, puffed. "Course, Sabrina ain't much better. Chit has feathers for brains. Horatia's too indulgent with her. Suppose she had ter put more attention on Hester, as she's the eldest and set to take over."

"What was Mrs. Mercer's relationship with Mr. Pascoe?" Sam asked, thinking of Kendra's contention that the killer could have been a woman.

"Same as her husband's, I expect," Mrs. Doyle with a dismissive wave.

Sam said nothing for the moment, then asked, "What will Mrs. Gavenston do if they run through the girl's fortune?"

The old woman leaned back, clamping the stem of the pipe between her lips. "Well, she ain't likely ter throw them out. They've got shares in the brewery from Sabrina's portion, so they'll get an allowance from that."

"Could they sell their shares?" And would Mr.—or Mrs.—Mercer, Sam wondered silently, approach Mr. Pascoe about it?

Mrs. Doyle frowned at him. "Now, why would they go and do a fool thing like that? It might be a smaller allowance than they're used ter, but it's not like they'll be going ter debtor's prison."

"What about the uncle?" Sam asked, circling back to the main subject. "I heard Captain Sinclair is back because he ain't satisfied with his previous inheritance. Wants a hand in running Barrett Brewery. Seems ter think females don't have a head for business."

"Bloody sod!" The old woman plucked the pipe out of her mouth and pointed it at Sam. "Horatia and his ma—and all the women that came before—are the reason Barrett Brewery is where it's at! Ye wanna know why Lucian came back? Because he saw Barrett ale being served over in that foreign country that he's been living for the past forty years, that's why! Probably never gave it a thought since the day he left home."

Mrs. Doyle was outraged on Mrs. Gavenston's behalf again. Sam couldn't blame her.

"Mrs. Gavenston is shipping Barrett ale ter India?" he asked to diffuse the tension.

"Horatia's keen on foreign markets. Now that we've made peace with America and France again, she'll probably be lookin' there as well."

"Captain Sinclair can't have any legal standing in getting his hands on the business."

Mrs. Doyle gave him a cynical look. "The courts ain't exactly sympathetic ter me sex. Thought that was why Horatia hired Mr. Pascoe. Horatia is a wily creature, but it made no sense that she hired the man." She finished her whiskey and signaled the barmaid for another.

"What's wrong with Mr. Pascoe?" Sam asked.

"Nothin' wrong with him, but he ain't—wasn't—a brewer, didn't know heads or tails about the ale business. Was a clerk at a bank in Maidenhead, so I reckon he knew money. But folks thought it peculiar that she'd choose someone wet behind the ears when there are better men for the job." She paused when the barmaid delivered their drinks, and Sam fished out another coin. "But I think Horatia was being canny. Mr. Pascoe didn't have a brewing background, but that allowed her ter groom him ter be the man ter represent Barrett Brewery. To stop her uncle from trying ter take control."

"But I thought the brewery is always passed ter the eldest daughter."

"Aye. But right now, Horatia's eldest daughter ain't wed."

Sam blinked. "Hor—Mrs. Gavenston was hoping for a match between Hester and Mr. Pascoe?"

"Ack, I can't be sure of that, but it wouldn't surprise me. Horatia has a ruthless streak in her," she said. "I'm not speaking ill of her. Any woman in business needs ter be able ter be ruthless, meself included. But if the shifting winds mean havin' a man at the helm—a man ye've picked for your daughter and mayhap can control . . ." She shrugged. "That fancy finishing school didn't jest polish up her manners. It polished some hardness inter her too. She was softer afore she was sent off there."

Mrs. Doyle finished her drink, then went through another fit of coughing. "Gawd. I'm done up," she muttered, looking suddenly exhausted. Slowly, the old woman hoisted herself to her feet. "A rest will do me wonders."

Sam scrambled to his feet as well. He hadn't yet quizzed her about Albion Miller or Mr. Fletcher, but he saw the grayness of her complexion and said only, "I'd like ter speak with you again when you feel better."

The old woman nodded and turned away, allowing her companion to help her through the thinning crowd. Slowly, Sam sat down again. He took a long sip of whiskey as he thought about everything Mrs. Doyle had said.

Arranged marriages were common enough in the Polite World, but Sam didn't think it put Mrs. Gavenston in an entirely flattering light. It certainly revealed a more ruthless side to the brewster than he'd first imagined.

He thought of Kendra's supposition that Mrs. Gavenston could have killed her manager in a fit of temper, and then remorse had propelled her into wanting his body found. Maybe it wasn't quite as outlandish an idea as he had first thought.

20

S am scowled at Phineas Muldoon when he slipped into the seat that Mrs. Doyle had vacated.

"So, do you believe Mrs. Gavenston was hoping for a match between her manager and her daughter?" the reporter asked.

"You've got sharp ears, lad. And that ain't a compliment."

Muldoon grinned, unfazed. When the barmaid circled around again, Sam ordered a whiskey and Muldoon an ale.

"I spoke with Mr. Shaw," Muldoon said. "He was distressed to hear about Mr. Pascoe's demise. He'd been his clerk for nearly nine years."

Sam had to think a moment. "Ah. Mr. Pascoe's employer at the Maidenhead Banking Company. He's here?"

"He's gone now," Muldoon said when Sam turned to seek the man out. "Here's the odd thing. Turns out Mrs. Gavenston is one of their largest depositors. She's been banking there for nigh on fifteen years."

Sam raised his eyebrows. "If she knew Mr. Pascoe before, saw the kind of man he was, maybe she took a liking ter him. And when her manager was ready ter be pensioned off, she naturally thought of him as a replacement."

"Possible," Muldoon conceded, inclining his head. "Or maybe that's when she got the idea to do a little matchmaking. Either way, it's odd that Mrs. Gavenston never mentioned she knew Mr. Pascoe prior to her hiring him."

Sam frowned. "I'm not certain what that has ter do with the man's murder."

Muldoon shrugged. "I'm not certain either." He grinned at the barmaid when she returned. "A moment of your time, my good woman," he said, handing her a coin.

"What can I do for ye?" She eyed him warily as she tucked the coin into her blouse.

"Everyone in the village must pass through here. What can you tell us about Mr. Pascoe?"

She pursed her lips. "A gentleman, he was," she said. "Real polite and quick with the coin—not like some of the coves around here. He came in for meals mostly."

"Alone or with anyone?"

"Depends. When he was alone, he was always scribbling. Must've been interested in . . . what do ye call it when ye look up at the stars?"

"Astronomy? Astrology?"

"Aye, one of those. Told me once that he was paying homage to a star." She shook her head and laughed lightly at the memory. "Thought he was dicked in the knob, I did, but it weren't that. He was interested in poetry, of all things. Can you imagine? I never learned ter read or write, so I can't say I cared one way or the other, but he got all dreamy-eyed when he was scribbling his verses."

"When he wasn't alone, who'd he come in with?" Sam asked.

"Sometimes he'd come in with Mr. Elwes. He's a schoolmaster here. I think they both liked ter read and write poetry. Sometimes he'd come in with Mrs. Gavenston or Miss Gavenston."

Muldoon leaned forward. "He'd be with Miss Gavenston alone?"

"She's not gentry, needin' a chaperone," the barmaid pointed out. "Everyone knows they work—*worked*—together at the brewery. They probably were alone over in their offices more than they were here with the village keeping their peepers on them. I told ye, he was an honorable cove. It's a shame what happened, really." She shifted on her feet, glancing around. "I gotta get back ter work."

Sam held up a finger. "One more question. Did you see him argue with anyone in particular? Or hear that he might've gotten into a quarrel with someone?"

"Not that I remember."

"Any thought ter who may have killed him?"

"Nay." She shivered a little. "Other than whoever did it had ter be mad."

"It's a puzzle," Muldoon murmured, drinking his ale with a thoughtful frown after she'd departed. "Who kills a man who was essentially a clerk, whose hobby was writing verses?"

"Like Miss Donovan said, whoever did the deed got angry and then stabbed him. Unfortunately, that means it could've been anybody."

"Yes and no. Yes, anyone with a temper could be the fiend who attacked Mr. Pascoe. And I don't know anyone on God's green earth that doesn't fly off the boughs every once in a while, with the exception of my sainted mother. And no, because the possibilities are narrowed down to people who knew him and what he may have been involved in—as Miss Donovan also said."

"Victimology," Sam said. "That's what Miss Donovan calls it. Says by studying the victim, you can figure out the killer."

Muldoon cocked his head to the side. "She's an Original, isn't she? What do you know about Miss Donovan? *Truly* know?"

Sam narrowed his eyes at the reporter. He'd come to have great affection for the American and wasn't about to put up with anyone disparaging her. "What are you gettin' at?"

"I meant no offense," Muldoon said. "I've just never met anyone like her. You have to admit that she's a strange one."

"Oh, you're not giving offense at all," Sam muttered drily.

"Lady Rebecca is as fiery, independent, and intelligent as Miss Donovan, but she has a sense of what is proper. Most ladies would not attend an inquest. His Grace only had to send word, and no one would have thought her absence odd."

"She attends autopsies. Why would she not attend an inquest?"

"Exactly." Muldoon jabbed a finger at him. "I'm only saying she's a strange creature. Strange in a good way, if you take my meaning. Different."

Sam had the same thoughts but would never admit to them. Now he shrugged. "She's an American. They set great store in liberty. They started a whole war over that notion. I even heard tales of females dressin' as men so they could fight us when they started their war of independence."

"I haven't been to America, but it sounds like the womenfolk there are a fearsome lot, if those tales are true. As fearsome as Scottish lasses. It's not difficult to envision Miss Donovan doing such a thing, but I feel like there's something more . . ." He tapped his nose and grinned. "There's a story with Miss Donovan. I can feel it in me Irish bones."

"Your Irish bones will be broken if you cause Miss Donovan one bit of embarrassment," Sam snapped. "The Duke of Aldridge ain't a man ter be trifled with, for all his geniality. He protects his own. And I don't think the marquis would simply stand aside either. You'll find yourself at Leighton Field at dawn with your dueling pistol."

"I would never cause Miss Donovan a moment of embarrassment. And that's not because me poor blood runs cold at the thought of facing his lordship over a pair of barking irons. I happen to like Miss Donovan. She may be a peculiar creature, but I admire her courage and cleverness, and her commitment to avenging those who suffered an untimely death."

"Oh, you like her, do you? And here I thought you were reserving your affection for Lady Rebecca," Sam teased, chuckling. He was surprised when Muldoon turned red.

"I have great admiration for Lady Rebecca, as well," the younger man said stiffly.

Sam eyed him carefully. "Well, as long as you admire her from afar. Lord Blackburn will hardly look kindly upon a romance between his daughter and an Irish scribbler. You're beneath her touch, me lad."

"You think I don't know *that*?" Muldoon stood suddenly, his eyes ablaze with temper. "You think . . . oh, to hell with you!"

Sam gaped as the reporter spun on his heel and shoved his way through the knots of men, disappearing out the door with a bang.

"What was that about?"

Sam glanced at Munroe as he materialized next to the table. "The folly of youth," Sam murmured, lifting his whiskey for a long, slow sip. He sighed, feeling older than his forty-two years and unaccountably depressed. "And dreaming of a world that doesn't exist."

21

Kendra spotted Captain Sinclair as he was crossing the street. She called his name, not only capturing the captain's attention but that of several bystanders, and sprinted across the cobblestones after him. "I'd like to speak to you, if I may."

Up close, Kendra noticed that his eyes were hazel, the same shade as his niece's. He didn't smile, inspecting her like she was a new recruit that he found wanting.

"Miss Donovan, my lord." Sinclair nodded, his gaze sliding past her to Alec. "I'm afraid that I do not have much time to spare. I am scheduled to meet Lord Davies at his estate in Wycombe for a fox hunt." He pulled out his watch fob. "In exactly one hour."

"This won't take long. Are you going now to Wycombe?"

He looked at Kendra with scorn. "Of course not. I must change into my riding habit."

"I planned to go to White Pond Manor as well. Do you mind if I get a ride with you?"

Even Kendra knew this was audacious. His eyes widened with shock, but he recovered almost instantly.

"As you can see, my gig is not built for four people—"

"Lord Sutcliffe and my maid will follow us in the carriage," Kendra broke in. The last thing she wanted to do was to go hurtling across the countryside with Sinclair, but this was too good an opportunity to miss. It wasn't like he could jump off if he didn't like her questions.

Sinclair's lips tightened, but like any military man, he knew when he'd been outmaneuvered. "Very well, Miss Donovan."

Alec stepped forward to help Kendra into the gig. His eyes gleamed with humor. "The royals could take lessons on being imperious from you, my sweet," he whispered as he lifted her.

"Whatever works," she murmured back.

Captain Sinclair clambered up on the other side and picked up the reins. He steered the horse onto the street behind two riders. Even though they couldn't have been going more than two miles an hour, Kendra's heart jolted. She grabbed the bottom of the seat to secure herself.

"I am aware that my niece had asked you to look into Mr. Pascoe's disappearance—and now his murder," Sinclair said, his gaze on the road ahead. "I hope you do not take offense, but I find your involvement in this affair quite peculiar."

Kendra had always wondered why people bothered saying "no offense" when they usually followed it by saying something offensive. "You think it's peculiar to want justice for a man who was murdered?"

He gave her a sideways look. "I think you are well aware to what I'm referring, Miss Donovan. In India, women understand the natural order and are content to be nurturers in the home, to provide succor to their husbands and tend their children."

"I find that interesting coming from you, given that your own mother was in charge of Barrett Brewery."

For the first time, Kendra wondered if that might have caused resentment. He'd basically been bypassed in favor of his sister in a time when males usually inherited. She thought she might have struck a nerve by the way his hands clenched on the reins.

"It's probably strange to be in a family that rebels against traditional primogeniture," she remarked.

He sighed angrily. "My family is in trade—there is no primogeniture, as such. And there is no estate. White Pond Manor belongs to me as much as it does to my niece or anyone else in the family."

Which was probably why Mrs. Gavenston hadn't booted him out on his ass when he started trying to insert himself into running the brewery.

"My mother had ridiculous notions fostered by Violet Barrett." His nostrils flared. "My father should have put a stop to the nonsense, but he did not. I joined the British Army and was sent to India."

"Did you marry an Indian woman?" she asked curiously.

"*What*?" He looked genuinely appalled. "Good God, no! My wife was a good, God-fearing Englishwoman, the daughter of a lieutenant colonel. I would never have married a pagan. The very idea is absurd."

She decided not to point out his hypocrisy in venerating an Indian woman's subservient behavior, and yet reviling the natural-born citizens of an entire country in which he'd lived. Instead, she asked, "Why did you come back? If there's nothing here for you at Barrett Brewery?"

"I returned because I realized the brewery is as much my heritage as my niece's. 'Tis time for me to take a more active role in the company. I have connections that would be of use in business."

"Connections?"

His expression turned smug. "Lord Davies, for one. He is influential in the West Indies trade, having considerable investments in that area," he said. "And I have many contacts in India, as well as the British military. I don't expect you to understand the nuances of business, Miss Donovan. Suffice to say, I would be a great asset to Barrett Brewery in these matters."

"It's not that complicated. You're hoping to leverage your connections—and the promise of increasing the brewery's markets internationally—for a position in your niece's company." *Asshole.*

"Barrett Brewery is *my* family's company," he snapped.

"Maybe in spirit. But in reality, Mrs. Gavenston is in control."

Her fingers tightened on the seat when the gig's wheel hit a rut in the road, and her heart lurched into her throat. They were leaving the village.

On one side of the country lane was the familiar patchwork farmland, on the other, thick woods. She recognized some of the landscape. They were going in the same direction as Squire Prebble's land, where Pascoe had been found.

"Horatia has to realize that if Barrett Brewery is to compete internationally, certain sensibilities must be recognized. Men—even savages—do not want to do business with the female sex. 'Tis beneath them. Horatia cannot even go into a gentleman's club in London. Where do you think most business is done, Miss Donovan? In the *drawing* room?"

He sounded exactly like Fletcher. Unfortunately, as appalled as she was by both men, she knew there was truth in those snide words.

"That's why Mrs. Gavenston had Mr. Pascoe—to negotiate on her behalf," she said, watching him carefully. "Is that why you disliked him? As long as he was around, offering that *manly* handshake when it came to making deals, you couldn't get your foot in the door."

He gave her a sharp look. "Who said that I disliked him?"

"I heard that you were upset when you asked him to support you in having more say in Barrett Brewery and he refused to go against Mrs. Gavenston. Did you threaten him?"

"Don't be preposterous. Why would I bother?"

"Because Mrs. Gavenston gave Mr. Pascoe a lot of responsibility at Barrett Brewery. More, it sounds like, than she is willing to give you."

That got a rise out of him, just as she'd intended.

"Bah! It only proves what I've been saying. Horatia is too soft. Mr. Pascoe had no experience in the brewery business. He was a bank clerk, for God's sakes. Tallying up numbers for a living."

"And you were a captain in the army."

"Barrett Brewery is in my blood. Before I joined the army, I worked at the brewery with my family."

"Well, I'd say tallying up numbers is what a good manager is supposed to do," she said.

"Mr. Pascoe was more than a good manager, I think," he retorted, lips curling. "My niece invited him often to dine with us. I saw the way that she looked at him."

Kendra's skin prickled at the implication. She tried to keep her expression blank and asked steadily, "How did she look at him?"

Sinclair gave her another sideways look. "In a way no woman her age should be looking at a pup like him. It was revolting."

Kendra said nothing. She'd sensed that Mrs. Gavenston had been hiding something from her. Was this it? An illicit love affair? Was their argument on Saturday a lover's quarrel?

Mrs. Gavenston was perhaps forty-five. Pascoe had just turned twenty-nine. So, only a fifteen- or sixteen-year age gap. Which wouldn't have raised eyebrows at all if the man had been the older one. Even in the 21st century, more people were likely to disapprove of an older woman falling in love with a younger man. If Mrs. Gavenston had been having an affair with Pascoe, Kendra could see her not wanting that to become known.

"You're saying that Mrs. Gavenston and Mr. Pascoe were having an affair?" she asked directly, done with innuendo.

He shrugged, but seemed reluctant to put his suspicion into actual words. "Whatever their relationship, it was not appropriate."

Kendra frowned, clutching again at the seat as Sinclair turned the gig down another lane, the Duke's carriage following some distance behind. Ancient oaks rose up on either side of the road, creating a tunnel of spreading foliage. Kendra caught glimpses of blond stone and glass through the greenery. She got the impression of size, but still wasn't prepared for the majesty and beauty of White Pond Manor when they emerged from the long, leafy tunnel and she had her first unobstructed view of the house. It wasn't as enormous as Aldridge Castle. But then what was? Nor did it evoke the sheer power of the castle's gray stones. Instead, White Pond Manor was four stories of elegance, its architecture paying homage to the romantic Renaissance style.

Apparently, the beer business was quite lucrative.

"How long has your family lived here?" she asked.

"My father purchased the property from a lord who was sent to debtor's prison. The house had fallen into disrepair." Sinclair actually smiled, the first flicker of genuine amusement that Kendra had seen from him. "Most of my childhood was spent dodging mason workers and scaffolding."

She thought of the Yarborough residence back in London, and let her eyes travel over the lush green lawns, carefully placed trees, and the glimmer of blue from a small lake curving gracefully around the manor on its left side. "It's beautiful."

Sinclair acknowledged that with a brief incline of his head. He concentrated on driving the gig around to the stables. Stable hands rushed forward to take the reins he threw at them. Kendra hopped down from the contraption before he could come around to give her assistance, earning a disapproving frown from Sinclair.

She glanced around when she heard the distinct crack of gunfire in the distance. Instinct nearly had her diving into her reticule for her muff pistol, but since Sinclair and the stable hands didn't appear disturbed by the noise, she relaxed her hands.

"Someone's shooting?" she asked Sinclair.

His lips thinned. "No doubt that dandy that Sabrina married. Horatia ought to be at the brewery at this time of day. If you wish to speak to her, you'll need to send word."

"I suppose Hester is at the brewery as well, since she'll be taking over one day."

It was a deliberate jibe, which Sinclair must have recognized, because he smiled like the cat that ate the canary. "We shall see," was all he said, and he fished out his pocket watch. "I must be off. Unless you wish to wait for Lord Sutcliffe here, I shall escort you into the manor. Brentworth will see to tea and get word to Horatia."

Brentworth, she assumed, was the butler. A place like White Pond Manor would have a butler. And a housekeeper. And an army of servants.

"I'd love some tea," Kendra lied, falling into step beside the captain. "By the way, where were you on Saturday afternoon and Sunday?"

He looked at her sharply. He knew what she was asking, and, by the way he pursed his lips, he didn't like it. Kendra wondered if he was going to ignore her question, but he finally said, "I had business in London on Saturday. On Sunday, I attended a cricket match in Windsor."

"Anyone to verify your whereabouts on both days?"

"My business is private. As far as Sunday goes, speak to Sir William Lloyd, as I joined his party. But anyone who attended the match between Harlequins and Lewes would be able to confirm my attendance."

"It would be helpful if you could tell me your business on Saturday to eliminate you as a suspect."

"Ah, but that is just it, Miss Donovan." His smiled humorlessly. "I don't feel particularly helpful. You have no authority to compel me to state my private business."

Usually her connection to the Duke was enough to motivate people to talk, even if they lied to her. But she had no power in this era beyond that.

"People who are reluctant to talk about their whereabouts during a murder makes me wonder what they're hiding," she tried.

But Captain Sinclair had spent forty years in the British military, occupying a country that didn't necessarily want to be occupied. He was not easily intimidated. "You may wonder all you like, Miss Donovan."

More gunfire sounded in the distance. The sharp reports were oddly spaced out. Two shots in rapid succession, then silence, and then two more shots.

Kendra walked with Sinclair on the flagstone path that angled away from the stables, up an incline. At the crest of the hill, Kendra paused to survey the rolling hills and woodlands.

"Isn't that Squire Prebble's land over there?" she asked, pointing.

He glanced briefly in the direction she indicated. "Yes."

Standing here, Kendra had a pretty good idea that as the crow flies, the cottage was maybe a mile, a mile and a half away, over rough fields and through dense woods.

Not an easy hike, but still close enough to walk.

22

Brentworth, Mrs. Gavenston's old, stoop-shouldered butler, ushered Kendra into a drawing room decorated in light, bright seafoam greens and pearl grays. The windows were large, letting in the afternoon sun, and evenly spaced. French doors led out to a stone verandah and overlooked a lawn that sloped down toward the lake and woods.

"I shall send word to Mrs. Gavenston," the butler said, "and see if Miss Hester is at home."

Which meant that she was, but might not want to see anyone. Kendra was getting used to the shorthand in this era.

She thanked him, and then instead of sitting, she wandered to the window. She saw a handful of people gathered near the lake. Here was the source of the gunfire.

They made an interesting tableau, Kendra thought. A woman was sitting next to a small round table draped in pristine white linen. Sunlight bounced off the silver tea service, porcelain, and crystal. Though the woman wore a bonnet with a wide brim and topped with what looked like a bouquet of flowers and two luxurious ostrich feathers that fluttered in the wind, she also held a tiny parasol angled to keep her face in the shade.

Three men and a young boy stood several paces away from the woman. The boy held the leash of a yellow Labrador retriever while an old man loaded a large-bore, single-barrel flintlock shotgun. A younger man was standing with a similar shotgun tucked under his arm. Another older man seemed to be keeping a watchful eye on a wooden crate filled with pigeons. Both old men and the boy wore working attire. The younger man was blond and dashing in a navy greatcoat over a scarlet jacket, deerskin breeches, and shiny black hessians.

Behind her, Brentworth arrived with Alec and Molly in tow. "Miss Hester is at home," he informed them. "She has not been well. She shall be with you shortly."

Kendra nodded, then indicated the group outside. "Who are they?"

"That is Miss Sabrina . . . ah, Mrs. Mercer, I should say. And her husband, Mr. Mercer." The butler bowed out of the room.

"I suppose it's bad manners to go down there and introduce ourselves?" Kendra murmured.

"Very shabby indeed," Alec replied.

She glanced at him and grinned. "So let's go."

He laughed and they started for the French doors that opened to the gardens. Kendra paused, looking pointedly at Molly. "I don't think I need a chaperone. Why don't you see if you can get a cup of tea in the kitchens?"

"Oh, but—"

"And maybe you can find out where everybody was on Saturday and Sunday."

Understanding dawned in Molly's eyes. "Oh. Aye, miss. Oi'm suddenly parched."

Alec cocked an eyebrow at Kendra as Molly left the drawing room. "That's inventive, darling."

"The servants will be more comfortable talking to Molly than me," she said with a shrug.

Alec offered his elbow to her and opened the French doors. The yellow Lab was the first to see them, yipping excitedly, his body quivering in excitement as he strained at his leash. The boy brought him back. "Whoa, boy! Sit! *Sit*!"

The dog sat, tail thumping on the ground. Everyone turned their heads to look at them.

"Good day," Alec said easily. "Forgive the intrusion, but we saw you from the drawing room. Is that a James Purdey?"

The younger man—Mr. Mercer—glanced at the gun in his hands with the same kind of affection that a proud papa would display in showing off his firstborn. "It is. I bought both of them last month."

"Mr. Purdey only set up his shop a couple of years ago, but everyone is speaking of him in the same admiring tones as they speak of Manton. Of course, given that Mr. Purdey once worked for Joseph Manton, the skill he's demonstrated in gun making is hardly surprising. A true craftsman. I am Sutcliffe, by the by, and this is Miss Donovan."

"Mr. Mercer," said the man. He gestured to the woman sitting. "And my wife, Mrs. Mercer." He turned to regard Alec with curious eyes. "You are the Marquis of Sutcliffe?"

Alec inclined his head to indicate this was true.

Mercer smiled. "My father is Lord Redgrave."

"We have been introduced."

Sabrina tilted her head to look at Kendra. "Miss Donovan, my mother has spoken of you. You found poor Mr. Pascoe. The inquest was today, was it not? I suppose that's why you are here in Cookham."

"Yes," Kendra said, studying the other woman. She had the look of both her sister and her mother in her bone structure. But her hair was ash blond and her eyes a deeper, darker blue, twinkling now with inquisitiveness. Her skin was creamy but flushed from the cool breeze blowing off the lake waters.

"Would you like to try it, my lord? We both can have a go." Mr. Mercer reached for the other shotgun that the older man was holding and offered it to Alec. "Unfortunately, we had to set up the pigeons in the old way. We don't have spring traps yet."

He waved his hand to indicate the two top hats on the ground about fifty feet away from where they were standing.

"Fair warning, your lordship, Mr. Mercer is a crack shot," his wife said with a laugh.

Mr. Mercer gave her a charming, playful bow. "As always, madam, I am your humble servant."

"Please, sit down, Miss Donovan." Sabrina offered the chair on the other side of the table as Mercer and Alec took their positions.

"Pull!" Mercer yelled.

The old man jerked the string, sending the top hats tumbling to the side. Instantly, two pigeons flew out of shallow holes that had been dug into the earth. The birds darted toward the trees. Both Alec and Mercer squeezed their triggers, gunfire cracking the air. One pigeon kept flying into the safety of the woods; the other spiraled to the ground. The boy released the yellow Lab and the dog sprang into action to retrieve the fallen bird.

"Excellent shot, my lord," complimented Mercer, but Kendra thought the dandy's smile was a little forced.

Kendra watched the two older men reset the traps—which meant taking two more pigeons from the cage and stuffing them into the holes, then replacing the top hats for another round. She'd seen a lot of strange things in this era, but this might have been the strangest.

She shifted her gaze to Sabrina. "How well did you know Mr. Pascoe?"

"He is—*was*—Mama's manager," said Sabrina. "He came to dinner at White Pond Manor many times."

"Highly irregular," her husband said, overhearing. "I tried to advise your mother on the matter, to explain that one does not invite one's man of affairs to family dinners. 'Tis simply not *done*."

Kendra could imagine how Mrs. Gavenston had reacted to that advice.

"Mama has done things her way for so long . . . since Papa died." Sabrina shrugged lightly. "That's been seven years now. And even when Papa was alive, he indulged her."

"Did your mother invite her previous business manager to dinner?" asked Kendra. "I understand that Mr. Pascoe has only worked for Barrett Brewery for about a year."

Sabrina looked surprised. "Mr. Carter? Good heavens, no. I hadn't realized it before, but . . . no. She only invited Mr. Pascoe."

"Did they discuss business at dinner?" Kendra wondered.

Sabrina frowned. "Sometimes."

"'Tis what I said," Mercer put in, in that same, puffed-up, authoritative tone. "'Tis ill-mannered to discuss business at the dinner table."

"It wasn't often," Sabrina said mildly. "They—well, everyone, really—would speak about books, art, poetry. Mama and Hester were quite taken with Mr. Pascoe's interest in poetry. He dabbled, you know."

Mercer shook his head. "Why would she encourage him to pursue such frivolous interests outside his position at the brewery? And a poet, of all things! Mr. Pascoe was already too bookish by half. Comes from being a schoolmaster's son, I suppose."

Sabrina smiled slightly. "I suspect that Mama secretly had such yearnings when she was a young girl. However, the brewery was her legacy. Her destiny."

Sabrina's words opened up a new perspective. Kendra had been quick to admire how Mrs. Gavenston's mother and grandmother had set up their business, allowing their daughters to flourish. She hadn't considered that Barrett Brewery might not have been Mrs. Gavenston's dream. And Kendra understood only too well the weight of family expectations.

Had Mrs. Gavenston wanted to be a writer instead—one of the few socially accepted hobbies for women of the era? Literary salons were popular among the ladies of the Ton, although if women were *too* enthusiastic about the written word—whether they were reading or writing—they could be mocked as bluestockings. The key, of course, was to keep it a hobby. If they wanted their works published, ladies would either take a male non de plume like Amantine Lucile Aurore Dupin, who became famous as George Sand, or publish anonymously, like Jane Austen, a fact that had tripped Kendra up when she'd first found herself in this timeline.

Women brewsters were in the same position, Kendra realized. Society was fine with them brewing their ale in their homes. But when they stepped outside the home and made it into a business, all hell broke loose.

"I cannot imagine who would want to hurt Mr. Pascoe," Sabrina was saying now.

Kendra turned to look at her. "He didn't mention having difficulties with anyone?"

"Well, not with *me*." Sabrina laughed at the idea. "You ought to ask Mama and Hester."

"What about your uncle, Captain Sinclair?"

Sabrina was silent, her eyes narrowing as she appeared to debate how much she should say.

Her husband had no such qualms. He glanced at her as he accepted the newly loaded shotgun from the old man and said, "Captain Sinclair felt Mr. Pascoe was too inexperienced to hold such an important position at Barrett Brewery. I must say, I agreed with him. Mrs. Gavenston allowed Mr. Pascoe too much freedom, letting him be her voice."

"I heard that Captain Sinclair and Mr. Pascoe argued. What do you know about that?"

"My uncle is of the mind that a woman's place is in the home," Sabrina said. "I think he actually thought to persuade Mr. Pascoe to his side, but Mr. Pascoe was quite loyal to Mama."

Mercer said, "The captain makes a persuasive argument. Your mother should at least consider it."

Sabrina smiled lazily. "Oh, darling, what would poor Hester do if Uncle Lucian took over?"

Kendra eyed the other woman. "What about you? Would you be upset?"

Sabrina looked surprised. "Me?" She smiled at her husband. "I have Mr. Mercer."

Mercer laughed, pleased.

It took tremendous effort for Kendra not to roll her eyes, especially when she caught the amused glint in Alec's eyes. She switched topics. "Where were you on Saturday afternoon—three to eight—and Sunday during the day?"

For a moment, Mercer eyed her as though trying to figure out if he should be insulted or amused. Then he shrugged, apparently settling on amusement. "Saturday afternoon I was at the Tip & Ship."

"Tip and Ship?" She wondered if that was slang for something.

"*The* Tip & Ship—'tis a public hostelry. They have mills twice a month on Saturday. Tom Belcher himself actually was said to have been in a boxing match there."

Kendra had never heard of the man, but Mercer said his name with the same kind of veneration that someone would have said Muhammad Ali or Joe Louis.

"So, you attended a boxing match at the Tip & Ship. What time?"

"The match was at four, but I was there at two. I wanted to get a good spot to view the fight. I'm not certain what time I came home. Eleven?" He looked at his wife for confirmation.

Sabrina nodded. "I believe so. You can ask Brentworth. He would have still been awake."

"And Frederick. The head groomsman. He took care of my horse."

"What about you, Mrs. Mercer?" Kendra asked. "If you don't mind . . ."

"I went into the village after nuncheon. I had a dress fitting with my modiste, spent a few hours looking over fashion plates." She smiled. "You have my permission to speak with Mrs. Browne, my dressmaker. She has a shop on High Street."

"Thanks, I will."

Sabrina laughed. "I spent most of the afternoon with her. The latest styles coming out of Paris are simply divine, don't you think? No one does fashion like the French. Thank heavens the war is over so we ladies can dress properly again. Then I went to the millinery shop and purchased this." She touched her bonnet, stroked one of the plumes. "I thought it quite dashing."

"You are a diamond of the first water," her husband complimented.

"I nearly purchased another—it was exquisite. A primrose satin, with silk flowers and the most amusing feather placed on the side."

"What about Sunday?" Kendra persisted. She didn't think either of the Mercers were good for Pascoe's murder, but she'd follow up with their alibis to cross them off completely.

Sabrina said, "We attended church, of course. And spent the day here. Right here, actually." She smiled and spread her gloved hands to indicate the table and chairs. "Mr. Mercer was pigeon shooting. I was watching. You can ask Walter and George over there."

"Aye, that they were, miss," one of the old men spoke up.

Kendra smiled at the man but knew that servants might lie to keep their jobs and not contradict their so-called betters. She asked Sabrina, "Was your mother home on Sunday?"

"Yes. I told you. We attended church. Well, except Hester. She's been ill. Then we had our nuncheon. I think Mama went into her study, I assume to work."

Her husband shook his head. "No, she went riding. I saw her when I walked out here."

"Oh. Well, she has been known to do that on occasion as well."

Kendra asked, "How about Captain Sinclair?"

Sabrina's eyes gleamed with humor. "Pray tell, Miss Donovan, are you going to inquire about every member of my family? I have no notion where my uncle was on Saturday or Sunday during the day. I suggest you ask him. He dined with us on both evenings, though. And Hester has been in her sickbed, as I said. Does this satisfy your gauche curiosity?"

"Oh, my gauche curiosity tends to be insatiable." Kendra smiled at her. "But this helps. For now."

23

Alec and Mercer were on their third round of shooting pigeons when Kendra saw Mrs. Gavenston striding toward them, not Hester, as she'd expected. She wore a hunter green merino pelisse trimmed with chinchilla along the hem, cuffs, and shawl collar. Her quick stride made the pelisse flare open to reveal a somber, umber-colored walking dress beneath. Maybe Mrs. Gavenston would have worn the gown any other time, but Kendra thought the dark color resembled widow's weeds. Only family members—and maybe servants—wore mourning colors to honor their dead.

"Good afternoon," Mrs. Gavenston said, a little breathlessly, as she came to a stop next to her daughter. She looked at Kendra. "Brentworth sent a message that you were here. I was at the brewery. I . . . I suppose you went to the inquest?"

"Yes."

Mrs. Gavenston's jaw tightened and she looked away. "I couldn't go. I simply couldn't go."

Sabrina looked up at her mother. "No one would expect you to, Mama. It's hardly the thing."

Mrs. Gavenston looked back to Kendra. "Have you any news, Miss Donovan?"

Kendra studied Mrs. Gavenston for a long moment. Her eyes were slightly swollen and red. She'd been crying. Her complexion was pale. Her grief appeared genuine. But that would fit with the scenario that she'd laid out. One instant of fury, a lifetime of regret.

"Could we walk?" Kendra asked.

She watched Mrs. Gavenston's eyes slide to Mercer and Alec, to her daughter, and then back to Kendra. She nodded. "Of course."

They began walking toward the manor house, but as they neared the stone verandah, Mrs. Gavenston veered away, in the direction of the formal gardens. Kendra admired the way the flagstone path curled around colorful rose, lilac, lavender, abelia, and hydrangea bushes, meticulously trimmed hedges. Insects droned in the scented air. It was peaceful except for the *crack-boom* of pigeon shooting that continued behind them.

"Your home and gardens are beautiful," Kendra finally said when the silence stretched out and Mrs. Gavenston seemed in no hurry to break it.

"My grandfather designed the gardens." Mrs. Gavenston smiled slightly, correctly reading Kendra's surprise. "He was fascinated by horticulture, I was told. He died when I was a little girl. I have very few memories of him."

Kendra couldn't help but think of Carlotta and her vague memories of childhood.

Mrs. Gavenston continued, "I remember my grandmother, Daisy. She was a frightfully competent woman, I thought. I admired her and was terrified of her at the same time. I was eleven when she passed away, but she and my mother had already taken me in hand, teaching me the beer trade. My own father died shortly after my grandfather. So, for a time, my grandmother and mother were both widows. My great-grandmother—Violet—had envisioned the brewery being passed down the female line, but I have often wondered if my grandmother and mother would have been as ambitious as Violet had been if they hadn't lost their husbands. I'm not certain about my mother. The brewery became her entire life after my father died."

She blew out a breath. "Forgive me, Miss Donovan. I'm rambling."

"I don't mind. I find it interesting." And it was always helpful to know the background of those involved in a murder investigation. It wasn't like Kendra could Google her suspects or check their social media.

They stopped in front of a small oval man-made pool with lily pads dotting the placid gray-green water, and a sleek Carrara marble statue rising from its center. It was a woman, carved life-size in exquisite detail, wearing an ancient headdress and attire. Her back was gently arched, her head thrown back, eyes closed in an expression of ecstasy or exultation. Her stone arms were uplifted to the sky, the hands holding a chalice.

"The Sumerian goddess Ninkasi," Mrs. Gavenston commented. "She was said to have been born in sparkling freshwater to the King of Uruk and the high priestess Inanna. Her duty was to prepare beer daily. Scholars only recently translated ancient clay tablets from the Mesopotamia region, including what they called a hymn to Ninkasi, but it's actually a recipe for brewing beer. Beer making has always been a respected occupation for women, often done in tandem with bread making."

Kendra studied Mrs. Gavenston's face. She seemed . . . older, sadder. Jeremy Pascoe's death had clearly taken its toll. Again, she thought there was more to the woman's sorrow. If she scraped away the grief, would she see guilt?

Mrs. Gavenston went on, "In Egypt, Tenenet was the goddess of childbirth and beer, although the goddess Hathor was also believed to have created beer and was celebrated as the goddess of drunkenness. The ancient Finns believed the goddess Kalevatar mixed a bear's saliva, wild honey, and beer to create ale."

"I'm not sure that should be put in an advertisement."

Mrs. Gavenston smiled. "I am merely emphasizing the historical significance women have always played in beer making."

"I understand," Kendra nodded. "And not just myths. In reality. It must be hard for you to have to fight against a culture that now says women have no place in the business. I spoke to Mr. Fletcher."

Mrs. Gavenston pressed her lips together. "Indeed."

"He wants to buy Barrett Brewery, and has a reputation for getting what he wants."

"I am aware of his reputation."

"Are you aware that he killed a man in a fight years ago, and many of his competitors have suffered unfortunate accidents?"

"As I said, I am aware of his reputation." She looked at Kendra. "Do you think he killed Jeremy? For what purpose? I own Barrett Brewery. Jeremy's death would not further his cause."

"If Mr. Pascoe was killed in cold blood, I would agree with you. But that's not what happened. It was done in a flash of temper, a loss of control." She eyed Mrs. Gavenston closely. "The killer may have regretted it afterwards."

Mrs. Gavenston gazed into the distance, her expression revealing nothing. Then she seemed to rouse herself, shaking her head. "Mr. Fletcher is not a man to lose control—or have regrets."

"What about Captain Sinclair?"

"Why should my uncle harm Jeremy?"

"No one set out to harm Mr. Pascoe," Kendra repeated. "But he could have followed him to the cottage. Argued with him. Again, killed him in a moment of anger." She waited a moment, but when Mrs. Gavenston said nothing, she continued, "Your uncle seems to have the same views as Mr. Fletcher about a woman's role in the brewery business. He wants to take a more active part in Barrett Brewery. He told me that deals are made in clubs that women have no access to. Did you ever send Mr. Pascoe to make deals on your behalf?"

The older woman frowned. "There have been a few such times. But I still control Barrett Brewery. I approve all deals, regardless of who negotiates them. Hurting Jeremy would not alter that fact."

Jeremy. Not the more formal address of Mr. Pascoe. She remembered what Sinclair had suggested, that his niece may have had an intimate relationship with her younger employee.

"No, but it might cause an argument," Kendra replied. There was no delicate way to ask the next question. "Mrs. Gavenston, were you and Mr. Pascoe . . . involved?"

"Involved?" The other woman seemed genuinely perplexed, then stiffened in shock. "What are you implying, Miss Donovan?"

"I'm not implying anything. I'm asking outright. Were you having an affair with Mr. Pascoe?"

"No! Of course not!" She clenched her hand into a tight fist, her knuckles blanching. "My God, why would you ask such a thing? That is . . . that is absolutely ridiculous!"

"It's not unheard of. You are an attractive woman and he was—"

"*No*! I was not . . . we were not having an affair."

Kendra tried a different tack. "What did you argue about when you last saw him on Saturday?"

"What?" The change of subject threw Mrs. Gavenston. She focused on the statue of Ninkasi. "I told you this. It was business. He was upset about the new machinery."

She's lying. What else was she lying about? Kendra let it go for the moment, and asked instead, "After you argued and Mr. Pascoe left the brewery, what did you do?"

"I worked, of course."

"How long did you stay at the brewery working?"

"I don't know. Late."

"You never looked at a clock?"

Mrs. Gavenston sighed, frustrated. "I was home for dinner at seven."

"Can anyone verify that you were at the brewery after Mr. Pascoe left? Your clerk, Mr. West?"

"No, he was ill. What *is* this?" The older woman was no longer pale. Her cheeks burned with anger as she turned to face Kendra fully. "Are you, perchance, suggesting that *I* am responsible for Jeremy's death? That *I* could have hurt him? Have you forgotten that I was the one who asked you to look into his disappearance?"

"No, I haven't forgotten." Kendra didn't bother to explain her theories. If Mrs. Gavenston was the killer, she already knew. "Where did you ride to on Sunday?"

That startled Mrs. Gavenston. "How do you know I rode anywhere?"

"Was it supposed to be a secret?"

"No," she snapped. "I went riding. I had no particular destination."

"Did you go into the village? Did anyone see you?"

"I rode into the woods, by the river. I was not looking for company."

Kendra deliberately switched subjects again. "Why did you hire Mr. Pascoe?" she asked, and saw something flicker across Mrs. Gavenston's face—Surprise? Anger? *Fear?*—before it smoothed back into careful impassivity.

"I needed a manager, of course. I think we're done here."

"I will find Mr. Pascoe's killer."

Mrs. Gavenston looked at her. "I hope so. But your questions are beyond the pale. If you think that I . . . I would never hurt Jeremy," she asserted.

"I told you from the beginning that I would be asking uncomfortable questions," Kendra replied steadily. The other woman's lips tightened at the reminder. Kendra sighed. "Mrs. Gavenston—"

"What is this?"

Hester was coming toward them. She was wearing a brown velvet pelisse over a dark violet walking gown trimmed with three ribbons at the hem, but she still looked like she'd just crawled out of bed. Which, Kendra realized, she probably had. Her face was pinched and as pale as a wraith, except for the tip of her nose, which was bright red, and her eyes, also crimson. Her bright hair, though she'd taken the time to have it styled into a topknot and curled, hung listlessly, and her blue eyes appeared dull.

"Did I hear correctly?" she demanded. "Are you accusing Mama of hurting Jeremy?"

Mrs. Gavenston spoke up quickly. "This is nothing for you to be concerned about, darling." She looked at Kendra and there was almost a pleading look in her eyes. "My daughter has had a relapse and has been confined to bed. She does not need to be disturbed."

"I'm sorry that you aren't feeling well, Miss Gavenston." Kendra studied the younger woman's eyes. More than sickness had robbed Hester of her alertness. If Kendra wasn't mistaken, she'd taken laudanum. It was a common enough practice during this era.

"Today was the inquest," Hester said foggily. "You attended, didn't you, Miss Donovan?"

"Yes."

"Did anyone . . . ? What was said?"

"Mr. Pascoe's death was determined a homicide." *Like it could have been anything else.* She waited a beat, then said, "I spoke to Mr. Fletcher."

Hester frowned vaguely. "Mr. Fletcher from Appleton Ale? Jeremy didn't like him. He'd offered to pay Jeremy if he could give him our recipes."

Mrs. Gavenston stared at her daughter. "Mr. Fletcher tried to bribe Jeremy?"

Hester blinked at her mother's sharp tone. "I-I—"

"Why didn't you tell me? Why didn't Jeremy?"

"Because he . . . we didn't want to worry you, Mama. Jeremy would never had done such a thing. He found the suggestion repugnant. He would never betray you in such a way, Mama." Tears rose in Hester's eyes. "He wouldn't have betrayed you."

"Of course not," Mrs. Gavenston murmured, looking troubled. "Still, you should have told me."

Kendra looked at Hester. "Why didn't you tell me when I first spoke to you? You mentioned Mr. Pascoe's altercation with Mr. Logan, but not with Mr. Fletcher."

"I-I don't know," she admitted. "You asked about who quarreled with Jeremy. Mr. Logan had quarreled with him. I don't think Jeremy and Mr. Fletcher actually argued."

"How did Mr. Fletcher react when Mr. Pascoe refused him?" Kendra asked.

"He told Jeremy to think about it."

Kendra remembered the gleam of amusement in Fletcher's eyes when he'd agreed that Barrett Brewery's recipes were excellent. She asked, "How valuable are your recipes?"

"Very valuable," Mrs. Gavenston responded tersely. "Hester and I are experimenting with new recipes all the time, but Barrett is known for certain ales and stouts that come from recipes that have been passed down from generation to generation, even before my great-grandmother Violet's time. Naturally, there is considerable secrecy involved."

Mrs. Gavenston stepped forward to put her arm around her daughter. "I don't wish to be rude, Miss Donovan, but I must take Hester back to her bedchamber."

"Oh, Mama . . ." Hester began to protest, but her mother hustled her down the path toward the manor.

Kendra followed behind, her mind on this new possibility. Industrial espionage. The FBI had an entire corporate espionage unit devoted to busting companies and countries involved in stealing trade secrets. The public generally thought of corporate espionage as a white-collar crime, and therefore less harmful. But it cost millions (and in her era, billions and sometimes trillions) in lost revenue. Whenever you were dealing with that kind of money, there was no such thing as harmless stealing. In fact, a few people would kill for it.

Pascoe hadn't been murdered to silence him after Fletcher tried to bribe him to steal Barrett Brewery's recipes. But Fletcher could have approached him about it again at the cottage. And if Pascoe said the wrong thing, maybe threatened to expose the other brewer . . .

It was definitely a possibility. And that was the problem. Right now, there were too damn many possibilities.

24

While Kendra conducted her interviews, Sam found Mr. Logan inside his stone barn, the other man's big, calloused hands wrapped around a pitchfork as he mucked one of the stalls. The man was in his mid-forties, with a weather-beaten face, currently glistening with sweat, and a hard-muscled body reflecting the long days he spent toiling in his fields.

The farmer paused, eyes narrowing with suspicion when he saw Sam. He demanded, "Who are you?"

Sam fished out the baton from his greatcoat. "Sam Kelly—Bow Street."

Logan grunted and went back to work, stabbing clumps of rotten hay with the pitchfork. "This is about Mr. Pascoe. I don't know what I can tell you. It ain't got nothing ter do with me."

"You were seen quarreling with Mr. Pascoe."

Logan paused again, leaning against his pitchfork as he eyed Sam incredulously. "That was business. I've been dealin' with Barrett Brewery all me life. Before me, me da dealt with Mrs. Dyer and Mrs. Sinclair.

Plenty of folks think it's peculiar tradin' with a woman, but I don't care about that."

He lifted his arm, wiping the sweat that ran in dirty rivulets down his face with the sleeve of his work smock. "We made our deal last year. How was I ter know that this bloody cold weather would ruin half me crops and grain prices would be what they are? Seems ter me that I should be able ter renegotiate the terms of our deal, especially since I had other parties interested in me harvest."

"Other parties, or one other party—Appleton Ale?"

Logan scowled. "Aye, Mr. Fletcher approached me about selling me harvest ter him. He offered me a sum that was considerably more than Barrett Brewery, I can tell you that. I'd have been a fool not ter consider it. I ain't no welcher, but I have a family ter feed too. The way I figured it, it didn't hurt ter talk ter Mr. Pascoe when I saw him havin' a meal at the Green Knight. I explained the situation ter him."

"I take it he wasn't accommodating ter any new arrangement with you."

"Well, he wasn't *un*sympathetic. He said that he'd need ter speak ter Mrs. Gavenston about it, but he doubted she'd change her mind. Blathered on about how margins were tight at Barrett Brewery, with the bloody grain prices rising everywhere in the kingdom. Like I don't know grain prices are rising?"

"If he was going ter speak ter Mrs. Gavenston, what did you quarrel about?"

"It was when I mentioned Mr. Fletcher's name and told him that he was offering ter buy me harvest that Mr. Pascoe got all het up. Said I should be ashamed ter deal with the cove! Why should I be ashamed? If you were offered twice as much for yer services, wouldn't you take it?"

"It would certainly be tempting," Sam conceded diplomatically.

"Damned right it is! I don't need no greenhead who'd never broken a sweat afore tellin' me what's what." He grabbed the pitchfork again, starting again on the hay. "Bloody whelp."

"Sounds like you were quite aggravated with Mr. Pascoe."

Logan shot him a sideways look. "I'll admit that he got me back up, lookin' down his nose at me like he was. It wasn't like I was cheatin' Barrett Brewery. That's why I spoke ter him in the first place, ter tell him about Fletcher's offer. If I was gonna kill him, it would have been then. I certainly wouldn't seek him out ter knife the bugger. What do you take me for?"

"Maybe you wanted ter talk ter him more about your arrangement with Barrett Brewery, and you flew up into the boughs." *Just as Kendra described.*

Logan snorted. "I saw him at the tavern, that's the only reason I spoke ter him in the first place. I didn't seek him out deliberate-like, and I certainly didn't seek him out afterwards. Christ, I didn't even know that he was makin' use of that cottage on Squire Prebble's land! Why'd he do that when Barrett Brewery supplied him with a perfectly fine house in the village? Sounds mighty fishy ter me. Like *he* was the one who had somethin' ter hide."

"He was a writer. Sometimes they get fool notions in their heads."

"Aye, well, I had no reason ter kill him." Logan stopped forking up the straw and manure long enough to scowl at Sam. "It's not like killin' him would change me contract with Barrett Brewery."

Sam scratched his nose. "Do you know if Mr. Fletcher had any dealings with Mr. Pascoe? Maybe he approached him like he approached you?"

"If he did, it wouldn't have been a pleasant encounter. I told you—it was when I mentioned Mr. Fletcher's name that Mr. Pascoe got right put out." Logan sighed. "Can't say I blame 'em for being on guard against Mr. Fletcher. He wants Barrett Brewery, and I expect he'll do just about anythin' ter get it."

"I heard Mrs. Gavenston's uncle, Captain Sinclair, has been trying ter get his hands in the business. Spent his life in India, then returns ter Cookham thinking he can just take over."

"You think it's a shabby thing for him ter do, do you?"

"Aye. Don't you?"

"Oh, I do." Logan turned his head to spit on the ground. "Except it weren't Captain Sinclair who's the weasel in Mrs. Gavenston's hen house."

Sam didn't think he was successful at hiding his surprise because Logan smiled and nodded.

"Aye. It's the other one," the farmer said. "The fancy nob. The viscount's son."

"Mr. Mercer."

"Aye." Logan nodded. "That's the one."

"You're saying Mr. Mercer had some sort of deal goin' on with Mr. Fletcher? How do you know?"

"'Cause I saw them together. Once was at the Tip & Ship. Maybe that weren't nothin', but I also saw Mr. Mercer leavin' Appleton Ale when I went up ter talk ter Mr. Fletcher about me crop. Mr. Fletcher *said* that it weren't him, but I've got peepers. I *know* it was him. Got me thinking. Why lie about it? What are they hidin'?"

25

By the time the Duke's carriage rolled to a stop outside of No. 29 Grosvenor Square, the sky had darkened into murky twilight, with clouds and fog beginning to drift in, along with a hint of rain. The oil lamps were already lit outside the square's residences, but unlike the gas lamps that were being installed throughout London, the light was so meager that it could do little more than highlight the brass knocker on the door.

The square seemed unnaturally quiet. Kendra attributed that to the lack of construction noise at the Yarborough mansion. The mason workers had gone home for the evening.

"Molly, go on ahead," she told her maid. When Molly frowned, she added drily, "I promise you that his lordship won't molest me out here on the street."

"Aye, miss." Molly blushed, hesitating for a brief moment before scurrying off.

Alec captured one of Kendra's gloved hands, leaning down to brush his lips tantalizingly against her ear. "Are you so certain about that, Miss Donovan?"

Kendra laughed, even though her stomach fluttered. "You're coming in for dinner, right?"

"If I dare show up to the dinner table in these clothes, my aunt will box my ears. I'll go home first and change into evening dress. But first I'll walk you to the door."

"I'm a big girl. I can walk myself." But she squeezed his hand before letting go. "Hurry back."

"Because you miss me or because you need a shield against my aunt?"

"What do you think?" she said, almost feeling giddy as they looked at each other. Christ, she was flirting. At least, she thought she was flirting. She'd never flirted before she'd ended up in the 19th century.

Before she made a complete fool of herself, she picked up her skirts and hurried up the path. She paused halfway and turned around to wave. Alec tipped his hat, then disappeared into the cab of the carriage.

Kendra glanced at Benjamin, who was frowning down at her from his perch. Definitely a mood killer.

She stayed where she was, watching as Benjamin snapped the lines. The clip-clop of hooves and rumble of wagon wheels broke the silence of the square as the carriage moved away. Kendra counted under her breath as she stood and waited. It took twenty seconds, but the man finally materialized out of the shadows.

"How long have you been lurking around?" she asked, turning to face Albion Miller.

"Long enough to see you turnin' it up sweet with his lordship." His lips twisted into a sneer, apparently a habitual expression for the man. "Heard you've been askin' around for me."

Because he was a bully, he edged closer, deliberately invading her personal space, ready to exploit any sign of weakness. And because Kendra knew what he was doing, she maintained her position. Although her hand dipped into her reticule to close over the muff pistol.

She got right to the point. "How well did you know Jeremy Pascoe?"

"I hardly knew him at all. I had no reason ter kill him. That's what you're really askin', ain't it?"

She tilted her head. "Since you're so accommodating, you wouldn't mind telling me where you were on Saturday after three, and all day Sunday?"

"Well, here now, if we're talkin' accommodating . . ." He stepped even closer, brushing a beefy hand against her arm. His stale breath fanned her cheek. "What are you offerin' me in return?"

Kendra's fingers tightened on the muff pistol for a fraction of a second. Albion was bigger than she was, but she'd taken down bigger opponents. Krav Maga had been part of her defensive training. The technique wasn't subtle, but it was brutally effective. A simple palm strike would probably be sufficient. Albion was a street brawler, not a strategist.

"Just answer the question," she snapped. "If you have nothing to hide, it shouldn't be that difficult."

Surprise flickered across his face. He had expected her to cower. Still, bullies like Albion didn't back away until they were given a reason.

"Don't take that tone with me, missy," he said, and took firm hold of her arm.

Kendra pressed her lips together to keep from crying out.

"You're no better than Horatia, puttin' on airs. Both of you thinkin' that you're better than you are. I saw you with your lord. Too cozy by half!"

Kendra twisted her arm out of his grasp and shoved him back a step. "What did you threaten Mrs. Gavenston with at the Tower?"

"Who says I was threatenin' her? Did Horatia tell you that?"

"No, she didn't. In fact, she dismissed you. Said that you weren't anything to be concerned about," Kendra goaded and watched his face turn purple. If he didn't collapse from a stroke, Albion might actually say something interesting.

"Did she? Did she indeed? Well, let's see if she would be happy to have her reputation in tatters. She acts like the grand lady of the manor, when she's nothin' more than a trollop." He thrust a thick finger out at Kendra, jabbing the air in an angry beat. "Wait and see what those fine gentlemen from the British East India Company think about dealin' with the likes of her!"

Kendra said nothing.

Albion sneered and went on, "What would her daughters think, eh? Hester so proper and ladylike. And the youngest marrying that lord's son." It was dark, but Kendra recognized the gleeful malice that lit the small eyes. "I know that Mr. Fletcher has been sniffin' around, hoping to buy the brewery. He might be interested to hear what I have to say!"

For the first time, Kendra became alarmed. Whatever the situation between Mrs. Gavenston and Albion Miller, it had existed for a long time. She'd wanted her bad cop routine to push the man, but she didn't want to push him over the edge into destroying Mrs. Gavenston.

"Okay." She held up a hand. Albion Miller was, she reminded herself, a man who exploited weaknesses. She kept her voice cold and disinterested. "Sure, you can do that. Of course, you'll lose your leverage with Mrs. Gavenston. How much money has she paid you over the years?"

"Are you all right, miss?"

Surprised, Kendra glanced at the man who'd emerged from the Yarborough construction site. He was little more than a shadow, but she recognized the Scottish mason worker. He was giving Albion a hard look.

"I'm fine, thanks," she assured him, stifling her irritation at the interruption.

Albion maintained his pugnacious front but seemed to size up the Scotsman as his real threat and began to back away.

Damn it. "You never told me where you were Saturday and Sunday," she called out as Albion turned and scurried away into the street.

He paused briefly, glancing back. Even with the distance and the dark, Kendra saw the taunt in his eyes. "Nay, I didn't, did I?"

Kendra scowled after him.

"Do you want me ter walk you ter your door?" her would-be rescuer asked.

She sighed, some of her irritation sliding into amusement. Everyone wanted to walk her to the door. "I think I can make it on my own, but thanks." She started down the path, aware that the mason worker's eyes followed her all the way.

At dinner that evening Kendra couldn't have felt more like an outsider than if she had taken her plate to dine in the stables. As she watched across the table gleaming with silver and lit candelabras, Lady Atwood threw her head back and laughed—*laughed*—while Carlotta recounted a story to Alec about meeting one of the countess's acquaintances on their ride through the park that afternoon. Well-bred ladies did not laugh out loud. Goddamn it, that was one of the *rules*. Last night, the countess had expressed the same hardnosed suspicion about Carlotta that she'd always had for Kendra. Last night, they'd been on the same damn page.

Apparently, Lady Atwood and Carlotta had bonded over fabrics and fittings at the dressmaker and a spin through Hyde Park. Now they were laughing and chatting like old pals. Kendra had been here almost a year and had yet to achieve that kind of rapport with Lady Atwood.

Not that she actually *wanted* to be pals with the woman. But it would be nice if the countess wouldn't look at her like she'd found an insect swimming in her soup.

How did Carlotta do it? Kendra wondered. She was beautiful, of course. That didn't hurt. It was called the halo effect. People were predisposed to like attractive people. But there was more to it than Carlotta being pleasing to the eye. She was, Kendra supposed, *personable*. Carlotta took delight in the latest fashions; she enjoyed gossiping about the foibles of the Beau Monde. The only interest Kendra had in fashion was to realize how much she missed the comfort and freedom that jeans had offered her in the 21st century. The only gossip that she'd cared about revolved around murder investigations.

And Kendra knew that she had never been personable. You couldn't be a fourteen-year-old freshman in college without feeling awkward. The only points of interest that she'd shared with her fellow college students had been academia. She'd never had Carlotta's skill at whipping up conversation out of thin air.

And it *was* a skill. As Kendra sipped her Beaujolais and sliced into the ham glazed with wild honey and cooked to succulent perfection by the Duke's temperamental chef, Monsieur Anton, she had to admire how cleverly Carlotta played her audience. Was she the only one who noticed how the other woman complimented Lady Atwood's taste on selecting her gowns at the modiste while demurring her own sense of style? How

Carlotta enthused about the Duke's interest in the natural philosophies with admiration shining in her dark eyes?

Kendra tried to use that to her advantage when she quizzed Carlotta about her own thoughts on natural philosophies. The daughter of people as brilliant as the Duke and his wife should have been naturally predisposed to having some kind of idea about science, right? That's what her own parents had counted on when they'd decided to have a child. But the questions only gave Carlotta the opportunity to play the victim. With eyes downcast, she quietly apologized, explaining that she hadn't been allowed to pursue such interests.

"Carlotta's childhood played out in a war-torn country, not as a daughter of privilege," the Duke reminded Kendra. "Her focus was on survival, not something as high-minded as scientific thought."

It was a subtle rebuke that left Kendra feeling like a complete asshole. Worse, her clumsy attempt to show them that Carlotta was not an intellectual equal had made her *look* like an asshole, while putting Carlotta in an even more sympathetic light.

Damn, damn, and double damn.

Kendra fell silent after that, an outsider in this family unit. Like a sorceress in the dark arts, Carlotta continued to weave a spell of enchantment. Hell, even Alec smiled when Carlotta told of meeting a certain nobleman known for his penchant for powdered wigs and corsets during their ride around Hyde Park's Ring.

Throughout the meal, she was aware of Carlotta glancing at her from the corner of her eye. She thought the other woman's dark eyes held smug laughter, but she might have been projecting her own feelings of inadequacy. *If this is war, I'm losing.*

"Remember, tomorrow evening we will be attending the Merriweather ball," Lady Atwood reminded everyone. "We shall be leaving at eight o'clock. And we have the masquerade ball at Vauxhall on Saturday. Carlotta and I shall be shopping for our costumes tomorrow."

"In the afternoon, as I will be accompanying His Grace to the Royal Society in the morning," Carlotta put in, smiling at the Duke.

Kendra stiffened. For someone who had never thought about science, Carlotta had apparently developed a fascination for natural philosophy.

"I thought Carlotta would find it interesting," the Duke said. "Friedrich Bessel is scheduled to speak. He's the director of the Königsberg Observatory. Brilliant young man." He hesitated, his eyes brightening as he looked to Kendra. "Have you heard of him, my dear . . . in your America?"

Your America was the Duke's code word for the future. She was always careful not to reveal too much. She'd grown up with Chaos Theory as a cautionary tale, where one tiny seed of information could twist the natural timeline in unexpected, possibly disastrous ways. Still . . .

"As you say, he was . . . *is* a brilliant man. I'm certain he'll come up with many great contributions to science." She allowed herself a small smile. This was an area that Carlotta couldn't encroach upon, she thought, as she exchanged a look with the Duke.

Carlotta may be more personable than me; she may know how to engage her audience and hold court with polite conversation. But I have the future to capture the Duke's interest.

For the first time, though, she wondered if it would be enough.

Kendra had two half-siblings that she'd never met. She'd grown up as an only child, so she'd never been involved in the typical familial dynamics, including sibling rivalry. As she prowled the drawing room where everyone had gathered after dinner, she wondered if that was what she was feeling now. As ridiculous as it sounded, Kendra had to admit to herself that her dislike for Carlotta could have just as much to do with jealousy as it did suspicion.

Which made her feel stupid. She was too old to think this way, *feel* this way. It was so . . . illogical.

She sipped her cognac, her gaze traveling to the claw-footed table where Lady Atwood and Alec were engaged in a game of backgammon, then moving on to Carlotta and the Duke, who were sitting at the pianoforte. Carlotta played and sang—she had a beautiful voice, damn it—while the Duke turned the pages of the music book. They made a cozy picture. Kendra eyed the paintings on the wall of Arabella and

Charlotte. She couldn't deny the resemblance between the child and the woman. Or the mother and the woman.

Which is what Carlotta was counting on, she was sure. Because it was all an act. She was an imposter whose goal was . . . *what*? If it had been Carlotta at the study door, then she knew that they'd sent Bow Street Runners to Spain. It was a sizeable country and could take years to dig out her real identity. But eventually the truth would come out. Even if she convinced the Duke that she was his daughter and he publicly acknowledged her, he could just as easily disavow her when the truth came to light.

Of course, a hell of a lot could happen in the meantime. Carlotta could use her position as the Duke's daughter to contract an advantageous marriage. Then there was jewelry. The Rutherford family jewels were entailed to the Duchess of Aldridge, she supposed, like the castle and estate were entailed to whoever held the title of Duke of Aldridge. But there was probably more easily pawned jewelry in the family vault. Or maybe new pieces that, with time, Carlotta could cajole the Duke to purchase for her. Kendra didn't need to stretch her imagination too far to see how much damage the other woman could do before she was exposed.

Kendra sighed. It was pointless to speculate. She should be doing something more worthwhile. Like going to the study, where she could focus on the investigation into Jeremy Pascoe's death.

She was trying to figure out a polite way to leave when Carlotta got up from the pianoforte. Retrieving her wineglass, she glided toward Kendra. Behind her, the Duke stood up as well. But instead of following Carlotta, he walked over to observe the backgammon game that his sister and Alec were playing.

"Will you be accompanying her ladyship and me to find our costumes for Saturday night's ball?" Carlotta asked, her dark eyes on Kendra as she joined her near the window.

"No."

Carlotta smiled faintly. "I am aware that you do not trust me, Miss Donovan."

Kendra got the impression that she was waiting for her to deny it. When Kendra said nothing, she gave a small laugh.

"You do not make this easy for me," Carlotta said. "I would not wish us to be enemies."

"We're not enemies." *Exactly.*

Carlotta shot her a shrewd sideways glance. "You dislike me."

"I don't know you." Kendra rocked back on her heels and surveyed the other woman through narrowed eyes. "I only know what you claim to be."

"And you don't believe me." Regret crossed Carlotta's beautiful face. She looked over at the Duke. "I would never wish harm on His Grace," she said softly. "He is a good man. A truly good man."

Kendra heard the wonder in the other woman's voice. She actually sounded sincere. "You seem surprised."

Carlotta sipped her wine thoughtfully. "Not many men who are in the Duke's position, who have his kind of power and wealth, are good men," she said slowly. "So, you are correct, Miss Donovan. I have been surprised by his kindness and generosity."

"I can see that you appreciate his generosity," Kendra said, allowing her gaze to slide over the striking scarlet gown Carlotta was wearing. In truth, she probably would have assumed the evening gown was Carlotta's, if Molly hadn't told her—via Lady Atwood's maid, Miss Beckett—that the dress had been purchased that afternoon for a considerable sum.

Carlotta's lush lips thinned. "I did not ask for a new wardrobe."

"No, you didn't ask. But I doubt you resisted either. In fact, I think you're a very good actress, Mrs. Garcia Desoto. Your timing is impeccable. You say just the right thing in just the right way at just the right time."

Carlotta's face paled. "You must really despise me."

"I despise those who try to take advantage of good people. If you're not who you say you are, I would advise you to run, Carlotta. Run before you do more damage. You say you don't want to hurt the Duke. What do you think it will do to him when the truth comes out and he learns that you're not his daughter, but some imposter using his dead daughter's identity?"

"How can you be so certain I am not Charlotte?" She tilted her chin up in challenge.

Kendra made a point of looking into Carlotta's eyes. "I'll find out the truth, you know."

"The truth." Carlotta's eyes went flat as she studied Kendra. "And what is the truth with you, Miss Donovan? You accuse me of taking advantage of His Grace's generosity, but who are you to speak? I know all about you too."

Kendra said nothing. They had been keeping their voices low so as not to be heard across the room, but Carlotta nearly hissed the last sentence.

"You speak of me taking advantage of His Grace's generosity," she went on. "But what of you? The clothes on your back were purchased with his coin. I know you were a servant before His Grace made you his ward." She laughed suddenly, but there was no humor in the sound. "Ah, I can see that surprises you."

"I guess somebody's been talking," said Kendra, careful to keep all expression off her face and out of her voice. *Never let them see you sweat.*

Carlotta's smile was catty. "You are a hypocrite, Miss Donovan. An upstart from the colonies who has managed to ingratiate herself into the household of one of the wealthiest men in England."

"I have never lied to His Grace." *Not since admitting to being from the future,* she amended silently. "I've never asked him for anything."

Kendra was assailed by a sense of déjà vu. She'd had the same argument with Lady Atwood.

"And I sure as hell didn't want to be here," she concluded. At least that was completely true.

Carlotta raised an eyebrow. "And yet I do not see you attempting to leave."

Kendra said nothing. What could she say?

Carlotta's dark eyes searched her face. "You and I are the same, Miss Donovan," she said finally. "We have both been adrift in a world that can be cruel to women. Why do you begrudge me the comfort of a loving family and home that you yourself have found?"

"Because I never pretended to be the Duke's daughter." She drew in an unsteady breath. "Are you admitting that you are not Charlotte?"

They stared at each other, measuring each other's strengths and weaknesses. Then Carlotta laughed. "Certainly not! I *am* Charlotte."

"I'll find out the truth," Kendra said again, the warning unmistakable. "It's something I am quite good at, you know."

"Because you sent your Bow Street Runners to Spain?"

Kendra remembered the footsteps, the skirt disappearing around the corner. "What are you going to do when they find out who you really are?" she pressed.

"What makes you think that they will find out anything that does not support my claim?" Carlotta replied, adopting a coy look. "I wish you would believe me, Miss Donovan. I wish we could be friends. When my father publicly acknowledges me, I will not look kindly on those who have distressed me."

Kendra raised her glass, but kept her eyes leveled on Carlotta as she took a deliberate sip of cognac. "Are you threatening me?"

"What an imagination you have, Miss Donovan! I wonder, though . . . who would His Grace choose if things became too strained in his household? His daughter or his ward?"

The question was so closely aligned to her earlier thoughts that all Kendra could do was frown. Carlotta smiled.

"What are you two whispering about?" the Duke asked as he strolled toward them.

Carlotta's smile widened as she stepped toward him, threading her hand in the crook of his arm. "Women's gossip. Tell me, what should I wear tomorrow at the Royal Society?"

Kendra watched as Carlotta maneuvered the Duke away from her. Was it a warning? Or was she reading too much into it? Becoming paranoid?

Her stomach churned and her head began to pound. Carlotta had the instincts of a street fighter. Certainly, she'd drawn blood when she'd called Kendra a hypocrite. Kendra finished her cognac, which probably wouldn't help either her stomach or her headache and set down the glass on a nearby table. She wasn't good at this family stuff. She needed to get back to work, to focus on Pascoe's murder. That was what she was good at, what she was trained to do.

She was formulating her excuses when Carlotta screamed and shoved the Duke to the floor. Kendra froze, her heart leaping into her throat. In the next second, there was the crack of a gunshot and the window that Carlotta and the Duke had been standing in front of exploded, glass shards showering down on them. The bookcase on the other wall splintered.

"Get down! *Get down!*" Kendra yelled, and dove for the floor.

26

Kendra's heart was galloping in her chest as she lifted her head just enough to scan the room. Alec had yanked Lady Atwood to the floor, half covering her with his body. Carlotta was doing the same with the Duke. There'd only been one shot, but Kendra felt like they were in a war zone.

The door flew open and Harding and two footmen came through at a jog.

"Get down!" Kendra shouted at them and waved wildly. All three crouched and ducked, wide eyes darting around the drawing room, trying to find the enemy.

Alec shifted his weight and looked across the room at Kendra. "I think the danger has passed," he said and before Kendra could protest, he pushed himself to his feet with lithe grace. After a moment, she did the same. They moved swiftly to the window. Alec pressed his body against the wall, angling his head to peer out the shattered window. Kendra did the same from the other side of the window. All she could see was darkness. Cold night air blew into the drawing room, chilling her cheeks and making her eyes water.

"Call the watch," the Duke ordered Harding as he got to his feet. He helped Carlotta up, then his sister.

"Yes, sir," the butler said, snapping his fingers at one of the footmen, who ran from the room.

"And send word to Mr. Kelly," Kendra yelled after him. Adrenaline continued to thrum through her bloodstream. She clenched and unclenched her hands as she gazed out into the darkness.

"He's gone," Alec said, correctly interpreting the look on her face.

Harding said, "I shall find supplies to board up the window tonight."

He didn't ask what had caused the window to break. He'd heard the report of the shotgun blast and was even now frowning at the splintered wood and hole in the bookcase.

After Harding and the footman left, Kendra whipped around to look at Carlotta. "What happened?"

"Do we need to discuss this now?" the Duke asked, putting his arm around Carlotta, who was shaking violently. "Her nerves are shattered."

"Then get her some smelling salts," Kendra said tersely. "What did you see, Carlotta? You screamed—"

"She saved Bertie's life," said Lady Atwood. She looked as white and shaken as Carlotta. She stumbled to a chair, sank down. "Dear heavens . . ."

Alec poured two glasses of brandy, which he brought to his aunt and Carlotta. "This might be better than smelling salts."

The countess tossed back most of the contents in a shocking display of unladylike behavior. The Duke led Carlotta to the sofa.

"I . . . we were talking . . . I do not even remember what we were talking about, Your Grace . . ." Carlotta took a sip of brandy. Her hands were trembling so violently that the liquid sloshed dangerously in the glass. She gave a little laugh that had just a touch of hysteria in it. "*Perdóname*—forgive me. I-I . . . looked out the window just for a moment. I saw a man standing across the street. H-he had a rifle."

"It's dark," Kendra pointed out.

Carlotta nodded. "I don't think I would have noticed, except he lifted the weapon. It wasn't the man, but the motion that I saw."

"So, you couldn't see whether the shooter was a man or a woman?" Kendra asked.

Carlotta's mouth parted in surprise. "But it must have been a man. It couldn't have been a woman."

"Why? A woman can shoot a rifle as well as a man."

"But . . ." Carlotta seemed shocked by the possibility but shook her head. "I really didn't see anything."

Alec observed, "You reacted swiftly."

Carlotta smiled slightly. "It is perhaps the benefits of growing up in war." Then her smile vanished, and she shook her head, bewildered. "What is happening?" She looked at the Duke. "Why would anyone shoot at you, Your Grace?"

"I don't believe they were shooting at His Grace," Alec said slowly.

Carlotta's eyebrows rose. "I have made no enemies in England."

"Are you so sure about that?" Kendra asked. It was a nasty thing to say, she supposed, because she didn't think anyone had been shooting at Carlotta. She opened her mouth to take back what she'd said, but Lady Atwood spoke first.

"Don't be stupid," she snapped. The brandy had fortified her. She glared at Kendra. "We know what happened. Look at you two." She wave her hand to indicate Kendra and Carlotta. "From a distance, you could be sisters. The monster was not shooting at Carlotta, he was shooting at *you*, Miss Donovan. You—and your damnable determination to associate with the criminal element—nearly killed my brother."

An hour and a half later, Sam had arrived at the house and Kendra, Sam, Alec, and the Duke had ventured to the study after seeing Carlotta and the countess off to bed and dealing with the watch, who promised to scour the area that very night for the fiend.

Kendra hadn't bothered voicing her opinion that they wouldn't find anything. The sniper was long gone. They'd left Harding to supervise the footmen boarding up the window.

"You're making someone nervous, lass," Sam said, looking across the study to where Kendra stood in front of the slate board.

She looked back at the Bow Street Runner and didn't deny what he said. It was the only thing that made sense.

"Who?" asked the Duke.

Kendra rolled her shoulders. "I don't know. We've just begun questioning possible suspects. That's always . . . sensitive."

The Duke said, "People object to being thought a murderer."

Kendra laughed. "That's one way to look at it. Another is that I just piss people off." She felt a spasm of anxiety when Alec strolled to the window. "How about everyone stay away from all windows for the rest of the night?"

"The watch is in the park, at least six men. I can see their lanterns. I think we're quite safe tonight," Alec said, but complied with her wishes. His expression turned brooding. "I think most of us are safe except for you, Miss Donovan."

"I . . ." *Can take care of myself*, she almost said, but she knew that annoyed Alec. She instead tried, "I promise to be extra careful."

Sam said, "It's fortunate that Mrs. Garcia Desoto was there to push you to the side, Your Grace. Although it's unfortunate that she didn't see the sniper."

"I owe Carlotta a debt that I can never repay," the Duke agreed quietly.

There was a moment of silence. In her mind, Kendra heard Lady Atwood's accusing words again: *You—and your damnable determination to associate with the criminal element—nearly killed my brother.* Guilt pierced her.

Kendra looked at the slate board, then at Sam. "Did you learn anything from Mrs. Doyle, Mr. Kelly?" The question shocked her audience.

Frowning, the Duke glanced at the clock. "It's past midnight. Perhaps we ought to wait until tomorrow morning to pursue this matter?"

"If someone shot at me because of my investigation into Pascoe's murder, then Mr. Kelly is right—I'm making someone nervous." She rubbed her arms, feeling chilled. "I don't want to waste time. Mr. Kelly is here. All I need is ten minutes for him to brief me on what he learned."

The Duke seemed ready to voice another objection, but then instead nodded slowly. "Very well. Ten minutes. Mr. Kelly, do you want a whiskey?"

Sam's face brightened. "Well, if it ain't no trouble . . ."

Kendra picked up a jagged piece of slate, jiggling it while she waited for the Bow Street Runner to settle in with his drink. The Duke sank into the seat behind his desk, while Alec dropped into another chair, stretching out his long legs, his fingers laced together and resting on his flat stomach as he regarded her. The pose appeared as lazy as the tiger at the Royal Menagerie and, Kendra thought, just as deceptive.

Sam said, "Mrs. Doyle gave me a history lesson of Barrett Brewery—which I'll speak more about tomorrow, if it's important. She said that Mr. Mercer eloped with Mrs. Gavenston's youngest daughter ter Gretna Green."

Kendra nodded. She'd heard people gossip about Gretna Green. It was, she thought, the Las Vegas of her day.

"Mr. Mercer's family cut him off, but sounds like they don't have a feather ter fly with anyways."

"We met Mercer and his wife," Alec spoke up. "Mercer undoubtedly was attracted to the fortune she brought, but they appear to have genuine affection for each other."

"Mrs. Doyle is of the mind that Mr. Mercer is going through that fortune fast. Which brings me ter my conversation later with Mr. Logan. He said he quarreled with Mr. Pascoe, wantin' ter change the price he was getting for his grain, because his crops failed and prices rose after the cold weather. Mrs. Gavenston negotiated a price with him last year. He said Mr. Fletcher offered him more."

"Fletcher is trying to cut off Mrs. Gavenston's supply line," Kendra mused.

Sam nodded. "I think we can eliminate Mr. Logan from the list. He admits he had words with Mr. Pascoe, but he was going forward with the deal this year. Mrs. Gavenston will have more difficulty with him next year. But there wasn't no reason for him ter approach Mr. Pascoe ter talk further on it. He didn't even seem ter know that Mr. Pascoe was making use of the cottage on the squire's land." He took a swallow of whiskey. "And I don't see the farmer comin' here and shootin' at you, lass."

"Logan was never high on the list, and I agree with you on all counts." Kendra grabbed a linen rag and wet it with water from the jug on the side table.

"How does Mercer connect to the farmer?" asked Alec.

"'Cause Mr. Logan happened to see Mr. Mercer meeting with Mr. Fletcher."

"What?" Kendra paused in scrubbing down the slate board.

"Mr. Logan saw Mr. Mercer—"

"Yeah, I get that," she cut him off, frowning. "I spoke with Hester today. She said that Fletcher approached Pascoe about stealing Barrett Brewery recipes, but Pascoe refused."

The Duke looked at her. "You believe Mr. Fletcher approached Mr. Mercer to steal Barrett Brewery recipes?"

"I doubt if Fletcher would have stopped at Pascoe. And Mr. Mercer would have access," she pointed out with a shrug. "If he needed money and Fletcher offered it in exchange for a little corporate espionage . . ."

"They most likely have an allowance of some kind, maybe shares in the business," Sam said, "but it ain't always enough. And money has a way of tempting saints ter become sinners."

"Mercer didn't strike me as a saint to begin with," Kendra said drily. "He's charming and self-indulgent. How long ago did he marry Sabrina?"

"Two years," Sam supplied.

Alec stared at the tips of his shoes. "I've known plenty a lord who've laid waste to their fortunes in far less time. Mercer is a dandy. His coat and hessians were high quality. And those James Purdy weapons are very expensive. If he attends mills on a regular basis as he did at the Tip & Ship, he most likely is placing wagers."

"His wife isn't frugal, either," Kendra added. "She likes shopping and doesn't seem to be on a budget. You'd think that someone as astute as Mrs. Gavenston would know that her son-in-law has gone through her daughter's money."

"Maybe she does know," said the Duke. "'Tis not something you would want bandied about."

Alec met Kendra's eyes. "Tomorrow I shall see what I can find out about Mr. Mercer's financial situation."

"How will you do that?"

He gave her a lazy smile. "My club, of course. As the son of Lord Redgrave, Mr. Mercer's marriage and financial situation has undoubtedly been thoroughly dissected and discussed."

Kendra thought about Captain Sinclair's comment about how much business was conducted in gentleman's clubs. She nodded. "Anything you can find out would be helpful."

"Are we certain Mr. Fletcher approached Mr. Mercer about stealing Mrs. Gavenston's recipes?" the Duke asked. "Or did Mr. Logan misinterpret a meeting between Mr. Fletcher and Mr. Mercer?"

"Mr. Logan said that he saw them together once outside the Tip & Ship in a deep discussion—but he admitted that could've been nothin' more than the typical friendliness one finds in such places," Sam explained. "But he also spotted Mr. Mercer leaving Appleton Ale. Mr. Logan had driven up ter see Mr. Fletcher shortly after Fletcher had approached him about purchasing his harvest. He saw Mr. Mercer and asked about it. Fletcher said he must've been mistaken."

The Duke frowned. "If Mr. Pascoe found out about it, that might be a motive for murder."

Kendra jiggled the piece of slate again, mulling it over. "If Pascoe learned of Mercer's theft, he might have said something to Mercer. Mercer could have gone to the cottage to try to reason with him." She paused. "Or his wife could have done it."

Alec's eyebrows shot up. "You think *Mrs.* Mercer may have killed Mr. Pascoe?"

"Why not? And don't say because she's a woman," Kendra warned.

He shrugged. "She seems a foolish creature."

"We're not dealing with a criminal mastermind here."

That earned a crooked smile from Alec. "Even so, if she had stabbed Mr. Pascoe in a moment of passion, I'd think she would have been in hysterics afterward. She spoke to you of the latest fashions, for God's sake."

"I don't think one has to do with the other. People compartmentalize. Some people are really good at playacting . . ."

Another thought, unrelated to Pascoe's murder, crossed her mind, and Kendra frowned. She put it aside for the moment, then cleared her throat and continued, "If Sabrina knew that her husband stole the recipes for Fletcher and Pascoe found out, she could have gone to the cottage to reason with him. There is nothing that precludes her from being the murderer."

No one said anything, but Kendra sensed their skepticism. She shrugged. "She's low on the list, but we can't ignore her. I'm going to visit her dressmaker tomorrow in Cookham about her alibi. If the dressmaker confirms her whereabouts, we can cross her off. Molly confirmed from the other servants that both Mercer and his wife were at the manor pigeon shooting on Sunday, like they said."

"Good ter know, but Pascoe was most likely done in on Saturday," Sam commented.

"According to the servants, Hester spent both days in her bedroom, sick. But she could have sneaked out. White Pond Manor is big enough to do it without attracting attention, I think. Mrs. Gavenston was at the brewery on Saturday and at home on Sunday, although she went off riding. Again, she could have slipped out of the brewery or the manor with no one the wiser."

"Why would Hester kill Mr. Pascoe?" asked the Duke.

"I'm just going through alibis—or non-alibis. Sabrina might have the best alibi, if she was shopping Saturday. Plenty of witnesses."

Sam scratched the side of his nose. "What I can't figure is why Mr. Mercer would be so foolish as ter steal from Barrett Brewery. Even if he needed the blunt. Ain't that a little like biting the hand that feeds you?"

"Fletcher is going after Barrett Brewery," Kendra replied. "Maybe Mercer thinks he will eventually win."

There was a soft knock at the door and Harding stepped in. "Sir, the watch has finished their search," he told the Duke. "They found nothing."

The Duke sighed. "Thank you, Harding. You may retire."

Harding hesitated, then bowed slightly. "Very good, sir." As he withdrew, he glanced at Kendra. She had no trouble deciphering that look. He blamed her for this latest craziness. Before she'd arrived, they'd never had drawing room windows shot out in the middle of the night.

You—and your damnable determination to associate with the criminal element—nearly killed my brother.

Sam took that as a signal, drained the last swallow of his whiskey, and pushed himself to his feet. "I'll take my leave."

"Just a minute, Mr. Kelly," Kendra said, then stopped abruptly. A day ago, she would never have been reticent about saying something in front of the Duke. But the relationship between the Duke and Carlotta had changed. And, by extension, her relationship with the Duke had changed.

"Lass?" Sam gave her a quizzical look when she remained silent.

Kendra cleared her throat. The Duke and Alec's eyes were on her. She could feel her face grow hot, the moment becoming more uncomfortable. "Ah, actually . . . why don't I walk you out, Mr. Kelly?"

The Duke wasn't fooled by her awkward attempt at 19th century manners. "Is there something you don't wish me to know?" he asked, his tone mild.

"No. Of course not." She went quiet for a moment, then blew out a breath, impatient with herself. "Look, it occurred to me that Mr. Kelly's men will be running around Spain trying to check out Carlotta's story, which could be bogus." *Is more than likely bogus.*

"Bogus?" Alec lifted an inquiring eyebrow.

"Fake," she explained. "Anyway, I wondered if there was a way to get out ahead of it. A shortcut of some kind." She paused, then said pointedly, "If Carlotta is an imposter, she's a very good imposter."

The Duke said nothing. Sam and Alec seemed like they were waiting for her to wow them with her insight.

"It makes me wonder if she's done this before," she went on. "Or . . . or there's another possibility. She knows how to play a part. In fact, I'd say she's excellent in that regard."

Alec was the first to understand. "You think she's an actress?"

Kendra had seen the woman's face pale at her comment about her acting skills. She chose her words carefully, keenly aware of the Duke's solemn regard. "I think it's a possibility. I think that in addition to knocking on doors checking out the story she gave us, Mr. Kelly's men should go to theaters, show the sketches Rebecca drew of her—"

The Duke interrupted, "Sketches?"

"I thought it would be more helpful if Rebecca made a couple of sketches of Carlotta for them to show around as opposed to only giving her description."

"I see. I suppose that would be more helpful," the Duke said, not smiling.

Sam shifted uneasily and glanced between the Duke and Kendra. There was no denying the crackling tension that had sprung up between them.

"Aye, well, I'd best be leavin'. But that's good thinking, lass. I'll send a message ter me men first thing."

"I'll see you tomorrow morning?"

"Aye."

"I'll show you out, Mr. Kelly," said the Duke. He smiled a little crookedly as he rose to his feet. "I have no hidden agenda behind my offer. I think everything that needed to be discussed has been discussed openly."

Kendra bit her lip. He'd never rebuked her like this before Carlotta.

The Duke paused at the door, his expression stern as he gazed at his nephew. "As it's late, Alec, I think you should give Mr. Kelly a ride to his home, on your way to yours."

Alec didn't bat an eyelash. "Certainly," he agreed, pushing himself to his feet. "I shall be with you both momentarily."

For a long moment, the Duke and Alec eyed each other.

"We'll be waiting," his uncle finally said. He looked at Kendra. "Good evening, my dear."

Kendra mumbled a response.

The Duke didn't shut the door to allow them any privacy, but Alec crossed the room anyway and swept her up into a long kiss that left her breathless after he eased back. His green eyes were intense as he searched her face. "I don't like this," he muttered. "Someone tried to kill you tonight, Kendra."

"But they didn't."

"The danger may have passed for tonight." He brushed a stray tendril of hair from her face.

There was nothing to say to that. She couldn't reassure him that there would be no more danger, because whoever had fired the shot was still out there. Instead, she raised herself up on the balls of her feet to kiss him.

"Good night, Alec," she said softly. "His Grace is waiting."

"You'll be going to bed?"

"Absolutely."

"Then I shall see you tomorrow morning."

"Technically, it's already tomorrow morning."

He smiled a little at that and pressed a surprisingly chaste kiss on her forehead before he dropped his arms. His gaze, when he looked into her eyes, was too perceptive. "You mustn't worry about my uncle, you know. He wants to find out the truth about Carlotta as much as anyone."

"Does he?" Kendra wondered quietly, her breath hitching only slightly before she managed to even it out. "Because I think he wants her to be his daughter."

"Wanting Carlotta to be Charlotte doesn't mean he will turn a blind eye to the truth."

"Maybe." She thought of what Lady Atwood had said the other night and repeated, "He might hate the messenger who tells him the truth."

Alec took her chin in his hand, tilting it so he could gaze into her eyes. "He will never hate you, Kendra. Don't torment yourself in this way. He holds you in the highest regard."

Kendra swallowed against the hot lump that had risen in her throat. "Maybe before. But everything is changing. *He* is changing."

"Is he? Or are you? From where I'm standing, you are the one who hasn't included him in the investigation into Carlotta."

"Maybe you need to move to another spot," she retorted with some asperity. But was he right? The Duke had made the decision to take Carlotta with him to the Royal Society and around town instead of attending the inquest or talking to her about the investigation, but she hadn't asked for his help either.

"Think about it, love." Alec kissed her again, a light, feathery touch, then headed for the door. When he reached it, he turned back, offering her a slight bow. "Good night, Miss Donovan. Stay away from the windows."

Twenty minutes later, Kendra crawled into bed with the pages of foolscap that she'd taken from the cottage. In the flickering light from the single candle on the nightstand and the flames that crackled in the fireplace, she tried to make sense of Pascoe's writings. His penmanship was surprisingly good, so it wasn't hard to read the words. But much of the scribblings were disjointed thoughts, just ideas and themes, many of which had to do with stars in the night sky. Hardly a new concept. Heavenly bodies had fired the imagination of writers throughout history. John Keats's famous sonnet, "Bright Star," which wouldn't be published for another couple of years, had always been one of her favorites.

She scanned the pages, which had many stanzas crossed over almost violently. A few sentences remained, almost untouched.

I spend my days dreaming of the night
For the Star that has bewitched me
To chase away my darkness with thy light

She didn't know what she'd hoped to find. Notes on what was going on in Pascoe's life, like pages in a diary? Clearly, Pascoe's interest in poetry didn't have anything to do with his murder. The only thing it did was give her insight into his state of mind at the time of his death—and even that was an assumption. The angry crossing out of words and torn foolscap could have been done at any time, really, not just the day of his murder.

Exhaustion blurred the words on the page. She forced herself to continue to read for another ten minutes, but there were no hidden messages, no names written in the margins. She gathered up the foolscap into a neat stack and put it on the nightstand before blowing out the candle.

Sleep didn't come easily. Even though she was physically drained, her mind continued to race. The shooting had surprised her. Not that you could ever anticipate something like that, but it would make more sense if she actually felt like she was getting somewhere on Pascoe's murder. Sure, she had plenty of theories, speculation . . . and a nagging sense that she was missing something vital. But nothing to deserve someone panicking and taking a shot at her.

At least she didn't think so.

With a groan, she rolled over and burrowed into the pillows. Maybe the shooting would help. She couldn't imagine Mrs. Gavenston or her daughters pulling the trigger. Or was she being sexist? How ironic would that be? But it was difficult to envision any of the women traveling to London, waiting in the cold and the dark, on the off chance that they'd spot her—or someone who they thought was her—in the window and shoot.

So who *would* do such a thing?

Albion Miller came to mind. He struck her as the kind of slimeball who'd enjoy waiting in the dark and shooting somebody in the back.

Captain Sinclair was another possibility, given his military background.

Oddly, despite Fletcher's violent history, Kendra had a harder time imagining the brewer waiting for the opportunity to shoot at her. Same with Mercer. A vision rose up in her mind of him shooting at pigeons, but she just couldn't see Mercer putting himself through the discomfort of the cold or having the patience to wait to pull the trigger.

Of course, there was another possibility. Any one of them could have paid someone to do it. But why? Who thought she knew more than she did? Who was panicking?

The problem with panic was that it was an emotional response, not a logical one. Anyone could give in to panic. She thought of her own reaction to Carlotta's growing closeness to the Duke—and his affection for her. If that wasn't panic, she didn't know what was. She knew she was messing things up, but she didn't know how to stop it.

Carlotta's words came back to her: *You and I are the same, Miss Donovan.* The woman was right. Against all odds, incredible odds, Kendra had found a home within the Duke's household. It wasn't always easy. It wasn't always comfortable. But it was a haven. How would she have survived without the Duke's generosity?

Her last thought before sleep finally overtook her was that she'd once had a home . . . well, if not a home, then a house with two parents. She knew how quickly it could change, that all she could do was stand by and watch it all slip away.

27

The next morning, Molly took one look at the shadows beneath Kendra's eyes as she determinedly went through her yoga routine, then pivoted and marched out the door again. She returned ten minutes later carrying a tray with—God bless her—a pot of coffee, a sugar bowl, and a cup. Kendra calculated she'd need the entire pot to feel human again, although yoga helped push a lot of the fuzziness from her brain. She drank her first cup—almost in one swallow—as Molly selected a walking dress of pale peach. A frill of lace edged the neckline and cuffs of the long sleeves. Delicate open embroidery decorated the hem.

Kendra took her time with the second cup of coffee, enjoying the aroma as well as the punch of caffeine as it flooded her system, while Molly brushed and pinned up her hair.

She was on her fourth cup by the time she finished dressing and made her way to the drawing room to inspect the damage from the previous night. She wasn't entirely surprised to find Harding inside with one of the workers from the Yarborough residence. He was measuring the window.

Harding glanced at her as she entered the room. "Miss Donovan, may I be of assistance?" he inquired, his tone carefully composed.

"I just came to . . ." She trailed off and waved her hand in a vague gesture, encompassing the scene. Her eyes traveled from the window to the bookcase. Like the rest of the mansion, the ceilings were extraordinarily high here—at least fourteen feet—and the bookcase ran floor to ceiling. Setting her coffee cup down on a table, Kendra dragged one of the chairs over to the bookcase. It weighed a ton.

"What in heaven's name are you doing?" Harding demanded in alarm, starting forward. Kendra wasn't sure if he was going to wrestle the chair away from her, but in the end, he helped her. Probably to avoid drag marks across the wooden floor.

"Thanks," she huffed, a little winded by the time they had the chair in position. As Harding and the worker stared at her in bewilderment, she clambered on top of the seat and raised herself to the tip of her toes. She still fell short of where she saw the bullet had burrowed into the bookcases' crown molding.

"I don't suppose you have a rod or a stick about so big?" She made a small O shape to indicate the diameter with her thumb and forefinger.

The worker scratched his head. "I could probably find one next door."

Harding asked, "Why?"

"I just need . . ." She gave another vague gesture. But how could she explain bullet trajectory reconstruction? It wasn't even her field of expertise. She'd always relied on real experts, who used lasers. Not an option here. Still, she might be able to ballpark it.

Harding shook his head, obviously bewildered. But he told the worker, "Go down to the kitchens. Ask for Mrs. Danbury. She should be able to provide you with a dowel."

"Aye, sir."

The man hurried from the room. Kendra considered jumping down, feeling awkward standing on the chair, but she'd just have to climb back up again when the worker came back. She was aware of Harding's gaze on her. The silence pooled.

She shifted on the chair and finally shrugged. "I might be able to figure out where the shooter was standing last night," she finally told the butler.

"And why would that matter, if I may ask? It doesn't change what happened."

"Details always matter."

Harding looked skeptical. A footman came to the door and gave Kendra a sideways look, but then turned to the butler.

"Mr. Kelly is at the door for Miss Donovan." Another sideways look. "Where shall I put him?"

Kendra said, "Bring him here."

The footman waited for Harding to nod and agree, "Yes, bring him here."

Five minutes later, the Bow Street Runner entered, then stopped when he saw Kendra standing on the chair. "Have you seen a mouse?"

Kendra stared at him blankly.

"In my experience, women jump on chairs when they see mice."

"I'll keep that in mind. Actually, I'm trying to conduct an experiment. Ah, good."

The worker came back, carrying a wooden dowel about a yard long. He handed it to her and then stood back to watch, avid curiosity on his face.

"Do you need help, lass?" Sam asked as she raised herself up on her toes again and attempted to shove the tip of the dowel into the hole.

Sam wasn't that much taller than she was. But Harding had maybe two more inches on the Bow Street Runner. She lowered her arms and looked at the butler. "Mr. Harding, you could actually be of assistance. Would you please try to stick this rod in that bullet hole?"

He seemed to think it over. Whether he didn't want to say no to the Duke's ward or he was honestly intrigued, he agreed. He waited for her to jump off the chair before taking her place with as much dignity as he could muster.

Kendra surveyed him as he stretched up. "Don't force the rod in; follow path that was made by the bullet."

He fiddled a bit; the rod wobbled. Finally, the dowel steadied. Kendra studied it and then shifted her gaze to follow the trajectory to which the tip of the rod pointed.

She crossed the room to the broken window. Outside, the sky was a solid whitish gray. The noise from the Yarborough construction zone drifted through the empty window frame. It was still early enough that the only people outside were servants—mostly milkmaids, kitchen maids, and laundresses, all carrying buckets and hemp bags.

"What are you looking for?" the worker asked, joining her and Sam at the window.

Kendra glanced back again at the direction the rod was pointing. "Based on the trajectory, I think the bullet struck here." She pointed at a spot where the window had been. "If you follow the angle, the shooter was probably standing right there at the edge of the park, near that elm tree."

"Suppose that makes sense," Sam said, scanning the trees and bushes. "Easy enough for the fiend ter hide in the shadows and wait for his chance."

Kendra replied, "I don't think the shooter last night intended to kill me—or Carlotta, thinking she's me."

Sam's eyebrows shot up. "Why do you say that, lass?"

"Look at the trajectory." Again, she made a motion with her finger from the window back to where Harding held the dowel. "It's too high. I'd have to be at least eleven feet tall for him to hit me. So, either he missed on purpose or he's the worst shot in England."

Sam scratched the side of his nose. "Aye, I reckon you've got a point. But what does it matter? Obviously, someone doesn't like you sniffing around. They might not be afraid of what you know now—but they're worried what your gonna find out."

Kendra frowned, still feeling like she was missing something. It didn't make sense. But, as she'd thought last night, paranoia was an emotional response. The killer could be getting paranoid for no reason.

Kendra realized the worker was listening. She told Sam, "We should go to the study."

"Miss? Are my services no longer required?" Harding asked, still holding the rod from his position on top of the chair.

She grinned. "Yes, thank you, Harding. Your service was invaluable."

"Very good, miss." He eyed the floor uncertainly, then looked across at her. "Do you wish breakfast to be sent to the study?"

"Ah. Yes, thank you. I'm expecting Lady Rebecca, Mr. Muldoon, and Lord Sutcliffe as well." She suppressed a smile and, because she didn't want to cause Harding any more embarrassment, she picked up her coffee cup and moved to the door.

"How long do you reckon he'll be up on that chair?" Sam whispered as he followed her down the hall to the study.

Kendra laughed. "It's going to be another black mark against me, I'm afraid."

"It was clever of you ter think of that with the dowel."

Kendra felt the curious probe of the Bow Street Runner's gaze, but shrugged. "It proves that the shot went high. Even if it was a warning or meant to frighten me, rather than kill me, we're no closer to knowing who's behind it."

Sam said nothing for a moment. "Did you manage ter get a good night's sleep?" he finally asked when they walked into the study.

"Yes," Kendra lied, and even as she said it, she knew that Sam would recognize it as a lie. It was hard to conceal the shadows under her eyes. "Can you go to the Tip & Ship today to see about verifying Mercer's alibi for Saturday?"

He nodded. "I sent another man ter Spain with the note about checking theaters."

"Good. Maybe it won't pan out—" Another slang term, this one not to be coined until the days of America's Gold Rush. "I don't know if it will turn out to be useful, but it's a lead."

"I also wanted ter tell you that one of me men returned this mornin' from Aldridge Castle and the village."

That perked Kendra up even more than her coffee. "What did he find out?"

"No one remembers any strangers comin' around and askin' about the Duke's family."

"But that only means that no one wants to admit that they might have been gossiping about the Duke and his family."

"Who has been gossiping about my family?"

Kendra glanced at the Duke as he strolled into the room. Some of the awkwardness that she'd felt the night before returned. She exchanged a quick look with Sam.

The Bow Street Runner said, "Me man returned from Aldridge Village. He says that no one's been around quizzing folks about your daughter or family."

"No one has *admitted* to gossiping about your family," Kendra emphasized. "They could be covering."

"True. However, they could mention a stranger in the village asking questions without implicating themselves as gossipmongers," the Duke pointed out.

"Yes, but human nature is to lie," Kendra said.

The Duke eyed her. "You have a very dim view of humanity, my dear."

She wondered if that was an observation or a criticism. "I'm rarely disappointed."

"I would remind you that no one from the village knew about my daughter's ritual of tapping three times."

"Not that you know."

"Not that I know," he agreed.

The door opened, and two maids came in bearing trays with an array of silver domes and pots of tea and coffee, as well as a pitcher of ale. The room fell silent as they put out the dishes, curtsied, and left.

"'Tis true that anyone in the household could have passed the knowledge on," the Duke continued quietly, moving to the sideboard, where he lifted one of the silver domes to inspect the scrambled eggs beneath. "Many of the castle's servants come from the village. I suppose at the time they may have discussed it with their families. Nanny MacTavish was concerned about the night terrors. She may have confided in someone."

"Where is the nanny?" Kendra asked.

"She was a good woman—completely devoted to Charlotte," the Duke said. He picked up a serving spoon and dished eggs onto a plate, then followed that with baked beans, stewed tomatoes, and plump sausages. "She was as heartbroken as I was when she was lost at sea. I gave her a character reference and enough money to return to her native Scotland. A village called Shandwick in the Highlands, if my memory serves."

A smile flickered on his face, then disappeared. "However, she said she liked the warmer temps in the South. She found a position in Sussex, as a nanny to Lord and Lady Thorpe's three children." He looked at Kendra and Sam, his eyes sharp. "I can assure you, Nanny MacTavish was not the sort of woman to spread tales, especially not about the idiosyncrasies of a child she once adored. Of that I am certain."

He sat down at the table, picked up his knife and fork, and concluded, "Nanny MacTavish died a long time ago. At least fifteen years. Consumption, I believe. Lady Thorpe told me when we met at a ball several years ago."

Kendra frowned as she refilled her coffee cup.

"You are chasing shadows from the past, my dear," said the Duke. He cut into his sausage, spearing half with his fork. "Why would anyone in the village be gossiping about Charlotte now?"

Kendra said, "They wouldn't. Not without prodding."

"Aye, but someone would have noticed an outsider was snooping around, making conversation about a child who'd been lost at sea twenty years ago," said Sam as he filled up his plate.

He was right, Kendra decided. Secrecy was not easy in a small village like Aldridge. The villagers were friendly enough, but outsiders were noticed. Even without telephones or the Internet, everyone in the village would have known everything by nightfall.

"There are only four possible ways that Carlotta could have come by her knowledge," the Duke said. "One, my household and two, the villagers. Mr. Kelly has just eliminated the possibility that it was my household or the villagers. Then there is my family. Caro has assured me that she has spoken to no one—then or now. I have written to my other two sisters. I have yet to receive a reply."

He fell silent as he picked up his tea, took a long sip.

Sam frowned. "And the fourth possibility?"

Kendra knew what was behind door number four, but let him say it.

"That Carlotta really is Charlotte," he returned softly.

Kendra still felt that a few careful inquiries—so careful that the mark wouldn't even know he was being pumped—could have elicited the necessary information. The name of Charlotte's doll, for instance. A question, or an educated guess. It was a Queen Anne doll, for Christ's sake. You didn't have to be a rocket scientist to figure out that a little girl might have named her Queen Anne doll Annie. And Arabella's scent would have been easy enough to find out, or another educated guess. Lavender was a popular perfume. If Carlotta hadn't been correct, then she would have fallen back on the fact that she had been a young child at the time. Her memories were vague or faulty.

As for the child's superstitious tapping, though Kendra knew that the information could have made its way into the general public, who would be talking about it now? How had Carlotta found that out?

She became aware that the Duke was staring at her, waiting for her to reply. She roused herself to murmur, "There might be another possibility that hasn't occurred to us yet."

The Duke raised his eyebrows in inquiry. "Such as?"

"I'll let you know when it comes to me."

By the time Rebecca and Muldoon came in, flushed with the cold and laughing, the Duke had already finished his breakfast and left. Kendra was a little surprised at the baleful way Sam glared at the reporter. She reminded him, "I invited Mr. Muldoon."

Sam grunted, still glowering at the younger man. "As long as he doesn't forget his place."

Overhearing, Muldoon's jaw tightened and his eyes flashed with sudden temper. "I'm not forgetting anything."

Kendra decided to ignore their hostility. Friction between law enforcement and the Fourth Estate wasn't anything new for her. She waited until they filled their plates and sat down at the table before she informed them about the previous evening's shooting.

"Dear heavens," Rebecca breathed, her eyes wide. "Are you are all right?"

"I'm fine. The shooter didn't mean to kill me. It was meant as a warning."

"How can you be so certain?"

"That's what I would like to know," Alec drawled from the doorway. He'd obviously been out riding. He wore his bottle-green riding jacket over dark brown vest and doeskin breeches tucked into gleaming black

Hessians. As he came into the room, he tugged off his gloves, his gaze on Kendra.

"The trajectory of the bullet was too high," she replied. "We either have a blind shooter or someone who deliberately missed."

Muldoon asked, "Did Mrs. Garcia Desoto offer a description of the gunman?"

"She says she didn't see anything. It was too dark. She only saw the motion when he raised the gun and pushed His Grace to the floor," Kendra said.

"Well, thank heaven for her quick reflexes, but it still must have been frightening," Rebecca remarked.

Muldoon chewed his food thoughtfully. "You haven't eliminated a woman from being the fiend who killed Mr. Pascoe, but I cannot imagine our fairer sex doing such a thing. Not because they cannot shoot," he added hastily, even though Rebecca didn't seem ready to argue the point with him. He hesitated, apparently not certain how to go on. He finally shrugged, finishing lamely, "It just doesn't seem right."

"I understand what you mean," Kendra admitted, since he was echoing her thoughts from the previous night. "But nothing precludes anyone from hiring someone to take the shot."

"In other words, no one can be eliminated from the list of suspects," said Muldoon.

"Yes and no. I met Fletcher after the inquest."

Muldoon raised an eyebrow. "And do you think God made a mistake putting feet on that creature, because it'd be more natural for him to be slithering about on his belly?"

She had to smile. "Descriptive. I agree that he's a snake. That doesn't mean he's a murderer—at least not of Pascoe," she added when he opened his mouth to contradict her. "He says he was at Appleton Ale on both Saturday and Sunday, and if we need to confirm it, he has plenty of witnesses."

Muldoon snorted. "And if they don't confirm his story, they'll be looking for new employment or be found floating facedown in the Thames."

"I didn't say his alibi was good. But it needs to be checked out."

He grinned. "I'll give it a go."

"This man sounds dangerous," Rebecca said, frowning. "Are you certain it's safe?"

Muldoon's grin widened as he glanced at her. "Can't be any more dangerous than sniffing around Parliament."

Sam mumbled something under his breath.

"However, I have a problem with Fletcher being behind the attack last night," Kendra said, standing to refill her coffee cup. "I don't see him bothering with a warning. I think he would shoot to kill—or give that order."

Muldoon agreed reluctantly. "I can't deny that."

"I'm not so certain," Alec said. "Killing the ward of a duke—or a duke himself—is serious business. You're not some chit selling flowers on the street corner, Miss Donovan. The crown would have every magistrate, thief-taker, and constable in London hunting for the shooter. Would Mr. Fletcher want to draw this sort of attention to himself?"

"Probably not, but there's another reason he drops down the list. Hester said that he tried to bribe Pascoe into stealing recipes from Barrett Brewery—"

"Seems to me a fine motive for murder," Muldoon interrupted, bewildered.

"Except it looks as though he found someone else," Kendra told him, taking a sip of her coffee. "Given that, I don't know why he would bother with Pascoe."

"Who did he find?" Rebecca asked.

"Mrs. Gavenston's son-in-law, Mr. Mercer—possibly. They were seen together." She looked at Alec. "Maybe you'll be able to get more information about Mercer and his family's financial situation at your club today."

His eyes narrowed. "Someone tried to kill you—"

"No. Someone sent a warning."

"I'm not leaving you alone."

She frowned at him. The last thing she wanted was Alec to act as her shield. Her blood ran cold to think of anything happening to him.

"I'm not going to be alone," she said. "Mr. Kelly is going with me. Besides, my plan is to visit a dressmaker. I doubt if anything is going to happen there, except I may accidentally step on a needle."

Alec didn't look convinced.

She continued, "If Mercer's alibi holds up, we can eliminate him. Same goes for his wife." She glanced at the names she'd written on the slate board. If they were lucky, they could start crossing off more than Mr. Logan by nightfall. "Captain Sinclair wouldn't tell me where he was on Saturday, but said he attended a cricket match in Windsor on Sunday with Sir William Lloyd."

"The Harlequins and Lewes." Muldoon nodded. "After I'm finished with Appleton Ale, I shall see what I can find out there." He looked at Sam. "Did you tell Miss Donovan about Mr. Shaw?"

"Pascoe's former employer?" Kendra asked, as Sam shook his head.

Muldoon turned toward Kendra. "I spoke to him at the inquest. He told me that Mrs. Gavenston is one of his bank's largest depositors."

"Why is Mrs. Gavenston using a bank in Maidenhead rather than Cookham?" Rebecca wondered.

But that wasn't the most interesting thing, Kendra thought. "Mrs. Pascoe mentioned that Mrs. Gavenston offered Pascoe his job. I assumed she'd put an ad in the newspaper, and he applied for it. Mrs. Gavenston must have known Pascoe before he came to work for her, but she never mentioned it."

"You make it sound like she was trying to hide something," said Rebecca. "It might have not occurred to her. What could that have to do with Mr. Pascoe's murder, anyway?"

Kendra said nothing, but this was another instance of Mrs. Gavenston being less than forthcoming, and that bothered her.

"Mrs. Doyle had the idea that Mrs. Gavenston might have an ulterior motive for hiring Mr. Pascoe," said Sam.

Alec looked at the Bow Street Runner. "What would that be, pray tell?"

"She was hoping ter make a match between him and her daughter, Hester. Mr. Pascoe was a greenhorn in the beer trade, which would give her the opportunity ter groom him—according ter Mrs. Doyle."

"Mrs. Gavenston is not considering changing her family's tradition of allowing the first-born female to inherit, is she?" Rebecca sounded alarmed.

"Nay, I don't think so," Sam assured her. "Mrs. Doyle was of the mind that Mrs. Gavenston needed a cove on her side as a countermeasure against her uncle."

"I'll bet Mrs. Gavenston is good at playing chess," Kendra murmured. She tapped her coffee cup with her index finger, thinking. "Is it just gossip that Mrs. Gavenston wanted a match between Hester and Pascoe?"

"As far as I can tell, it's conjecture. Mrs. Doyle said that Mrs. Gavenston may have learned pretty manners when her ma sent her off ter a fancy finishin' school as a young lass, but she's got a ruthless streak in her—no disrespect," Sam added, obviously not wanting to slander the brewster and annoy Rebecca. "Mrs. Doyle said that if Mrs. Gavenston thought it would be advantageous to Barrett Brewery to encourage a match between her daughter and Mr. Pascoe, she'd be doin' it. But it ain't as though folks don't get leg-shackled for business reasons every day."

"Almack's would close down otherwise," Alec drawled with a lazy smile. "It's called the Marriage Mart for a reason."

Rebecca said stiffly, "There's a difference between forcing your daughter into an unwanted marriage, Sutcliffe, and encouraging a match that you believe would be beneficial. I do not see Mrs. Gavenston bullying her daughter into an undesirable arrangement."

Kendra recognized the defensive tilt to Rebecca's chin. Clearly, she was having a difficult time thinking that a woman she admired might have feet of clay.

"Well, whatever might be going on between Hester and Pascoe, I think Hester cared for him," Kendra said finally. The desolation swimming in Hester's eyes when they'd informed her of Pascoe's death hadn't seemed fake. Of course, it didn't let her off the hook. As Kendra had told them, a great many people ended up dead at the hand of someone who professed to care for them.

"Mrs. Gavenston might have wanted Pascoe around for another reason," she said carefully.

"What's that, lass?" Sam asked.

"She might have been the one who was interested in Pascoe." She wasn't surprised by the stunned silence that followed. It was controversial, but only because, as she'd thought earlier, Mrs. Gavenston was the older one in the match.

Muldoon was the first to speak. *"Romantically?"*

She eyed him with some amusement. "Mrs. Gavenston isn't that old. I asked her, but she denied that they were having an affair."

Sam choked on the swallow of ale he'd just taken. *"God's teeth*! You actually asked her if she and Mr. Pascoe . . ." He stared at her. Everyone was staring at her.

"It needed to be asked."

Alec laughed. "And how did she respond?"

"She denied it and appeared horrified by the idea."

Muldoon gazed at her. "You don't believe her?"

"I don't know. She's hiding something. Maybe she was just trying to push Hester and Pascoe together." Kendra drank her coffee, pacing. "The timing works," she finally said. "Her uncle returned to England from India shortly before she hired Pascoe. Captain Sinclair hasn't exactly been subtle in his desire to take more control of the brewery. He says suppliers and export agents want to deal with a man rather than a woman—"

"Which is outrageously unfair!" interjected Rebecca, eyes flashing.

"It is, but Mrs. Gavenston doesn't strike me as an idealist. I think she's a realist. She's not going to waste her time fighting that kind of prejudice. So, instead she makes a strategic move by bringing Pascoe in as the brewery's manager to act as her liaison."

Muldoon cocked his head. "But she already had a business manager who was a man."

"Mr. Carter was old, so he was probably going to retire anyway. She had to prepare for that eventuality. It makes sense, her knowing Pascoe. She wouldn't bring in a man she didn't know. Pascoe was perfect. By all accounts, he was good with numbers, and at the same time, he was a poet. A dreamer. His mother said that he sometimes had his head in the clouds. I don't think Mrs. Gavenston would have been worried about him. He wouldn't be a threat to her."

Sam whistled softly. "Mrs. Doyle is right. Put like that, Mrs. Gavenston does seem ter be a bit ruthless."

"A realist," Kendra corrected. "Barrett Brewery is her legacy. She has every right to fight for it. Captain Sinclair was the one who implied that Mrs. Gavenston and Pascoe were involved, but he's not exactly an objective witness."

She thought of Albion Miller. He'd also implied that Mrs. Gavenston had done something improper, something that would shock her daughters and bring scandal to her family. Nothing beat sex when it came to scandalous behavior. And Albion was a shifty son of a bitch. He followed people, watched them from afar. Had he seen Pascoe and Mrs. Gavenston together in a compromising position?

Or was he leveraging something that happened years ago? It sounded like Mrs. Gavenston and his brother, Robby, would have married if Robby hadn't died suddenly. If they had had an *indiscretion*—that was the euphemism of the day, if she wasn't mistaken—could Mrs. Gavenston's reputation still be tarnished all these years later?

Kendra didn't have to think about that one too long—yes, women were held to a standard that was never imposed on men, who were encouraged to sow their wild oats before they married. If Mrs. Gavenston and her beau hadn't waited for wedlock, society would be outraged at her lapse and the shame would follow her to the end of her days. Her disgrace would spill over and contaminate her family and Barrett Brewery.

"How does any of this relate ter Mr. Pascoe's murder?" Sam asked, bringing Kendra's attention back to the present. "Unless it was a lover's quarrel?"

That would actually fit the crime scene. Domestic disputes that started in the kitchen had a higher percentage of becoming deadly for the very reason Pascoe ended up dead—that's where the knives were. It was too easy to grab a weapon in the heat of anger, too easy to lash out.

"Maybe," Kendra said. A spidery sensation tripped down her spine. *I'm missing something*, she thought again. All the pieces to the puzzle weren't there. Or they were all there, but jumbled up.

She glanced at the clock. "I need to go to Cookham. Dressmakers in small towns might have as much gossip as tavern owners."

Rebecca laughed. "I think you are right. In fact, I have a fitting at my own modiste this afternoon." She pushed herself to her feet. "I shall see you at the Merriweather ball tonight?"

"I don't think I can get out of it," Kendra admitted.

Sam drained the rest of his ale and thrust himself to his feet. "We should go then. The quicker we get ter Cookham, the quicker we'll get back."

Alec grasped Kendra's arm to detain her as everyone filed out the door. "I'm going to speak with Coachman Benjamin to make certain he and his grooms are prepared for any misadventures on the road to Cookham. Whoever was behind the shooting last night might decide to advance his agenda beyond a warning."

28

The village modiste, Mrs. Browne, was easy enough to find, since there was only one dressmaker on High Street. Probably only one dressmaker in Cookham, period. The shop itself was a narrow redbrick Georgian sandwiched between a tobacco shop and haberdashery. It was two stories and boasted a large bow window on the ground floor, where two evening gowns were displayed on headless mannequins made out of wicker.

A bell chimed when Kendra and Molly entered the shop. The interior was cluttered with bolts of fabric on shelves, leaning against the walls, and stacked on the end of a long table. There was another, smaller table, the surface covered with fashion plates and magazines, with four spindly-looking wicker chairs arranged around it. A dozen dolls stared back at them from two shelves, which Kendra thought was weird until she realized that they were simply miniature mannequins, dressed in the latest styles. The air smelled of something spicy, exotic and uniquely feminine.

"Good afternoon, ladies!" greeted a woman as she sailed through a curtained doorway. She looked to be in her mid-forties, with her light brown hair covered by a tiny frill of French lace. She wore a fashionable embroidered, high-waisted, pearl-gray muslin with a colorfully patterned cashmere shawl wrapped elegantly around her shoulders to ward off the room's chill.

The modiste's gaze dismissed Molly as of no importance and fixed on Kendra. "I am Mrs. Browne. How may I assist you?"

"Kendra Donovan, and my maid, Molly."

Mrs. Browne's eyebrows rose a little. Servants were to be treated like pieces of furniture—useful, but generally ignored. Kendra knew the rules; she just didn't always follow them.

Mrs. Browne asked, "Is there anything specific you are looking for, Miss Donovan? Or is it Mrs. . . . ?"

"Miss. Actually, Mrs. Mercer recommended you," Kendra lied. "She said that she was here on Saturday afternoon, and you showed her fashion plates from Paris."

"Yes, Miss Sabrina—Mrs. Mercer—is one of my best customers, as are her sister and her mother. Horatia—Mrs. Gavenston—and I have known each other since we were in leading strings." she said. Kendra loved this kind of chatty, guileless manner when she was conducting interviews. The dressmaker gestured to the table with the wicker chairs. "Please, won't you have a seat. Would you like tea? Or coffee? I can tell by your accent that you are American."

"Thank you, tea would be fine." Kendra smiled at Mrs. Browne as she and Molly sat.

"Let me put on the teakettle." Mrs. Browne disappeared through the curtain.

Kendra tugged off her gloves and set them aside. "You said that you and Mrs. Gavenston are friends," she said when Mrs. Browne reappeared again.

"I don't know if I would be so bold as to say we are friends—not now," she demurred, sitting down at the table. "We are still friendly, but it's not like when we were young misses." She leaned back with a sigh. "'Tis difficult to believe how many years have passed since we were so young and gay. The time has simply flown!"

A modern lament, Kendra thought, that apparently wasn't so modern. Once again it brought home to her the biggest difference between the early 19th century and the twenty-first was technology, not humanity.

She asked, "How well do you know Albion Miller? I heard that he grew up with Mrs. Gavenston as well."

Mrs. Browne wrinkled her nose like she'd just smelled something rotten. "A ne'er-do-well, if there ever was one! I simply cannot fathom it. He comes from good family. Common stock, but still *good*. His sister, Beth, and I were friends. In fact, it was through Beth that I formed a connection with Horatia. She was part of our little group for a time because of Robby."

"Robby?" Kendra feigned ignorance.

"Oh. Yes. Robby Miller—Beth's older brother. Oh, my, he was a handsome devil. Such beautiful blue eyes. If I hadn't already set my cap for Mr. Browne, I know I would have been quite smitten."

"How old were you?"

"Fourteen." She laughed at the memory. "I suppose you can't imagine an old woman like me being so foolishly in love? My daughters are around that age now. They think that their father and I do not understand what they feel when they flutter their lashes at a boy—and when he looks back."

What Kendra couldn't imagine was falling in love with a boy at that age, marrying him, and still being married to that same boy decades later. At fourteen, she'd been terrified after her parents walked away. Romance had been the absolute last thing on her mind.

The shriek of the teakettle's whistle pierced the air. Mrs. Brown stood up. "Pardon me." She disappeared through the curtains.

She bustled back into the room a moment later, carrying a tea service. "We'll let it steep a bit, shall we?" Kendra watched her unload the tray. "It was quite tragic, really," she sighed as she sat.

"What happened?" Kendra asked, although she didn't think she needed to prod Mrs. Browne to keep her talking. She was happy enough to gossip about old times.

It wasn't that difficult to get someone to talk about ancient history, especially when a tragic event had happened. That sort of thing became embedded in people's minds. If someone passing through Aldridge

Village mentioned losing a child at sea, it would be entirely natural for a villager to remember the Duke losing Charlotte. And plenty of information could be mined from that one comment. She was sure that Mrs. Browne didn't even realize how much information she was supplying to a virtual stranger.

"Robby left Cookham to apprentice for his father's uncle," Mrs. Browne explained. "A silversmith, I believe. I think Horatia was happy for him, but it was difficult too. Young love is like that, isn't it? It's so very vexing to be parted. You think the world is at end, don't you?"

Kendra made the appropriate noise of agreement.

The modiste frowned. "Of course, for Horatia and Robby, it turned out to be true. We received word that Robby had taken ill. Cholera. Such a shock. It made no sense how he could have been affected. He wasn't living in one of those dreadful slums where you breathe in all those vapors that can contaminate the lungs."

Kendra pressed her lips together to stop herself from explaining that cholera was actually contracted from contaminated food and water and could be easily be passed along by an infected person handling food—not by breathing in vapors.

Mrs. Browne picked up the small cream pitcher and poured a thimbleful into her teacup. "Naturally, Horatia traveled to London to see him. It's been almost thirty years, but I remember the poor dear when she returned. He'd died, of course." She passed the cream pitcher to Kendra and lifted the teapot. "Horatia was devastated. Simply devastated. Beth tried to offer Horatia comfort—even though she was devastated herself. So did I. But she sank into this ghastly melancholy."

Mrs. Browne *tsk*ed as she poured tea into all the cups. "She was pale and hollow-eyed. We thought the poor dear would simply waste away. Mrs. Dyer—her mother—finally put a stop to it by sending her off to a finishing school for young ladies."

"It wasn't to teach her pretty manners?" Kendra asked, remembering what Sam had said.

"Heavens, no!" The modiste laughed. "Horatia had quite nice manners already. She certainly didn't need to be sent away to learn to behave properly." She shook her head and took a quick swallow of tea before setting down the delicate cup on its saucer. "No, Mrs. Dyer wanted to break the horrible spell of melancholy that Horatia found herself under."

"It must have worked," Kendra said cautiously.

"It took a while. Even when she returned to the village, she was so sad, really. She drifted away from our little group. I suppose without Robby, she didn't see the point in continuing the association. And it must have been painful for her, to see Beth with her young man and me with Daniel." She let out a heavy sigh and shook her head. "Oh, she was friendly enough at the local assemblies and White Pond Manor's ball, but the poor creature always seemed to be staring off into the distance with such sorrow. Remembering dear Robby."

"How terrible," Kendra murmured, sipping her tea.

Mrs. Browne nodded. "Of course, Horatia had been involved in the brewery since she was a babe in her mother's arms, but she quite threw herself into work after that. Everyone needs to heal at their own pace, I suppose. Several years later, Mr. Gavenston came to the village. Big, strapping young man. He began to pay court to Horatia and the next thing we knew, they married. Goodness," she said, blinking with surprise. "How did I ever get on such a topic?"

"Albion Miller," Kendra reminded her.

"Oh, yes! He was a horrid boy and is a horrid man. A sneak. Even when Beth and I were little girls, he'd follow us and threaten to tattle if he caught us in some mischief. Not that there were many times we were in mischief, mind you." She shot Kendra a cheeky grin. "Still, if we didn't supply him with some treat or do what he demanded, he'd threaten to tell. Born bad, that's what he was. Mr. Miller should have taken a switch to Albion's backside. I think Robby threatened to wallop him a few times, but . . ." She shrugged helplessly.

She lifted her teacup again and studied Kendra over the rim. "Why do you ask about Albion?"

"I was wondering how connected he was to Mr. Pascoe?"

Mrs. Browne looked at her in surprise. "What a strange question! I don't know if there is any connection, except living in the same village. And they both are connected to Horatia—Mrs. Gavenston," she corrected herself belatedly. "I can't imagine that Mr. Pascoe was even acquainted with Albion."

Kendra tried instead, "How well do you know Captain Sinclair?"

"Captain Sinclair? Not at all. I was a babe when he left Cookham. I was reintroduced to him at White Pond Manor's Michaelmas ball. He attended only one assembly, and I seem to recall that he spent his time in the card room, not on the dance floor." She leaned forward and lowered her voice even though there was no one else was in the shop. "Everyone knows that he's been trying to get his hands on Barrett Brewery. Shoddy behavior, if you ask me. The women of that family have spent their lives making a go of it. Mrs. Dyer is the one who began selling her ale and stout to the rest of England and Scotland, and Horatia was the one who thought to expand to foreign markets."

"So, people here are unhappy with Captain Sinclair trying to take control of the brewery?"

The modiste let out a heavy sigh. "Unfortunately, there are plenty of villagers who share Captain Sinclair's belief that a female shouldn't be running a business that size. Horatia is wily, but I'm afraid she may eventually be forced to give up some control or lose it altogether. There are simply some things that are impossible to fight against."

Kendra lifted her teacup as she considered that. It dovetailed with the idea that Mrs. Gavenston might have sought out Pascoe because she thought she could control him more easily. Maybe it was a ruthless move, but Kendra wasn't unsympathetic. The woman was surrounded by vipers who by fair means or foul were working against her.

Sex was often used to control. Had Mrs. Gavenston's ruthlessness extended to that? Had she deliberately engaged in an affair with Pascoe to control him more readily? Or, had she tried to control the winds of fate by pushing him toward her daughter, Hester?

"When Mrs. Gavenston came into your shop, did she mention any of what was going on at the brewery?" she finally asked.

Mrs. Browne shook her head. "Horatia is not one to share confidences. We gossip a bit about what's going on in the village while she has her fittings or selects new gowns, but nothing more. Certainly nothing about the brewery business."

"What about Mrs. Mercer or Miss Gavenston? Do they talk about Barrett Brewery when they come in?"

She laughed. "Mrs. Mercer—no. She's only interested in fashion and is quite headstrong about her opinions on the matter. Thankfully, she has an unerring eye and knows what suits her. Miss Gavenston, on the other hand, needs a bit of guidance. She has become more interested in fashion in the last year, but nothing like her sister. If Mrs. Mercer didn't have her annual stipend from Barrett Brewery, I would worry that she would set herself up as my competition."

"And Mrs. Mercer *was* in here on Saturday afternoon?"

"Oh, yes. Didn't I mention that? We went over the fashion plates I received from Paris. She selected two gowns but wanted different trimmings than what I have available in my shop. I've ordered them."

"What time did she leave?"

"Half past five. I believe she wanted to go to the millinery next." Mrs. Browne's eyes had begun to narrow, as though it had just occurred to her the direction the questions were taking.

Kendra returned to the earlier topic. "And Hester—Miss Gavenston—never mentioned the troubles at Barrett Brewery with Captain Sinclair or Mr. Pascoe?"

Mrs. Browne hesitated, but then shrugged. "I don't recall her speaking of any troubles. She appeared to quite admire Mr. Pascoe, though. Did you know that he was something of a poet?"

"Miss Gavenston told you that?"

"Yes. She appeared to be taken with the notion. But what young lady isn't intrigued by a gentleman who can spin together a flowery phrase or two? Look at that Lord Byron. More tea?"

"Thank you." Kendra waited until Mrs. Browne refilled all their cups before asking, "What did you think of Mr. Pascoe?"

"I only met him a handful of times at our assemblies, but I found him charming. He invited me to dance a few times when he noticed Mr. Browne was in the card room, just as he danced with Horatia. Not many young men would take note of us older ladies. But he was always attentive. I cannot imagine why anyone would harm him. And *murder . . .*" She shook her head, perplexed. "It's not something that happens here in Cookham. We're not like London, where fiends and cutthroats lurk behind every bush."

Mrs. Browne put down her teacup. "Now . . . shall we view the Parisian fashion plates?"

Apparently the gossip portion of the visit had concluded. Kendra lowered her teacup as well. "Actually, I have to go to a masquerade ball. Maybe you can help me with my costume?"

"I don't usually do costumes." But Mrs. Browne looked intrigued. "What are you thinking? I believe Mary, Queen of Scots is quite popular at fancy dress balls. Milkmaids, lady's maids, and Roman empresses as well."

"I was thinking more George Washington."

Mrs. Browne's eyes widened in shock.

Molly gasped, speaking up for the first time. "But, miss, 'e's a cove! Ye can't dress like a *cove*."

"I don't see why not. It's a costume ball."

"But ye'd be wearing *breeches*."

Which was sort of the point. Just for one night, she wanted to have the freedom of movement that she'd once had. Still, Washington might have been a poor choice. He'd died almost two decades earlier, but she didn't know how hostile the British might still be toward America's founding father.

"Gypsies are popular. And flower girls," Mrs. Browne said faintly.

"How about a coachman?" Kendra said, thinking of the dour Benjamin. She might even be able to tuck a blunderbuss in her belt.

"But ye'd still be dressing as a man," Molly fretted. "It ain't done, miss!"

"Well, it would certainly be adventurous, which is what fancy dress balls are all about, aren't they?" Mrs. Browne's shock had subsided. "I'm not a tailor, though. I do not know how to fashion a jacket . . . and you'd need a jacket, shirt, waistcoat, greatcoat, breeches, and cravat. I could shop these items for you. They'd have to be resized, considerably. I would need to take your measurements." A glimmer of excitement began to shine in the modiste's eyes. "You'll need boots, as well . . ."

Kendra smiled. She'd engaged personal shoppers in her own timeline. This was along those lines.

"Would you want me to supply the mask, as well?" Mrs. Browne asked.

"Sure."

"When will you need the costume?"

"The ball is Saturday night at Vauxhall."

The modiste paled a bit. "That is very soon."

"It is. Could you have everything delivered to Number 29 Grosvenor Square?"

Mrs. Browne's eyebrow's shot up at the address. "You live in Grosvenor Square?"

"It's the Duke of Aldridge's residence."

"You live with the *Duke of Aldridge*?"

"She's 'is ward," Molly said, then frowned at Kendra. "Lady Atwood ain't gonna like this, miss. Maybe ye should go ter her modiste in London ter get yer costume."

Maybe it was the thought of losing business to a London dressmaker or maybe it was the Duke of Aldridge's name, but Mrs. Browne's chin went up. "I'll do it." She stood. "If you will follow me to the back room, Miss Donovan. You'll need to take off your dress so I can take accurate measurements."

Kendra glanced at her reticule. Inside, she had the muff pistol and a few coins. "I don't have enough money with me—"

"You are the Duke of Aldridge's ward—your credit is good here," Mrs. Browne cut her off with a smile and a wave of her hand. "When I send you the clothes, I'll send the bill."

Kendra had never had a fitting in the middle of an investigation before, but if she had to go to a damn masquerade ball, then she'd get the costume of her choice. Once Mrs. Browne's work was done, Kendra walked to the millinery down the street. She'd all but crossed Sabrina off her list, but it still helped when she heard the shopkeeper's confirmation that the very fashionable Mrs. Mercer had indeed been in her establishment on Saturday afternoon and purchased one of her best creations.

Coachman Benjamin had dropped Kendra and Molly off at the dressmaker's shop before taking Sam to the Tip & Ship to verify Mercer's alibi. Without the convenience of cell phones, Kendra had been forced to calculate the time it would take her to conduct her interviews beforehand.

She'd suggested meeting at Barrett Brewery at four o'clock, which she figured would give her enough time to interview the shopkeepers, walk to the boys' school to speak to Pascoe's friend, Mr. Elwes, and fit in a quick lunch at the Green Knight, where she hoped to speak to Mrs. Doyle. What she hadn't factored in was her much lengthier conversation with Mrs. Browne and going through the process of having her measurements taken. Kendra recalculated her schedule and mentally scratched off the Green Knight.

"Are you hungry?" she asked Molly, her gaze on a sign outside a bakery shop.

"Oi'm feelin' a bit peckish," Molly allowed.

"Come on, then. I'll buy you lunch."

The yeasty aroma of baked goods hit Kendra the second that she opened the door to the small shop. She hadn't thought herself hungry until that moment, but her mouth began to water at the heavenly scent. A girl who looked about twelve but was probably older was behind the wood and glass counter. Kendra ordered two beef pasties.

"Can you tell me where the Cookham Grammar School is?" Kendra asked as the girl put the pasties on what looked like a flat iron shovel and slid them into a brick wood-fire oven.

"At the end of Bigfrith Lane."

"And that is where?"

The girl put her elbows on the counter. "When ye leave the shop, take a right, yeah? Walk ter the end of High Street, then take another right until ye come ter Cookham Road, yeah? Go left. Ye'll run into Bigfrith Lane, then go left. The lane's a bit higgledy-piggledy, but if ye stay on it, the school will be on yer left. Unless ye're blind, ye can't miss it."

"Thanks. How much?" Kendra asked, and fished out a couple of coins from her reticule to cover the price of the pasties. The girl removed the hot pasties and carefully wrapped them in scraps of muslin before handing them to Kendra. Pasties were like the fast food of the day, easily eaten on the run. Or, in her and Molly's case, while walking, since Cookham, unlike London, didn't have hackney drivers queued up, waiting for fares.

Outside, she gave one pasty to Molly and as they walked, she partially unwrapped hers and let it cool a little before taking a bite. Kendra set a brisk pace as they moved down the high street. It wasn't congested like London, but there were plenty of men around, loading and unloading wagons.

As a 21st century urbanite, Kendra had rarely been around live cattle. She'd seen a variety of farm animals in the distance, while driving through rural areas, but her closest relationship with a cow was the occasional steak or burger she ordered at a restaurant. When she'd first arrived in the 19th century, she'd been mildly shocked by the number of animals that were part of the daily life. Anyone who had studied history in school—or seen the cinematic version of the Wild West in movies and TV shows—knew it was true. But the photos, movies, and newsreels could never capture the reality of having horses and cattle on the streets, flies buzzing around the beasts as they lifted their tails to defecate while they lumbered along.

In London, an army of children were employed as streetsweepers to clean up the feces. Here in Cookham, either the streetsweepers had the day off or weren't doing a very good job.

Kendra had been bemused to see how many other animals roamed the streets and alleyways, in addition to cattle. By the time they turned onto Bigfrith Lane, she counted at least two pigs, seven chickens, five dogs—one with feathers haphazardly sticking in its fur, making Kendra think there might have been eight chickens at one point—and two cats on the loose.

The girl at the shop was right; it would be impossible to miss Cookham Grammar School, a large gray-stone, gothic-style structure centered on a swathe of green lawn. Because the Church of England was responsible for educating many lower- and middle-income children, Kendra wasn't entirely surprised to see that half of the structure was a church with an imposing façade and bell tower. The school was attached to the church, and thick ivy crawled nearly to the roof, only hacked back around the long, skinny windows so that light could get inside. It would save on oil for the lamps and candles.

"Seems a bit dour, don't it?" Molly whispered as they walked the path that led to the pair of heavy oak doors set in an archway.

"It's not the most cheerful atmosphere," Kendra agreed, pulling open the doors.

It was even less cheerful inside. The hallway was wide, with darkly paneled walls and a dull wood floor. The fan window above the door and the lit wall sconces did little to dispel the gloom. Most of the doors were shut, but a few were slightly ajar. Sounds drifted toward them: the low-timbered murmur of men's voices, the higher timbre from a child, the shuffle of papers, the squeak of chairs, the now familiar scratch of slate against slate board.

"W'ot'll we do now?" Molly asked, looking around nervously. "'Ow will we find Mr. Elwes?"

Kendra hadn't anticipated the anonymity of this hallway. There was probably an office for the principal—or headmaster—somewhere. Instead of searching, Kendra decided to take a shortcut and approached the first door that was slightly ajar.

"W'ot are ye doin', miss?" Molly whispered furiously behind her.

Kendra pushed the door open with her shoulder and gave a light rap against the frame with her gloved fist. She found herself in an old-fashioned classroom with about fifteen children—all boys, about eight years old. The schoolmaster stood in front of the slate board with a long pointer, holding a book. He was probably in his fifties, with a bald pate and muttonchop sideburns. He'd obviously been reading to the class but broke off at Kendra's entrance. All the boys perked up, swiveling to stare at her with unabashed interest. Kendra found the experience of being studied by fifteen pairs of eyes a little unnerving. And she'd sat across from serial killers.

"I'm sorry to interrupt." She summoned a smile for her audience. She looked at the schoolmaster. "I'm looking for Mr. Elwes. Perhaps you can help me?"

"Who are you?" demanded a sandy-haired boy with a pug nose and bold blue eyes. "Are you Mr. Elwes's wife?"

"'E ain't gotta wife," another boy muttered.

"Then maybe she's his beloved." The pug-nosed boy grinned, causing the other boys in the room to titter.

"Master James, that will be enough!" the schoolmaster said in a tone that suggested he'd had many dealings with Master James. He glared at the boy, then hurried toward Kendra. "We are in the middle of class, my good woman," he whispered.

"I realize that, and apologize for the interruption," she said again. From her vantage point, she could see James roll a piece of paper into a tube. He ripped off a corner, sticking the paper into his mouth to create a small wad. A few of the other boys made faces at each other while they wriggled in their seats.

"Mr. Elwes is also in class," he said disapprovingly.

"I understand, but if you could point out his classroom, I would appreciate it."

A boy howled when James beaned him with a spitball.

"Silence!" The schoolmaster turned to glare at his class. Then he pivoted back to glare at Kendra, clearly holding her responsible for him losing whatever tenuous control he had had over the students. "I shall escort you to Mr. Elwes. And you lot"—he tossed an ominous frown at the boys, most of whom were still squirming—"begin reading chapter seven. There shall be a quiz when I return!"

The kids groaned as Kendra followed the schoolmaster out the door. He stopped briefly when he spotted Molly. "Good heavens, we're being invaded," he said beneath his breath. He walked so briskly down the hall that the tails of his coat fluttered behind him. He stopped at a door across from a staircase. "Please stay here while I go in and speak to Mr. Elwes." He opened the door and slipped inside.

"'E's not very friendly-like," Molly muttered, frowning after him.

"Would you be in a good mood if you had Master James in your class?"

Molly grinned. "'E seems a bit of a devil."

The door opened again and the schoolmaster returned, followed by a young man with russet hair and an expression that was both baffled and curious. "You wish to speak to me?" He kept his voice low, closing the door firmly behind him.

Kendra wasn't sure if he closed the door to keep his class from overhearing them or the students from escaping.

Kendra offered her hand. He eyed it in surprise, but, after a moment, shook it. "Yes, I'm Miss Donovan. And this is Molly."

"You're an American."

The other man muttered something indecipherable under his breath. "I shall leave you, Mr. Elwes," he said aloud, scowling at Kendra and

Molly. "I advise you to be quick about . . . whatever this is. We must not have any disruptions."

"I understand. Thank you, Mr. Norton."

They watched the other man scuttle down the hall, and then he screeched when he yanked open the door to his classroom. "Master James! Get down this insta—" The rest of his sentence was cut off when he slammed shut the door.

Elwes gave Kendra an apologetic look. "We don't get many visitors, especially women. I only have a few minutes. What can I do for you?"

"I understand that you were friends with Mr. Pascoe. I need to ask you a few questions about him."

The schoolmaster's face seemed to lengthen in sorrow. "I am honored to have counted Mr. Pascoe among my friends. I confess I have been dreadfully shocked by his . . . by what happened. However, I don't know how I can help you, Miss Donovan. Constable Leech approached me the other day and I had nothing to tell him. I don't know what I can tell you."

"I would still appreciate it if you can make some time for me."

"I must return to my class." A smile ghosted around his lips. "I have a Master James as well. I shudder to think what Master Marcus may be conspiring to do behind this closed door." He paused. "I'll be finished in twenty minutes and then the boys are required to go to the church for prayers. If you wish to wait, I can speak with you then."

"We'll wait."

"I can meet you outside in the park. Unless it's too cold for you? It's shocking to think we're in the month of May."

"The park is fine," Kendra replied. "We'll see you in twenty minutes."

Kendra and Molly spent the time wandering around the stretch of greenery that rose behind the school. The landscape crested and then tumbled down toward dappled woods, thick with oak, ash, and alder trees. The breeze was cool enough to cut through Kendra's coat and carried the scent of the Thames, which made her think that the river was just on the other side of the forest. She imagined the boys inside the school released from their lessons and prayers, enjoying racing around this area.

Molly tried to use the time to dissuade her from dressing like a man for the masquerade ball. "'Oo's gonna want ter dance with ye, miss, with ye wearing breeches?" the maid demanded, twisting her hands.

Kendra grinned. "Another point in my favor."

"'Er ladyship is gonna fly up into the boughs, mark me words." Molly's tone was dire.

"So, what else is new? Lady Atwood is always upset with me."

"She may order ye ter stay 'ome."

"Let's hope."

Molly's face twisted in distress. "It ain't *natural*, miss."

Kendra rolled her eyes. "It's a costume party, not an audience with the pope."

That had Molly pursing her mouth in disapproval. Like most of Protestant England, the maid viewed the pope with a great deal of suspicion.

Kendra caught sight of Mr. Elwes striding toward them. He'd put on a wool overcoat and tricorn hat. Molly moved slightly away to give them privacy.

"Forgive me for keeping you waiting, Miss Donovan," he apologized as he approached.

"Thank you for meeting with me."

He sighed. "'Tis a difficult time for me. As I said, Mr. Pascoe's death was shocking. I miss him."

"You weren't at the inquest."

His mouth twisted and he shook his head. "No. I couldn't . . . I've been to inquests in the past and have found them to be raucous affairs. Mr. Pascoe would have hated to be . . . *displayed* in such an indecent manner."

Kendra couldn't argue with that. She asked, "Did you know Mr. Pascoe from Maidenhead?"

"No, I met him when he moved to Cookham. I noticed him at the tavern. He was reading Thomas Gray's 'Elegy Written in a Country Churchyard.' Do you know it?"

"I'm not familiar with it, sorry."

"It is one of my favorite poems. I approached him about it, and we began a conversation that turned into a friendship. I have tried my hand at writing a verse or two." He gave her a self-deprecating smile. "Mr. Pascoe was much more talented than I. In fact, I was encouraging him to send his works to a publisher."

Kendra remembered the heavy, almost violent editing marks that Pascoe had done on the pages she'd found in the cottage. "But Mr. Pascoe didn't feel himself good enough?"

"The curse of an artist, I'm afraid. He was plagued by self-doubt, despite my encouragement. I thought his recent attempt at an epic poem quite good. *My Star*—that was the title. Or at least it was the most *recent* title." Another smile flickered across his face. "He tended to quibble over that as well. I wonder if I ought to approach Mr. and Mrs. Pascoe to inquire if they would lend me his writings. I could send them to a publisher on their behalf, to possibly publish posthumously."

"That sounds like it would be a fitting tribute to your friend." She waited a beat. "Did Mr. Pascoe talk to you about his job at all? Or mention if he was dealing with any stress recently?"

"Nothing that would have gotten him killed."

"What about something that may have gotten him into an argument?"

Elwes's brow furrowed. "Well, that is different, isn't it? I know that Mr. Pascoe had a few disagreements with Mrs. Gavenston's uncle, Captain Sinclair. He was distressed over them."

"Captain Sinclair is trying to take over Barrett Brewery," Kendra said.

"Yes, but it was more than that. It was the insidious way he was going about it. Captain Sinclair approached Mr. Pascoe for his support and even threatened him if he chose to stand with Mrs. Gavenston."

"Mr. Pascoe—Senior . . . ah, the Elder," she managed. "He mentioned that Captain Sinclair had tried to intimidate his son."

"The captain warned Mr. Pascoe that he would win this war for control of Barrett Brewery and he would remember his disloyalty. He told him that he would have him sacked without references once he took over the brewery."

"Dramatic," Kendra said. "Was Mr. Pascoe worried?"

"I think so. He mentioned that he ought to look elsewhere for employment. I believe he approached his former employer about returning to his former position at the bank."

"Really? When?"

Elwes pursed his lips, remembering. "A few days before he died, I think. But that can't have anything to do with his murder, can it?"

"I don't know."

But it might have had something to do with the argument that Pascoe and Mrs. Gavenston had on the day he was killed. Mr. Shaw might have felt the need to warn Mrs. Gavenston of Pascoe's possible defection, hoping to ingratiate himself with one of the bank's largest depositors.

She asked, "Did Mr. Pascoe mention Mr. Fletcher to you? Or Mr. Mercer?"

"Mr. Fletcher is another sneaksby. Came right out and asked Mr. Pascoe to filch Barrett Brewery recipes for him! Bloody—oh, pardon me. The man is nothing more than a pirate. Mr. Pascoe was quite rightly appalled when he told me the tale."

"Did he and Mr. Fletcher argue over it?"

"I don't know if it was so much an argument as Mr. Pascoe telling him that he would never do such a thing, and would report him to Mrs. Gavenston."

"Mrs. Gavenston or *Miss* Gavenston?" Kendra asked. Hester had known about the bribe, not her mother.

Elwes frowned. "Mrs. Gavenston—or so I thought. I know he worked quite closely with Miss Gavenston, though. So perhaps he meant her. I don't know. Does it matter?"

"I don't think so. But what about Mr. Mercer?"

"He thought he was a bit of a dandy, if you must know." Elwes smiled slightly. "Mr. Mercer played up being the viscount's son, even though his family appears to have disowned him for marrying beneath him. *And* we had heard the chap didn't have a feather to fly with before his marriage." That was said with quiet satisfaction. "Mr. Pascoe had a closer association with the man than I because he often dined at White Pond Manor. I was introduced to Mr. Mercer at a village assembly and have seen him occasionally around the village. I believe that he tends to travel to London for his amusements."

"Did Mr. Pascoe mention Mr. Mercer's association with Mr. Fletcher?" she asked carefully.

He looked surprised but it wasn't for the reason she thought. "How did you find out?"

"So, Mr. Pascoe *did* know about the association?"

"A local farmer—Mr. Logan—told him that Mr. Fletcher was offering him more money if he sold his harvest to him rather than Mrs. Gavenston, as he had promised. Mr. Pascoe had words with him about it, and then went to London to speak with Mr. Fletcher at Appleton Ale. While he was there, he saw Mr. Mercer. Or at least he believed it was Mr. Mercer. Mr. Pascoe confessed to me that he only saw him at a distance. When he hailed him, the man hurried away, and got into a hackney before Mr. Pascoe could come upon him."

"Did Mr. Pascoe speak to Mr. Mercer later about it?"

"Mr. Mercer denied it."

"But Mr. Pascoe didn't believe him?"

"No. But he could hardly call Mr. Mercer a liar to his face, could he? Especially when he only observed the man from afar. Still, Mr. Pascoe told me that he would be keeping an eye on him."

The low gong of church bells sounded. Elwes glanced back at the school, then let out a sigh. "I'm afraid I must go, Miss Donovan. My class will be back from prayers shortly."

"One more question. Did Mr. Pascoe say anything about Albion Miller?"

Elwes frowned. "No. I don't recall him doing so, anyway."

"Thank you, Mr. Elwes. And I'm sorry for your loss."

He smiled sadly. "I appreciate that, Miss Donovan. Mr. Pascoe and I had much in common. Our interest in literature and poetry. And, of course, our unfortunate beginnings. I fear I shan't find another friend like Mr. Pascoe."

"Unfortunate beginnings?"

Elwes had begun turning, but paused, looking back at her. "Yes, we were both foundlings. We shared many of the same interests, and I confess that there were occasions when I wondered if perhaps . . . but it is of no matter."

Kendra looked at the schoolmaster in surprise. "You're saying Mr. Pascoe was adopted by the Pascoes?"

"You didn't know? It wasn't a secret, but I suppose it isn't something one speaks about either. I only know because I had mentioned my own situation to Mr. Pascoe, and he confided to me that he was from similar circumstances, except he'd been fortunate. The Pascoes took him in when he was not yet five days old.

"I confess that I was envious of Mr. Pascoe," Elwes continued. "I spent my childhood at a foundling home. Thankfully, it was run by a reverend and his wife who were academic minded—and I was interested in academics." A wry smile pulled up the corners of his mouth as he looked at Kendra. "Not many of the children in the Home wanted to learn to read or write, you know."

Kendra said nothing, her mind racing to add this new information to what she already knew. She felt like she'd been painting with the primary colors and now a tiny drop of yellow had bled into the blue and red. Only a small difference, really, but it changed the entire picture.

"I met Mr. and Mrs. Pascoe once when they came to Cookham," Elwes said softly. "They'd accompanied Mr. Pascoe to dinner at the tavern. You must have met them?"

"Yes."

"They're lovely people, aren't they? That was when I felt a bit covetous. I am embarrassed to admit that I wondered how fate could have been so generous to my friend and so miserly to me. And yet look at us now." His eyes darkened and he was quiet for a moment. Then he let out a heavy sigh and shook his head. "Mayhap the Bard said it best. 'Death, a necessary end, will come when it will come.'"

"Did Mr. Pascoe know anything about his biological parents?" Kendra asked.

Elwes looked surprised at the question. "How could he? Mrs. Pascoe told him that he'd been a gift from God when someone put him on her doorstep in the middle of the night."

"God will uplift," she murmured softly, and shrugged when Elwes raised his eyebrows at her. "Mrs. Pascoe told me that's what Jeremy means—'God will uplift.' She's got a thing for searching out the etymology of names."

"Ah."

It occurred to Kendra that she had no idea how adoption was done in this era. "Were Mr. and Mrs. Pascoe trying to adopt a child before? How would a young woman know to put her child on their doorstep?"

Elwes looked baffled by the question. "I have no idea. In truth, Mr. Pascoe and I never discussed it beyond us confiding in each other the circumstances of our births. It was a point of interest between us, nothing more. As I said, I thought him most fortunate. My own mother dropped me off in a church, with no parents on hand to take me into the warm bosom of their family." He looked at Kendra. "Why are you asking me about something that happened so long ago, Miss Donovan? What does Mr. Pascoe's birth have to do with his death? There can be no possible connection."

"You'll have to forgive me, Mr. Elwes. I have a tendency to ask a lot of questions about a lot of random things. It helps me understand the victim. Of course, many times the questions and answers lead to nowhere in particular." She shivered slightly as the wind picked up and drew her collar closer to her throat. "Thank you for your time, Mr. Elwes. You've been very helpful."

He shook his head, still bewildered. "I don't see how, but . . . I must go. I will not have a classroom if I tarry any longer. Good day, Miss Donovan."

Kendra watched Elwes hurry across the lawn. He disappeared a moment later through the school's door.

Many times random questions and answers didn't lead anywhere.

And yet there were times, she thought, when they did.

29

It took almost twenty-five minutes to walk to Barrett Brewery, and Kendra spent the time mulling over the idea that had come to her. It could change everything, but did it have anything to do with Pascoe's murder?

She spotted the Duke's carriage as she and Molly approached the brewery. Coachman Benjamin and two grooms loitered next to the vehicle. She scanned the area for the Bow Street Runner and saw him in the open bay doors, chatting with the same two coopers that she and Alec had talked to the other day. Sam noticed her and quickly excused himself to meet her.

Kendra waited until he was near enough to ask in a low voice, "Did you find out anything at the Tip & Ship?"

There was the normal bustle of activity, with deliveries coming and going, the clang of steel from the area that the coopers were in. No one was close enough to overhear their conversation, but she caught a few curious looks tossed in their direction.

"The proprietor—a Mr. Davis—remembered Mr. Mercer comin' ter the mill. Made a big show of putting down his wager. According ter Mr. Davis, that ain't unusual, though the cove never has any blunt in his purse. Tends ter write vowels—IOUs," he added for Kendra's benefit. "Mr. Davis said that Mr. Mercer lost. Didn't see him around for a while after the mill. Thought maybe he'd run off. But then he came up ter Mr. Davis near ten o'clock and paid him in cash."

Kendra frowned. "Mr. Mercer said that he went to the match early, around two. The match didn't start until four. How long did it last?"

"Boxing mills don't last more than an hour. There were two mills that day. So, I reckon they were finished by six, no later than seven."

"But it took Mr. Mercer almost three more hours to find Mr. Davis and pay his wager."

"I thought it peculiar too. Mr. Davis thought he went somewhere ter get the money."

"So he broke his usual pattern of giving an IOU." Kendra shook her head. "Something's not adding up. Did Mr. Davis see him the entire time?"

"He couldn't swear ter it. Nor could anyone else who worked there. It wasn't like they were keeping their peepers on him the entire time."

In the 21st century, they could ping cell phones and tap into a car's GPS to find out where Mercer had gone.

"In other words, he could have left and come back," Kendra said, her gaze traveling to the stable boy combing down a horse near one of the stalls, then to the Duke's carriage with the coachman and grooms. "How'd Mercer get there? Did you speak to the stable hands on whether he left for any period of time and then came back later?"

Sam grinned at her. "Do you know that some of me lads on Bow Street wouldn't have thought of that?"

"But you did." It wasn't a question.

"Aye. Spoke ter the Tip & Ship's grooms. Mr. Mercer rode horseback. The problem is the lads in the stables are just as interested in boxing as anyone else. They couldn't say when Mr. Mercer left, but both mills were over by the time he came back."

"He didn't happen to mention why he'd left?"

"Nay, and they're not gonna ask one of their betters what he was doin'."

"It looks like we can scratch his wife off the suspect list, but not her husband."

"You confirmed Mrs. Mercer was shopping, then?"

"Yes. I also learned a few other things. I need to speak to Mrs. Gavenston." She hesitated. "Alone."

While Molly seemed fine with that, scooting back into the carriage, Sam raised his eyebrows, waiting for an explanation.

Kendra released a sigh. "I may have learned something . . . actually, it's pure speculation at this point. I need to talk to Mrs. Gavenston about it. It's sensitive. I can't say anything more. Can you please wait for me here?"

"All right, lass."

Kendra could feel Sam's curious gaze follow her as she crossed the courtyard.

Inside, the brewster's clerk, Mr. West, was at his desk. He looked much better than the last time she saw him. When she told him that, he looked both pleased and flustered.

"I need to speak with Mrs. Gavenston. Is she here?" she asked.

"Just a moment." He stood up and disappeared down the hall. Less than a minute later, he was back. "Mrs. Gavenston will see you. If you will follow me . . ."

She followed the clerk to Mrs. Gavenston's office where he knocked briskly on the door before opening it. He stepped back so Kendra could pass through, then departed, closing the door quietly behind him.

Mrs. Gavenston stood behind her desk, her gaze wary. There was no smile of greeting today. Kendra could only imagine how Mrs. Gavenston would behave toward her after this conversation. For a fleeting moment, she felt a pang of regret. Like Rebecca, she admired the woman. But she couldn't let that influence her. The truth was the only thing that mattered in a murder investigation.

"Miss Donovan, good afternoon," Mrs. Gavenston said. "What can I help you with? Have you learned anything new?"

"Yes, as a matter of fact, I think I have," Kendra said slowly. "And you can help me by being completely honest."

Mrs. Gavenston stiffened. "Are you implying that I have not been honest with you?"

"I'm pretty sure you haven't been honest about a great many things." She kept her gaze fixed on the other woman. "You weren't honest about what you and Mr. Pascoe argued about on Saturday. It wasn't about you bringing in new machinery. I think you argued about something much more personal."

"I don't know wh—"

"Mr. Pascoe just had a birthday," Kendra talked over the other woman. "Maybe that was the trigger. Did you tell Mr. Pascoe that you had given him away twenty-nine years ago?"

Mrs. Gavenston's mouth parted and her face paled as she stared at Kendra in utter shock. In the silence, the heavy tick of the clock on the shelf and the sizzle of the coal fire in the hearth seemed acutely loud.

"I don't know what you are saying, Miss Donovan," Mrs. Gavenston finally said, her voice coming out low and harsh. "You must be mad. That is all I can think for you to throw around these slanderous accusations. I must insist that you leave. And I do not want you to return. My God, I wish I had never asked you to help me!" She raised her voice so the last words were a shout. "Get out!"

"I'm sorry," Kendra said, and meant it. "I don't mean to upset you—"

Mrs. Gavenston scoffed. "We are done here, Miss Donovan."

"Not quite." Kendra moved forward and sat down in one of the visitor's chairs uninvited, which earned a gasp of outrage from the brewster. "It doesn't work like that, you know. Mr. Pascoe was murdered, and I intend to find who killed him. To do that, I need the truth. The *entire* truth, Mrs. Gavenston." She paused, allowing the other woman a moment to digest that. "Don't you want to know what happened to your . . . to Jeremy?"

Mrs. Gavenston swallowed. "I'd like you to leave." But she sank down in her chair, her eyes locked on Kendra.

"Let's try it this way, shall we? Let me tell you a story. It's actually a very old story—a young girl and boy meet . . . or maybe they'd always known each other. But one day, they looked at each other a little differently. It happens. Maybe it was springtime." She smiled a little as she embellished the story. "They began to spend more time together. They fell in love. And they *did* love each other. They planned to marry. Maybe not then—they were both very young, after all. But eventually."

She waited. But Mrs. Gavenston said nothing, gazing into the fire and wearing an indecipherable expression.

After a moment, Kendra continued softly, "The boy wanted to be worthy of this girl before he could ask for her hand in marriage, so he went off to London to apprentice to become a silversmith. Unfortunately, while he was in London, he fell gravely ill and died. I'm certain the girl's heart was broken. She grieved for her lost love. Then she realized something else. She realized she was going to have his baby."

Mrs. Gavenston's lips trembled and she pressed them together into a tight seam.

"It must have been a horrible time for this young girl. What was she? Fifteen? Sixteen?" She paused to allow comment, but when none was forthcoming, she continued, "When her mother realized her secret, she came up with a solution. She would tell everyone that she was sending her daughter to a finishing school. The girl would have to give up the child, of course."

Let's see if she would be happy to have to have her reputation in tatters, Albion Miller had said. This was an era when unmarried girls could be ruined forever if their indiscretion was ever known.

"That must have been painful for this girl," Kendra said. "She lost the boy that she loved, and then she was forced to give up her son.

"I'm not sure how the girl found out about this couple who wanted to have a child," she said slowly. "But instead of leaving her baby at a home for foundlings, she made sure he went to a good home, with loving parents. It was a maternal act, I think. She left him there, but she kept an eye on him. Even when she grew older and married and had two more children that she would never have to give away. I wonder, did she move her money to the bank where her son found employment, or did she move her money there and get the manager to hire her son?"

Mrs. Gavenston said nothing, but Kendra thought she saw the other woman's eyelashes flicker slightly.

"These details are probably easy enough to find out," said Kendra. "The story doesn't end there, of course. Years later, this woman was given an opportunity to really have a relationship with her son when she was able to hire him herself. She invited him to dine with the family, which was not always understood. She probably looked at him with an affection . . . a love that might have been misconstrued."

Kendra studied Mrs. Gavenston's averted face. "How am I doing?"

There was no response, so she nodded and said, "I'll go on, shall I? The woman's son had a birthday. It probably brought up a lot of memories, good and bad. Maybe it motivated her to tell him the truth. Or maybe it was a spur of the moment decision? I suppose *why* she told him the truth doesn't matter compared to what happened afterward."

Kendra lowered her voice and said softly, "He was angry, wasn't he? She must have been devastated. She probably thought—had *hoped*—that he would be happy to learn the truth after all these years. At least she thought he'd be a little understanding. But he wasn't understanding at all, and they argued until he stormed off."

Kendra fell silent. There was a chance that Mrs. Gavenston had followed Pascoe to the cottage to try to reason with him. She could still be Pascoe's murderer. The fact that she was his mother changed very little.

Mrs. Gavenston sat very still. The silence seemed to throb between them. Finally, she drew in a deep breath. "You have a very active imagination, Miss Donovan." She looked at Kendra directly. Her hazel eyes were like chips of stone. "If you dare share this . . . this *fiction* with anyone, I shall speak to my attorney. Do I make myself perfectly clear?"

"So, you're denying it?"

"If you are implying that I had a child out of wedlock and that child . . . that child was Jeremy Pascoe, I categorically deny it. And even if . . ." Her breath hitched, and she was forced to clear her throat. "Even if this was not some twisted Banbury Tale—*which it is*—I don't know what it could have to do with Jeremy's murder."

"It could have everything to do with Mr. Pascoe's murder," Kendra argued. "You and your uncle are in the middle of a power struggle—"

Mrs. Gavenston made a derisive sound.

"—where he believes he has the upper hand because he's a man," Kendra went on. "What do you think he would do if he found out that you had a son who could be in line to inherit Barrett Brewery?" she asked, dropping all pretense.

"*If* I had a son matters naught," Mrs. Gavenston shot back. "Barrett Brewery has always been passed down the female line. Hester will be taking over. Besides, you said that no one targeted Jeremy. Why would my uncle try to harm him?"

"What I said before still stands. Captain Sinclair could have found out your connection to Mr. Pascoe. He could have approached him at the cottage. Maybe he tried to buy him off. Mr. Pascoe was already upset from what happened with you . . ." She let her words trail off. The picture was clear.

Mrs. Gavenston flinched, then shook her head. "No. I won't hear any more of this. It's not true. None of this is true." She thrust herself to her feet. She was trembling. "I want you to leave now, Miss Donovan. I have no desire to speak of this again. I have no desire to speak to you again. You are no longer welcome here."

Kendra heard the implacable note in the other woman's voice and slowly rose. She only hoped that once Mrs. Gavenston had time to think it over, she'd feel differently. "You have a choice, Mrs. Gavenston. You can try to help me find your son's murderer, or you can protect Barrett Brewery from scandal. You won't be able to do both."

In answer, Mrs. Gavenston turned away to stare out the window. After a moment, Kendra left the office.

Once Sam, Kendra, and Molly were back in the carriage returning to London, Kendra filled him in on her conversation with Mrs. Gavenston.

"God's teeth," Sam said at the end of the story, staring at Kendra in astonishment.

His body swayed gently with the motion of the vehicle, the wheels traveling over the macadam. Molly stayed silent, but was wide-eyed. Sam wasn't sure what shocked him more, the story itself or the fact that the American had dared to ask Mrs. Gavenston about it.

"Do you reckon it's true?" he asked.

"She denied it, but yes. I think it's true."

"If folks knew she had a bastard, they'd stop buying Barrett ale and stout." Bloody unfair, if you asked Sam, especially given that many of the men who drank Barrett no doubt had a few by-blows running about themselves.

"That's why we need to be careful with this information."

Sam scratched his nose. "'Tis scandalous, for certain. But what does it have ter do with Mr. Pascoe's murder . . . unless Mrs. Gavenston is the one who killed him?"

"However the topic of Pascoe's parentage came up, it's a strong motive for her to approach him again to reason with him. Only something happened. The argument escalated and Mrs. Gavenston snapped."

Sam could envision the scene. "If he was angry enough, he might've threatened ter tell everyone. Mrs. Gavenston has worked all her life for Barrett Brewery. I can see her flying off the handle if she thought he'd put it at risk."

"And be filled with remorse afterward." Kendra nodded. "But it opens up other possibilities as well. Captain Sinclair might be able to fight Pascoe as the brewery's manager, but if Pascoe had a blood tie to the family . . . Would Pascoe's illegitimacy change things, though? Maybe Captain Sinclair wouldn't view him as a threat because of it."

"Nay. It ain't as though he'd be inheriting a title or an estate that was entailed. Nothing stopping him from legally takin' over if Mrs. Gavenston wished it."

"So, both Captain Sinclair and Mr. Mercer might have approached Pascoe at the cottage if they found out the truth. Mrs. Gavenston said that nobody knew—then she insisted there was nothing to know, since it wasn't true."

Sam looked out the window. Clouds were knitting together on the horizon, teasing the possibility of rain. "Why would Mr. Mercer care if Mr. Pascoe turned out to be Mrs. Gavenston's by-blow? He's not angling for a position in the company."

"Maybe he wouldn't. Maybe this has nothing to do with Pascoe's death, but it adds a new element. It bumps Hester up on the list. We know Mrs. Gavenston is under a lot of pressure to change the tradition of passing the brewery down the female line. If Hester found out that Pascoe was her half-brother, she might have felt threatened enough to at least confront him about it."

"Wasn't she in her sickbed?"

"She has a cold—she still can walk. White Pond Manor isn't that far from the cottage, really. She could have snuck out."

Sam frowned. "How'd she know he was there? She wasn't at the brewery that day when her ma and Mr. Pascoe argued. She wouldn't have known that he'd left. *If* she even knew about the cottage in the first place."

"I don't know," Kendra confessed, looking increasingly frustrated. "Something's not adding up. There's still a missing piece to the puzzle."

"Sometimes when something's nagging at the back of me brain, I need ter let it rest a bit. Go ter your ball tonight, lass. Chances are, it'll come ter you."

"On the middle of the dance floor?" Her mouth twisted with both amusement and irritation.

He grinned at her. "If you're thinking about Pascoe's murder in the middle of the dance floor, lass, then you're not dancing with the right man."

She gave a reluctant laugh. "I'd rather skip the ball . . . but Lady Atwood terrifies me."

Sam laughed as well. He didn't believe that for a minute—the lass had more courage than anyone he knew—but her annoyance at having to attend the fancy soiree was genuine. Not many women . . . nay, *no* woman he knew would prefer to spend an evening puzzling over a brutal crime rather than dressing in a beautiful gown, dancing all evening. He thought about what Muldoon said the other day, and, while he'd never admit it to the reporter, he had to agree with him. Kendra Donovan *was* a strange creature. But strange in a good way.

30

L ady Merriweather, a tall, thin octogenarian draped heavily in beaded purple silk, her hair covered by a towering turban of matching fabric, wore the pleased, slightly smug expression of a matron who knew her ball was a success. The measuring stick of success, of course, was having most of the Ton pressed together with almost indecent intimacy—known as a crush—inside the fashionable Hanover Square mansion.

The ballroom was a showpiece. Its high ceilings glittered with moldings slathered in gilt. Three crystal chandeliers were ablaze with candles. The walls were covered in crimson velvet damask and decorated with enormous gilt-framed mirrors and paintings. If Kendra wasn't mistaken, the largest portrait in the room, that of a young, fresh-faced beauty, was Lady Merriweather herself, painted at least half a century earlier.

The room was large enough to fit a full orchestra, now playing a quadrille. Doors opened to another room that had been set up for refreshments, although liveried footmen were circulating with cut crystal glasses filled with lemonade and wine on silver trays. There was also a cardroom for non-dancers and withdrawing rooms for ladies to fan their flushed cheeks or take a respite from an overaggressive suitor. Thankfully, Lady Merriweather had the foresight to open the French doors, which led out onto a large verandah overlooking the shadowy gardens. Even though the night air was cold, it was a welcome draft in a ballroom overheated with so many bodies.

It had taken Kendra, the Duke, Alec, Lady Atwood, and Carlotta fifteen minutes to go through the receiving line and find this spot near the French doors.

"How delightful," Carlotta remarked, her dark eyes lit with almost childlike wonder as she stared at the beautifully dressed throngs. She looked at the Duke and Lady Atwood. "Thank you for allowing me to come with you."

"I would not think to deprive myself of your company," the Duke offered gallantly. "You are in excellent looks this evening, my dear. As are all you ladies," he added with a hasty smile at his sister and Kendra. "Sutcliffe and I are fortunate men to be in your company."

Alec gave one of his lazy smiles. "Indeed."

"This lovely gown deserves the credit, not I," Carlotta demurred, lifting her hand to touch the simple strand of pearls around her throat. "And the loan of the necklace."

Kendra's stomach knotted as she watched the slender fingers stroke the luminescent pearls. There was no denying Carlotta's beauty. Lady Atwood's maid had arranged her raven hair into a high bouffant adorned with seed pearls. Her gown was the palest blush pink organza overskirt, the bodice a slightly deeper shade of pink and tied with long ribbons beneath her breasts. Tiny capped sleeves allowed Carlotta to wear long, white gloves. A creamy expanse of her bosom was revealed by the gown's low neckline. Though she was supposedly twenty-six—the same age as Kendra—and had been married, Carlotta looked both young and surprisingly innocent. And nothing brought out the protective instincts more than youth and innocence.

Kendra had a feeling that Carlotta knew exactly the image she was projecting. And it was working, damn her. Every moment the Duke spent in the woman's company, he seemed to fall more under her spell.

"Soon we shall have to think about throwing a ball of our own," the Duke said with a smile.

The statement sent a bolt of electricity through Kendra. She could tell that Lady Atwood and Alec were also taken aback. Even Carlotta appeared surprised. The Duke hadn't said the ball would be used to introduce her to society as his daughter, but they could all read between the lines. It was one step closer. A big step.

He's not going to wait months for the Bow Street Runners in Spain to send their reports, Kendra realized with an almost frantic flutter in her belly.

The Duke looked at Carlotta. "I would be honored to take you out for your first dance."

"*Do* you know how to dance?" Kendra asked, more sharply than she'd intended. "You grew up in a time of war, always moving. I wasn't sure if you ever had the time to learn."

Carlotta's fine eyebrows drew together, more perplexed than worried. "Everyone knows how to dance, Miss Donovan," she finally said. "Even soldiers dance."

"Many of our English dances originated from the French court," the Duke added, looking at Kendra, "and I believe the waltz was actually first introduced in Vienna ballrooms."

Kendra could feel her face heat up under their scrutiny. The question had been a colossal mistake. It was a reminder that *she* was the one in this group who had not known how to dance—not these old-fashioned steps. She'd never done much dancing in the 21st century, either, but she'd recently learned the polonaise, the Scottish reel, the quadrille, the minuet, and the waltz, which was slightly different than the modern waltz. The latter had only been accepted by English society in the last year. Even Lady Atwood—a huge opponent of the waltz—had begun to frown a little less when it was mentioned.

She was relieved when the Duke escorted Carlotta out on the dance floor and Lady Atwood excused herself to join her friends, mostly older widows who sat in a group of chairs on the sidelines, allowing them an unrestricted view of the dancers and the rest of the ballroom.

Alec raised an eyebrow at her. "Would you like to dance, Miss Donovan?"

She smiled faintly. "Maybe later. Right now, I would like to stroll."

Alec offered his elbow, and they joined the people who were walking the outer circle of the ballroom.

"Did you learn anything about Mr. Mercer in your club?" she asked in a low voice.

Alec laughed. "I should have known you wanted to talk about the murder."

"What else do you have in mind? Telling me how fine my eyes are, or how pleasant my conversation?"

"Well, now that you mention it, you do have very fine eyes, Miss Donovan. Your conversation, on the other hand, could be a little less macabre."

"I'll work on it," she replied with a laugh. "Now tell me about your day, my lord. Before anyone interrupts us."

"Lord Redgrave and his family are up the River Tick, which we already knew. He's to inherit the earldom when his father cocks up his toes—which, according to the betting books, might not be in too many months. Unfortunately, the estate has been in dire straits for generations. The entire family has a reputation for being spendthrifts. So, Mr. Mercer comes by his profligate ways naturally."

"You'd think they would have been more receptive to Mr. Mercer marrying an heiress," Kendra murmured.

"Not a chance. Lord Redgrave is a starched shirt, if there ever was one. He didn't deepen the family debt by gaming. He demands only the best. Spent a fortune that he doesn't have refurbishing his London townhouse. There's a possible match brewing between Lord Redgrave's eldest and Lord Dasher's youngest daughter. Apparently, the chit's a bit horse-faced and is going through her fourth season in Town with no takers, despite a sizeable dowry. The honorable Mr. Thaddeus Mercer—the eldest son—is less than enthusiastic, but the betting is that he and Miss Whyte will be engaged by fall."

"Good God."

"From their description of Miss Whyte, I'd say that Mr. Mercer—the youngest—ended up with the better deal marrying the former Miss Gavenston, even if his family cut him off. Still, I was told that the younger Mr. Mercer often comes to town to partake in its amusements."

"And what exactly are those?"

"The same sort many young men are drawn to—boxing, swordplay, the occasional opera dancer."

"The *occasional* opera dancer? You make it sound like he indulges in that like an order of fries at a McDonald's drive-through window."

"What, pray tell, are these fries, and why would anyone drive through a window, especially a Scotsman's?"

"Fried potato slices that actually originated in Belgium. And in America—*my* America—time is precious, so we don't want to get out of our horseless carriages. We wait in long lines to pick up our food—which, I know, doesn't save that much time." She squeezed his arm. "And none of that matters right now. Are you saying that Mr. Mercer is unfaithful to his wife?"

"He isn't keeping a mistress, but . . ." He lifted one shoulder in a half shrug. "How does this connect to Mr. Pascoe?"

"I don't know if it does." But it certainly added another layer to the kind of man that Mercer was. "Doesn't put him in a flattering light, does it?"

"Was he *in* a flattering light and I missed it?"

"Good point. I thought him a narcissist. I guess he is."

Alec looked at her. "And what did you learn today in Cookham, Miss Donovan?"

Kendra let her gaze travel around the throngs of people. The orchestra had switched to a Scottish reel. "For that story, my lord, we're going to have to do several more spins around the ballroom."

Two hours later, Kendra stood in front of the French doors, where her most recent dance partner, Mr. Humphrey, had deposited her while he fought his way through the masses to get her a glass of lemonade. She'd actually met Mr. Humphrey during her last visit to London and found him to be an affable guy, so time with him was never as excruciating as time with some of the other young men.

Carlotta came up to her, fanning her flushed face. "I am quite overheated."

Kendra eyed the woman. "You've danced every dance since we arrived. I guess you're a success. Congratulations. The Duke had better get ready for callers knocking on his door tomorrow."

"And you do not approve."

"It's not for me to approve or disapprove," Kendra said stiffly.

Carlotta sighed in frustration. "I have told you, Miss Donovan, that I do not wish us to be enemies. Why are you so threatened by me?"

"I'm not threatened by you."

"Perhaps we ought to speak more privately," Carlotta said, pointing her fan at the open French doors. "I wish to—"

"Ah, there you are, my dear," the Duke said, smiling as he approached. His gaze was on Carlotta, not Kendra. "Do you have a moment? I would like to introduce you to an old friend of mine, who has just arrived. Miss Donovan, you don't mind if I steal Carlotta away from you?"

Kendra forced a smile. "Steal away."

Carlotta hesitated only for a second, then inclined her head in acceptance. "I would be honored, sir," she said, smiling as she put her hand on the crook of his elbow and allowed him to usher her through the packed ballroom.

The Duke led Carlotta to an older gentleman, who bowed while Carlotta curtsied. There was something terribly intimate about the scene. Kendra felt like she was standing outside a window, her nose pressed up against the glass, watching a father proudly introduce his daughter to an old friend.

The flutter she'd felt earlier in the pit of her stomach spread to her chest. There was no denying the expression that she saw on the Duke's face. Protective, proud . . . *loving.*

A strange desire to weep assailed her. It stunned her even as she swallowed hard to overcome it. She *never* cried. What the hell was wrong with her?

"Miss Donovan, would you like—What's the matter?" Alec's voice sharpened as he came up next to her, his gaze fixed on her face.

"I . . ." Her breath hitched. She had to force herself to swallow. "They look like they belong together, don't they?"

He didn't ask who. Instead, he turned to scan the ballroom, his eyes narrowing when he found his uncle and Carlotta.

"Do you want to get married?" Kendra blurted out, and she was shocked as soon as the words left her mouth. *What the hell did I just say?* It was like some alien had invaded her body, hijacked her emotions, taken control of her mouth.

Alec's head whipped around, his green eyes intense as he locked his gaze on her. "Pardon?"

Her blood thundered in her ears and she had to lick her suddenly dry lips. She could take it back. Say it was a joke. Say that she had a brain tumor. Maybe she *did* have a brain tumor.

But she heard herself say, "Marry. Let's get married."

Alec stared at her. From a long distance, she heard the music of the orchestra, the laughter and murmur of conversation swirling around her. He didn't respond. He glanced again at the Duke and Carlotta before shifting his eyes back to her. Why wasn't he saying anything? The earlier panic that had flooded Kendra was now sliding into something else, something that might be described as acute embarrassment. They were in the middle of a bloody ballroom, although—thank God—everyone was well occupied with their own conversations. No one to witness her mental breakdown. No one except Alec, who was staring at her like she'd just suggested they steal the crown jewels.

"No," Alec finally said.

She sucked in a surprisingly painful breath and took a step back.

"Kendra—"

"No." She jerked away when he tried to capture her hand with his. "Let's forget it, shall we?"

"Devil take it," he hissed. "Listen—"

"No. No, I—"

"You know that I—"

"Sutcliffe! Miss Donovan!" Lady Rebecca materialized beside them, holding a glass of lemonade. "Dear heaven, I think everyone in Town is here this evening. Lady Roberta is holding a musical recital. I can't imagine anyone is there." She smiled, but it began to falter as she peered at Kendra and Alec. "What's the matter? Did you learn something about Mr. Pascoe's murder?"

"Yes." Kendra managed to keep her voice steady. She didn't look at Alec. "I'll tell you later, but now Sutcliffe would love to dance with you."

"Oh." Rebecca appeared nonplussed.

"Miss Donovan—"

Kendra forced herself to look at Alec now. "I need a moment." She thought she sounded fine—at least, not as desperate as she felt.

Whatever Alec saw on her face, he nodded slowly, then glanced at Rebecca. "I would be honored if you would accompany to the dance floor, Becca," he said, offering his hand.

Rebecca narrowed her eyes at both of them.

"I'll take your glass for you," Kendra offered. *Please, please, go*, she prayed silently. She needed a moment to compose herself, and she couldn't do it with Alec staring at her or, worse, apologizing for his rejection.

"Very well," Rebecca agreed finally, handing Kendra her glass. She gave her a pointed look. "We shall have a word afterward, though." She put her hand on Alec's arm. "Come along, Sutcliffe."

He hesitated, his eyes still on Kendra.

"Sutcliffe . . ." Rebecca tugged on his arm and Alec reluctantly turned away.

Kendra gave a sigh of relief. Alec glanced back once as he led Rebecca out onto the dance floor where the set was forming. Mr. Humphrey was probably returning with her glass of lemonade, but she needed to escape the stiflingly hot ballroom. She took a sip of Rebecca's lemonade to ease the dryness of her throat and slipped out the French doors. The evening air was wonderfully cold against her feverish cheeks. The verandah was empty, but she needed more distance between here and her recent humiliation. She kept walking, down the steps, into the gardens full of dense foliage. Clouds drifted across the moon, which made the shadows even deeper. She craved the dark right now. *What have I done?*

Pausing next to a marble bench in front of a rose bush, she closed her eyes and focused on her breathing. She needed to find a sense of equilibrium in a world that had spun dangerously out of control.

Maybe if she hadn't been so focused inward on her embarrassment over making a complete fool of herself, she would have been more aware of her surroundings. But she heard nothing until the man was right behind her, his hot, foul breath feathering her ear.

"Look at w'ot we got here, eh? She came right ter us, all on her own," he said in a guttural voice. "It must be our lucky night. It ain't yer lucky night, though, is it, bitch?"

Kendra froze when she heard the ominous click of a hammer being pulled back and the cold metal of the pistol's barrel as it was pressed against the back of her head.

Kendra dropped the glass, what was left of the lemonade soaking into the grass. "What's this about?" she demanded and was pleased that her voice remained cool and measured, revealing none of the inner tension that sent her pulse beating in a wild tattoo at her wrists and throat.

There were two men, dressed in rough wools. The one who held the gun pointed at the base of her skull now pushed her so that she marched in front of him through the gardens to the street.

"Shut it!" he snarled.

"Yer certain that she's the one?" whispered his partner. He was the taller of the two, with a long weasely face and a nervous tic that caused his right eye to wink at her periodically and his mouth to spasm.

"She matches the description," said gunman. He was a little shorter than Weasel Face, with a heftier build. He had thick lips and heavy jowls. He was the more menacing of the two. Still, if she had to have a gun pointed at the back of her skull, Kendra thought Jowls was a better choice than his skittish pal. If Weasel Face's tic extended to his trigger finger, he could accidentally blow her head off.

On the other hand, Jowls might have not any compunction about pulling the trigger. She was in an unenviable catch-22 situation.

"If it's money you're after, I can pay," she said.

"Didn't I tell ye ter shut yer hole?" Jowls shoved her forward with his free hand.

Kendra stumbled, but caught herself from falling flat on her face. Picking up her skirts with one hand, she scurried forward. Her mind raced with possibilities. It wasn't a good sign that the two criminals didn't feel the need to hide their identities. Either they were walking her away from the Merriweather mansion because they had been ordered to bring her to the mastermind behind the kidnapping or they wanted more privacy to kill her and dispose of her body.

Her heart pounded in her chest and there was a vinegary taste in her mouth that she recognized as fear. *Not good.* Fear could be as deadly as the bullets in the double-chambered flintlock pointed at her head.

She drew in a slow, deep breath, and felt her lungs expand and her mind clear. She let it out. Negotiate first. They'd been hired, obviously. That meant money was the motivating factor. Jowls might not be thinking too clearly himself. She had to remind herself that they were most likely dealing with the same wild adrenaline rush that she was. Except they had a weapon. They were in control.

The vegetation cleared and they emerged in a narrow alley that ran along the backside of the Merriweather property. There were three streetlamps burning, the yellowish glow limning the carriage waiting next to the curb. A hulking figure was on top of the carriage, his hands fisted around the reins, controlling the two horses.

"'Urry up, ye bastards," the coachman growled from his seat.

Weasel Face rushed forward to open the door. Inside, a brass lamp revealed a black interior that smelled like dirty socks. Weasel Face grabbed her arm with surprising strength and threw her inside. Kendra managed to right herself on the leather seat before her abductors scrambled in behind her, slamming the door. They settled on the seat opposite her, Weasel Face directly across from her and Jowls next to him. Instead of the back of her skull, the pistol was now trained on her forehead.

"*Go!*" Jowls yelled. The carriage jolted forward.

"Do you know who I am?" Kendra tried again.

Jowls's thick lips twisted into an unpleasant smile. "The Nob's ward." He let his eyes rove over her. The shadows in the carriage couldn't hide the lascivious glint. "Yer a prime article, ter be sure. Maybe we'll have some fun."

Kendra began calmly to remove her long white gloves. Fingers and fingernails could be turned into weapons if you knew the proper defense strategies. "You both look like businessmen." *If your business was crime.* "We should be able to negotiate."

"W'ot are ye doing?" demanded Weasel Face. He blinked rapidly as he looked at his partner. "W'ot's she doin'?"

"Looks like she's preparing ter negotiate."

Kendra smiled. The carriage was rolling at a steady pace, roughly three miles an hour. She glanced at Weasel Face. He didn't seem to have a weapon. The coachman most likely had a blunderbuss, as that seemed standard for coachmen. But Jowls was her immediate concern. The gun in his hand hadn't wavered.

"How much money do you want?" she said. "I'll double whatever you were offered."

"Aye, and once ye bring us the blunt, ye'll just be on yer merry way? Ye won't be goin' ter the nearest beak or ask yer Bow Street Runner ter find us? We won't be sent ter meet Jack Ketch?"

Jack Ketch was the name used in this era for all of England's executioners. She tilted her head as she considered Jowls. He wasn't stupid. And she wasn't a good enough an actress to convince him otherwise.

"I suppose I can't argue with that," she admitted. She inhaled again, let it out slowly as she gathered her nerve for what she must do. When the carriage stopped, she suspected there would be more men waiting. Right now, she was outnumbered two to one, not counting the coachman outside. She didn't want to increase those odds against her, which meant it would have to be now or never.

"Think we're fokking stupid," said Jowls.

"Aye, she thinks we're stupid—"

Weasel Face started to chortle and Kendra sprang forward, striking out with brutal efficiency. The soft tracheal cartilage of his throat dipped beneath the force of her fingers, cutting off his words abruptly. He gasped and choked, his hands coming up too late to protect his throat.

She was already launching herself across the seat at Jowls, grasping the hand that was holding the pistol. Kendra managed to thrust the weapon upward just as he squeezed the trigger. The shot was loud enough to make her ears ring and the bullet tore through the carriage's ceiling. The coachman screamed and the horses bolted. The burst of speed over cobblestone made the carriage swing dangerously from side to side. But Kendra barely noticed the teetering carriage as she and Jowls grappled for the gun.

"*Bitch*!" he shouted and swung at her with enough force to break her jaw, had she not dodged to the side.

Kendra countered with her own attack, striking him on the nose, and blood spurted from it. She aimed for the groin with her knee, but he managed to throw her off him. She landed hard on the other seat and scrambled up just as he raised the gun. He had one shot left, but at this range, there was no way he'd miss. Kendra sucked in a breath, tensing for the impact of the bullet.

The carriage, already wobbling wildly, jerked sharply to the left. She saw Jowls's eyes widen in horror, and then all three of them went flying as the carriage began to roll. Their screams mingled with the high-pitched shriek of the horses. The glass on the brass lamps and the windows shattered as the carriage tumbled, then began to career on its side, the horses dragging it down the street. Kendra covered her head with her arms, trying to protect it as her body slammed into the carriage's wall, which was now the floor. Jowls and Weasel Face fell beside her, shouting and groaning. There was an ominous snap as the harness broke. No longer attached to the panicking beasts, the carriage spun like a top for three dizzying rotations. Finally it came to a stop.

Kendra lay where she was for a second, her entire body pulsing with pain. Slowly, she became aware that she wasn't the only one breathing in the dark confines of the carriage. *Shit*. Gritting her teeth, she forced her limbs to move before her captors revived and tried to stop her.

The door was now above them. Kendra pushed herself to her feet, stepping on something soft—maybe the leather seat, maybe a stomach—and thrust open the door above her like it was a hatch in a submarine. She saw the outline of the moon through a thin curtain of clouds. She grasped the sides of the door and began to heave herself up.

"Fokking bitch, where do ye think ye're going?" Jowls growled.

Kendra gasped as thick fingers closed over her ankle. She kicked out hard. Jowls grunted and cursed, and the fingers fell away. Her arms trembled with the effort as she hoisted herself through the door.

"Get the bitch!" Weasel Face croaked in a broken voice. "I'm gonna cut her!"

Damn. Kendra had hoped at least he'd be dead. She rolled off the carriage and dropped to the ground. Pain sang up her legs, jarring her bones. *Fuck!* Blood, warm and sticky, trickled down the side of her face and oozed out of cuts and scrapes on her body. She wiped it out of her eyes, glancing wildly around. Her gaze landed on the coachman. He was lying on the ground, his legs crushed under the carriage, blood caking his battered face. His eyes were open, glassy with death.

She dragged her gaze away, trying to get her bearings. They were obviously in one of the business sections of London. Flickering streetlamps revealed dark, shuttered retail shops lining one side of the cobblestone lane. On the other side was a medieval-looking church. Next to it were black, iron-wrought gates, and more ironwork arching across the entrance that showed the name: Saint Michael Cemetery.

Inside the carriage, Jowls and Weasel Face were moving around, cursing and muttering. She saw shadowy hands reach out of the opening to grasp the frame of the carriage doors.

Time's up.

Hoping it wasn't a bad omen, Kendra began limping toward the cemetery.

31

A lec finished the intricate dance steps and bowed over Becca's hand. His gaze traveled the length of the ballroom for the third time since leading Becca out on the floor, but once again he did not see Kendra. Devil take it, where was the blasted woman?

"If it's any consolation, I do not see her either," Rebecca murmured.

His gaze returned to Rebecca. He smiled wryly. "I am being unpardonably rude."

"Don't be stupid. Are you going to tell me what you two are having a row about?" she asked as they moved off the dance floor and threaded their way through the crowds to the periphery of the ballroom.

"We aren't having a row," he said, and avoided Rebecca's too-perceptive gaze by searching the room for Kendra. Uneasiness prickled the back of his neck when he couldn't find her. "Do you want a lemonade?"

"Not particularly, but let's go there. Perhaps Miss Donovan is getting a refreshment," Rebecca said drily.

He had to force himself to keep to the languid pace that was appropriate for such an event. His muscles tensed with the desire to sprint through the rooms. The refreshment room had a handful of people sampling the lemonades and wines, but no Kendra. With Rebecca on his arm, he continued to stroll to the cardroom, although he couldn't imagine Kendra sitting down for a game of piquet, Loo, or Faro. They only paused long enough to determine Kendra wasn't there before moving quickly onto the formal dining room, which had been converted into a buffet for the midnight supper. His gaze roamed over the guests circulating around the plates laden with an assortment of cheeses, fruit, breads, and pastries. Where was she?

Rebecca offered, "I'll look in the ladies withdrawing rooms."

Alec nodded. "Thank you."

As she hurried down the hall, Alec leaned against the wall, absently nodding at the many familiar faces that greeted him as they walked by. Carefully, he schooled his features into a cold aloofness that discouraged anyone from tarrying to speak with him. It wasn't difficult; his mind was replaying the earlier scene with Kendra.

Marry. Let's get married.

Like a bloody fool, he'd just gaped at her. Hell and damnation! She'd caught him flat-footed. What lady proposed to a gentleman in the middle of a ball? What lady proposed to a gentleman *ever*?

Kendra Donovan, that was who.

He almost regretted not taking advantage of her momentary weakness . . . except he'd known that it *had* been a weakness. He'd seen her looking at the Duke and Carlotta. He'd seen something in her eyes that looked perilously close to fear. Not fear that Carlotta was a charlatan, but that she was not.

For such an intelligent woman, Kendra could be shockingly foolish. While she placed a great deal of value on her skills as an investigator—and rightly so—she placed almost no value on herself as a human being. On one level it baffled him how easily she thought she could be replaced in his uncle's heart, and yet on another, he understood. She'd told him how her parents had left her to fend for herself when she'd disagreed with the path that they'd laid out for her. She always adopted a nonchalant tone when she spoke of that time, but he'd been cognizant of the pain beneath the surface, a wound that outwardly had healed but deep inside still festered.

He'd been asking her to marry him for months. He should have said yes and damn the consequences. Devil take it, he couldn't even claim chivalry for his refusal. He'd said no because he wanted . . . *more*. He didn't want Kendra to marry him because he was a safe harbor for whatever imaginary fears she was dealing with regarding Carlotta. He didn't want to be second choice.

"She's not in the withdrawing rooms," Rebecca said as she returned, interrupting his brooding thoughts. She looked worried. "Let us return to the ballroom. Mayhap we missed her the first time."

Ice settled in his belly. "I don't think she's here."

"But where would she go? Why would she leave?" Rebecca paused, then suggested, "She might be out in the gardens."

Alec grasped Rebecca's elbow, steering her down the hall to the ballroom. Briefly, they paused to scan the ballroom, in case Kendra had been outside and returned. When they couldn't find her, they continued on to the French doors.

"Perhaps you should wait here while I search the gardens," Alec said, hesitating.

Rebecca gave him a look. "I think my reputation can survive walking with a man I've known since childhood in the gardens. Come on, Sutcliffe. I'm as concerned about Miss Donovan as you are."

Alec decided it was pointless to argue. They slipped outside. The light from the ballroom spilled across the empty stone verandah. They crossed it and went down the steps to the garden, which was shrouded in shadows.

"I don't see her," Rebecca said. "If you had a quarrel, do you think she would leave? Go home?"

"It's Kendra Donovan. Anything is possible." He strode forward. His foot landed on something and he heard a sharp crack. "Damnation!"

"What is it?"

He bent to carefully retrieve what was left of the shattered glass.

"I gave Miss Donovan my lemonade," Rebecca said, and there was a note of dawning horror in her voice. She looked up, her face paler than normal in the moonlight. "Did she drop it?"

The ball of ice already in Alec's stomach spread through his bloodstream. "Not voluntarily."

"You think . . . you think someone has taken her?"

He tossed the glass to the side and grabbed Rebecca's elbow, spinning around to sprint toward the verandah. "Come on."

"What are we going to do?"

"I'm going to find Mr. Kelly. And then I'm going to find Kendra, if I have to scour the entire city."

Kendra's bruised knee felt like it had swelled to the size of a Macy's Thanksgiving Day balloon and the side of her face was on fire. Tightening her jaw, she blocked out the pain as she stumbled through the cemetery gates. The moon was playing hopscotch with the clouds in the evening sky. Thin ribbons of mist were beginning to crawl across the uneven ground, slithering around the ancient headstones and markers. Despite the sense of urgency driving her, Kendra took a moment to scan the graveyard. Many of the tombstones were cockeyed where the earth had shifted and settled. Angel statues stood watch over lichen-draped crypts. A shadowy mausoleum that looked like a miniature White House was at the far end of the cemetery. Gnarled trees and flowering shrubs dotted the landscape. In the sunshine, the cemetery was probably beautiful. Maybe even peaceful. At nearly midnight, with the moon and mist, it was as creepy as hell.

But beggars can't be choosers.

"Where's my bleeding pistol?" she heard Jowls demand, his voice clearer in the crisp night air. She tossed a swift glance over her shoulder and saw that he was sprawled on top of the crippled carriage, peering through the door. Weasel Face's voice was muffled as he answered. He was still inside, probably searching for the lost weapon.

Kendra started for the cluster of trees. She'd already devised a plan in her head. She needed to get to the opposite end of the cemetery. She'd have to climb over the high wrought iron fence that surrounded the property, but she didn't think that would be a problem—

"*Holy crap!*" She gasped, startled, and skidded to a stop. Her heart pounded in her chest as her gaze fixed on a small figure crouched next to one of the crypts. It was a boy of about six or seven, with tumbling dark locks that framed an intelligent, attractive face.

"Are you real?" she asked.

"Are *you?*" he shot back.

She blinked. The boy was flesh and bone, she decided. No ghost would be so insolent. What the hell was a young child doing out in the middle of the night in a cemetery? He wasn't one of London's street urchins either. She could tell that his clothing was well-made. He was very thin, but he didn't have the half-starved look of the city's poor.

On the street, Jowls give a pained grunt as he leapt to the ground. It jolted her back to reality.

"Come on, kid," she whispered, extending her hand. The boy had nothing to do with the two men chasing her, but she doubted that they'd leave any witnesses if they came across him. "We've got to move."

He jerked away from her. "Why should I go anywhere with you?"

She stared at him. "Because right now I've got two men who want me dead, and you will be collateral damage if I don't get you to safety."

As if on cue, Jowls shouted, "Gonna kill ye, ye bitch!"

The kid glanced sharply toward the entrance of the cemetery.

"Come on," Kendra said again, and this time when she reached for the kid, he put his small hand in hers.

Keeping low, they crept among the larger tombstones. Kendra prayed that the clouds would swallow up the moon to give them cover of darkness.

"Why are the ruffians chasing you?" whispered the boy. "Are they graverobbers?"

"Shush."

On some level, it registered—and surprised her—that the kid sounded American. She tightened her hand on his and dragged him over to a tombstone that had a sculptured stone angel smiling down at the mound of earth. She rubbed her swollen knee absently as she peeked around the wings of the statue. Her would-be kidnappers were standing at the gated entrance. Jowls had retrieved his gun and Weasel Face now was brandishing a knife.

Shit.

"Ye stay 'ere," Jowls ordered. "I'll flush 'er out."

Kendra pulled back, sucking in a deep breath as she reconsidered her strategy. With the men breaking ranks, she could go on the offensive. Try to take out Jowls and then go back for Weasel Face. First things first, though—the kid was a liability. She needed to find a hiding spot for him so he would be safe no matter what happened to her.

Sweat—or was it blood?—trickled down her cheek. Irritated, she wiped it away as her gaze searched the area.

"What are we waiting for?" the kid quizzed her with a trace of impatience.

She shushed him again, but her gaze had already locked on the classical granite mausoleum. She estimated that it was about twenty feet high, with two columns on either side of the double doors.

The moon disappeared behind a cloud, plunging the world into darkness. Jowls stumbled on a marker somewhere behind them, letting out an oath. Kendra tugged on the kid's hand and they took off across the graveyard. The statues and markers were now little more than inky shadows veiled by the night. For whatever reason, Jowls wasn't attempting to be stealthy. He continued to curse, his footsteps thudding against the ground as he swept the graveyard. He probably thought the fence had trapped her inside the cemetery and so he didn't need to be quiet.

Kendra and the kid skirted a rosebush and skidded to a halt in front of a yawning abyss. Not quite an abyss. Only six feet deep. A freshly dug grave, so fresh that a worker had left behind his shovel, the handle sticking out of the mounds of dirt.

"This is auspicious," the kid whispered.

Kendra glanced at the boy in surprise. She reached over and yanked the shovel out of the soil. Loose dirt and pebbles cascaded over the lip of the hole. Wincing a little at the noise, she clutched the shovel with one hand, grabbed the boy with the other, and scrambled up the sloping hill. She nearly tripped twice, her feet tangling with the long skirt of her evening dress. They closed the distance to the mausoleum.

"W'ot's happening?" Weasel Face shouted, his voice sounding broken and scratchy from her earlier attack. "Have ye found the bitch?"

"Does it *look* like I've found her?"

"I don't know! I can't see a bloody thing!"

"Shut it, will ye!"

Kendra dropped the child's hand when they made it to the door of the mausoleum. She reached out to grasp the doorknob.

"Damn," she muttered when the door didn't budge.

"It's locked. Probably to prevent graverobbers," said the kid.

"Thanks, Sherlock," she muttered. She plucked two pins from her tumbling hair and knelt down, inserting them into the lock.

"My name's Edgar. What are you doing?"

"Kid . . ." She huffed out a sigh of exasperation and went to work. When the tumblers clicked into place, she pushed open the door a crack. "Okay. Get in."

He stared at her.

"You won't be locked in," she assured him. "It's big." It probably held at least eight crypts, but she didn't think reminding the child that he'd be sharing the space with a number of corpses would be smart. "You can hide in here, okay?"

He gave her a strangely adult look. "What will you be doing?"

"Don't worry about me, kid. But if I don't come back, wait an hour before coming out. Then go home."

She heard Jowls moving around below. Closer now. *Shit.* She was running out of time. Rather than argue anymore, she shoved the kid through the door and shut it as quietly as possible. Then she picked up the shovel again, moving down the hill to the angel statue and open grave.

Shivering, she settled down to wait.

Jowls was methodical in searching the cemetery, going from side to side in a zigzag pattern, working his way down from the entrance where Weasel Face was standing guard. The strategy wasn't a bad one, Kendra had to admit. But he made two mistakes. He assumed that she would be trapped within the grounds because she wouldn't be able to scale the high wrought iron fence which enclosed the cemetery. It would be difficult, especially with her banged up knee, evening dress, and dancing slippers. But Kendra was confident that she would be able to get over the fence, if that's what she wanted to do.

And that was mistake number two. Jowls expected to find her cowering like a frightened animal. She had the element of surprise on her side, because he didn't expect her to fight back.

Kendra crouched next to the angel statue with the shovel gripped in both hands. She clenched her jaw tight to keep her teeth from chattering, listening to Jowls as he stumbled over stone grave markers, muttering curses. Every once in a while, Weasel Face would ask how the search was going, and Jowls would bark back a reply. Then Jowls would taunt her, promising to do the most hideous things to her when he finally found her.

And that was mistake number three. She knew exactly where he was as he thrashed his way through the graveyard.

She focused on her breathing as he came closer.

Her nerves stretched taut. She tightened her grip on the handle of the shovel. Adrenaline kicked in like a wild animal inside her as she silently counted his steps.

Closer.

Kendra sprang to her feet. She barely felt the agony of her knee; her entire focus was on swinging the shovel around. Her arms reverberated with the impact of the spade against Jowls's chest. He let out a yell and flew backward.

Had he dropped the gun? She couldn't see.

"W'ot's happening?" Weasel Face shouted in his hoarse voice.

Kendra didn't wait. She swung the shovel up in an arc and downward with vicious force, but Jowls was already rolling to the side. The shovel blade clipped him on the shoulder. He hissed out a breath and managed to lurch to his feet.

Aware that she'd lost her advantage, Kendra recalibrated, shifting the shovel to swing it like a baseball bat. This time the blade caught him in the face. She heard a sickening crunch of cartilage and bone, saw his shadowy form spin over the mounds of loose dirt. Then he was gone, plunging into the open grave.

Breathing heavily, her blood pounding in her ears, Kendra waited for Jowls to climb out of the grave. Instead, she heard in the distance a strange clattering sound. Her hands were clammy with sweat as she grasped the shovel's handle, braced for another attack. Her eyes darted around. But Weasel Face wasn't charging at her. Jowls was still in the open grave—ominously silent. Unconscious or dead?

Then she identified the clattering: a watchman's rattle. Two watchmen were at the cemetery entrance, holding lanterns.

"Hey!" Kendra shouted. "Over here!"

"Who goes there?" demanded one of the watchmen. Their lanterns bobbed in the dark as they jogged up the hill toward her.

"Blimey!" A watchman gasped when the light from his lantern caught her. "Were you in the carriage that rolled over outside? What's your name, miss?"

"Kendra Donovan. I was kidnapped . . ." She frowned, lifting a hand when the other watchman moved the lantern closer, blinding her.

"Kidnapped, were you?" The second watchman didn't sound like he believed her. "And just who kidnapped you? Bonnie Prince Charlie?"

"One kidnapper is there." She pointed at the open grave. "The other seems to have escaped."

"Right here, you say?" He swung the lantern around to peer into the dark pit. "Sweet Jesus. Vince, look! She ain't lying. There's a man down there. I think he's dead."

Vince crept up to the edge of the grave with his lantern. "Good God. What happened ter his face?"

"He ran into my shovel." Kendra stuck the shovel in the ground and propped herself on it, feeling suddenly weak. "Can someone send a note to Lady Merriweather's ball? A few people might be looking for me."

The first watchman gaped at her. "Lady Merriweather?"

"Yes. That's where I was before . . . I was here." She was starting to shiver. "Why are you here?"

"We were sent out by the lady and gent down there," Vince jerked a thumb toward the street. For the first time, Kendra noticed a carriage parked outside the cemetery gate. "Seems like their son was dared to come to the cemetery by a couple of mates. Then we saw the overturned carriage."

Edgar. Kendra let go of the shovel handle. Now that the danger had passed, her knee was throbbing again. She began to limp up the hill to the mausoleum.

"Now where are you off to, miss?"

She ignored him, throwing open the mausoleum door. The darkness was impenetrable. "Edgar?"

The watchman followed, stretching out his hand with the lantern just as the boy came forward. Edgar blinked in the circle of light.

"Master Allan," the watchman tutted in an avuncular way. "You've caused plenty of mayhem tonight, haven't you?"

Kendra wondered if she should thank the boy. After all, if he hadn't snuck off to the cemetery on a dare, his parents wouldn't have called the watch and she'd still be dealing with a very pissed off Weasel Face.

The boy looked up at her. "You got the villains?"

"One. The other got away."

"Let's go," the watchman said, shooing them down the hill. The moon reappeared, making their journey easier.

The second watchman was now staring down into the open grave. Kendra overheard the other man say, "Seems a waste of time ter haul him outta there, don't you think?"

They kept walking, skirting tombstones and grave markers.

Edgar shot her a glance. "Did you know that this cemetery was named Saint Michael?"

"I saw the name at the entrance."

"Michael wasn't a saint, though. He was an archangel," the boy said. "You are supposed to pray to him for protection from your most lethal enemies."

Kendra looked at the kid. "Did you pray to him?"

He nodded slowly.

"Then I guess it worked. Thank you."

He grinned at her.

"Edgar!"

A woman rushed forward from the cemetery entrance. Edgar broke into a run. She opened her arms to envelop her son in a hug.

Kendra's gaze traveled past them, surprised to see Alec, the Duke, and Sam coming through the gate. While the Duke and Sam paused, Alec kept striding forward. A moment later, she was enveloped in her own hug.

"My God, I thought I'd lost you!" Alec whispered against her hair.

She hugged him back. "How'd you know I was here?" she asked when she finally pulled away.

"After Alec realized you had vanished, we located Mr. Kelly and organized a search," the Duke said, coming up to them. His gaze fixed on Kendra, filled with concern. "My God . . . Are you all right?"

Kendra nodded, shivering. "But how'd you find me *here*?"

Alec took off his greatcoat and wrapped it around her shoulders. He smiled, his white teeth a glimmer in the darkness. "Mr. Kelly heard that a carriage had overturned. We figured that you must have been involved."

"What happened, lass?" Sam asked her.

"I stepped outside. Two men were waiting for me." She frowned, aware of a whispery sensation running down her spine. "I'm pretty sure they were hired by someone. I decided it would be best not to wait to meet that person. So I . . . voiced my objections. The carriage overturned. The coachman was killed."

"And the two abductors?" asked the Duke.

"One is up there, dead. The other one escaped."

Sam looked like he was going to say something but closed his mouth when Edgar's parents stepped toward Kendra. The woman wiped tears from her eyes. "Thank you for protecting Edgar, Miss . . . ?"

"Donovan. Kendra Donovan."

The woman nodded. "Thank you, Miss Donovan. I don't know what I would have done if we had lost Edgar to this misadventure. He was very naughty to have snuck out." She shot him a look that was both reproving and loving, then glanced at Kendra. "Mr. Allan and I are grateful to you, keeping Edgar safe."

Kendra decided not to point out that Edgar's nocturnal adventure would have probably been harmless. She was the one who had led the criminals into the cemetery.

"Edgar was very brave," she said.

The boy smiled.

"Yes, well. Thank you," Mr. Allan said gruffly. He had a faint Scottish accent. He frowned at his son. "And you, young man, I'll have to figure out a suitable punishment for this night!"

Kendra smiled slightly and started to turn away. But she paused to look back at the boy, transfixed by the small face, the intelligent eyes studying her. Wait. *Edgar Allan Poe.*

"Do not be too severe with Master Allan," the Duke added to the boy's father. "All boys need a great adventure once in a while."

"Ah, yes . . . well, good evening, Your Grace, Miss Donovan, sir."

"Take care of yourself, Edgar," she managed to say.

Mr. Allan clamped a hand down on Edgar's narrow shoulder and pushed him toward the carriage.

Kendra couldn't seem to tear her gaze away from the small figure as his foster parents—the Allans, she knew, never adopted their foster son—led him to the carriage. Edgar looked back at her over his shoulder, his gaze intense, and then they climbed in the carriage. The coachman shut the door and clambered onto his perch, then set the horses trotting. Kendra watched until the vehicle disappeared around the corner.

Holy crap.

"What's wrong?" It took a few minutes for Alec's words to penetrate her strange daze.

"Nothing." *I just met Edgar Allan Poe when he was a child.*

The Bow Street Runner frowned, his gold eyes flat as he looked at her. "It would appear that someone is getting even more nervous. They're no longer content with just a warning, lass. They want you dead."

32

I 'm sorry I ruined your evening," Kendra said carefully. She was sitting next to Alec and across from the Duke as his carriage barreled down the street toward Grosvenor Square. Sam had stayed behind to deal with Jowls's body. Now that the danger had passed, she couldn't stop shivering, even though she still wore Alec's greatcoat and was sitting close enough to him to be warmed by his body heat. The adrenaline boost was wearing off.

And, truth be told, she suspected that she was still in shock over her unexpected encounter with one of America's greatest writers.

"Don't be ridiculous," the Duke replied, eyeing her with concern. "I cannot believe that someone was so bold as to have you abducted from Hanover Square. In the middle of a party, for God's sakes. Who would *do* such a thing? What kind of madman are we dealing with?"

Kendra felt gratified by his use of pronouns. We, as in *we* are in this together. Instead of you, as in *you* are on your own.

"Why the escalation? Mr. Kelly was correct. This wasn't a kidnapping. You were meant to die tonight." In the glow of the brass lamp, Alec's green eyes blazed. "Who is behind this?"

She leaned back against the seat, suddenly exhausted. Disjointed thoughts flitted through her brain. "I don't know," she finally said, and glanced out the window. The fine mist was thickening into a pea-soup fog. "Aren't we going back to the Merriweather ball for Lady Atwood and Carlotta?"

The Duke shook his head. "Lord Blackburn promised to escort them home. Are you certain you are all right, my dear?" He fished out a white handkerchief. "You've got blood on your face."

"Thanks." She took the linen square, dabbed at her face, then gingerly touched the injury on her scalp.

"When we're home, I shall send for a doctor—"

"No, I'm fine. Just cut from flying glass when the carriage overturned."

"Your cheek is bruised," the Duke said, inspecting her face.

"So's my knee. I'll live."

A muscle twitched along Alec's jaw as he clasped her hand. He looked into her eyes. "I don't want you going anywhere alone."

"I never do." Well, almost never. "I've got a chaperone."

"I'm not talking about your maid," he snapped.

"I don't need a bodyguard shadowing me. I guess you failed to notice, but I saved myself tonight."

"And what happens when your luck runs out?" he demanded furiously.

She snatched her hand back and straightened, glaring at him. "It wasn't *luck* that saved me tonight. I am a trained FBI agent. I know how to take care of myself."

"You—"

"Enough, Alec." The Duke's voice was calm. "Enough, both of you. All our nerves are overwrought."

They fell silent for a moment.

"Who was the boy?" the Duke spoke up again, his gaze on Kendra. "I saw the way you looked at him. He means something to you?"

"You could say that," she replied. "I think I've read everything he's written. He's a literary genius."

The Duke's eyebrows went up. "Fascinating. He is . . . or, rather, will one day be a writer?"

"A writer and a poet. In my time, he's considered the father of the detective genre and one of the pioneers of science fiction. Edgar Allan Poe will probably become best known for transforming the horror genre . . ." Her breath caught in her throat. "One of his literary themes was being buried alive. And I just pushed him into a mausoleum!"

"You think you perhaps inspired his fascination for the topic?" The Duke's gaze sharpened, intrigued with the possibility.

Alec shook his head. "Impossible. Kendra read his books in her time *before* she came here. This boy became who he was and lived his life long before she was even born."

She gave him a wry look. *Impossible* was not a word she could throw around with any certainty anymore.

"Intriguing," the Duke breathed. "This would suggest that you were always meant to come to this timeline, my dear. And your fear of changing the future is overblown, because your presence here has already changed whatever future you know."

"It's called a predestination paradox." She had to take a breath to steady her voice. Even though she was now living in the 19th century, it still gave her a panicky sensation in the pit of her stomach to consider all the theories of time travel. She'd accepted it as a reality—how could she not?—but it remained a bizarre phenomenon. "It suggests that mankind does not have free will, that we are not masters of our own fate."

The Duke said quietly, "I rather think we delude ourselves into thinking that we have any control over our own fate."

"It defies logic," Kendra muttered.

Now the Duke smiled at her. "And that troubles you."

"It should trouble everyone."

"Not everyone is as averse as you are to the unexplained and the miraculous."

Kendra wondered if the conversation had shifted.

He continued, "However, I don't think you're dealing with . . . what did you call it? A predestination paradox. The child clearly had an interest in the macabre before he met you. Otherwise he would not have been in a graveyard in the middle of the night." He raised an eyebrow at her. "Does that assure you?"

"I guess it will have to."

Alec spoke up, "I'm more concerned with who is trying to kill you than your encounter with the boy. Do you think Mrs. Gavenston sent those men?"

The Duke stared at them. "Good God, why would Mrs. Gavenston do such a thing?"

Kendra told him about her encounter with the businesswoman, and her suspicion that Jeremy Pascoe was her son.

"Dear heavens," he muttered. "A secret like that might be worth killing for. Though I cannot fathom her murdering her own son to keep him from exposing her."

"Except that's not what happened."

"Yes, you said it was a moment of rage. That, too, I cannot fathom."

Kendra shook her head. "Whatever happened, we might be conflating Pascoe's murder with the secrecy surrounding his birth."

"Meaning she may not have killed her own son, but she sent two ruffians after you to keep her secret," the Duke said.

"That's one possibility."

"You forget that someone took a shot at you before you confronted her about her possible connection to Mr. Pascoe," Alec said.

The Duke frowned. "That was a warning. Mrs. Gavenston could have feared you were getting close to the truth and wished to send you a message."

"Possible," Kendra conceded.

The Duke eyed her closely. "Do you have another theory, my dear?"

She did, but it was only beginning to form. Like an experiment in a petri dish, she needed to put it aside, let it germinate for a bit. And if she was right . . .

"I always have theories, Your Grace," she said, and turned to look out the dark window to avoid the Duke's too perceptive gaze.

"Are you certain I shouldn't send for the doctor? You're limping," the Duke said as they moved toward the door of No. 29.

"I banged up my knee, that's all. I'll be fine—no doctor," Kendra said, but a moment later wondered just how bad she looked when she caught the horrified looks of Harding and one of the footmen as they entered the foyer.

"Good evening, sir . . . ah, should I have a bath prepared for you, Miss Donovan?" Harding asked with remarkable aplomb, as though he was used to her coming home with her hair in disarray, her evening gown torn, her face bloodied. Then again, he had seen her in a similar state before.

The Duke spoke up before Kendra could answer. "Yes, a bath, and rouse Miss Donovan's maid to put together a poultice for her knee. Have my sister and Carlotta returned?"

"Not yet, Your Grace."

"Very good. Hopefully, they're enjoying themselves." The Duke looked at Kendra. "I shall send up a warm brandy for you to drink before you go to bed. You need rest."

"Thanks." She started toward the stairs.

Alec joined her, putting an arm around her waist. "I shall help Kendra to her room," he told his uncle.

"I'm fine," she began.

Alec gave her a look. "Do you want me to carry you?"

"No."

"Then be quiet."

"Alec shall escort you to your bedchamber door," the Duke said, placing a slight emphasis on *door*. He had an almost stern look on his face as he watched them ascend the stairs. "I shall wait for you in the study, nephew. Perhaps we can have a drink before you venture to your own home."

"I shall meet you there shortly," Alec agreed, then lowered his voice for Kendra's ears alone. "My God, he's as bad as a mother hen clucking over a chick. It's not like you're in a fit state to be ravished."

Kendra laughed softly.

When they reached her door, Alec dropped his arm from her waist and picked up her hand. Kendra had never thought herself to be a hand-holding kind of gal, but heat shot through her as Alec stared at their laced fingers for a long moment.

"I wish to speak to you about our conversation before you went out into the garden," he said, fixing an intense gaze upon her.

Kendra's stomach clenched at the memory. "Can we forget it?"

"No." He kept his eyes on hers. "You do know that there is nothing that I wish more than to marry you?"

"Alec—"

"I love you. But I don't want you to marry me to run from your present circumstances; I want you to be running toward me."

She sighed. "It was dumb. I don't even know why I said it."

"Don't you?" He looked deep into her eyes. "You know that the Duke loves you. That will not change, no matter what happens with Carlotta or who she turns out to be. I wish you would believe that."

Kendra swallowed against the lump in her throat. She tried to disengage her hand. "I'd rather not talk about it. I feel stupid enough."

"Kendra—" he began, but broke off with a frustrated oath when the door opened.

Molly gave a startled yelp. "Oh, pardon me. Gor!" Her eyes rounded as she caught sight of Kendra. "W'ot 'appened? Ye look like ye've been in a mill, miss!"

"A boxing analogy is apt," Kendra admitted drily. She turned to face the maid when Alec released her hand.

"Oi'll 'ave a bath brought up."

"The Duke has already ordered a bath and a hot brandy. Can you fix a poultice for my knee? It's swelled up."

"Aye, Oi'll do that." Molly hesitated, looking at them.

"It would be nice to get the poultice tonight," Kendra commented.

"Oh. Aye." The maid hurried down the hall, passing two maids carrying steaming buckets of water. They kept their eyes averted as they went through the door.

Alec leaned forward and pressed a chaste kiss on her forehead. "Take your bath, drink your brandy, and get a good night's sleep, Kendra. I shall see you tomorrow morning." He smiled a little, then turned away.

"Alec?"

He paused and looked back at her. "Yes?"

"Thanks for not taking me up on my foolish proposal."

He shook his head. "Don't thank me. I'm already regretting it."

33

The next morning was bleak with gray skies and a cold drizzle. Kendra crawled out of bed, feeling every bruise on her body. Her knee wasn't quite as swollen—maybe the poultice had worked—but her leg had stiffened overnight. She did a few stretches to ease the tenderness before moving into the dressing room, where she inspected her reflection. The gash on her head had scabbed over and was concealed by her hair, and most of the contusions on her body would be covered by clothes. The only bruise that she couldn't hide was the one on her cheek.

"Gor, miss. 'Ow are ye?" Molly asked.

"A lot better than the other guy."

"Gave me nightmares ter think of ye in that graveyard last night. Oi brought ye coffee."

"You're a saint."

Molly handed her the cup. "W'ot are ye going ter be doing this mornin'? Stayin' indoors?"

Kendra glanced at the rivulets running down the windowpane. "For a while, at least." She sipped her coffee, thinking. She needed to review her notes again. She was missing something. "Mr. Kelly will probably be arriving soon. And Mr. Muldoon and Lady Rebecca."

Her gaze fell on the stack of foolscap that contained Jeremy Pascoe's writing. She would have to return them to Mrs. Pascoe, she thought, wandering over to the elegant desk to leaf through the pages marked with angry slashes. She remembered Mr. Elwes's idea of taking Pascoe's writing and see if he could get it published posthumously. Since she'd never heard of a poet named Jeremy Pascoe, either it never happened, or his work failed to rise above obscurity.

"Miss?"

Molly held up a loose-fitting cream sprigged muslin. Kendra set down her cup and the sheaves of foolscap to slip on the morning gown, then let Molly pin up her hair, followed by a green velvet bandeau.

"Maybe Oi can get some rice powder ter cover yer face."

"It's not going to work." Kendra inspected the bruise. At least it was on her cheek, not swelling her eye shut.

Someone knocked at the door. Molly put down the hairbrush and hurried over to the door, peeking out. "Aye? W'ot is it?" Kendra heard a low murmur, then Molly closed the door, and brought over a note. "This was sent for ye. Is it from that Irish scribbler again?"

Kendra frowned as she opened the piece of paper. "I don't think so . . ."

"W'ot's it say?"

But Kendra was already on her feet, moving to the wardrobe. She pulled out her heaviest hooded cloak. "Whoever sent it wants me to meet them. They're waiting in a carriage down the street."

"'Oo sent it?" Molly demanded.

"I don't know. It doesn't say." She went to the dresser, opened her reticule to retrieve the muff pistol. "I'll find out when I get to the carriage."

"But . . . ye can't go, miss!" The maid was alarmed. "It could be a trap. Ye've already been shot at and kidnapped!"

"You don't have to remind me."

"But ye're goin' anyways?"

"Yes. Don't worry. This time I'm prepared."

"Oi'm goin' with ye."

"No."

"Miss—"

"I doubt if the person behind last night's attack has had a chance to regroup yet. I think this is something else. If I'm wrong, though, I don't want to worry about you getting caught in the crossfire."

"Oh, miss. We ought ter tell 'Is Grace."

"I don't want him caught in the crossfire either." That didn't seem to reassure the maid. Kendra sighed. "Look, I really don't think there's anything to be concerned about. But if I'm wrong, I'd rather you stay here because then you can alert the Duke if I don't return in . . . say, twenty minutes. How does that sound?"

"*Terrible!* A lot can 'appen in twenty minutes!"

If someone wanted her dead, they only needed half a minute to point a gun in her face and pull the trigger. But since that would hardly comfort the maid, Kendra kept quiet. She put on the cloak and pulled the hood over her head. She kept her hand on the pistol.

"Twenty minutes," she reminded Molly, walking to the door. She glanced back at the maid's pale, tense face. "I'm not that easy to kill, you know. I've survived more than what happened last night."

"Aye, ye've been lucky, so far. But everybody's luck runs out eventually."

Kendra's luck held, at least in allowing her to slip out the servant's entrance without attracting any attention. She considered that a win as she hurried down the alley and past the mews. Her hood protected her from the light rain, but the cobblestones were slick, and she was careful to avoid the shallow puddles.

A short time later, she emerged on the street. The rain and early hour had kept servants indoors for the moment. The silence seemed odd. Kendra realized that she'd grown used to the noise at the Yarborough residence, but the bad weather had put a temporary halt to the construction. Now the only sound coming from that area was a light tapping as raindrops hit the oiled canvas tarps stretched across bricks, tools, and stacked timber.

Kendra let her gaze travel down the road, locking on the only carriage that was parked next to the curb. The coachman was huddled on his seat, dressed all in black, smoking a cigarette. He watched her approach, then tossed the cigarette to the side, clambering down.

"Yer the Yank?"

Kendra arched her eyebrows. "Who are you?"

"Come ter fetch ye."

She allowed her hand to inch forward, so the gun wasn't concealed by the cloak anymore. "Not until we come to an understanding."

His mouth dropped open as his gaze landed on the gun. "Jesus, are ye mad? Yer pointing a barkin' iron at me? She's pointing a barkin' iron at me!" he yelled to someone inside the carriage.

There was a rumble inside the carriage that sounded a lot like laughter. "God's blood. I told ye that she was a peculiar wench!"

Kendra's lips parted in surprise. She knew that voice.

"Open the door!" she ordered, gun still in hand and trained on the coachman.

With a wary eye on Kendra, the coachman yanked open the door. She glanced passed him to the man sitting inside: Guy Ackerman, better known as Bear. The rumor was that he'd earned the nickname by fighting a bear. Anyone else, Kendra would have dismissed it as hyperbole. With Bear, she wasn't so sure. He was gigantic. His gleaming bald pate nearly touched the ceiling, six-foot seven-inches of beefy muscle. He was also a crime lord.

"What are you doing here?" she demanded.

"Are ye gonna stand out in the rain quizzing me?"

Kendra frowned, debating the wisdom of getting into the carriage. They had a strange relationship. He'd once threatened to kill Alec and do some very nasty things to her. She'd threatened to make him sing in soprano for the rest of his life. But as far as she was concerned, they'd reached a détente. It reminded her of the relationships she'd developed with some unsavory informants when she was an FBI agent.

"I ain't gonna harm ye," he said, and smiled, little more than baring his teeth. The smile narrowed his eyes and the puckered scar near his left eye wriggled like a worm.

"Someone has been trying to kill me, so forgive me if I'm a little cautious," she said drily.

The smile, if that was what it could be called, vanished. His face hardened with ruthless purpose. "Aye, and that's what I want ter talk ter ye about."

Kendra regarded him for a moment longer, then nodded. "Okay. You." She pointed her pistol at the coachman. "Put both of your hands on the carriage."

"W'ot?"

Bear's smile returned. Amusement glinted in his flat brown eyes. "Do as she says."

The coachman complied. Kendra shoved the muzzle of her gun at the base of his skull, patting him down while she kept an eye on Bear. The crime lord's smile grew wider, as though he found the scene genuinely funny. The coachman gave a squawk of outrage when she took his blunderbuss and the knife from his pocket.

The coachman turned to her "Oy, ye can't just—"

"Shut it," Bear said. He didn't raise his voice; he didn't have to. The coachman's mouth snapped shut.

Kendra swiveled the gun in Bear's direction. "Now, you. Sit back as far as you can go and put your palms on the ceiling."

For a second, he looked startled. Then he laughed, sliding backward on the leather seat and raising his arms, splaying his hands as instructed. It wasn't much of a comfort, as he'd still be within arm's reach of her, and one swipe from those giant hands could break her jaw. Still, she'd be able to get off one shot.

And if things went sideways, one shot was all she needed.

Kendra kept her gun trained on him as she climbed into the carriage and settled on the seat opposite him.

"Can I rest me arms?"

She nodded. "No sudden moves, though."

He grinned. "Let's take a drive. Just around the square," he added when she stiffened. "The watch might find a parked carriage with no crest on its door a might peculiar."

"Okay."

The coachman glared at her as he slammed the door shut. She heard him fold the steps. The carriage rocked slightly as he climbed onto his seat. A moment later, the vehicle jolted forward, wheels splashing through puddles.

"Yer still with yer tulip?" asked Bear.

Kendra suppressed a shudder. Bear called Alec a tulip. The fact that he always asked whether they were still together was a little creepy.

"I don't think you're calling on me to ask about my love life. What's this about? Snake?"

Snake was a young street thief who'd worked for Bear until she'd lured him away a couple of months ago. Now the boy was being trained to be a stable hand at Aldridge Castle. And hopefully a law-abiding citizen, although given the number of pies that had gone missing from the kitchens, she wasn't so sure about that.

Bear gave her a blank look. "What about Snake?"

"I thought you might be checking up on him."

"He's workin' for a duke. He's landed in cream."

"Okay, then what's this about?"

His gaze traveled over her face, lingering on the bruise. "I heard about last night. Ye were kidnapped out of some swell's party. Heard that there were two blokes and ye killed one of them. With a shovel. Is that true?"

"Why do you want to know?"

The glint in his eyes was one of admiration. "It's true," he decided. "Ye're a bloodthirsty wench."

"I take exception to someone trying to kill me. And there were technically three blokes. The coachman was killed when the carriage rolled over."

"Aye. Can ye describe the bloke who got away?"

"Why?"

In a blink, the humor vanished, leaving Bear's face merciless. "Because *I* take exception ter someone operating in me city without me permission."

Kendra lifted her eyebrows. "Your territory is the whole of London?"

The flat brown eyes were hard. "Your lot sees London Town in its finery. Me lot lives in the real London. And I'm its lord."

It wasn't a boast, but a cold declaration. Kendra asked, "Every petty criminal asks for your permission to commit a crime?"

"Nabbing a gentry mort from a countess's party ain't a petty crime. It's the kind of thing that brings out the beaks and thief-takers. We don't need that kind of attention from the law or swells."

Kendra nodded. Now Bear's unprecedented visit was making sense. It was less about her, and more about keeping control of his own operation. In his own way, Bear held as much power as the Prince Regent, except he did it like any mafia don, by murdering his opponents and exacting retribution on those who didn't follow his rules.

Then again, thinking about how the British monarchy and its nobility rose to power, there wasn't that much difference between the lords of the realm and a lord of London's underworld.

She said, "You object to someone going freelance."

"Freelance . . ." He tested the word out on his tongue, like he was unfamiliar with it.

Which he probably was, Kendra realized. The word was originally two—*free lance*—referring to mercenaries in medieval times who rented out their lances. The word *freelance* probably hadn't been invented yet.

Bear got the gist of it. He smiled his scary smile and nodded. "Aye, I object ter me men going freelance. Tell me about the blokes who took ye."

"We didn't exactly exchange calling cards. I don't know their names. The one that got away was tall, maybe six-foot. Thin. Long face. Weaselly looking. He had a nervous tic in his right eye."

"Ah." Bear settled back in his seat with a satisfied grunt. "Twitch."

"Yeah, he had a twitch in his right eye . . . oh. That's his nickname. Makes sense."

"It's 'cause of that, but mostly on account that he's a cloak twitcher. He hides in alleys and snatches cloaks from those goin' by."

She eyed Bear. "Do you think you'll be able to find him?"

"Course I'll find the bastard. He can try ter disguise himself, but he won't be able ter hide from me."

"I want to—"

The words ended in a sharp intake of breath. *Nickname. Disguise.*

Kendra's mental shift was so sudden it was disorienting. The truth—or what she believed was the truth—became clear. "Stop the carriage!"

Bear stared at her. "Ye know we've moved a bit, don't ye?"

"Take me home then."

"What's ailing ye? Something ter do with last night?"

"No. I have another idea about that. When you find Twitch, I want to talk to him. I need to know who hired him and his friend."

"That's what I mean ter find out. I'll let you know what he says."

Kendra studied the criminal. Bear hadn't promised to bring her to her assailant. By the time Bear extracted the information from the man who'd dared become a freelancer, she had a feeling that Twitch was as good as dead.

Kendra didn't bother with the servant's entrance upon her return. She sprinted up the front steps, throwing open the door The maid and footman in the foyer turned to gape at her. Harding came in as she hiked up her skirts and raced to the grand staircase.

"Miss Donovan . . ."

The rest of the butler's words were lost to her as she rushed down the corridor to her bedchamber.

Molly sprang out of the chair. "Oh, miss, Oi've been ever so worried!"

Kendra ignored her. Laying the pistol down on the nightstand, she crossed the room to the desk. She snatched up the pages of foolscap containing the words that Pascoe had written.

"'Oo'd ye meet?"

"Bear," she mumbled absently, her eyes focusing on the angrily slashed out words on each page.

"Good 'eavens."

She'd been wrong, she thought now, as she sifted through the pages. She'd mistaken the stricken words as a poet's frustration. Now she realized it was something else. There was a pattern here that made sense, if you looked at it from a different perspective.

She straightened abruptly, gathering the pages into a neat pile. "I need to go to Maidenhead."

Molly looked confused. "W'ot? Now?"

"Yes."

"Oi'll get a carriage dress for ye ter change into." She moved to the wardrobe.

"Don't bother. This isn't a social call."

"Oi'm going with ye."

"That's fine. I'm not expecting trouble." Still, she slipped her pistol back into the reticule, and rolled up the foolscap, tucking the pages into the pouch as well.

"Oi 'ave ter get me coat and bonnet."

They left the room. The maid peeled off toward the servant's stairs; Kendra headed to the grand staircase, pulling up short when she saw the Duke and Carlotta on the verge of descending. They both paused to look at her.

"Good morning. How are you feeling, my dear?" the Duke asked as she joined them.

"Fine, thanks. Can I borrow the carriage?" She was aware of Carlotta's gaze on her, but she kept her attention on the Duke.

His eyebrows shot up. "Certainly. What's this about? Have you been outside this morning?" he asked suddenly, his gaze roaming over the damp cloak she was wearing and the wetness of her skirt's hem.

"Yes. I have to go to Maidenhead."

"Maidenhead? To Mr. and Mrs. Pascoe?"

"They'll be my first stop."

His gaze was shrewd as he searched her face. "You know who killed Mr. Pascoe," he stated.

"I think so, but I need to follow up on something first."

"I shall come with you."

"No, that's all right. I'll be fine."

"Are you certain you should venture out alone?" Carlotta said. "His Grace told me what happened last evening. I shudder to think what you must have endured."

Kendra turned to eye the other woman. "Do you?"

"Of course. It must have been frightening."

"I'm not letting you go to Maidenhead alone," the Duke said firmly.

A knock sounded in the foyer below. Harding opened the door to Sam Kelly.

Kendra smiled. "I won't be alone. I'll have Mr. Kelly with me. Mr. Kelly, you'll come to Maidenhead with me, won't you?" she called down to him.

The Bow Street Runner glanced up as he removed his hat. "Certainly, lass. Why are we going to Maidenhead?"

"Following a lead."

Kendra saw that the Duke still looked troubled. She assured him, "Don't worry. I told you Pascoe wasn't murdered cold-bloodedly. I won't be in any danger."

"That's what I thought last night at the Merriweather ball. But we were wrong."

The drive to Maidenhead seemed to take forever. Maybe it was the drizzle that at times turned into rain, which forced Coachman Benjamin to slow. Or maybe it was the anticipation building in Kendra's chest. Molly sat silently in the corner while Sam explained that he'd had his men canvasing the seedier areas of London to identify Kendra's assailants. They'd managed to discover the dead man as Stanley Butler, a known footpad with a violent reputation. They figured the other man was Vernon Melling, also known as—

"Twitch," Kendra finished for him. "Partly because of his facial tic and party because he's a cloak twitcher."

Sam stared at her.

"Bear paid me a visit this morning."

The Bow Street Runner's jaw dropped. "God's teeth, *why?*"

"He wasn't happy that the chain of command was broken. I guess Twitch and Stanley should have asked permission first before accepting the job to abduct me."

Sam frowned, his gold eyes searching her face as though he were perplexed about something. "So, why'd he come ter see you?" he asked finally.

"He wanted a description of the man who'd gotten away."

"Hmm," was all Sam said.

They both went quiet for a moment. The only noise was the rumbling of wheels over macadam and the steely tap of rain against the carriage top. Kendra felt a pinch of guilt that Coachman Benjamin and the other groomsman were getting soaked.

Sam spoke up. "Tell me why we're gonna visit Mr. and Mrs. Pascoe." So, Kendra told him.

The Pascoes' maid-of-all-work, Martha, answered the door and stepped back so that Kendra and Sam could crowd into the foyer. Molly had stayed behind in the carriage.

Mrs. Pascoe came bustling in from the kitchen, her eyes behind her gold-rimmed spectacles widening. The desperation in her eyes was almost painful as she fixed her gaze on Kendra.

"Miss Donovan, have you news? Do you know who killed Jeremy?"

Her gaze flickered over the bruise on Kendra's face, but she didn't inquire about it.

Kendra hesitated. "I wanted to bring you back some of your son's papers." She opened her reticule and withdrew the rolled foolscap.

"Oh. Thank you." Mrs. Pascoe started forward, her hand outstretched.

"Actually, I was hoping you could help me." Kendra unrolled the pages. "It's about your pastime. You said that you and Jeremy would research names. Can you tell me if this word is connected to any particular name?"

Mrs. Pascoe frowned as she took the paper. "*Star*? It's crossed out."

"I know, but you can still see what it is. I want to know if there's a name connected to it."

"I'm not certain. I shall have to consult my book. If you would wait in the parlor . . . Martha will take your coats. Would you like tea? 'Tis a miserable day."

"No, thanks. We'll wait here for you."

"Very well."

The older woman left and Martha stood for a moment staring at them, apparently not sure what to do. She eventually drifted back into the kitchen. They heard the repetitive *thunk* of a knife against a cutting board and the soft tick of a clock.

It took probably about ten minutes for Mrs. Pascoe to return, holding an enormous leather-bound book to her bosom. "I found several references, actually," she told them. "Tara means *star* in Gaelic. And in ancient Greek, there's Astara. And, of course, the Hebrew name Esther."

Kendra didn't need to look in Mrs. Pascoe's book to know the English variant.

Hester.

34

The cold drizzle had eased into a clammy mist by the time the carriage pulled up to Barrett Brewery. Again, Molly stayed in the carriage while Kendra and Sam jumped down and hurried into the building. Mr. West was working at his desk when they came down the corridor.

He glanced up, quill pen poised. "May I help you?"

"We need ter speak ter Miss Gavenston," Sam said, bringing out his baton.

Mr. West's eyes widened at the sight of the gold tip. He rose. "I-I must speak to Mrs. Gavenston."

Kendra ignored the clerk, striding past him to the hall that led to the offices.

"Now, see here! You can't go back there!" Mr. West gasped, chasing after her.

"Watch me."

"Stay back," Sam warned the clerk as he hurried after Kendra.

Kendra threw open the door to Hester's office, but the room was empty. She was turning away when the door to Mrs. Gavenston's office opened. The older woman stared at Kendra and Sam, shocked. Then anger tightened her face.

"What are you doing here?" she demanded. "I have nothing to say to you, Miss Donovan. I told you that you are no longer welcome here."

"I'm sorry you feel that way. I need to speak with your daughter, Hester."

"Why?"

"Where is she? Is she in there?" Kendra looked beyond Mrs. Gavenston but saw no movement in her office. Hester, she was certain, would have come to the door when she heard her name.

"No. She's unwell." The brewster glared at Kendra. "Why do you want to speak to my daughter?" Then her face paled. "You are not going to tell her . . . ?"

Mrs. Gavenston glanced at Sam, then looked back to Kendra, panic darkening the hazel eyes. "You cannot tell Hester about our conversation yesterday. Because it's not true. I told you that your suspicions are not true. I will *not* have you telling my family these unfounded lies."

"I'm sorry," Kendra said again, and had never meant those words more. She shot a look at Sam, and they both turned to retrace their footsteps back down the hall.

"Where are you going? I will not have you disturbing her!" Mrs. Gavenston called after them. "Have my carriage readied immediately," she ordered her clerk, who'd been watching the exchange with wide-eyed astonishment.

Kendra's stomach churned, but she and Sam kept walking. One quick glance at the Bow Street Runner's set face told her he wasn't looking forward to what happened next either. But it had to be done.

Leaves still dripped with rainwater as they drove through the green tunnel of trees. Emerging on the other side, Kendra thought that White Pond Manor looked as beautiful as it did the first time that she'd seen it.

Except today, under the sullen skies and patches of ghostly white mist creeping across the ground, there was a sense of melancholy that hadn't been there before. The windows were dark and unwelcoming.

The carriage stopped in front of the steps. Coachman Benjamin clambered down from his seat, unfolded the steps, and opened the door. Kendra and Sam climbed out. There would be no calling card today.

By the time they strode up the steps, Brentworth, Mrs. Gavenston's butler, was already opening the door.

"We've come to speak to Hester—Miss Gavenston," Kendra said, sweeping past the butler. Her manners were high-handed to the point of rudeness, but she didn't want to give him the chance of slamming the door in her face.

"Miss Hester is ill," Brentworth said. His gaze moved past Kendra and Sam to the other carriage rumbling down the drive. "Ah, that is Mrs. Gavenston now. You may speak to her."

"We've already spoken to her. We need to speak to Miss Gavenston," said Kendra, glancing at Sam.

He yanked out his gold-tipped baton and thrust it forward. "This is Crown business. Tell Miss Gavenston that we must speak with her. Immediately."

"I . . . I . . ."

"Immediately," Sam repeated, his flat cop-eyes burrowing into the other man.

Brentwood looked quickly at the carriage still moving down the drive, clearly torn between yielding to a man representing the Crown and waiting for the mistress that he served. It took a few seconds before he bowed briefly, obviously coming to the conclusion that the worst that could happen to him with Mrs. Gavenston was being sacked without references, while resisting a man of the Crown could mean prison.

"I shall inform Miss Hester that you wish a word," he intoned stiffly. He left them standing in the foyer, with the door open. An insult, Kendra knew.

Outside, the carriage drew up behind the Duke's. Kendra watched Mrs. Gavenston's coachman leap down and throw open the doors, assisting Mrs. Gavenston to the ground. The brewster raised her eyes to lock on Kendra. She picked up her skirts and hurried up the steps, into the foyer.

"I don't want you to upset Hester," she said tightly. "I-I don't know what you need to speak with her about."

Don't you? thought Kendra. She studied the other woman's face, flushed with anger and anxiety.

"Your suspicions . . . she didn't *know*," Mrs. Gavenston hissed, her gaze intense, as though she could force Kendra into agreeing with her. "My family didn't know about Jeremy. They would have no cause to wish him ill."

Brentwood walked back into the foyer with a maid in tow. He looked at Mrs. Gavenston. "Ma'am, Miss Donovan and this . . . this person have asked to speak to Miss Hester. He said it was business of the King."

"I am aware." She let out a breath, suddenly resigned. "Let's go into my study for privacy. Have Hester meet us there."

"Ah, that's just it, ma'am," the maid blurted out. "Miss Hester ain't here."

The butler frowned at the maid. "What she is saying is Miss Hester went out for a walk."

Mrs. Gavenston stared at the girl. "In this weather?"

The maid nodded unhappily. "I told her she oughtn't go outside, not when she's been feeling so poorly and it's so cold and bleak. I told her she could catch her death of cold. But she said it didn't make no difference."

The back of Kendra's neck prickled. "She said that?"

The maid nodded. "Aye. I told ye; Miss Hester's been feeling ever so poorly."

"Where did she go?" Kendra asked sharply.

"I told ye. Out for a walk."

"*Where?* What direction?"

The maid pulled back, intimidated by Kendra's aggressive manner. She made a vague gesture to indicate the back of the mansion. "Toward the woods."

"What is it, Miss Donovan?" Mrs. Gavenston asked.

Kendra pivoted, ready to bolt out the door, but then she realized it would be quicker to go through the house and out the French doors. She swung around and started down the hallway.

"Miss Donovan!"

"I don't think Hester just went for a walk in the woods," she said without stopping. "I think she has a destination in mind."

"The cottage," Sam guessed, falling into step beside her.

She glanced at the Bow Street Runner and nodded grimly. "The cottage."

The cottage was closer to White Pond Manor than anyone realized, about a mile if you cut through the woods. She wondered how many times Hester had walked that route. Maybe bringing a picnic basket with her. Maybe just popping by to talk. *Poetry happens to be an interest of mine, as well*, Kendra recalled Hester saying.

It should have taken around fifteen minutes at a brisk pace to walk to the cottage. But the ground was sodden from the rain, making it more difficult. Kendra's sore knee ached with the strain of walking fast. The forest was a dripping mess, and they had to travail over fallen branches, dead leaves, and weedy clumps of vegetation. The loamy scent of the earth and trees was almost too cloying as she, Sam, and Mrs. Gavenston made a silent journey through the trees, each burdened with their own thoughts. The clearing came upon them suddenly, the tiny cottage in its center.

Free of the tangles of vegetation in the woods, Kendra hiked up her skirts and ran the rest of the way. Heart pounding, she thrust open the door, her eyes immediately zeroing in on the woman sitting on the narrow cot across the room.

Hester's expression was almost dreamy, and it didn't change when she glanced at Kendra.

Kendra's breath caught painfully in her throat. She slowly lowered her gaze to where Hester's hands were resting almost primly on her lap. One hand held a large knife. The other was resting, palm up, dark red blood oozing out of the gash across her wrist, soaking her skirt and dripping onto the floor.

"Oh, my God!" Mrs. Gavenston cried as she came through the door. "Hester! What are you doing? *Stop!*"

Some of the dreaminess vanished from Hester's eyes when she saw her mother. She lifted the knife, bringing the blade back to her wrist. "Stay back, Mama."

"Stop right now!" Mrs. Gavenston's voice rose in a wave of panic.

Kendra grabbed the other woman's arm and squeezed in warning. "Mrs. Gavenston, please let me talk to Hester."

"I don't want to talk," Hester whispered, her gaze dropping to the blade pressed against her delicate skin, slightly above her seeping wound. A new bubble of blood appeared.

Kendra studied the laceration on Hester's wrist. The blood was dark, like a good burgundy wine, indicating the self-inflicted wound was shallow as opposed to a deeper, more deadly arterial injury. The blood would then have been bright red, spraying out with each beat of Hester's heart. She'd managed to cut a superficial vein—messy, but not necessarily fatal. But the knife that she was currently pressing against her flesh could change everything.

"Hester . . . Hester, look at me." Kendra kept her voice calm, steady.

Hester said softly, "It's too late."

"It's not too late," Kendra insisted.

Hester shook her head. Tears filled her eyes. "You don't understand. I-I didn't mean to do it. I don't even know how it happened."

"Tell me what happened," Kendra encouraged, taking a step inside the room. "How long have you been meeting Jeremy here?" Her gaze strayed to the plush turquoise pillows next to Hester on the cot. They matched Hester's eyes.

"I am the one who told him about the cottage." She looked around the tiny interior as though seeing it for the first time. "We came here together. I helped clean it for him."

And for yourself, thought Kendra. A place that Hester could walk to, to meet Pascoe without the curious eyes of the brewery and town on them.

"You brought blankets and pillows," Kendra said.

"We would sit here and talk." Even though the tears were now spilling down her cheeks, her expression became dreamy again. "We talked about everything. I've never met anybody like him, you know. He was so kind and caring. He read me his poetry. He said . . . he said that I was his muse."

Kendra thought of the stanza that Pascoe had written that she'd read.

I spend my days dreaming of the night
For the Star that has bewitched me . . .

Hester whispered, "I-I loved him. I thought he loved me."

Mrs. Gavenston gave a horrified moan, finally understanding. "What did you do? What did you and Jeremy *do?*"

Hester looked at her mother, misinterpreting the appalled look on her face. "We talked about marriage, Mama. He feared that people would think that he was a fortune hunter."

Mrs. Gavenston pressed a hand against her trembling mouth, her own eyes brightening with tears. "Did you . . . did you . . . ?"

Hester's lips twisted in a sad smile. "He didn't seduce me, Mama, if that's what you are asking. Although I would have allowed myself to be seduced. I know that shocks you, but we would have eventually married."

"Oh, my God."

Hester's brow puckered at the dismay in her mother's eyes. "I thought that you would be pleased, Mama. You cared for Jeremy. I know you did."

The enormity of her thirty-year-old secret was reflected in Mrs. Gavenston's eyes. A sob escaped the hand over her mouth.

"I don't know what happened, what changed," Hester continued, her eyes glazing over again. "I knew he would be coming here. He always came here on Saturday afternoon, after work. I came to wait for him, but he was already here."

Kendra thought of the argument Mrs. Gavenston and Pascoe had at the brewery. Mrs. Gavenston had finally told him that she was his mother. He'd reacted with repulsion not because he'd been angry that Mrs. Gavenston had abandoned him, but because of the feelings he had for Hester, his half-sister. Kendra could only imagine the shock and disgust that he'd felt as he'd tried to erase all references to the manifestation of that love, even tearing holes in the foolscap.

Hester whispered, "He was so cold to me, so cruel. He said . . . he said things . . . I don't remember what happened. I only wanted him to stop. I *begged* for him to stop."

Kendra imagined Pascoe turning his anger and disgust on Hester. Maybe as an outlet for his own pain. Maybe to drive her away.

Mrs. Gavenston moaned.

"I'm sorry, Mama. I don't remember picking up the knife. I truly don't." Hester's gaze dropped to the knife that she held now. "The next thing I knew, Jeremy was on the floor. I-I ran. I ran back home and went to bed. I took some laudanum and went to bed. It didn't seem real. It was a horrible nightmare. I-I didn't want to remember, but I couldn't stop crying."

Kendra thought of Hester's red eyes and nose. She hadn't been battling the common cold all this time; she'd been weeping.

"I tried to pretend that it didn't happen, but then you asked Miss Donovan to find Jeremy . . . and she did." Hester raised her tearstained face to look at her mother. "I tried to focus only on work, but it was no use. Jeremy haunted me. Every time I walked past his office . . . I couldn't take it. I can't live with what I've done, Mama. I want it to be over."

Mrs. Gavenston dropped her hand. Her fingers had left red welts on her face. "No, my darling. Please, put down the knife. This is my fault . . . this is all my fault. I should have seen . . ." A sob caught in her throat. "Oh, my God, what have I done?"

"You did nothing, Mama. I bear the weight of this sin. I killed Jeremy." Hester pressed the blade against her wrist.

"You kill yourself now and you'll be condemning your own mother to the fate that you're trying to escape," Kendra said, her gaze locked on Hester. "Do you want that? Do you really want your death to haunt her, just as Jeremy's death haunts you? Would *you* really be so cruel?"

Hester hesitated.

"Please, put down the knife, darling," Mrs. Gavenston entreated again. "*Please*, I beg of you."

Hester's face twisted in anguish as she stared at her mother. "I don't want to hurt you."

"Then put down the knife. Please, Hester, don't break my heart."

Kendra held her breath as she watched the emotions flit across Hester's face. Then with a harsh cry, she dropped the knife.

Mrs. Gavenston flew across the room to gather her daughter in a tight hug, rocking her as though she were a child. Both women were sobbing.

"Bloody hell," Sam muttered, and sagged against the doorframe. He glanced at her, his gold eyes dark with shock, his face a pasty white. "I don't know about you, lass, but I could use a whiskey."

"I'll take you up on that. But first things first . . . do you have a handkerchief?"

"Aye. It ain't even used." He handed her a clean linen square. "What do you need it for?"

"Hester. After the time we spent saving her, it would be a damn shame if she bled out."

35

But what had they saved her from? That was the question that circled Kendra's brain like a ball on a roulette wheel.

Constable Leech was sent for and when he arrived, he admitted that Hester could end up dangling from the hangman's noose after she was convicted, which, given her confession, was inevitable. She couldn't even claim self-defense. Maybe, if she was lucky, she would be transported to Australia. If she survived the harsh conditions on the voyage, where convicts often died of typhoid and cholera, and female convicts raped, she'd end up doing hard labor in that Godforsaken land.

And they call that lucky, Kendra thought, shaking her head.

The third option was the madhouse. While the very idea made Kendra shudder, she knew that would probably be the kindest scenario. Diminished capacity could definitely be argued at the trial; Hester slashing her own wrist was proof enough. But more importantly, Mrs. Gavenston was wealthy. She could afford to have her daughter incarcerated in a well-appointed private room in a mental institution for the rest of her life, or until the mad-doctors agreed that she was mentally stable and could be released.

There was no happy ending. Not that there ever was in a murder investigation. Jeremy Pascoe was still dead and nothing could change that. But the usual satisfaction of bringing the perpetrator to justice was absent.

Kendra and Sam waited at White Pond Manor while Mr. Hobbs was called in to take care of Hester's injuries. They had attempted to leave—what else could they do?—but Mrs. Gavenston had asked them to wait. Taking one look at her shattered countenance, neither Kendra nor Sam had the heart to say no.

So, they waited in the drawing room with the French doors. The sky darkened again with pewter clouds that let loose another downpour. A servant lit candles around the room and put more kindling in the fireplace. A maid brought in tea. Kendra and Sam both politely sipped from dainty cups, silently wishing for something a lot stronger.

"Thank you for waiting," Mrs. Gavenston said, coming into the room. Her face had aged in a matter of hours from grief and guilt. "I wanted to . . . I don't know. I suppose apologize for my behavior. For not admitting the truth about Jeremy."

"You have nothing to apologize for," Kendra said.

Tears filled her eyes. "When you carry a secret like I have, it's not a simple matter to confess it." She sighed heavily. "You know everything, but I wanted to say . . . I *need* to say that I loved Jeremy's father, Robby. If things had been different, we would have married."

"Did Albion know about Jeremy?" Kendra asked. "Did he know that Jeremy was his nephew?"

"He knew that Robby and I . . . But he didn't know that I was increasing when Robby went to London. Only my mother and I knew about the baby."

"But you've been paying him off all these years."

"I've given him money sometimes. Not always. It seemed easier that way. Just as it was easier to bring Jeremy to the brewery as my business manager rather than tell him that he was my son." Her mouth trembled until she firmed it. "I never thought that he and Hester . . . I didn't see it." She paused. "I have a favor. I know I have no right to ask this of you, but I would prefer Jeremy's circumstance to remain a secret."

Kendra stared at the other woman.

Whatever Mrs. Gavenston saw on her face prodded her to continue. "Not for me, you understand. But for Hester. It wouldn't *change* anything. And it could cause her more harm. For her to realize . . ." She had to take a breath. "The scandal would hurt my family."

"And Barrett Brewery," Kendra couldn't stop herself from adding, her cynical side reasserting itself. How much was Mrs. Gavenston's request for their silence about protecting Hester and Sabrina, and how much was about protecting the family business? She saw the quick flare of anger in the older woman's eyes.

"You may think me a monster, Miss Donovan, but this *is* about my family," she said with quiet dignity.

Kendra let it go. If Mrs. Gavenston's motivation was something besides shielding her daughter from the truth, she wouldn't be able to prove it. "What about Barrett Brewery? Will Sabrina inherit?" Kendra couldn't imagine the younger woman toiling away behind a desk.

Apparently, Mrs. Gavenston had a difficult time imagining it as well. She looked away. "I don't know."

Kendra felt sorry for the other woman. Mrs. Gavenston had a fight on her hands to keep the brewery, with both her uncle and Fletcher circling like sharks. If the truth about Jeremy got out, it would be like chum in the water. Maybe it would be the very thing that they needed to wrest control away from her. The tide of history was already turning against women brewsters. Did Kendra really want to be responsible for helping Captain Sinclair and Fletcher?

Kendra sighed. "It's your secret," she finally said, looking at Mrs. Gavenston. "I won't say anything."

"I won't either—if you answer one question," Sam said.

Mrs. Gavenston regarded the Bow Street Runner warily. "What is the question?"

"Did you hire ruffians ter try ter kill Miss Donovan because you feared your secret was about ter be exposed?"

Mrs. Gavenston's lips parted in shock. "I did no such thing!"

Sam watched her for a long moment, then nodded. "I'll keep your secret."

Mrs. Gavenston released a sigh. "Thank you."

Kendra put down the teacup and saucer and stood. "Goodbye, Mrs. Gavenston, and good luck."

She tried not to limp when she walked to the door with Sam. Her knee was really sore. She thought she might ask for another poultice when they got back to Grosvenor Square.

"One more thing," Kendra said, pausing to turn back to Mrs. Gavenston. "Be careful of your son-in-law. I think he might be selling your recipes to Mr. Fletcher."

Mrs. Gavenston's lips twisted into a mirthless smile. "I know. He's been selling what he *thinks* are Barrett Brewery recipes. I was surprised that Mr. Fletcher had tried to corrupt Jeremy. But I know about my son-in-law's failings." She gave a bitter laugh at the expression on Kendra's face. "I'm not quite the fool you think I am, Miss Donovan. At least not when it comes to Barrett Brewery. It's everywhere else that my wits have fled."

36

Kendra waited until everyone—Alec, the Duke, Rebecca, and Muldoon—had gathered in the study before briefing them on what had transpired with Hester. First, though, she swore them to secrecy. Of course, Muldoon resisted, sensing that he would be letting a prime story slip through his fingers. Apparently Fleet Street reporters were as tenacious in the 19th century as they were in her day. It was only when Rebecca accused him of caring more about his wretched newspaper than the human beings involved that he grudgingly backed down.

As Rebecca and Muldoon regarded each other, Kendra's inner antennae quivered again. Maybe Mrs. Gavenston wasn't the only one who failed to see a romance blooming beneath her nose. Kendra put aside her suspicions to tell them who'd murdered Pascoe—and why.

The silence was profound when she finished, broken only by the crackle of logs in the hearth, the rain tapping against the windowpanes, the tick of the clock on the mantel. Kendra took a slow sip of brandy.

"Dear heaven," Rebecca finally breathed. "Poor Mrs. Gavenston. She must have been terrified when she realized that she was with child. There is no greater shame for a woman."

How different it would be in another two hundred years. Not everywhere, of course. But the stigma of having a child out of wedlock would no longer force a young mother to give away her baby to avoid becoming a social pariah. Every family reacted differently to such news, but society overall had changed. There was more sympathy, less censure. *Thank God.*

Muldoon shook his head. "Unfortunately, Mrs. Gavenston paid for her indiscretion."

Rebecca let out a heavy sigh. "To think a secret from thirty years ago could cause so much destruction. Mrs. Gavenston could have had no idea what would happen between Hester and Jeremy."

Kendra wondered if Mrs. Gavenston should have considered the possibility. This was, after all, a society of tightly controlled courtships. How freeing it must have been for Hester and Jeremy to work closely together, to have their business relationship turn into a friendship to so easily fall in love. Siblings who grew up together rarely formed a sexual attraction. Not only were there societal taboos, but Finnish anthropologist Edvard Westermarck had come up with the hypothesis that children raised together from birth to six had a form of reverse sexual imprinting, giving them a sort of immunity from becoming attracted to each other. Yet there had been cases when siblings had met each other as adults and, unaware of their genetic connection, had fallen in love. *Hello, Dr. Phil.*

"I wonder if we're doing Hester any kindness by keeping the truth from her," Rebecca said. "She will go to her grave believing the man that she loved had turned against her for no reason."

"Do you think it would be kinder for her to learn that the man she loved was her own brother?" Alec asked.

"No, I suppose not." Rebecca took a swallow of her sherry. "I dare say that's why Mrs. Gavenston was so desperate to keep the secret that she hired someone to harm Kendra."

Kendra shook her head. "Mrs. Gavenston only learned today of the consequences of keeping Jeremy a secret."

"Aye. And I asked her about that, but she denied it," said Sam.

Muldoon shrugged. "She's obviously lying. Conspiracy to commit murder is a serious charge. The woman would be in gaol or the madhouse along with her daughter."

Sam said nothing, his gaze on the glass of whiskey that he held.

"Or it was Fletcher," the reporter said, eyes narrowing. "He's evil."

Kendra thought Muldoon was speaking more out of dislike for the brewer than a specific reason.

"He would also have to be mad," the Duke said with a steely note in his voice. "Kendra is a member of my family. Mr. Kelly, I want your men to continue to investigate the matter. Even though the danger most likely has passed, I want to know who was brazen enough to order these attacks."

Kendra's throat tightened unexpectedly at his words.

"Perhaps Miss Donovan already knows," Alec murmured. He was sprawled on a chair, his legs outstretched, holding his whiskey. The pose appeared indolent, but his green eyes were sharp as he studied her. *He sees too much*, she thought.

She cleared her throat and said, "If I knew, why would I keep it a secret? I want the person responsible for the attacks caught as well."

"Of course, you do. Mr. Kelly shall find the fiend." Rebecca finished her sherry and set aside the glass. "I shall take my leave. Tomorrow night is the masquerade ball at Vauxhall—although I fear it may be cancelled if this rain continues."

"I doubt that. The party will simply be moved to inside," the Duke said.

Rebecca smiled a little. "It's hardly the same, sir. I was quite looking forward to the dark walks in the pleasure gardens."

Alec shook his head. "Not without a chaperone."

"Don't be such a stuffed shirt, Sutcliffe," she said, pushing herself to her feet.

Muldoon eyed her with interest. "And what is your costume?"

"I shall be going as Athena."

He smiled. "Ah, the goddess of wisdom and war. It suits you. Maybe I ought to sneak in as Hercules. Would you grant me a dance?"

The Duke and Alec stared at the reporter, surprised, while Rebecca blushed.

"That would be very bold of you, Mr. Muldoon," she said.

"It would be very stupid of him," Sam growled, glaring at the Irishman. "It ain't for the likes of us."

Muldoon gave the Bow Street Runner a taunting look. "With everyone wearing masks, it will be difficult to distinguish a prince from a pauper. Vauxhall has as many common folks wandering the dark paths as gentry, you know. It only requires three-and-six-pence as the entrance fee."

That caught Kendra's attention. "This is a public venue?"

"Yes, with private parties, such as Sir Howe's," the Duke said.

"How big are these entertainments at Vauxhall?" she asked.

"It depends on the entertainment." The Duke glanced at the window, streaked in rain. "And the weather. When I was a young buck, Arabella and I attended the fancy-dress jubilee. More than sixty thousand attended that celebration."

"*Sixty* thousand? I didn't realize it was so large a venue," Kendra said, turning away to think it over. Easy access, everyone wearing masks. If she wanted to target someone, she couldn't ask for a better location.

"Who will you be going as, Miss Donovan?" Muldoon asked. He smiled when she glanced back at him. "Still thinking to dress up as a woman from the future?"

"I think the future is out—for now. My costume . . . it's a surprise."

The Duke raised his eyebrows. "I didn't realize you had time to shop for anything, my dear. I believe Caro purchased something for you to wear."

"Then I guess my costume is going to be a surprise for her as well."

The Duke cocked his head. "Do I need to be worried?"

Kendra smiled. "There should be minimal bloodshed."

"Well, I'm intrigued to see what you have come up with, Miss Donovan," Rebecca said. "Mama said that we shall be meeting here before we go to Vauxhall."

"I shall escort you to your carriage," Muldoon offered, standing.

"Me too," Sam said, earning an irritated frown from the Irishman.

The Duke waited until both men escorted Rebecca from the room. "Pray tell, you don't think Mr. Muldoon was serious when he spoke of sneaking into the masquerade ball to dance with Becca, do you?"

"It's Muldoon," Alec said with a shrug.

"Hmm. Well, I suppose it is none of my affair." He glanced at the clock on the mantel. "Caro and Carlotta ought to be in the drawing room. Alec, I assume you will be staying for dinner."

"Thank you, yes."

Alec rose after the Duke left. He crossed the room to Kendra and lifted his hands to frame her face, looking into her eyes. "What are you plotting?"

"Plotting?" Her eyes widened. "What makes you think I'm plotting anything?"

"Because I'm not stupid. I saw your face when we were discussing who was behind the attacks, and when you asked about Vauxhall."

"I'll never play poker with you."

"You have a lamentable tendency to try to take control of situations by yourself, Miss Donovan. I'd say you're a managing female—"

"You make it sound like an insult," she interrupted, annoyed. "I'm used to managing my own life. It wasn't until I came here, in this blasted backward century, that that became a problem."

"It's not a problem. At least, not with me. What is a problem is your lack of trust in me."

"I trust you. No, seriously, I trust you," she insisted when she saw the skepticism flash in his eyes. "But you don't trust me to handle myself."

His thumb brushed the bruise on her cheek. "Maybe I don't like to see this."

"I can't say I like it either, but I handled myself. I need you to trust me to do that."

"And will you trust me enough to share your plan?"

" I'm not planning anything yet—I'm thinking about a plan, though," she admitted. "I want to get the person who tried to have me killed."

"Carlotta. That's who you think is behind the attempts to harm you, isn't it?"

"Clever boy." She smiled. "You're halfway right. I want her accomplice."

Later that night, as gusts of wind rattled the windowpanes, Molly helped Kendra out of the pink fringed evening dress and into her ivory lawn nightgown. She sat in front of the mirrored vanity and watched Molly brush out her hair.

"Any gossip about Carlotta?" she asked the maid.

"Miss Beckett says that Lady Atwood is lookin' ter 'ire 'er a lady's maid."

So, either the countess was tired of sharing her lady's maid or she was softening to Carlotta's claim to be Charlotte.

"Do you know if Carlotta left here to go anywhere on her own?" Kendra asked.

Molly frowned. "Like shopping?"

"Anywhere."

"Nay. Leastwise, Oi don't think so. 'Er ladyship is usually with 'er when they go out."

Kendra frowned. *Who is your accomplice, Carlotta? How do you communicate with him?*

"Has she sent messages out with the footman? Or a stable boy?"

"Ter where?"

"I don't know. Anywhere."

"She's went out ter the back gardens ter pick flowers."

"Are you sure she stayed in the garden?"

"As far as Oi know."

"And no one met with her?"

"Nay, Oi don't think so."

Kendra said nothing. She'd managed to sneak out of the house on several occasions. It was sneaking back when she was usually spotted.

"She accompanied the Duke to the Royal Society and went shopping with the countess," she said. "She's had opportunities to send or receive messages."

Molly eyed her as she set down the brush. "'Oo is she sending messages ter?"

"I don't know." But she damned well knew that Carlotta wasn't working alone.

"Will that be all, miss?"

"Yes, thank you, Molly. Good night."

Instead of crawling into bed, Kendra moved to the window. The nearly pitch-black darkness outside turned the wavy glass into a mirror, reflecting her pale face, the candles on the nightstand, the dancing flames in the fireplace. The events of the day suddenly washed over her, leaving her with a strange sense of despondency. Hester's situation left her feeling sad. She knew how one moment could change your life forever.

Behind her, the door opened. In the window's reflection, she watched Alec slip into the room.

"I was hoping you'd come," she said, turning.

He started to smile, but his lips fell as he searched her face. "What's wrong?"

She laughed softly. "I *really* can't ever play poker with you."

He crossed the room, resting his hands on her shoulders. "What's wrong?" he asked again.

"Nothing. Not really. I-I just can't help but think Jeremy Pascoe wasn't the only victim." She slid her hands around his waist, pressing herself against him. His arms came around her immediately. "Can you just hold me? Tonight. Just hold me?"

"Always."

"And I'll tell you about my plan."

37

A package came for you, miss."

Kendra had been wiping down the slate board, but now glanced over her shoulder at Harding, who had stepped into the study. "A package?"

"Yes. From a Mrs. Browne in Cookham."

"Oh. Okay. Thanks. Where is it?"

"Your maid brought it to your bedchamber." He hesitated, looking at the now blank slate board. "It's finished, then?"

Kendra tossed the wet rag aside. "The investigation into Mr. Pascoe's death is finished."

Harding nodded, then left.

Kendra stood for a moment, her gaze traveling to the window. The rain from the previous evening had dissipated. The sun was out and the sky was dotted with layers of marshmallow clouds. If the weather didn't change (and since this was England, that was always a possibility), she expected the masquerade at Vauxhall wouldn't be limited indoors, but spill outside, into the dark walks.

It's not finished, she thought. *But it soon will be.*

Molly had placed the package, wrapped in brown paper and tied together with raffia, on the bed, and was eyeing it with all the trepidation that a bomb disposal unit would an unattended backpack in an airport.

"Lady Atwood ain't gonna be pleased," she warned. "We still 'ave time ter get ye a new costume."

"I don't want a new costume. I want *this* costume."

Kendra untied the raffia, and pushed aside the paper to reveal leather boots, faun-colored breeches, a gray and ivory embroidered silk waistcoat, white cravat, and cream shirt with lacy cuffs, and a deep burgundy frock coat. Kendra grinned. Mrs. Browne had even included a black tricorn hat and a black silk domino mask.

Kendra kicked off her shoes. "Unbutton me. I need to make sure it fits."

Molly still didn't look happy, but she obeyed. Kendra peeled off her clothes, except for her stockings and garters, slipped on the shirt, and shimmied into the breeches. After nine months of only wearing long dresses, it was strange to wear pants again. In many ways, she knew she'd been fortunate that the fashions of this era were better than other times in history. She didn't even want to think of how fashion would change in the next couple of decades, with women literally strapped into cages as they donned crinoline hoops made out of steel and cotton beneath multiple petticoats and waists cinched into tight corsets to acquire the shape of a bell. She'd seen *Gone with the Wind*, so she had to admit that there was a certain visual appeal. Still, the trade-off—turning women into decorative dolls—was too much to contemplate.

Kendra pushed the thought away. It was always weird to think about the future. She might not know what was going to happen in her life tomorrow—or tonight, for that matter—but she knew what would happen in a broad historical context. She knew that in four years the Regency would come to an end when King George died and his son, the Prince Regent, was crowned king. And King George IV would die only a decade later, his health rapidly deteriorating, confined to his bedchambers. But what good was that knowledge?

"Oi don't know how to tie this," Molly said, interrupting her reverie. The maid was holding up the long silk cravat.

She smiled. "No, I don't suppose you do. Well, we'll figure it out. Or I'll borrow the Duke's valet."

Molly laughed. "Oi'd like ter watch that!"

"Mrs. Browne did a good job," Kendra said, picking up the frock coat and slipping it on. It was about a size too big, but Kendra didn't have any problem with that. The garment had what she wanted, something else that she'd taken for granted—pockets. "I won't need to carry my reticule," she said, slipping her hands into them.

"If yer gonna go as a gentry cove, it wouldn't look right if ye carried a reticule."

Kendra grinned. "True. This is almost perfect."

"Almost?"

"I want to get one more thing. Let's go shopping."

Molly's eyes widened. "*Ye* want ter go shopping?"

"Yes. And I'm swearing you to secrecy. I don't want anyone in the houschold to know. We should take a hackney."

Molly's shock turned into wariness. "Oh, no. This ain't gonna be good."

"Don't be so pessimistic."

"W'ot's that?"

"Negative. Having a negative attitude ages you, you know."

"Oi think being yer maid does that."

Kendra paused at the doorway to the drawing room later that evening, scanning the occupants in their fancy costumes. Lady Atwood looked downright regal in a sumptuous velvet Elizabethan-style dress the color of a ripe plum, trimmed in gold cord and decorated with pearls. She'd covered her hair with a beautifully embellished attifet headdress, which matched the colors of her gown. Diamonds glittered around her neck and in her ears. Carlotta had chosen to dress as a Flamenco dancer in a striking red and black *traje de lunares* polka-dot pattern, cascading with ruffles. She'd swept her hair up high into a chignon, anchored by combs, and wore a red rose behind her ear. Like his sister, the Duke wore an Elizabethan costume with a broad-collared shirt and laced leather doublet, slashed to reveal the azure lining. A short black velvet cape fell from his shoulders. On his head was a velvet flat hat decorated with two feathers. Her gaze slid to Alec, who'd dressed entirely in soft black leather. Like a goth huntsman.

As she gazed at them, she was suddenly assailed by a dizzying sense of déjà vu. This was how it had begun. She'd attended the fancy-dress ball at Aldridge Castle, disguising herself as a lady's maid, on the night everything changed. Then, her 21st century counterparts had dressed in Regency costume, not bothering to hide their tattoos and multiple piercings.

"Miss Donovan? Is that you?"

Carlotta's voice dragged Kendra back to the present. She was *in* the Regency era, and everyone was trying to dress in costume from *their* history.

"*What* are you wearing?" Lady Atwood demanded. "I sent a costume to your bedchamber."

The costume in question—a milkmaid's dress from the Elizabethan era (apparently a popular timeline)—was folded neatly and placed on the chair.

"I had already bought this," Kendra said.

"You cannot wear that! Bertie, tell her that she cannot wear . . . wear inexpressibles!"

Kendra nearly shook her head in exasperation. *Nothing ever changes.* The people in every era managed to be offended by something and language was always under assault. Here, it was considered indelicate for a lady to mention by name the garments—breeches, trousers, pantaloons—that would clothe a man's lower body, so the word inexpressibles had been adopted to mean the same thing.

"It is rather a bold choice, my dear," the Duke pointed out mildly.

That was probably an understatement. The outrage on Lady Atwood's face was very real. It would take another thirty-five years for early women's rights advocates to challenge the rules that forbade them from wearing inexpressibles. And it would take many more years of women being ridiculed and arrested for daring to dress themselves in a pair of pants. She knew she was being provocative—Molly and Mrs. Browne had warned her—but it was vital to her plan.

She also couldn't tell them that, because then she'd have to explain the plan that she'd come up with—which would open a new set of objections.

So, she fell back on the only argument she could make. "It's a *costume*."

"It's a *masculine* costume," snapped Lady Atwood. She staggered back a bit, looking like she was about to succumb to a fit of vapors. "This time you go too far, Miss Donovan. It is beyond the pale."

Alec pulled out a stopper on a decanter and splashed sherry into a crystal glass. "You are an Original, darling," he said, smiling slightly as he brought her the glass.

"This is not being an Original, Sutcliffe—this is being a hoyden," his aunt shot back. "Everyone in town shall be at Vauxhall. I don't think I can take the shame. This is too vexing! And, Sutcliffe, have care with your endearments. Though Miss Donovan's reputation will most likely be in tatters by the end of this evening for this—this brazen costume, you will be doing her no favors by being overfamiliar with her."

Alec gave an abbreviated bow, green eyes gleaming with humor. "Point taken, aunt. Still, I suspect that the Ton will be intrigued by Miss Donovan's unusual . . . ah, choice."

"Mark my words, we shall be a laughingstock," the countess predicted. "She will be lucky not to have someone give her a direct cut!"

"No one would dare," the Duke said, his upper-class accent sharpening like a scythe. "You make too much of this, Caro."

She pointed a finger at him. "And you make too little. There will come a time when our bloodline will not be enough to save us from her eccentricities." She shot Kendra a scathing look. "If you cared for our family's good name, you would change immediately."

Kendra almost wished she could. She'd known that Lady Atwood wouldn't like her choice of costumes, but she had no idea how furious she'd be. Carlotta was staring at Kendra, too, with a perplexed expression.

"Lord and Lady Blackburn and Lady Rebecca," Harding announced, stepping aside for Rebecca and her parents to enter the drawing room.

Lord Blackburn was dressed in a similar style to the Duke, and his wife had gone for Elizabeth I. They both regarded Kendra's costume with surprise and amusement.

"Now I know why you kept your costume a secret," Rebecca said, grinning at her and pulling her slightly away from the rest of the group. "How did Lady Atwood react?" she asked in a whisper.

"How do you think?" Alec raised an eyebrow at her as he arrived to hand her a drink.

"I didn't know whether I needed smelling salts or a shield," Kendra remarked drily. "I probably should have waited for you. I could have used the goddess of wisdom and war on my side. You look great, by the way." She gazed at the frothy, flowing golden robes Rebecca was wearing. She'd kept her hair auburn hair down, decorated with golden leaves.

Rebecca smiled, sipping her sherry. "Thank you. I confess, I do not usually enjoy London's soirees, but I am looking forward to this one. What say you, Miss Donovan?"

Kendra's eyes strayed to the group across the room. Carlotta looked over at her, and their eyes met. Kendra thought she recognized a certain tension tightening the other woman's face, although her dark eyes remained inscrutable. Kendra's heart pumped faster with anticipation.

"Oh, I'm looking forward to this evening as well. I think it will be very interesting."

Alec smiled slightly, raising his glass to clink against hers. "Here's to an interesting evening, then."

38

Vauxhall Gardens reminded Kendra of Carnival in Rio de Janeiro, with hordes of people and a circus-like atmosphere. Sir Howe's ball was in one of the pavilions, but the public—not the very poor, who had to pay to get in, but the merchant class, at least—had access to the other entertainments in the gardens. In one section, a musical troupe was performing to raucous cheers of revelers both on the ground and in supper boxes; in another Kendra was startled to see a high-wire act had been set up, tightrope walkers above entertaining the awestruck crowd while jugglers and court jesters drew applause below. The main thoroughfares were lit by thousands of lamps hanging from trees, but there were unlit paths—the close or dark walks that Rebecca had mentioned—that twisted off into carefully designed wilderness, still wet from the recent rain.

Maybe this wasn't Carnival. Maybe it was Disneyland.

The evening temperature had dropped a good ten degrees—another benefit of wearing the male frock coat, Kendra thought—but the night sky was clear, with a scattering of diamond-hard stars and the moon floating in an ocean of darkness. The air was filled with laughter and conversation, and carried the scent of smoke, vegetation, flowers, cooking meat, and brine, the latter traced to the Thames that bordered the gardens.

Kendra wore a look of vague amusement, revealing none of the keyed-up energy coursing through her bloodstream, as she followed her party through the reception line, where Sir Howe, an aging, plump Robin Hood, greeted his guests. The pavilion was set up like any ball. An orchestra was playing on the edge of a dance floor and a separate room was set up for refreshments. Doors opened to a large outdoor area, which was already crowded. Kendra's gaze traveled beyond the patio to the dark walks, convenient for amorous couples to disappear.

Perfect, Kendra thought.

The Duke invited Carlotta out onto the dance floor, followed by Lord and Lady Blackburn. Alec surprised his aunt by asking her to dance. Kendra snagged two champagne flutes from a passing footman, handing one to Rebecca, and they began strolling. Deliberately she maneuvered to a position near the door. *I want to make it easy for you.*

"Do you think Mr. Muldoon will come?" Rebecca asked suddenly, sipping her champagne, her gaze roaming the crowd.

People had dressed as Roman and Greek gods and goddesses, Romany, shepherdesses, chimney-sweepers, milkmaids, Turks, Indians, empresses, Iranians, and a couple of Harlequins.

Kendra glanced at her. "Do you want him to come?"

Rebecca shrugged. "It means naught to me. I am simply curious to see if he would be so brazen."

"I don't think Muldoon is too worried about being labeled brazen." She eyed Rebecca closely. The other woman was wearing a gold domino, but Kendra could see that her face was flushed. "You like him, don't you?"

"*Like* him? I barely know him."

"Attraction isn't necessarily tied to the length of time you know someone. Usually it happens immediately." She thought of the desire that had flickered to life in her with Alec. It had been as unexpected as it had been unwanted at the time. *It's still unwanted.*

342

"*Attracted*? You think I'm attracted to Mr. Muldoon?"

Kendra smiled. "For what it's worth, I'm pretty sure it's a mutual attraction. If Muldoon comes, he's not coming for the food."

Rebecca said nothing for the moment. Kendra couldn't see her expression beneath the mask.

"It would be impossible," Rebecca finally sighed. "We do not belong to the same social circles."

The domino shadowed Rebecca's eyes, but Kendra thought she saw misery. "If you like each other, you shouldn't let anything stand in your way of being together."

There was a short silence, then Rebecca laughed. "Well, that's rich, coming from you."

"What do you mean?"

Rebecca turned to fix her with her gaze. "It means that I see the way you and Sutcliffe look at each other. Why haven't you married?"

"It's complicated," Kendra muttered, taking a gulp of champagne as she wondered how the conversation had gotten turned around on her.

Rebecca laughed again. "A marriage between you and Sutcliffe is far less complicated than a union between me and Mr. Muldoon. You may be an American, but you are His Grace's ward, meaning you're now in the same social sphere as Sutcliffe. *You* don't have to sneak into this ball. The Ton will never welcome Mr. Muldoon into their drawing rooms."

Kendra wasn't sure how welcome she was by the Polite World, but she asked, "When did you start caring about what everyone thinks?"

"I don't. But . . ." Rebecca bit her lip. "I would happily live in the country without the dictates of Polite Society. But can you imagine Mr. Muldoon leaving London? For what? To become a farmer? Or, worse, to live off my father?"

Kendra had nothing to say to that. She hadn't really thought about it, but she realized now that Rebecca was right. What she knew of the Irishman, he loved his job. And he struck her as a true urbanite. Imagining his ink-stained fingers milking a cow was laughable.

Rebecca shook her head. "There is more to consider than me and Mr. Muldoon enjoying each other's company."

Kendra let out a sigh. This wasn't the first time she'd seen how ruthlessly this system separated the classes, not just in work but in love. That would change, of course, but it would take another century and the rise of the merchant class. Rebecca and Muldoon would be long dead. *She* would be long dead. The thought made her uncomfortable—to live out her life more than a century before she was born.

The music stopped. Kendra's gaze moved to the dance floor, where Carlotta was laughing up at the Duke as they wove their way through the crowd. She felt confident that she'd considered all the angles, but no plan was foolproof. She was taking an enormous risk. *I might not die of old age here; I might die tonight.*

She drew in a breath, let it out slowly. She edged a little closer to the door. And waited.

It took another hour. Kendra's eyes were on Rebecca and a masked Romeo on the dance floor. His face was covered but his bright reddish blond curls made her think that Muldoon had indeed crashed the party. *Good for him*, she thought, although she wished he'd chosen a different costume. Maybe he, like Rebecca, thought any romance between them was ultimately doomed, even if he couldn't resist a flirtation.

Her mind flashed to Pascoe and Hester. Not everyone had a happily ever after.

"Miss Donovan."

Kendra turned as Carlotta materialized beside her. "Mrs. Garcia Desoto."

The dark eyes glittered at Kendra from inside the eyeholes of her domino mask. "I never said anything before, but I applaud your choice of costume. It's very courageous."

Kendra said nothing.

After a moment, Carlotta spoke again. "Could I have a word?"

"You can have several." *Don't look too eager.*

Carlotta smiled faintly. "Shall we walk?"

"Of course."

She wasn't surprised when Carlotta headed for the door. She fell into step next to the woman as they threaded their way through the swirling eddies of people that spilled outside the pavilion. The other woman's tension was palpable. Or was it Kendra's own? Beneath her clothes, despite the cold night air, she was perspiring, her skin prickling. She tossed a casual glance around the throngs of people and slipped her hands into her pockets as she followed Carlotta across the main path to one of the dark walks.

"I thought you wanted to have a word with me," Kendra finally spoke up. "That usually entails words."

"*Si*—yes." Carlotta licked her lips, glancing around nervously. Trees and hedges lined the winding path. The moonlight and stars helped light the way, but it was increasingly dark the farther they moved from Vauxhall's busier, well-lit areas. The laughter, voices, and music receded, leaving only the hushed darkness of the path. Kendra heard the rustle of shrubbery—animal or the breeze? Or something more dangerous?

"I'm sorry, Miss Donovan," Carlotta said slowly. "I am sorry we could not be friends."

"No offense, Mrs. Garcia Desoto, but I don't think your purpose in His Grace's household was to become friends." She paused, forcing the other woman to stop. She let her gaze travel over Carlotta's frilly costume. *Have I miscalculated?* She dismissed the thought. Carlotta wasn't carrying a reticule; there was really no place for her to be carrying a weapon.

Slowly, she reached up and untied the strings to her domino. "I think it's time the masks come off, don't you?"

Carlotta hesitated, then nodded, removing her mask.

"How about telling me the truth?" Kendra asked, keeping her gaze steady on Carlotta even as she strained to hear the noises around them. Was that a footfall? The slither of damp leaves as someone moved through the foliage?

"All right . . . I'll tell you the truth."

Carlotta started walking again. *Luring me where she wants me to go,* Kendra thought.

After a moment, she followed.

39

Timothy Fox—aka Twitch—had never felt so cold. Not even when he'd been one of the thousands of raggedy children scrambling to find shelter in the dead of winter in London Town. It was common enough for children to freeze in the middle of the night, but Twitch had survived.

He wasn't so sure that he'd survive this.

It was that blasted American bitch's fault. Twitch sat on a single, sagging cot, anxiously biting his dirty fingernails, wondering how it had gone so wrong. He and old Stanley had been hired to kidnap the woman at the swell's party. That had been risky enough—she was a duke's ward, after all—but no one had warned them about the woman. They'd expected her to cower in fear, to beg for her life. Instead, she'd fought like a hellcat.

Timothy lifted a hand to his throat, which still ached from her unexpected jab. He broke into a cold sweat just thinking about how he'd gasped for air like a bleeding codfish. He'd thought he was going to expire on the spot. And then somehow she'd grabbed old Stanley's pistol and the fucking carriage had overturned . . .

It had been a miracle that he'd survived. Stanley too. Except the bitch had killed Stanley. Word on the street was she'd killed him with a blasted shovel. Twitch still couldn't believe it.

Now—and this was what really made his insides go all shivery—he'd heard that Bear wanted the men responsible. Last night, he'd stumbled back to his tiny room in Seven Dials. Thank Christ, his early morning visitor had roused him from his deep slumber, helped along with half a bottle of whiskey. The visitor had wanted him for another job . . . as if he'd do such a thing after the previous night's disaster.

He'd then gone to the apothecary to find something for his throat. That's where he'd first heard about Bear's displeasure; later, he'd seen several hard-looking men outside his flat. He'd fled Seven Dials to hide out here in Rachel's room. He'd taken up with the whore only a few weeks before, so he was certain no one would think to link them. At least not immediately. He hoped to be on a mail coach by early light. It was best to leave London Town until Bear's temper cooled.

The muscle around his eye tightened and twitched uncontrollably. He bounced to his feet, his nerves jangling. He needed to move around, but the space was so tiny. Where was the damn whore? Rachel had gone out over an hour ago to pick up food for them. She'd probably found a customer along the way, damn her eyes. When she got back, he'd show her the back of his hand, he would, to keep him waiting . . .

He turned sharply at a sound outside the door. Two steps and he was at the door, jerking it open.

"It's about goddamn time—" he snarled, his gaze fixed on the heavily rouged blonde, until he noticed the large shadows behind her. With a gasp, he fell back as Bear ducked his head low to step through the doorway, followed by a burly man carrying a cudgel. They filled up the small room.

"There 'e is, Bear, just like Oi told ye," Rachel said.

Bear dug into his into his breast pocket for a couple of coins and handed them to her.

"Bitch!" Twitch spat, watching her fingers close into a greedy fist around the coins.

She glared at him. "Oi'm a whore—Oi ain't a bitch!"

"Oi'm gonna kill ye—" Twitch let out a howl as the other man stepped forward and hit him on the shoulder with the cudgel. The pain drove him to his knees.

Fingers clutched around the coins, Rachel gave him a disparaging look, then disappeared.

He swallowed heavily. The tic on his eye pulsed erratically as his panic surged. Rachel's betrayal was the least of his problems.

"Oi know we shouldn't 'ave taken the job last night. Stanley was the one 'oo wanted ter do it," he sobbed, easily tossing his dearly departed friend to the hounds. "Oi never would 'ave! Oi swear on me mother's grave! That's why Oi told 'im that Oi wouldn't do tonight's job."

He was blubbering, unable to stop. "I said, nay, find someone else, cause Oi knew ye wouldn't be pleased if Oi went off and worked without yer say-so again."

Bear's eyes narrowed. "What job?"

"The one at Vauxhall. 'E still wants the gentry mort."

"Kendra Donovan."

"Aye, aye! The bitch is attending some fancy-dress ball. Easy pickings. If she's dead, it ain't me fault!"

Kendra kept her hand in her pocket, her finger positioned around the trigger guard of the muff pistol. Carlotta finally stopped again and turned to face her. Her face was bone-white in the moonlight that penetrated the path. Her eyes were wide and dark.

"I'm sorry," Carlotta whispered.

Inside her pocket, Kendra's fingers tightened as a large shadow materialized behind Carlotta. The moonlight limned his heavy, fleshy features beneath the knit cap, and the pistol he had pointed at her.

Even though she'd planned for this, had put herself out as bait, her mouth went dry and her ears buzzed like a swarm of angry mosquitos as she stared at the deadly muzzle. Deliberately, she drew in a deep breath, letting it fill her lungs. She exhaled slowly and shifted her eyes to Carlotta.

"You're not Charlotte, are you?"

Carlotta tilted her head to study her. "No," she finally said. "Sadly, I am not Charlotte."

"Who are you? How did you know all that information about Charlotte?" she asked.

"Well, now . . . that's a long story," said a new voice from behind her.

For the first time that evening, Kendra felt a jolt of surprise all the way down to her toes.

The voice belonged to a familiar face.

Sam Kelly was settling down in front of the fire of the Pig & Sail, sipping his first hot whiskey of the evening, when a young urchin pushed himself into his line of sight.

"Ye're Mr. Kelly—the thief-taker—ain't ye?"

Sam huffed out an aggravated sigh. "I am Mr. Kelly. And somebody had better be dead if you are gonna be asking me ter give up me comfortable spot here. What's this about?"

"Bear wants ter see ye outside, if ye please."

"Bear?" Sam's mouth sagged open at the mention of one of the most notorious crime lords in the whole of London Town.

"Aye. 'E says it's about some American wench."

"Kendra Donovan." Sam was already hoisting himself to his feet. With some regret, he set his whiskey glass in front of a surprised man. "Enjoy," he muttered, and made for the door. He paused briefly to reach into the pocket of his greatcoat for the pistol he carried. While he didn't think Bear had sought him out to do him harm, it was always best to be prepared.

The urchin had disappeared but there was a carriage several paces away and a coachman who looked like a cutthroat standing in front of the open carriage door. Sam approached the man. He hesitated, peering inside the cab where Bear sat on tufted leather cushions, the brass lamp casting a warm glow on his enormous frame.

"What's this about?" Sam demanded.

"I got word that someone wants ter put a period in Kendra Donovan's life tonight. Thought ye'd be interested in stopping her murder. Well?" Bear boomed out when Sam stared at him. "Are ye interested?"

"I'm interested."

"Get in, then."

40

The moonlight leached the color from the man, casting him in a silvery light, but Kendra knew his hair was bright red and his eyes were a brilliant blue.

"I guess you've finished your work at the Yarboroughs," she said.

The Scotsman grinned the same cocky grin that he'd bestowed upon her the first time they'd met. His expression was affable as ever, despite the gun that he had pointed at her head.

"Aye, lass. I have something more lucrative in me pocket."

Kendra did a quick mental review, the puzzle pieces shifting and falling into place. This was why Carlotta hadn't needed to send messages or travel to meet her accomplice; her accomplice had been right next door all along, watching the Duke's residence. Like the time he'd supposedly rescued her from Albion Miller. She should have realized something was odd then. The mason workers had been done for the day; there was no reason for the Scotsman to still be around.

"Lucky for you that the Yarboroughs decided to renovate their house," she murmured.

"Aye, it was convenient. I almost got hired at the stables three doors down. I prefer mason work ter shoveling horse shit."

His associate laughed.

Kendra said, "You must have been planning this for a long time."

"Well, now it's hard to say. I began ter think about it when me ma died last October, but maybe the notion was put in me head before that, when I was in London in September. Looking back, I think you put the notion in me head, Miss Donovan."

She remembered the time. She and the Duke had traveled to London when they'd heard that Alec had been under suspicion for killing his former mistress. Now she shook her head. "What does that have to do with anything?"

"Tongues were wagging about the Duke's ward, the brazen American. The gossipmongers suspected that the Duke was so indulgent with your peculiarities because you reminded him of his daughter."

"I still don't understand—"

"It got me ter thinking that if the Duke could be taken in by a chit that looked like his daughter, how would he react to someone who claimed ter be his kin? Seems ter me, he'd be just as indulgent." He tapped his temple. "At least that was the beginning of an idea."

"Cam," Carlotta plucked at his sleeve. "I should go back."

Kendra shot her a nasty look. "What's your real name, anyway? I doubt it's Carlotta."

Carlotta tilted her head as she regarded her. "Adelita."

"What's your endgame, Adelita? Do you really think that His Grace is going to publicly declare that you are his daughter? There are men in Spain searching for your real identity right now."

"Aye, and they're following the trail that we gave you," Cam scoffed. "It'll take them months, maybe even years, before they uncover anything. By then, the Duke will announce that poor Charlotte has come back from the grave. You want ter know why? Because he *wants* ter believe it. It's why he's been so quick ter take her into the bosom of his family. He's been treating her like a princess, proud ter show her off ter all of his friends."

"He did that because he's a good man. Don't mistake his kindness for him being a fool." Still, Kendra's stomach churned, recognizing a certain truth to the Scotsman's words.

"I'll wager in three months, the swell will be throwing a ball ter introduce Charlotte ter society formally."

Kendra forced a shrug. "So what? He introduces Carlotta—Adelita—to society, and then he finds out the truth. If you think he'll keep quiet to avoid the public humiliation of being duped, you don't know him very well. He won't continue the pretense."

Cam bared his teeth in a smile. "Aye, I suppose you've got the right of it. But I suspect he'll have an accident at some point. Maybe sooner rather than later. No sense tempting fate, not with so much blunt on the line."

Kendra's insides went cold at the thought of the Duke dying at the hands of this man. "You are going to kill the Duke of Aldridge? Are you crazy?"

Even Carlotta was looking at him wide-eyed. "That wasn't part of the plan."

"Plans change." He shot her a look. "How could we know that he would accept your tale so readily? He wants his daughter back." His mouth twisted. "Don't worry, pet. You won't have ter get your hands bloody."

Carlotta said nothing for a long moment, then she nodded. "I always did fancy jewels," she said in a throaty murmur, smiling slowly, seductively, at the Scotsman.

He laughed, leaning in to kiss her. "You'll have all the baubles you can wear, me beauty."

Kendra shifted slightly, letting her gaze travel the shadows around them. Her movement drew Cam and his associate's attention. Cam lifted the gun, as though to remind her of its presence.

Carlotta pulled away. "I have to get back before I'm missed." She shot a hard look at Kendra. "What are you going to do about her?"

"We'll be taking Miss Donovan for a boat ride tonight."

Kendra wondered if she'd be alive or dead by the time that she hit the water. Probably dead. But even if they tossed her out of the boat alive, she would have fifteen minutes, twenty tops, to battle the frigid waters of the Thames before hypothermia set in. Not that she was going to let it get that far. She drew in another deep breath and let it out slowly as her fingers tightened again around the gun in her pocket.

Carlotta laughed softly and began walking. The darkness swallowed up her departing figure in seconds.

"How did you find her?" Kendra asked.

"I knew Adelita from the war. You might say I was her protector in Spain for a period of time. I thought of her immediately when I came up with the plan. She's the right age and has the right coloring. Me aunt called Charlotte her dark beauty, went on about her raven hair and almost black eyes."

"Nanny MacTavish," Kendra said slowly. "You're Cam MacTavish."

"Cameron Armstrong. But MacTavish is me ma's maiden name."

"Your aunt told you about Charlotte, her tapping three times, her doll and her mother's perfume . . ."

"Not exactly. I barely knew the woman. She left Shandwick when I was a bairn."

"Then how?"

"When me ma died, I went home ter Shandwick ter settle things. Me da had died years ago and me sisters were married, so it was up ter me." His lips twisted. "Ma never threw anything out. I found the letters her sister posted ter her over the years. She was so proud ter be the nanny for such a grand household as the Duke of Aldridge. Living it up in a castle. Made it sound like they ate off gold plates. And how she would go on about the lass!

"She wrote to me ma about how her mistress was so *clever* ter have come up with a scheme ter comfort the child after her night terrors. Tapping three times. Telling her it was magic."

The other man shifted on his feet, as though bored by their conversation.

Kendra kept her gaze on the Scotsman. "Just enough knowledge to convince the Duke that his daughter might have returned from the dead."

Cam grinned. "It was perfect. The only problem was you."

Suddenly, he moved forward, pressing the muzzle against her forehead. Kendra went very still, barely breathing. She had thought she had a little more time.

He said softly, "You're the one who sent Runners to Spain and kept quizzing her, trying to catch her in a lie. You were the one who was always cautioning the Duke, telling him ter wait until there was proof."

"I'm not the only one."

He ignored her. "His Grace listens ter you. With you gone, the Duke is going ter want his daughter around even more. Tragedy brings families together, you know."

"Which is why you tried to have me kidnapped last night."

"You're surprisingly difficult ter kill."

With the cold muzzle pressed against her head, Kendra felt that she was only too easy to kill. She waited. There was no way she'd be able to draw her pistol before he squeezed his trigger.

Suddenly, Cam eased back. Kendra was exhaling when he plunged his hand into her pocket, closing over her fingers around the muff pistol. "Let it go," he said softly. He brought his weapon up to her head. "I won't ask again."

She loosened her hand and allowed him to take the muff pistol out of her pocket.

The roguish grin returned. "That's another thing about having someone in the Duke's household. You hear tales. You and this little pistol you carry around . . ."

He dropped the muff pistol into his pocket, then patted her other pocket. He stepped back after determining it was empty. He regarded her with laughing eyes. "You know, for a clever lass, it was very foolish of you ter come out here alone."

Kendra arched a brow at the Scotsman. "Who says I'm alone?"

41

Sam was huffing by the time he arrived at the pavilion where the masquerade ball was being held. A handful of masked Zeuses, four Cleopatras, and two Julius Caesars crowded outside the door, sipping from gold cups. God's teeth, how was he ever going to find Kendra Donovan in this crush when every reveler disguised themselves by wearing dominos or full-face masks? Sam didn't even know what kind of costume the American had chosen.

"You forgot your mask!" one of the Zeus's told him as he started to push through.

Without replying, he thrust his baton at the man.

"Oh, bloody good show—a Bow Street Runner," said the second Zeus. "Look, Stanford. He's a Bow Street Runner!"

"He still forgot his mask," the first Zeus said.

Sam's teeth snapped shut to prevent him from saying something improper to his betters and he plowed through the crowd. Once inside, he stopped again, scanning the exotic creatures swirling around the room.

He couldn't tell if Kendra Donovan was among them or not. Had she already been spirited away to meet her fate?

"Mr. Kelly?"

He turned to face a masked man in Elizabethan garb. It took him a moment to recognize the rather bold nose and pale eyes of the Duke of Aldridge. Relief washed through him.

"Your Grace, where is Kendra—Miss Donovan?"

"Why? What's wrong?"

"Bea—ah, I have it on good authority that Miss Donovan is in danger tonight." Sam decided to leave the crime lord's name out of it. The fact that Bear had given him the information was bizarre enough to be distracting. "I wanted ter see her myself." He surveyed the room. "You might need ter keep a close eye on her tonight, sir."

"The last I saw of my ward, she and Carlotta were stepping outside . . ." He also examined the merrymakers filling the room. "I don't see her or Carlotta."

The Duke turned abruptly and strode toward the door. Sam hurried after him, pushing through the same drinking group. The Duke began, "I don't—" but broke off as a small figure ran toward them from one of dark paths that crisscrossed the pleasure gardens.

For a moment, Sam thought it was Kendra, but he realized that the woman was Carlotta when she drew near enough and spoke.

"Your Grace, por favor . . ." She was breathing heavily. "You must come. It's Miss Donovan. He has her. She's in danger."

"Who?" the Duke asked sharply.

Carlotta shook her head, already spinning away. The Duke and Sam barreled after her as she started up one of the darkened paths.

They were fifteen yards in when they heard the shot.

Kendra had only a second to watch the confusion and surprise play out across her would-be attackers' faces when Alec stepped into view between the trees, his flintlock pistol raised. Cam's hireling let out a violent oath and reacted quicker than anyone could have anticipated, swinging his gun around and firing. The report was abnormally loud in the night air. Kendra was already reaching behind her for the second gun she'd bought earlier that afternoon and tucked into the waistband at the small of her back when Alec suddenly went down.

The breath evaporated from Kendra's lungs and her heart stopped. Terror like she'd never known before ripped through her. She whipped her gun around and fired. Her aim was off. Instead of hitting center mass, as she'd been trained, the bullet tore through the other man's throat. Blood spewed forth like a geyser as the man did a cartwheel back before falling into the shrubbery.

Cam let out a howl. His fist shot out, knocking the gun out of her hand with enough force that her fingers went numb. "Damn you! You're dead!"

Kendra believed it. Her heart slammed in her chest as she stared into the barrel of the pistol he held. Another shot rang out and Kendra couldn't stop herself from flinching. But she watched a strange expression cross the Scotsman's face. Even in the darkness, Kendra saw the ripped material and dark stain on the back of his coat as he fell forward. She looked at the man who'd been standing behind Cam, then kicked the Scotsman's gun away, before leaping over the body to Alec.

Tears sprang to her eyes and ran down her cheeks as she ran her hands over his chest, inspecting him for blood. "Are you hurt? Did he hurt you?"

"I'm fine. Darling, I'm fine!" He caught her frantic hands, looking beyond her to assure himself that the man was dead.

"You went down." Her breath hitched. "I saw you go down."

"Bloody rain soaked the grass. I slipped."

"Oh, Jesus."

Alec caught her and held her close when her knees sagged. They both jerked upright when they heard the sound of running feet. Alec brought up his gun. Kendra scrambled to pick up the dead Scotsman's weapon. But Sam Kelly and the Duke burst out of the shadows.

"Don't shoot!" Sam threw up his hands.

"Christ." Kendra lowered her weapon.

"What happened?" Sam asked, glancing at the dead bodies. "Who are they?"

"How did you find us?"

"Carlotta told us that you were in danger."

Kendra couldn't hide her shock. *"Carlotta?"*

"Yes . . ." The Duke glanced around. "She was with us."

Kendra followed his gaze as he scanned the twisty path from which they'd came, but she already knew. Carlotta was gone.

42

Her things are gone," the Duke said, his footsteps heavy as he entered the study where Alec was pouring a glass of sherry for Kendra and a whiskey for Sam. Outside, a distant church bell marked the hour: one A.M.

It had taken them over an hour to leave Vauxhall. Sam had sent for the local watch and Dr. Munroe to deal with the dead bodies. Unfortunately, he was also forced to deal with the crowd of merrymakers from the masquerade ball who'd heard about the incident. Hordes of drunken characters had descended on the crime scene to gawk.

Before they left, Kendra had managed to locate Rebecca in one of the pavilion's shadowy alcoves. As she approached, Kendra noticed Romeo standing next to her friend, but he melted into the crowd before she got there. Kendra was pretty sure she'd glimpsed a prominent chin and strawberry-gold hair before he had disappeared.

The traffic had been so heavy across Vauxhall Bridge and in the main thoroughfares of London that it had taken another hour before they'd made it back to Grosvenor Square. Harding informed them that Carlotta had returned two hours earlier, claiming she'd taken ill. Miss Beckett had helped her undress for the evening, which was the last time that the staff had seen her.

"The silver candlesticks in her bedchamber are gone, as well," the Duke said now. "And the pearl necklace that I loaned her the other evening. Caro says that several pieces of jewelry are missing from her jewelry box as well. She's beside herself. Miss Beckett is trying to calm her. I've asked Harding and Mrs. Danbury to go through the household to see what else might be missing."

Sam said, "We'll find her, sir."

A shadow passed across the Duke's face. "No. Let her go. She didn't take any family heirlooms."

"You can't know what she's stolen or not until there is a household accounting," Alec said, bringing his uncle a glass of brandy. "I think you ought to let Mr. Kelly at least try to find her, even if you choose not to press charges."

The Duke sighed, going over to the fireplace to study the burning logs. "I'd just as soon be done with this farce."

Kendra exchanged a glance with the Bow Street Runner. She wanted to talk to the woman, too, if just to voice her anger at how she'd hurt a good man like the Duke.

The Duke took a long swallow of brandy. "I was a fool," he finally said, turning to face them.

"You wanted her to be your daughter," Kendra said softly. "It's understandable."

Silence pooled for a long moment, then the Duke said, "When I lost Arabella and Charlotte, it was like having my heart ripped out of my chest. I wanted to die. Instead, I walked around with a hole inside me that no one else could see. Alec . . ." He looked at his nephew. "Alec remembers that terrible time."

Alec gave a small nod, his expression mirroring the pain on the Duke's face.

"When Carlotta claimed to be Charlotte, I suppose I wanted that second chance. Who doesn't want that with someone they've lost?"

"You didn't accept her story without reason," Sam said. "How did she know those things about your daughter?"

"They were found by Cameron Armstrong in the letters his aunt sent his mother years ago," Kendra explained.

"Nanny MacTavish," Alec elaborated. "Nanny MacTavish may not have gossiped to the rest of the staff while in your employ, but apparently she felt free to express her concerns and affection for her young charge in correspondence with her sister."

"I never considered that."

"Why would you?" Kendra said. "Armstrong had been planning this for some time." She decided not to mention his claim that their relationship might have planted the seed for the Scotsman. "He wanted to keep close tabs on his accomplice, which is why he ended up working at the Yarboroughs' next door."

Sam frowned. "Why did he want ter harm you, lass?"

Alec spoke up. "Because Kendra was the proverbial fly in the ointment."

"It's what I do." She smiled and lifted her brandy glass in a silent toast.

"And you do it so well, darling," Alec replied, then looked at the Duke. "Armstrong worried that she would block you from accepting Carlotta fully as your daughter. He also didn't like it when she had the clever idea of sending a sketch to aid the Runners in their search."

"I am aware that I have been a fool, but I like to think that I would not have done anything legal until Mr. Kelly's men returned with news," the Duke said.

Kendra wondered if that was true. If there had been no news, or the news had been inconclusive, she doubted that the Duke would have stayed in a state of limbo. Not when he had Carlotta charming him. Not when he desperately wanted to believe in the impossible.

Alec shook his head. "Armstrong thought you taking Carlotta around town while he planted the seeds that she was your daughter might be enough. If something happened to you . . . Carlotta might have been able to maintain her position as your daughter."

The Duke looked shaken. "My God. She was working toward my death all this time."

"I don't think so," Kendra said slowly. "I think she was surprised when Armstrong mentioned that. She left because she wanted to warn you. For what it's worth, I think she genuinely cared for you. It seems the original plan was to steal from you, but when Armstrong saw how you seemed to accept her, he got greedy."

They were silent for a beat. Then Sam said, "Armstrong was the one who shot at you, didn't he, as a warning? Didn't he recognize Carlotta?"

"It wasn't a warning. It was a stage performance," Kendra said. "Carlotta was the one who maneuvered the Duke to the window. She's the one who screamed and saved him. The bullet wasn't meant to hit anyone."

"Which you proved the next morning with your little experiment," said the Duke.

"Probably another reason Armstrong feared Kendra," Alec murmured. "If she could figure that out, what else could she figure out? I imagine Carlotta told him about Kendra's investigation into Mr. Pascoe's murder. He figured the murderer might be feeling the same thing about Kendra, maybe wanted to eliminate her. So he hired men to have her kidnapped from the Merriweather ball."

"Carlotta approached me that night to take a walk with her, but you interrupted the plan," Kendra said to him. "I went out that night without her assistance."

She avoided Alec's eyes. Thinking about her proposal was still embarrassing.

The Duke eyed Kendra. "But tonight was deliberate, wasn't it? You staked yourself out like a goat."

Kendra shrugged. "I wanted to push things. It seemed a good time to get a confession. I was pretty sure she hadn't been acting alone. *I* wasn't."

Alec smiled wryly. "I had my eye on her the entire time. Except when I slipped in the damn grass."

Sam drained his whiskey and stood. "At least now we know the truth," he said. "I'll keep you informed about the inquest and such."

"Alec, walk with Mr. Kelly to the door," the Duke ordered.

Alec's gaze slid from his uncle to Kendra and back again. He nodded, setting down his glass and gesturing to the door. "After you, Mr. Kelly."

The Duke waited until he and Kendra were alone to say, "I don't like that you put yourself in danger, my dear."

"I—"

He held up his hand to silence her. Kendra closed her mouth and waited.

"I like it even less that you didn't think you could come to me," he continued. "I am aware that I spent a great deal of time with Carlotta, thinking she may be my daughter. I am also aware that you have felt left out. This is something that I never intended. In fact, I hope you know how much I care for you."

He paused. Kendra didn't know if she could speak, even if she had anything to say.

The Duke went on, "I want you to know that even if Carlotta had turned out to be Charlotte, my regard for you would not have changed. The heart is an amazing organ, my dear." He smiled faintly. "I've found that it has limitless capacity to love."

Tears came to her eyes as she looked at the Duke. She had to clear her throat before she could speak. "Not everyone has a heart like that, you know. I guess I'm still learning the lesson."

Who would have thought she'd learn it in this era?

He smiled at her. "Charlotte would have liked you."

She wiped the tears that fell down her cheeks. She offered the Duke a tremulous smile, reaching out to squeeze his hand. "That is the nicest thing anyone has ever said to me."

43

Three days later.

Kendra's fingers, encased in black silk gloves, curled into fists to stop herself from pushing aside the ebony veil that was attached to the brim of her bonnet. The black netting was designed to cloak her in anonymity even as it identified her to the world as a widow. Better than running around London in a maid's uniform, she'd been told. But she felt a little bit like a goth beekeeper.

Maybe it wouldn't have been so bad if it had been a sunny day. Unfortunately, for the last three days, fog covered the city. On the plus side, the dense mist was why the *Blue Bess* was still docked in the London wharf rather than sailing to America. Unfortunately, Kendra's visibility was basically zero. She took great care with her steps, lifting her skirts to walk up the wobbly gangplank to the deck of the packet ship. The air around her was uncomfortably moist, and heavy with the smell of fish and salt. She heard the slap of water, the ominous creak of masts, the incessant cry of seagulls. Conversations drifted over to her from seamen on the docks and the decks of ships.

"Here, let me help you, ma'am." A tall man wearing a captain's uniform materialized out of the vapor.

"Captain Coleridge?"

"Aye, ma'am." He looked over her shoulder at the vague outline of the carriage. "Is Mr. Kelly with you?"

"No. But I'm not alone," she said, allowing him to help her the rest of the way up the gangway.

A handful of seamen were working on the deck. In the thick fog, they appeared ghostly. For a moment, she felt like she'd just boarded the *Flying Dutchman*, the doomed ship manned by phantoms.

The captain nodded and led her to the ship's saloon, a common area where a few men were sitting around a long wooden table. They stopped talking, eyeing her with interest as she walked with the captain to one of the doors that lined either side of the wall. At the last one, Coleridge knocked briskly. "Mrs. Martinez? It's Captain Coleridge. May I speak with you?"

There was a moment of silence. Then the door swung inward.

"What is it?" Carlotta froze, her dark eyes going wide at the sight of Kendra. Like Kendra, she was wearing widow's weeds. The plain black gown, with its lack of embellishments, oddly enhanced her natural beauty. Her pale skin glowed in the dimly lit room. She'd pulled her raven hair back into a loose chignon, tendrils floating delicately around her face.

"Mrs. Martinez is a widow too," the captain said, winking at Kendra before withdrawing. "I'll give you your privacy."

"Thank you."

Kendra stepped into the tiny room with a small bed, a washbasin, and a little night table. A small trunk took up most of the floor space.

Kendra closed the door and sat down on the trunk. She took off her bonnet with the concealing netting. "Hello, Carlotta."

Weary resignation crossed Carlotta's face as she sat down on the bed. She linked her slender fingers together and waited.

Kendra had thought she had a lot to say to the other woman, but now that she was sitting across from her, she was having trouble formulating the words.

"His Grace wanted to let you go," she said, surprising herself and Carlotta.

The dark lashes fluttered. "Why?"

"He cared for you." Kendra regarded her for a long moment. "And I think you cared for him. I remember when you told me that he was a good man. You didn't want him to get hurt. It's why you warned him the night of the masquerade ball, wasn't it?"

"It was never supposed to be like this," Carlotta said softly.

This, Kendra thought, was the image that Rebecca's artistic eye had captured when she'd sketched her. Gentler, more vulnerable.

"I met Cam during the war," Carlotta went on. "He was a soldier. I was—am—an actress."

Kendra nodded. "I thought so. There were a couple of moments when you seemed . . . theatrical, I suppose. I sent a note to Mr. Kelly's men in Spain to show a sketch of you around theaters."

"Then Cam and I had less time than we realized." She grimaced. "I've been in many theaters. I've been on the stage since I was fifteen."

"This was a different role, though. People would get hurt."

Carlotta looked away. "Cam said that I would only have to pose as His Grace's daughter long enough to get inside the house. One week. Maybe two. Enough time for us to walk away with a small fortune, really. But then His Grace sent me off with his sister to have a wardrobe made for me, and began introducing me to other members of society. We didn't expect that."

"Then you warned me that you wouldn't rest until you knew the truth about me. I told Cam. I didn't realize he meant to kill you until after the night of the Merriweather ball."

Kendra studied her. "You were supposed to lure me outside to the men waiting there. What did you think would happen?"

Carlotta said nothing.

"And during the night of the masquerade ball, you led me to Armstrong. What did you think would happen then?"

"I went to the Duke, so he could save you."

"You went to the Duke to warn him—not because of me. I think you did that only because Armstrong told you that he planned to kill the Duke."

Carlotta tilted her head to study Kendra, a puzzled frown pulling her eyebrows together. "What is it about you, Miss Donovan, that inspires so much love?"

Kendra stared at her, shocked. "What?"

"The Duke loves you. I've seen it in his eyes when he looks at you. I told that to Cam. He felt the Duke should have only one daughter. And then there's the marquis. He's in love with you, and you with him. And Lady Rebecca is a most loyal friend. You are surrounded by such love. Even that criminal . . . Bear, *si*? I heard how he searched London to find the men who tried to kill you.

"So, I ask myself again, what is it about *you*, Miss Donovan? Why are you so fortunate? What makes you so special that you attract this admiration and affection?"

Kendra didn't know what to say to that. It was too bizarre. She'd always been an outsider. Her parents had certainly never loved her. And while she'd loved her job as an FBI agent, and had been friendly enough with her colleagues, she'd never been part of the barbecues or happy hours. The girl that Carlotta was describing wasn't her.

Or it hadn't been in the 21st century.

"I am not so fortunate, it would seem," Carlotta said with a wry smile. "Will I have a trial before going to the gallows?"

"Do you think you'd get off if you had a trial?"

"It might depend on the men on the jury. I can enchant when I have to."

"Like you enchanted the Duke. And Lady Atwood—and I thought that was impossible."

Carlotta laughed, and seemed surprised that she had laughed. "I know people. What they want, their hopes and dreams. Except for you, Miss Donovan." The dark eyes examined her. "You remain a puzzle to me. You do not act like any young lady I have ever met. The countess doesn't understand you either. She would like to turn you into a proper English miss, but you seem not to care about her regard. You don't seem to care about society. You wore breeches."

"I needed pockets and the breeches for my guns."

"And you are not joking." Carlotta shook her head. "You are . . . what do the English call it? An Original."

"I'm getting tired of being called peculiar."

"I would give anything to be you, Miss Donovan. And I do not say this because I most likely will hang."

Kendra drew in a deep breath before turning back to the other woman. "Why are you on this ship? It's going to America."

Carlotta shrugged. "There is nothing for me in Spain."

Kendra stood then, and turned to open the trunk she'd been sitting on. "You were busy before you left," she murmured, letting her gaze travel over the silver candlesticks and a jewelry box. She picked it up and studied the glittery jewels inside. "Is this all the jewelry you stole from Lady Atwood?"

"I had to pawn her sapphire necklace for passage on this ship." She spread a hand to indicate the tiny room. "This is not grand, but it's better than being in steerage."

"What pawn shop?"

"Crane Treasures on Blackfriar Lane."

"Okay." Kendra tucked the box under her arm and let the trunk's lid fall shut. As much as she hated the netting, she put on the bonnet and pulled the veil over her face again. "I wish you luck on your new adventure, Mrs. Garcia Desoto, or Mrs. Martinez, or whatever your name really is."

"Wait!" Carlotta's eyes went wide. "Are you . . . you're letting me go? Why?"

"I hadn't intended to, you know. But you're right. I've been very fortunate." Kendra opened the door, glancing back. "Good luck in America."

"You let her go?" Alec lifted an eyebrow as Kendra settled on the carriage seat across from him and pushed up her veil. "Because the Duke wanted you to?"

"Because she reminded me how lucky I am, and how others aren't so lucky," she replied. "I have Lady Atwood's jewels. Most of them, anyway. We need to stop at Crane Treasures pawn shop on Blackfriar Lane. She sold a necklace to buy her ticket on the ship."

Alec knocked on the ceiling to get his coachman's attention, ordering him to travel to the pawn shop. As the carriage jerked forward, he looked at her. "What about the other items that she stole? There were more than jewels."

"They can be replaced. She can't arrive in America completely penniless."

"Your soft heart is showing, Miss Donovan."

"Shut up."

He laughed, snagged her wrist, and pulled her over to his side of the carriage. "Are you ever going to ask me to marry you again?"

She stared at him in surprise. "You want me to ask you?"

"Yes."

"Aren't you the one who should be asking me?"

"I have, and you have always said no." He brushed his lips against hers, smiling. "I have decided that ours has never been a conventional relationship, and if I ever do marry you, we will not have a conventional life. So, we might as well start how we shall go on."

She laughed. "You can't be serious."

"But I am. You asked me to marry you before and I foolishly wasted that opportunity to say yes. I shan't waste any more opportunities." He lifted his hands to frame her face. "Do you love me?"

The breath caught in Kendra's throat. "Yes."

"And I love you. Well, then? Do you have something to ask me?"

A rush of feeling rose up to swamp Kendra. She thought of the moment she believed he'd been shot. *I almost lost him.* Tears pricked her eyes, which both stunned and baffled her. She felt like she was teetering on the edge of an abyss, a moment that would change her life irrevocably. She swallowed against the hot lump that had become lodged in her throat.

"Alec, will you marry me?"

"My God." He lowered his lips to hers and breathed, "It's about time . . ."

Acknowledgments

I t is always a little bit daunting to begin a writing journey. Thankfully, I am never alone on this endeavor. As always, I am more grateful than I can say for Jill Grosjean, agent extraordinaire, and the wonderful team at Pegasus. Katie McGuire has once again proven herself to be the consummate editor with an unerring eye and fresh perspective, and I am truly grateful for the support of my publisher, Claiborne Hancock. I'd be remiss if I didn't acknowledge Deter Thornton, whose artistic vision for the covers continue to wow me.

I also consider myself to be the luckiest of women to be surrounded by wonderful family and friends. Bonnie McCarthy, Karre Jacobs, and Lori McCallister, you have been there since the beginning and continue to uplift me. And a big thank you to Olga Grimalt, who has been involved in California's bilingual school programs and was my go-to gal for anything related to the Spanish language and culture, and Lesley Smith, who never fails to impress me with her many talents. Also, a big shout-out to Ethan McCarthy, who is juggling being an EMT with his studies in microbiology at UCLA, and yet always found the time to answer my questions involving anything gruesome and gory.

I was hoping to be more hands-on in my research of breweries, but ended up delving into books, blogs and websites instead of a pub crawl like I had initially envisioned. Still, it's always wonderful to do firsthand research by interviewing experts. I was fortunate enough to speak with Jeffrey A. Savoye, who runs the Edgar Allan Poe Society in Baltimore. While Poe has only a brief cameo in the book, I appreciate the time Mr. Savoye spent talking to me about the literary genius. I am eternally grateful to librarians, who have given me such strong support over the years, and my wonderful readers, many of whom have reached out to me via Facebook and social media to say the nicest things and even help expand my knowledge on certain subjects. I want to thank Gail Soleski for pointing out to me that "reins" are used when one is on a horse, but "lines" are used when one is driving a carriage or some other conveyance. These little details are invaluable to a writer. As always, any errors are mine and mine alone.

Throughout the years, I have been fortunate to visit the Tower of London, so I was aware of its history with the Royal Menagerie. Still, I always learn new things in my research, such as how the Menagerie once allowed their visitors to mingle freely with the monkeys. Sadly, the story of the small child being attacked is true, and it prompted the zookeepers to change the exhibit. However, decorating the monkeys' habitat like a London drawing room came purely from my imagination. Similarly, I took creative license in closing the distance between London and the villages of Cookham and Maidenhead. In modern times, it doesn't take long for someone to travel that distance. Yet in the Regency period, it would have taken a couple of hours by carriage. As I didn't want Kendra to spend most of her time in a carriage, I used a little writer's magic and shortened the distance.